<u>ALL KINDS OF HEROES</u>

plus The Buddy Book - Home at Last

By

Carol Kern

This book is a work of fiction. Places are real, but characters, events, and situations in this story are purely fictional. Any resemblance to actual persons, living or dead, is coincidental.

ISBN: 1-4107-4359-4 (e-book)
ISBN: 1-4107-4360-8 (Paperback)

Library of Congress Control Number: 2003092550

This book is printed on acid free paper.

Printed in the United States of America
Bloomington, IN

1stBooks – rev. 6/17/03

PROLOGUE:

They would find him; he had made sure of that. It would all happen according to plan.

He smiled at his reflection on the computer screen, the flitting bursts of color from the screen saver exploding over his image as he feathered his fingertips lovingly over the keyboard. *'The greatest invention of mankind',* he thought, *'and the worst'.* He knew with absolute certainty now that all things carried the seeds of their own destruction. The computer did, his emaciated body did, the whole world did. *'Good and evil',* he mused. *'Good and evil in everything'.*

Sighing audibly, his breath shaky with tension, he glanced at the watch sitting askew on his thin wrist, marveling at the fact it was a great invention too. It could tell him what time it was in every part of the world, and it was almost time now on the eastern coast of North America.

He depressed a key on the computer, bringing up the program that had been his obsession for the past three and a half years. He had taken his time, been careful,...oh so careful, changing his location frequently, while planting the suggestion that *someone* could someday bring the world to a screeching halt. There had been speculations, warnings in the major newspapers, all according to plan; but nothing too alarming, nothing to make anyone search for him or stop him before he could complete what he thought of as his mission. He would be a hero.

He felt the familiar surge of rage at the thought of the necessity for the mission and the hate that prompted it. *'Did other heroes, other saviors and martyrs feel the same rage as they approached their final moments?'* he wondered. The rage made it easier somehow, though the outcome was never in question. They had taught him well in those American Universities, but they had failed to see what he was learning. To their peril, they had failed to see.

His eyes quickly scanned the computer screen then drifted to the syringe that lay in front of it.

"My vial of peace, my entry to paradise," he whispered.

His only regret was that he must be a dead hero rather than a living one. He would have preferred to see, to hear of and to know the crippling chaos that would be inflicted on the arrogant super-power that was the United States of America. But that wouldn't be possible. He was as good as dead anyway.

He glanced again at the message he had placed in the printer tray. It was important for the world to know that he acted alone, that he alone was the genius who made it happen, that the credit was all his. And they would know why he had done it and why he had ended his life.

It was time. One minute to midnight, December 31, 2004, Eastern Standard Time in North America. He visualized the glowing orb in Time Square as it made its descent to the chant of thousands of revelers,..."30, 29, 28...", and nimbly typed in the command that would set everything in motion.

"Happy New Year, America," he whispered, smiling. "Let the chaos begin."

CHAPTER ONE – DECEMBER 31, 2004

She could see it happening—could see the vague image, the insanity of the man who would change the world. The vision was so real she could smell his unwashed body, the acrid scent assaulting her, making her nauseous. She could see the squalor that surrounded him, feel his sickness and rage, and even witness his dying breath. Over and over again she saw. Only now, the vision was clearer and her whole body felt as though it was electrically charged. It would happen—of that she was certain.

Ruth felt another rush of adrenalin as she glanced at the digital clock on her microwave oven. *Have to stop checking the time,* she told herself, beginning to panic. *You'll wind up having a heart attack. Or even worse, a stroke!* The tingling in her midsection was growing more intense as the time for it to happen grew closer. *Still an hour and 40 minutes to go. I don't know if I can stand it!*

She reached for the notebook that lay on the kitchen table in front of her, hoping it would offer a distraction. But all the items that had been crossed off the list, all the things Matt had said "no!" to, only intensified her feelings of dread. Matt hadn't believed in her vision; still didn't for that matter. But thankfully he had agreed to most of the things on the list because they were sensible things that should be done anyway.

Ruth admitted to herself that at first she hadn't believed in the vision either. She had dismissed it as a figment of her overactive imagination because it came to her on the first anniversary of the September 11 attacks. And, it hadn't been at all like her other visions. Always before she had seen visions of little things that affected her personally, or of something good happening. And the tingling in her midsection had been like a feeling of happy anticipation. Like the time she saw the school bus turning up the lane, minutes before it actually did, bringing Buddy home that time he was lost. And the times when she *knew* their bull would be the top seller at the bull sale and their heifer calf would be the champion at the show in Toronto.

1

Always little things. Good things. Never anything tragic or earth shattering,…until a little over 2 years ago.

Ruth's mind shut out the pounding pulse in her temples as it drifted back to the summer of 1978 and the day she, her husband, Matt, daughter, Rachel and son, Michael, had moved onto the old farmstead in Nova Scotia. If she could have made time stand still, Ruth knew she would have chosen that day. It was a day so incredibly perfect, with the sun shining in a brilliantly blue sky, cooled by a slight breeze that kept the insects away and perfumed every breath with the intoxicating aromas of honeysuckle and freshly mown hay. She had never felt more alive than on that day, or more in love with the world and everything and everyone in it. It was a day of new beginnings, of old endings, the first day of a long-awaited adventure, the first day of the rest of her life.

It was also the day she had discovered a childishly scrawled, misspelled message written in chalk on the inside of a heavy plank door in the unused back section of the house. *Gost here,* the message read. Ruth had laughingly erased the message with her thumb, not wanting six – year old Michael, who had just learned to read, to see it. He would be experiencing enough of a culture shock as it was, what with seventeen year old Rachel soon leaving for college, the disruption of having to change schools and make new friends, along with moving into an old house in the country without indoor plumbing and with only rudimentary electrical service. She hadn't wanted him to think he was moving into a haunted house too.

Although Ruth hadn't ever believed in ghosts or things that go bump in the night, there were several unexplained incidents that began just a few days after they were somewhat settled in. There was often a faint tinkling sound in the house, like wind chimes in a light breeze, or glasses with varying amounts of water being tapped in a musical sequence, or perhaps even a harpsichord. It was mystifying, but never frightening. Whatever the source, it was a soothing, pleasant background sound, and was usually accompanied by a faint scent of roses. Other times there was the sound of two men calmly conversing at a distance. There were two distinct voices, but it was as though they were too far away to make out what was being said.

They all heard the sounds, and to Ruth, Michael and Rachel they were pleasantly intriguing, but Matt had dismissed them as being sounds conveyed from distant neighbors due to atmospheric conditions, or as sounds made by breezes blowing through cracks in the old house. Ruth didn't agree with that explanation, but didn't know the answer as to the source unless the scrawled message, *gost here* was true. If there was indeed a ghost there, Ruth thought, it was certainly a benevolent one, because she had never felt so safe and protected anywhere or at any time before in her life.

She distinctly remembered her first vision, although she hadn't thought of it as a vision at the time. They had noticed there were a lot of mice in the barn and talked about getting a cat to help with the problem. They had been so busy though installing a bathroom that they hadn't gotten around to it. Then one morning as she was cleaning up the makeshift kitchen after breakfast, she had a vivid mental picture of a buff colored cat having kittens in the barn loft. She dismissed it with a chuckled *you wish*, but the image persisted. An hour later she went to look in the barn and found a buff colored cat in the loft with four newborn kittens. When she told everyone about her vision and then her discovery that a cat had actually had kittens in the barn, they all had a good laugh about it, especially when Rachel, bug-eyed, sang doo doo – doo doo in parody of the Twilight Zone tune.

The second vision occurred about a month later, and it involved the cat in the barn and their old Samoyed, Sultan. Sultan had been six when Michael was born, and he was now a senior citizen in dog years. He had always been essentially a house dog, having previously only had a fenced in back yard to roam around in. But, with all the hammering and plaster dust from renovations in the old farmhouse, and so much wide open space to explore, he had decided to take up residence in the barn. He, and the cat they named Meggie Mae, got along as though they had been raised together. Although Meggie Mae's kittens had never been out of the loft, Ruth had a vision of them lined up along Sultan's back as he lay on the barn floor. Sure enough, when she looked in the barn later, there were the four kittens lying stretched out on the old dog's back.

As the months grew into years there were many more visions, and Ruth began trying to conjure up images when she wanted something particular to happen. She often tried to *'see'* the lottery numbers in upcoming draws but was never successful. The visions only came to her unbidden. She couldn't make them happen, she couldn't *see* anything in the future simply because she wanted to. It was now many years since she had tried to see what might be in her immediate future, resigning herself to the fact that whoever or whatever was causing her to see visions was in control, not her.

A loud screeching noise came from the living room, startling Ruth out of her reverie. Michael, Rachel, her husband, Ted and nine year old son, Chris, were all watching some infernal shoot 'em up chase movie to pass the time until they could all watch the ball drop in Times Square. Thirteen year old Carin and eleven year old Lindy weren't interested in watching the movie. They were in the dining room working on the 3-d puzzle they had gotten for Christmas. Matt had gone up to bed early to read, and had fallen asleep, as usual.

Ruth wished she hadn't agreed to let her 3 grandchildren stay up to watch the New Year festivities in New York City, but since she had, she wouldn't go back on her word. It would be one a.m. in Nova Scotia when the clock rolled past midnight in New York, but as Lindy pointed out, it wasn't as if tomorrow was a school day. "We've been watching it every year for as long as I can remember," she had argued.

"But its only ten o'clock in Edmonton when it turns midnight in New York," Ruth had countered, all to no avail. She let the kids win the argument because she didn't know how to tell them everything was going to change for them, or how she had flown them all to Nova Scotia, not just so they could all be together for the holidays, but so they would all be safe. Although she didn't know whether or not electrical systems would be affected our west, she had remembered reading somewhere that almost all of North America was connected to the same power grid so she wasn't taking any chances. Having them out in Edmonton and not being able to contact them and know whether or not they were okay would have been intolerable. So, early in what Ruth thought of as her "Survival Plan", the top priority had been to save up for plane tickets to fly Rachel and her family home for the holidays. Beyond that, they knew nothing about what was to happen.

Ruth glanced over at the clock again. Eleven thirty-six. She set her notebook aside and slowly got up from the hard kitchen chair thinking she felt every one of her 66 years. Her arthritis was acting up again; she needed to get up and move around, work out some of the stiffness. She walked to the living-room doorway and looked in on Michael, Rachel, Ted and young Chris, all completely engrossed in their movie.

"I'm going out to the barn to check on the cows," she announced. No one answered or acknowledged she was there. Shrugging, Ruth retraced her steps, walked back through the family room and kitchen then stood in the entrance to the dining- room. Carin and Lindy had their backs to her, leaning over the table, quietly searching for pieces to the intricate 3-D puzzle. She opened her mouth to announce she was going out to the barn then changed her mind. She knew Lindy would want to come along, and she really felt like being alone.

Turning toward the back door she noticed Buddy on the family-room couch. It was probably time for him to go out.

"Hey Buddy, ya wanna go pee?" she called, softly. Buddy stretched and yawned then snuggled deeper into the cushion, the twitching of his eyebrows clearly saying *'No, it's too cold out and I'm too comfortable right here.'*

"Okay Bud, but don't come whining to go out after everyone's gone to bed."

Ruth opened the door between the kitchen and the small, back entry room. "I guess I'd better go do what I wanted Buddy to do before I go out in the cold," she muttered to herself. Going through the laundry room, she paused at the door leading to the back of the house and the hidden tunnel. She felt as though she were intruding where she didn't belong as she hesitantly opened the door. The large, newly renovated room had been given over to Rachel and Ted so they would have a bit of privacy, and Ruth felt as though she were spying. She tiptoed over to the new bathroom, quietly closing the door behind her. Dirty underwear and damp towels littered the floor by the tub, and Ruth had to restrain herself from picking them up. Then, to her disgust, she saw that the seat was up. "Men!' she muttered. "I guess Rachel can't teach Ted to put the seat back down any more than I've been able to teach Matt!"

As she stepped back out into the large room, she surveyed it with pleasure. She acknowledged to herself that she had done a good job with it. The room had been the biggest expense in her Survival Plan. Always a *"some day"* project, it had taken twenty-one years for Ruth to justify the expense of renovating the unused back of the house. It was always intended that some day it would be her private getaway place, but that would have to wait. Right now it had a more important use.

The simple lines of the white pine furniture appealed to her, after living so long with the dark, ornately carved antiques Matt loved. Painting the walls and the ceiling between the beams a cream color and installing a brick hued carpet wall to wall lightened and brightened everything. The large open space in the center of the room was covered by a cream and forest green rug. It very effectively hid the trap door that led to the tunnel they had discovered when they began the renovation work.

Ruth recalled how they had speculated about the purpose of the tunnel and had come up with all sorts of fanciful ideas. Had it been a hiding place for valuables during the years when pirates terrorized the area? Was it a 'safe place' as part of the underground - railroad? Or perhaps a hiding place for illegal contraband when rum -runners plied the waters of the Annapolis River during the prohibition years? They had finally settled on the most logical explanation. More than likely it was just a cold room or root cellar under the original dwelling that had been built by Loyalists after the Acadians were expelled, and simply had never been connected to the cellar when the main part of the house had been built. Its history really didn't matter. To Ruth it was the perfect hiding place for all the food she had bought to see them through.

Reluctantly, Ruth left the room, turning off the light and shutting the door behind her. She went back through the laundry room and over to the closet in the entry room where her overalls and heavy barn coat were hanging on hooks. She put on her overalls, then her coat, heavy boots and gloves. Last of all, she pulled the hood of her coat up over her head, and tugging on the drawstrings, tied it snug around her face. "Winter is such a lot of bother," she groaned.

Before going outside, Ruth opened the door to the office on the other side of the entry room. "Good," she said out loud, after a quick glance around. "Everything's turned off." The room had been turned into a home office several years ago when it became obvious that it was going to be impossible to make a living anymore from farming alone. Now it was where Ruth kept the purebred cattle records, and it was Matt's engineering design office and Michael's home office for his fledgling promotions business. It stood as mute evidence that small farmers were becoming a dying breed.

Sighing heavily, Ruth fumbled to shut the office door with her gloved hands. Then, flipping on the outdoor floodlights that would light her way to the barn, she stepped out into the cold night air.

'Well, for once the weather report was right!' she thought. It was a crisp, cold, windless night and the light falling on the crusted snow made it sparkle and twinkle as though studded with millions of diamonds. Looking up, she saw the sky was like a black void with thousands of tiny pinpricks of brightness.

"Beautiful!" Ruth exclaimed. *'Who was it that said the best things in life are free? Or, was that a song?'* "Of course. It's a song!" Ruth declared as the melody popped into her head. She hummed the tune as she made her way over the crusty snow, all the way to the barn.

Ruth loved the smell of the barn. It was a warm comforting smell even when it was freezing cold. The hay, the sawdust and straw bedding, the moist, slightly fermented odor of the cows' breath, the earthy-grassy aroma of the manure all combined to make a country perfume that she found very appealing. Taking a deep, satisfied breath, Ruth flicked on the barn lights.

To her left were six calving pens running the length of the barn. The first three pens were occupied, each with a very pregnant looking cow lying in the straw, contentedly chewing a cud. Ruth entered the first pen and tapped the cow on the back.

"Get up, Zepher," she urged. Zepher rolled her eyes around at Ruth and groaned, still chewing her cud. "I know how it is, old girl,"

Ruth soothed. "But you have to get up so I can check you. C'mon Zeph, up!" she said, pulling off her glove and snapping her fingers. The cow laboriously stood, arched her back and stretched. Ruth felt for the tendons on either side of her tail-head. "Mmm, still tight," she murmured to the cow. Next, Ruth felt the udder. "Not quite there yet, are you old girl," Ruth said, while scratching Zepher behind the ear. "Looks like you have another day or two to go, at least."

In the next pen, Ruth repeated the process with the second cow. When the cow stood, it immediately lifted its tail and deposited a huge load of manure. "Ah Zoe," Ruth groused. "I can always depend on you to do that every time you stand up." She reached for a manure fork propped up against the outside of the pen, slid open the manure window on the outside wall, and heaved the steaming mass out the window onto the manure pile. Zepher, back in the first pen, was also engrossed in depositing a pile for Ruth to clean up while she was at it.

After checking the second cow, Zoe, Ruth determined that she was probably about a day closer to calving than Zepher. They were both 14 year- old cows, about to have their thirteenth calves. "Such good old girls you are," Ruth whispered softly. "Never a bit of trouble from either of you."

She opened the sliding gate into the third pen and the heifer there immediately stood and began thrashing her tail back and forth. "Well, what have we here, Melissa?" There were little piles of watery manure scattered all over the pen, a tale-tell sign of the early stages of labor. As Ruth stood there observing her, Melissa suddenly opened her eyes very wide, slowly lifted her tail and deposited another small spattering of manure, ending with the thrashing tail. Ruth felt for the tendons along the sides of the tail-head. Instead of taut tendons as there had been on the other two cows, there was a soft depression on either side of the tail. Melissa was definitely in labor. "Couldn't you have waited until morning?" Ruth sighed. "Looks like it's going to be a long night." Melissa would be two years old in another week and was having her first calf. With a first-timer, Ruth knew, anything could happen.

Stifling a yawn, Ruth walked down the center of the barn to the far door, flipped on the outside floodlights and stepped out into the corral. There were two cows at the long feeder licking up the last grains of feed, one was getting a drink from the waterer and two more were getting a final fill-up of hay before bedding down for the night. Ruth removed a glove and checked the tail-head tendons of the five cows that were still up.

Over in the free-stall shelter, most of the cows were contentedly dozing. It reminded Ruth of a big dormitory, with each stall *owned* by a particular cow. The more dominant cows took the stalls closest to the feeder, and it could easily be seen how each cow ranked in the herd. Sure enough, as she walked the length of the shelter, there was Amber in the stall on the left and Cherry across from her in the first stall on the right. Ruth chuckled to see that Zoe's and Zepher's usual stalls had been usurped by lower rank cows. They could both expect to be challenged when they rejoined the herd. The lowest ranked cows were always the coming two-year olds. Their status changed after calving, but they always had to fight for it!

Determining that there wouldn't be any surprise calves born outside that night, Ruth returned to the barn and turned off the spotlights. She watched Melissa for a few more minutes then left the barn, leaving the lights on.

Ruth walked up to the small heifer barn just to count heads and make sure none of the yearling heifers looked sick. All 14 of them were peacefully in their stalls, jaws busy masticating the hay they hadn't taken time to chew thoroughly, earlier.

Trudging wearily back to the house, the floodlights that had lit her way to the barn now half blinded her as she faced them. "Blasted lights!" Ruth muttered. "Blind me comin' back to the house but can't see without 'em comin' or goin. Lotta things like that in life. Things get ya comin' an' goin'."

Back at the house, she stripped out of her barn clothes, hung them on the pegs then went into the warmth of the kitchen. She washed her hands then took a pitcher of punch out of the refrigerator, filled 7 glasses, added a dash of white wine to the four for the adults, and called to the girls to hurry into the living room to toast the New Year, which was now mere seconds away. No one was all that enthusiastic, even acting as though they resented the interruption. It was obvious to Ruth that everyone wanted to wait for what they considered the *real* New Year celebration, when the ball dropped in Times Square. She went back to the kitchen and fished two 5-gallon jugs out from under the sink. Setting one in each side of the double sink, Ruth filled first one with cold water from the tap, then filled the other with hot water. She left them sitting where they were in the sink, then filled a small kettle with water and set it on the kitchen woodstove to heat. She put four heaping teaspoons of hot chocolate mix in a cup, and after a moment's hesitation, added another spoonful for good measure.

She glanced at the clock on the microwave. Twelve-sixteen, it read. On her tiptoes, she reached up to a high cupboard and took down two filled oil lamps and set them on the table, then placed a box of kitchen matches next to them. When the kettle began to whistle, Ruth poured the boiling water into the cup of chocolate, stirring thoroughly as though she had to get it just right. She set the cup on the table next to her open notebook then walked over to the living room doorway.

Ruth had to call out Michael's name twice before she got his attention.

"Melissa is in labor," she announced.

"How far along?" Michael asked, trying to keep an eye on the television.

"Not far. Still in the early stage."

"Uh, I think the movie will get over about one o'clock. Think she'll be okay 'til then?

"Probably. But I'll likely go back out to check on her again before that."

"Okay," Michael said, his attention back on the movie.

Ruth sipped her hot chocolate as she scanned the list in her notebook. **Food:** Check. There was enough stored in the freezers, the cellar and in plastic barrels hidden in the stone tunnel under the back section of the house to feed 10 or 12 people for a year. **Fuel:** Check. Two 200- gallon tanks filled with diesel for the tractors and the generator and another two with gas for the car. Plus, there were the solar panels on the south side of the house and the wind-powered generator for electricity. **Household and Medical Supplies:** Check. There should be enough of everything to last a year. **Cattle Feed:** Check. About 30 tons of it was stored in the feed bins, and enough hay put up for 2 years if necessary. **CB Radio** was next on the list. Check. The radio had been installed in the pickup truck. The next item, **Rifles** had been crossed out. They only had two .22 rifles and a shotgun, but there was plenty of ammunition for all three guns.

Ruth remembered how she had argued against registering those guns under the new gun control laws nearly two years before. *'I don't want anyone in government or anywhere else knowing there are guns here,'* Ruth had argued *'They might have cause to confiscate them and we may need them since we can't get any more.'* Matt had ignored her and had gone ahead and registered them anyway. It was the law. Ruth prayed that hadn't been a mistake.

Plane Tickets. Check. *'Well of course check,'* Ruth thought. *'Rachel and the kids are here, aren't they!'* Hadn't she given up smoking 20 months ago to pay for those tickets? Squirreling the money away, week after week, feeling virtuous, self-sacrificing and oh so out of sorts and crabby because never a minute went by in all those months that she hadn't craved a cigarette? With all the money she had saved, plus the air miles that had been accumulated from everything they'd had to buy, there had been almost $200 left over after paying for the plane tickets. A few days before Christmas, Ruth had used the money to buy 2 cartons of cigarettes and 2 three-gallon tubs of ice - cream. She hadn't opened any of them, thinking she could always take them back to the store in case nothing happened after all. Only, right that moment, she knew she wouldn't do that.

Taking her cup of hot chocolate with her, Ruth went out to the laundry room. She had stashed the cartons of cigarettes and a package of disposable lighters in a box wedged between the freezer and the wall. Eagerly, she opened a carton and pulled out a pack, then tore open the package of lighters. Feeling a bit like a kid sneaking that first illicit cigarette, she extracted an ashtray from the cupboard above the washer and giggled as she lit the cigarette.

11

'Don't inhale!' she warned herself, too late. Coughing softly, she told herself to take it slow and easy, but by the third puff she was inhaling again instinctively and beginning to feel dizzy.

"Ah, a revelation!" she said out loud. "Now I know why kids start smoking! It's got nothing to do with advertising, or cost, or looking cool. It's because it's so deliciously sinful without being a sin, so unacceptable without being illegal, as satisfying a shock as spiked, green hair and pierced body parts, without the grotesqueness and pain! What a gratifying way to thumb your nose at all the puritanical, sanctimonious, supercilious, health-nut prigs out there in their running shoes and jogging suits, eating tofu and bean sprouts, spouting philosophical jargon and…"

"Mom?" Michael said, opening the door. "I smell…" He stopped, seeing the lit cigarette Ruth held between her fingers. Embarrassed and defensive, Ruth gave him a warning look.

"Uh, who were you talking to?" Michael asked, looking around.

"No one. Just thinking out loud."

"Oh. How long have you been smoking again?"

"Just now. This is the first one."

"Is it maybe also the last one?"

"Nope! And that's definite!" Ruth gave him that warning look again then suddenly remembering, she gasped. "What time is it?"

"About 20 minutes to one."

"Then why are you out here? I thought you wanted to finish watching the movie?

"I did, but then I felt guilty about not going out to the barn."

"Why? I told you I would be going out again."

"Well what do you think made me feel guilty? You have a way of doing that, you know. You had just been out, and you were out a couple of hours before that, and a couple of hours before *that,* and I've just been sitting around watching…"

"There's a jug of hot water in the sink," Ruth interrupted. "For Melissa after she calves. You know how they like a warm drink, after."

"I saw it. I'll just pop out now for a quick look at her," he said, heading for the door.

"Take a battery lantern with…, Michael, your coat!" Ruth called, but she was too late. Michael was already out the door, running to the barn.

Ruth finished her cigarette and drank the rest of her hot chocolate, then put her cigarettes, lighter and ashtray up in the cupboard. Seeing a can of pine air-freshener there, she gave the laundry room a good spray. "No sense having a confrontation with Rachel before I have to," she muttered.

She had just gone back into the kitchen with her empty cup when Michael came back in. Her raised eyebrows asked the question for her.

"She's fine," Michael said. "She hasn't even had the first water bag yet. I'll go back out there and check on her as soon as the movie ends." He paused, giving his mother a long searching look.

"Everything really is going to be fine," he said softly.

When Michael went back into the living room, Ruth sat at the kitchen table again, lightheaded from the cigarette. Though she tried not to, she felt compelled to keep checking the time. She could feel the pulse beating in her ears as a rush of adrenalin hit her every time she looked at the clock. Twelve fifty-four. She reached for the box of matches and, hands shaking, lit one of the oil lamps, then went and turned off the kitchen light. The lamp cast a weak glow that reached no further than the edge of the table. "It's too little!" Ruth gasped, and quickly lit the second lamp. The light was only a little brighter, until she remembered she had to turn up the wicks. "Oh," she gasped. "Of course. There, that's better." She left the two lamps lit and turned the lights on again.

Twelve fifty-eight. Ruth felt her heart racing as she watched the seconds ticking past. She tried to concentrate on breathing in and out, in and out, but realized she was holding her breath and the room was spinning. She couldn't breathe! The face in the vision was clearer now, smiling grimly, sunken eyes glistening and dead looking, like glass. And the smell—oh God, the smell! It was like a blend of rotting food, randy male goat and sickening sweet incense.

The digital clock read one zero, zero. Dumbfounded, Ruth inhaled, exhaled, then inhaled again. Midnight in New York and nothing happened. She could hear the commentator on the TV in the other room, but couldn't make out what he was saying. The seconds continued to tick away and nothing happened.

Ruth was crying, great tears of relief rolling down her face when the lights went out. It was then, with the great shock of silence in the house, that Ruth remembered she always kept the clock on the microwave set a little ahead of time.

CHAPTER TWO – JANUARY 1, 2005

The light from the oil lamps pulled everyone out to the kitchen, Chris asking no one in particular "What happened?"

Carin and Lindy solemnly sat down in chairs on either side of Ruth, bewildered by the tears shining on their grandmother's cheeks and the look of astonishment on Michael's face. Michael couldn't find the words for what he wanted to say. No words were adequate for all that he was thinking and feeling right then.

"What happened?" Chris asked loudly, breaking the silence. "Right when the ball started to drop, everything went black!"

"Why don't you call the power company and see what they have to tell you," Ted suggested, looking at Michael.

Without speaking, Michael took the phone book off the corner shelf and looked up the number. Then, picking up the phone's receiver, he held it to his ear for several seconds, his other hand poised over the numbered buttons. Slowly, he set the receiver back down.

"The line is dead," he said softly.

"It can't be!" Ted exclaimed. "The phone doesn't go out when the power goes off!"

"Well it has," Michael said, his gesture toward the phone an invitation for Ted to see for himself.

He did so, clicking the disconnect -bar several times and depressing several numbers, as everyone watched him in anticipatory silence. Replacing the receiver, he looked in mute dismay at the family assembled around the table.

Ruth made eye contact with Michael then glanced at the battery - powered radio next to the phone book, and back at Michael again. Getting the message, Michael picked up the radio and placed it on the table. Turning it on he said, "This should give us some kind of answer. We can pick up stations here from New Brunswick, Maine and even Boston." He slowly turned the dial all the way to the end and back again. There was nothing but the faint sound of static.

"I don't get it!" Rachel exclaimed, bewildered.

"I'm hoping it's not what I think it *could* be," Ted said. "I've read about some of the possibilities if some hacker decided to create a problem. Frankly, I don't know what would shut down the electricity, the phone and radio broadcasts simultaneously *except* someone deliberately sabotaging them. If that's what's happened it could mean we've gone back in time to the early 1900's!"

"Oh cool!" breathed 9 year- old Chris, looking raptly up at his dad. "You mean like in that old movie we saw...I can't remember what it was called, but this guy..."

"No, not like that son," Ted told him. "I just meant that if there's no electricity we won't be able to use any of the things we're used to, like radios, TV's, microwaves, toasters, things that have to be plugged in to work. None of those things existed a hundred years ago."

"But the radio has a battery, Dad. It doesn't have to be plugged in, so how come there's nothing on it?"

"I don't know the answer to that, Chris. I know next to nothing about how electricity or radio waves work. All I know is, we all take things for granted; that if we plug something in and turn it on it will perform a particular function for us. It will be hard getting used to the idea that we won't have a whole lot of things we are used to having. Of course, that's only if the power's off for a long time."

"Well, why did the electricity go out? There's no storm or anything. The lights *will* come back on again, won't they?...Dad?"

"I wish I had some answers for you son," Ted said, squeezing Chris' shoulder. "Believe me, I wish I had some answers."

Michael kept glancing at his mother, wondering if she would reveal the vision she'd had and verify Ted's conclusion as to what had happened. But Ruth wasn't even thinking about doing that. She had just been sitting there dazedly thumbing the pages of her notebook, her mind tumbling from one thing after another, when suddenly the *important thing* that had been nagging at her came into focus and her hands flew to her mouth as she gasped, "Melissa! We forgot all about her!"

With a stricken look, Michael was in motion. "No need for you to come out Mom," he called over his shoulder.

"You'll need a lantern. They're in..."

"I know where they are," Michael said, flipping the light switch for the entry room, then flipping it off again. "Jeez, this is going to take some getting used to."

"That's what Dad said," Chris interjected.

"And *Mom* says it's high time you were in bed kiddo," Rachel said. "So go brush your teeth and get into your pajamas. I'll be up to tuck you in."

Chris gave his mother a pouting look. He wished he had never opened his mouth and drawn attention to himself. His two sisters hadn't said a word so no one was sending *them* off to bed. Carin was just sitting there with a gloomy face but Lindy looked pleased about something. He opened his mouth to protest that Lindy obviously thought she was going to get something he wasn't, but Rachel cut him off short.

"No arguments," she warned. "Go!"

"He can't very well *do* that Rachel," Ruth said. "There are no lights and no running water. I guess it's going to take a while for that to sink in."

Getting up and going over to a cupboard, Ruth took down a blue plastic cup with **CHRIS** printed on it and handed it to her grandson. "See that jug in the sink, Chris? The one on the left. Just pull up the lever and fill your cup about half full. That's your toothbrush cup."

Full of self-importance, Chris followed his grandmother's instructions, gratified that he had something his sisters didn't.

"Now, get that big flashlight with the handle from that cupboard down below. That's the one. Now you're all set. That's *your* flashlight and *your* cup. Use the water in the cup to wet your toothbrush and rinse out your mouth. Don't turn on the water in the sink and don't flush the toilet."

"That won't be hard to remember," Chris said. "I almost always forget to flush the toilet anyway, so now that will be a good thing instead of something I get yelled at for."

"Would you like some help son?" Ted asked.

"Nope," Chris replied, proudly walking into the hallway with his flashlight and cup. "I won't spill the water, Grandma," he called out.

"I know you won't," Ruth answered.

17

Smiling and confident, facing a new experience, Chris ascended the stairs.

"One down and two to go," Rachel said, eyeing her daughters.

"I'm ready," Carin said. "Is there a cup and flashlight for me too?"

"Yes, and for Lindy too. You girls can get everything ready, but don't go upstairs for a few more minutes. I think Chris would like to be completely on his own right now."

Lindy's look of pleasure had vanished. "Grandma," she asked. "Are you going out to the barn soon? Can I go too? I've never seen a calf born and it would be so special to experience that on the very first day of the new- year. Please?" Lindy was satisfied at the wording of her request. She thought it was very grown up sounding, and she watched apprehensively as her grandmother looked first at her mom and then her dad to see if they had any objections.

"I don't see why not," Ruth finally said. "Unless it's a problem birth. Your Uncle Michael should be coming back in soon to let me know how things are progressing."

Lindy fairly beamed with pleasure. Ever since they had arrived in Nova Scotia, the week before Christmas, she had spent every minute she had been allowed out in the barnyard with those beautiful reddish-brown cattle with the white faces. Herefords, Grandma had called them. There were about 60 of them and she already knew all their names and could tell them apart. Carin and Chris didn't know how she could do that. They thought the cows all looked alike. But they didn't. They all had different faces and different bodies, just like people. And *she* could tell them all apart, just like Grandma and Uncle Michael could. She had hoped to see a calf born so when she went back to Edmonton in a couple of days she would be able to tell her best friends Geena and Julie all about it. She'd been afraid one wouldn't be born before she had to leave and she just *had* to see it! And oh boy, she was going to!

While Lindy was basking in the warmth of anticipation at actually seeing a calf born, Rachel had gone upstairs to tuck Chris in, Ruth was replenishing the wood in the cook-stove and Ted was tucking large logs into the big woodstove in the family room. Carin was finding the flashlights and cups, suddenly laughing out loud.

18

"Look," she said. "There are cups that say **Rachel** and **Ted**. And mine is spelled with a **K** and Lindy's says **Linda**."

"Well, you two girls don't have common names so that was as close as I could get," Ruth called over her shoulder. "But at least you'll each have your own and won't get them mixed up."

"They're just great, Grandma," Carin said, stifling a yawn. She kissed Ruth on the cheek. "I'm going up to bed now. Goodnight."

Rachel passed Carin on the stairs, wished her sweet dreams then came back into the kitchen. Sitting down wearily, she stared at the cups labeled **Rachel** and **Ted** that Carin had set on the table.

Ruth kept her eyes on Rachel's face, noting first the puzzled look then the growing awareness as Rachel glanced over at the water jugs in the sink and the oil lamps on the kitchen table that had been lit in advance of the blackout.

"Did you *know* this was going to happen?" Rachel stammered, remembering that her mother sometimes saw things happening shortly before they actually did.

"Not for certain," Ruth said carefully. "But you know how I get these *gut feelings* sometimes and I thought there was enough of a chance something would happen to be prepared for *anything!*" Ruth continued, somewhat hesitantly, trying to choose the right words, not wanting to frighten Rachel unduly.

"I've spent the last year and a half, or more, getting ready for this. And I don't know if I've done enough or too much." Seeing the dazed look on Rachel's face, she quickly added, "I've probably gone way overboard with things. Your dad, for sure, and Michael, probably, think I have. And they could be right. Your Dad's asleep and doesn't know what's happened. Maybe he'll wake up in the morning and everything will be back to normal. Maybe he'll be able to have a good laugh at me. I don't know, but…"

"But you don't really believe that, do you," Rachel stated flatly. "You got us all out here on the pretense of wanting us here for Christmas and now we're probably stuck here without the comforts or necessities of life, while back home everything is still functioning." As a feeling of panic overwhelmed her, Rachel's voice rose steadily. "I've got a career back in Edmonton, Mom! So does Ted! The kids have their schools, their activities, and their friends! You've always

19

wanted us to move out here so you could be closer to the kids, and now you've had your way! Our lives are back in Edmonton, Mom, whether you want to accept that or not. If you wanted to be closer to the kids so bad, why didn't you just sell your precious farm and those stinking cattle and move out west? Why did you have to do this to us, Mom? Why?"

Lindy was aghast at her Mother's angry words, and afraid to look at her Grandmother in case she might be so hurt she was in tears. Lindy knew she wouldn't be able to stand that. She could never stand for anyone to be upset.

Ted was sitting on the couch, petting Buddy, embarrassed by what Rachel had said, but too much in agreement with her to attempt to soften any of her accusations.

Looking down at the table, Ruth said, "Rachel, do you realize what you are saying? You're actually accusing me of being *responsible* for the failure of all power and communications systems simply because I had a *vision* something would happen and was prepared in case it did." She looked sharply up at her daughter, her voice rising in volume as her daughter's had. "Those systems are just as likely to have failed in Edmonton as here. Maybe they have failed all across the country, all over North America, *hell,* even all over the world!

"But since I prepared for almost any eventuality, there's now a CB radio in the truck that can communicate with other CB's out there. We *will* find out how far-spread this is, and if everything is fine in Edmonton, you *will* get back there! If you want to accuse me of something, accuse me of caring enough about all of you to want you safe, of wanting not to have to worry about how things were in Edmonton if you were still there. Accuse me of putting your poor Dad in debt for the rest of his life by buying everything I thought we would possibly need for at least a year. Accuse me of being secretive and manipulative; but don't accuse me of doing *anything* for a purely selfish or self-serving motive. My only motive was wanting us all safe, and all of us here together was the only way I knew how to do that." Ruth paused. "I even made what was for me *the* supreme sacrifice so we could be together. I gave up smoking 20 months ago to save enough to send all 5 of you *round trip* plane tickets. Now, if you'll excuse me, I'm going out to the laundry room for a cigarette. *I've never wanted a smoke so bad in my life!"*

Rachel lowered her head and put her hand over her eyes, shaking her head. "Oh God, Mom, I'm sorry," she sobbed. "It's all just so scary, I mean, all the things that could happen because of this. Any one who isn't prepared, and I imagine that will be most people, will be in a panic." Rachel looked up at her Mother. "Just look at what fear did to me! Made me believe the things I was saying even though deep down I knew they weren't true." She reached for her mother's hand. "Tell me what you saw," she pleaded. "What was your vision and why didn't you tell anyone what was going to happen if you knew for so many months?"

Ruth carefully considered what she would say so that Rachel and Ted would get the picture, but she didn't want to unduly alarm Lindy who was sitting there avidly taking everything in. "It was a simple vision, rather obscure at first, more like an impression rather than a full-blown vision like I was used to. There was a man sitting in front of a computer, and I could see him working on a program and feel the progress he was making. The first time I saw it was on the first anniversary of the September 11 terrorist attacks, and I didn't believe it was real. Then I began having the vision over and over again as though something was trying to tell me to get prepared. So that's what I did. I knew when it was programmed to happen and I must have written 50 or more letters over the past two years, intending to send them to the Premier, the Prime Minister, the President—but I never sent them. Who would believe me? Even your dad and your brother thought I was nuts! I guess I wasn't prepared to be a laughingstock, thought of as some delusional old nutcase,—. The past couple of months the visions have been clearer, stronger. I've been able to see the person clearly, even smell him and his surroundings. It's been pretty unnerving" Ruth paused, then seriously addressed her daughter.

"Tell me honestly, Rachel, if I had told you about all this before, would you have believed me? Would you and Ted and the kids be here now, here where I know you will be safe?"

"Probably not," Rachel admitted, whispering.

Ted came over to the table, clearing his throat. "Got another flashlight for us, Mom?" he asked, taking Rachel by the hand and helping her out of her chair.

"No, you can use an oil lamp. I only got flashlights for the kids because they're safer. They aren't used to carrying fire around."

"I love you, Mom," Rachel said, throwing her arms around Ruth.

Ted kissed his Mother-in-Law on the cheek. "Me too Mom," he said. Then to Rachel, "Grab the toothbrush cups woman. We've likely got a busy day ahead of us tomorrow. Don't stay up too late," he added to Lindy, as Rachel put water in their cups.

Just the two of them in the kitchen now, Lindy said, "It's not really a lousy farm with stinky cows like Mom said. I love the farm, and especially the cows."

"I know sweetheart," Ruth said, stroking the back of Lindy's head. "People say things they don't mean when they're scared."

"That's what I don't understand. Why is Mom scared? Our lights went out before in Edmonton and she wasn't scared. And what does the lights going out have to do with you seeing a vision of a man sitting at a computer?"

"The man was some kind of computer genius who figured out how to shut down the electricity and computers and satellites. So this time the power going out is different. It's probably not something that's going to be fixed in a few hours. Most people who live in towns and cities don't have woodstoves, so they will be cold, are probably getting cold right now. Within a few days they will run out of food and will be hungry too. Hungry, cold, and scared. Most of the food in Nova Scotia comes from somewhere else, and if there's no way more food can be brought in, the stores will run out in a week, maybe two at the most. And when there's no more food in the stores, people will be desperate and will start coming out to the country to try to find something to eat."

"Will we have some food to give them?"

Sadly, Ruth shook her head. "No. People who are cold, hungry and scared won't be satisfied with just *some* food, and there would be too many for us to feed. They would try to take all we have. So, we won't be able to let anyone know we have food here, because we can't give people any. I know that sounds mean and selfish, but if we give away our food or let people take it, then we will starve too."

"You mean people here are going to starve, like in Africa when there's a famine?".

"I really hope not, but I think maybe some will. It depends on how long it takes to get things fixed. It could get pretty bad because it's winter here. It hurts a lot more to be hungry when you're cold than when you're warm."

Lindy didn't want to think about that. She saw no point in worrying about things that couldn't be changed. "When is Uncle Michael coming back in?"

"Well, that was a surprise change of subject!" Ruth laughed softly.

"You don't think the calf is already born, do you?"

"No, not likely. Michael would have come back in if it were. Besides, he knows how I like to be there when the calves are born, so he would have let me know if it's close. He probably hasn't come back in yet because he doesn't have anything to report."

"Oh. I just want to be sure I don't miss it!" A thoughtful look crossed Lindy's face. "Are the cows going to starve too? The new babies?"

"No, that's not likely. People are used to storing away food for their cows for the winter. We have enough stored away here for our cows to eat for about two years. Farmers will see to it that their cows are fed. People who have cows have them because they—love cows!"

"So do I. I wish we had a farm with cows back in Edmonton. I'd be…" Lindy hesitated, certain she had heard the back door close Facing the kitchen door, she held her breath as Michael came in, bringing a draft of cold air with him.

"The calf is backwards," Michael announced.

Ruth closed her eyes and sighed. "Do you want me to wake your Dad or will my help do?"

Michael grinned. "I think the two of us can manage. You're an old pro at this."

"Mmmm! Emphasis on the *old* the way I'm feeling right now."

"If you don't feel up to it…"

"No, I'm fine. Really. I'd be out there anyway, so may as well make myself useful."

Michael noticed Lindy sitting on the edge of her chair. "What are you still doing up, cute stuff?" he asked.

"Waiting for you. Grandma said I could see the calf being born."

"*If,* I said. *If* everything was all right. But it isn't. Sometimes a backward calf can drown before it is born. That's not something you want to see. I'm sorry Lindy. I know you were really looking forward to this, but I think there will be another calf born tomorrow, and you can see that one for sure."

Lindy couldn't say anything. She was swallowing hard, trying to erase the lump in her throat that was making her eyes water.

"Think you can get yourself up to bed alright?"'

Lindy nodded, trying to hold back the tears of disappointment that threatened to spill over and ruin her grown-up feeling.

"Well, let's get to it." Ruth said, going out to the entry room with Michael.

Lindy waited until she heard the back door close, then went over to the window. She could see the light from Michael's lantern bobbing over the snow packed ground then disappear as he and Grandma entered the barn. Grabbing her flashlight off the table, she rushed to the door and quickly put on her heavy coat and boots. She was out the door and running before she remembered to turn on the flashlight. When she reached the barn, Lindy turned the flashlight off and opened the door just enough to squeeze through. She could see a light down in the third pen. Creeping over the straw strewn floor, she stooped over the manger to peer into the pen, trying not to breathe.

Melissa was lying flat out on her side in the middle of the pen. Grandma and Uncle Michael were talking, bent down doing something at Melissa's back end, blocking her view. She couldn't see anything. Listening to what they were saying, Lindy went back to the second pen where Zoe lay chewing her cud. She climbed over the manger, felt the straw to make sure it was clean and dry, then sat down next to Zoe, her arm around the cow's neck.

"She's pretty exhausted but she's making good progress on her own now. I don't think I'll need to use the chains or calf-puller," Michael was saying.

"By the look of the feet the calf's not that big," she heard her Grandma say. "Just a little pull on those feet when Melissa pushes should help a lot. I'll let you know when the rib-cage is past the pelvis, then you can pull the calf out quickly."

Incredibly, Lindy saw her Grandmother put on a long plastic glove then ease her hand way up inside Melissa. She stood up and moved closer to get a better view.

"Come all the way in here if you really want to see this," her Grandmother said, not taking her eyes off what she was doing. It took Lindy a few seconds to realize the words were directed at her. Wasting no time, she opened the sliding gate between the pens just as Ruth said, "Okay Mike, one big pull now." And out came a wet, snorting, flopping, beautiful calf!

Michael pulled the calf past the cow's outstretched legs and deposited it next to its mother's head. Melissa's nostrils quivered as the scent of her calf reached her, and making a marvelous recovery, quickly rolled over onto her belly, tucking her feet beneath her. With soft grunting and gentle lowing that sounded like she was humming some kind of special lullaby for calves, Melissa began the process of cleaning and stimulating her baby with her rough tongue.

Lindy didn't even hear Michael say he was borrowing her flashlight and would go get the jug of warm water. She was completely enthralled with the calf.

"What is it, Grandma? A boy or a girl?"

"A girl."

"This is the year all the calves will have names that start with a P isn't it?"

"You sure don't forget anything when it comes to the cows, do you?" Knowing what Lindy was leading up to, Ruth added, "I think you should be the one to name her."

"Really? You're not mad at me for coming out here after you told me not to?"

Ruth paused, chuckled softly, and put her arm around Lindy's shoulders and squeezed. "You did what I thought all along you would do. Because, you see, in that way you are a lot like me. If I had been told to go to bed when a calf was being born, I know I would have been out here too."

Pleased to the point of bursting, Lindy said, "I'd like to name her Priscilla. Is that okay?"

"Priscilla. Yes, I think that's a good name for her. It really suits her. Now, how did you happen to think of that name in particular?"

"Oh, when I was littler, I had a special doll I named Priscilla. I don't have her anymore so I thought it would be nice to have something else with that name."

"What happened to your doll, Priscilla?"

"I let a little girl down the block play with her and she took her and wouldn't give her back."

"And you didn't do anything about that?"

Lindy shrugged. "I tried. I told her mother she had taken my doll and I wanted it back. But her mother said it was *her* doll, that she had bought it for her. So I didn't know what to do. Later, I thought of lots of things I could have said."

Ruth shook her head and sighed. "It's hard to think what to say when a situation like that happens because it's so unexpected. I feel sorry for the little girl. Maybe some day when that mother is visiting her daughter in a juvenile detention facility, she won't have to ask herself *'why'*."

Lindy looked up at her grandmother. "That *did* happen, in a way. She was taken away from her mother and put in a foster home. I felt sorry for her so I told her she was welcome to keep Priscilla, but I didn't really mean it. I would mean it if I could tell her now. I have a new Priscilla to play with that's a whole lot better!"

Michael returned a few minutes later to find his mother and Lindy sitting on the edge of the manger with their arms around one another, gazing raptly at the calf as it tried to stand for the first time. Melissa was on her feet, anxiously bawling, as her baby took one tumble after another. On her fourth try the calf had gotten her rear legs under her

26

and was trying to unbend her front legs when the hind legs started to slide apart on the wet, slippery straw. Michael placed his feet on either side of the calf's rear legs, and it was enough support for the calf to stand. She was wobbly and shaking from the cold, but she was standing. In less than a minute she was taking her first steps.

"Isn't that amazing!" Ruth exclaimed. "Could you imagine a human baby standing up and walking when it is just a few minutes old? And by this time tomorrow she will be able to run faster than her mama!" Ruth never tired of the miracle of a new calf, and knew that in her younger granddaughter, a kindred spirit had emerged.

"Can I stay here with her to see her eat for the first time?"

Ruth considered. Sometimes it took a while for a calf to learn to eat or for a first-time mama to let it nurse. But even as she was thinking that, the calf was heading toward Melissa's udder with obvious purpose. Michael helped the calf get a teat in its mouth and she began sucking lustily.

Suddenly Lindy laughed. "Priscilla has a happy tail," she giggled, as the calf's tail switched back and forth in obvious pleasure. "And Melissa has a happy face," she added, as the cow stood with her head lowered, eyes half closed, chewing her cud.

"Well, on that happy note, you and I are going to get ourselves out of here and leave the cleaning up to Michael," Ruth said, hauling Lindy to her feet. Picking up Lindy's flashlight that Michael had set beside her in the manger, Ruth escorted a contented little girl back to the house.

Michael cleaned and re-bedded Melissa's pen, made certain she drank her warm water, then gave her a scoop of feed. Zoe and Zepher in the other pens called out for some feed too, and Michael obliged them. '*Might as well cater to them while I can,*' he told himself.

He went out to the corral and checked on the rest of the herd. Then, on returning to the barn, he stood inside the door a few moments gazing down the length of that dark expanse…and had the distinct feeling that he was looking at the future; a long dark corridor to the unknown.

CHAPTER THREE – JANUARY 1, 2005

Lindy was too excited to sleep. She lay awake for what seemed a very long time thinking about the new calf in the barn and planning what she would do tomorrow. Unaware that she was doing so, she finally drifted off then woke with a start to see that it was beginning to get light outside. Quietly, she dressed herself in the clothes she had discarded on the floor by her bed just a few hours before, then carefully feeling her way, tiptoed along the upstairs hallway and down the stairs.

There was just enough light coming through the kitchen window for her to make her way across the large room without bumping into anything. Shivering as she went out into the cold entry room, Lindy hurriedly donned her heavy winter coat and boots, unlocked the back door then made a dash to the barn. She passed the first two stalls without glancing at the cows, her eyes glued to that third stall where Melissa and Priscilla were laying, the calf curled into a ball at her mother's head. It was too dark in the barn for Lindy to see the calf clearly. "Darn," she whispered. "It was too dark in here to get a good look at her when she was born and it's *still* too dark!" Then remembering the sliding panels that opened so manure could be tossed out onto a pile, Lindy slid the panel back in the third pen and a weak light filtered through the opening. Not satisfied, she went into the fourth pen and opened the panel there then went back over into the second pen where Zoe was and opened that one as well. That was better, and it was getting lighter all the time. Soon now, she would get a good look at Priscilla. Settling herself comfortably in the manger, she was prepared to wait for the sun to rise.

Matt prided himself on always being the first one up in the morning, no matter the season, at least an hour before anyone else stirred. He never stopped to consider that he was also in bed and asleep about three hours before anyone else, every night.

Grumbling to himself, he probed around in the half- light of the bedroom for fresh clothes. Ruth, lightly snoring on her side of the bed, would give him hell if he turned on the light so he could see properly. It had taken almost 40 years of marriage for her to break him of the inconsiderate habit of flooding the room with light at the crack of dawn, then leaving it on as he attended to his morning rituals in the bathroom.

Matt flipped the light switch in the bathroom. "Well shit," he muttered, as the room remained semi-dark. He peered at the note taped to the handle on the toilet. DO NOT FLUSH, it read. There was another note taped above the sink. DO NOT RUN WATER. It was then Matt noticed all the cups with names lined up by the sink. The one with his name was half filled with water. Brushing his teeth, he was aware of a nagging alarm in the back of his mind, but shrugging, dismissed it until he had further assessed the situation. He had never yet seen a winter in Nova Scotia that didn't include a temporary power outage, and quite often more than one. It was just part of the routine.

On the kitchen table there was another note informing Matt he would have to milk Felicity by hand and that everything he needed was ready for him, sitting on top of the freezer in the entry room. He stoked up the embers in the cook-stove, adding kindling and a couple of split logs. Once the fire was burning hotly, he filled the kettle from the jug of water sitting in the sink and set it on the stove. The big, old-fashioned drip pot was on the counter waiting for him, and while filling the basket with ground coffee, he reckoned this was the major benefit of a power outage. There was no better coffee in the world than coffee from that old pot, but unless the power was off it was never used. He wondered why, even though he was almost always the one to make the morning coffee.

While he waited for the water to boil, Matt went into the family room and refueled the big woodstove. He would have the house toasty warm for everyone when they all finally crawled out of bed. Buddy slowly stepped down off his bed on the couch, yawning and stretching. "Just you and me first thing every morning, right Bud?"

Matt said. Buddy lazily wagged his tail in acknowledgement that he was being spoken to then strode purposefully toward the kitchen door, stopping briefly to sniff at his dish in passing, in case some tidbit had magically appeared.

Matt let Buddy out into the frigid gray dawn, noting that the back door had been left unlocked. He would have to get after Michael, or maybe even Ruth, for being forgetful. It wasn't wise to leave doors unlocked anymore with all the hooligans prowling about nowadays. Besides, hadn't Ruth insisted on new dead-bolt locks for all the doors? Hadn't he installed them himself at her insistence? Well, she'd bloody well better use them!

Matt poured the now boiling water into the top of the old drip pot, appreciatively inhaling the invigorating aroma of the coffee. He poured himself apple juice from the fridge and had popped two slices of bread into the toaster before he remembered the power was off. "Well shit!" he said for the second time that morning. Setting his juice, buttered bread and coffee before him on the table, he reached to turn on the radio. Then, remembering, he reached for the battery radio instead. Turning the dial, he heard nothing but light static. His stomach muscles tensed as he went to the phone, his hand hesitating above it. He didn't want to know. He had to know. Slowly he raised the receiver to his ear and listened to the silence.

In a daze Matt methodically downed the food before him, his habitual pre-breakfast fortification before milking Felicity and gathering the eggs. Not wanting to think, he opened the back door and whistled for Buddy who came running, having finished his check of the perimeter of the farm- yard. Buddy sat waiting patiently while Matt found him a dog biscuit as payment for his services, and he immediately trotted with it over to the rug in front of the woodstove in the family room which he had decided long ago was the proper place to consume treats.

As Matt stepped out into the cold morning air, he sensed the change that was coming. Everything looked the same, but somehow everything was different too. And though he didn't want to think about it, the sound of his boots on the crusty, well-trodden path to the barn seemed to beat out a tattoo in his head. *'Ruth was right! Ruth was right!'*

Matt frowned when he saw that the door to the barn had been left unlatched. He felt a slight draft and noticed that three of the manure windows had been left open as well. "Somebody is really getting careless around here," he complained out loud. Going over to the first pen he looked at Zepher then glanced over at the other two cows. All were laying facing the corral at the end of the barn, their backs to him. Seeing nothing amiss, he crossed to the other side of the barn where the two little Jersey cows and the Hereford bull were penned. He gave the three of them some feed, thankful that he wouldn't have to tote buckets of water to them. The energy-free, gravity-fed water system that Ruth had insisted be installed in the barn was going to be worth the expense after all.

Securing Felicity in her stanchion, Matt perched on the little stool by her side, leaned his head into her flank, and began milking. *'I don't know why I don't do it this way more often,'* he mused. *'It's much nicer than the milking machine.'* He chuckled to himself, realizing he no longer had a choice, at least not for the time being. There was little more than half a bucket of milk, reminding Matt that it would soon be time to dry Felicity off. Ruefully, he looked over at the Jersey heifer, Mia, who was due to have her first calf in about ten days. He didn't relish what he knew was in store, trying to get a first-calf heifer to submit to hand milking. And about four months from now there would be *two* cows to milk, after Felicity produced her next calf.

Latching the barn door behind him, Matt returned to the house where he poured the milk through a filter into the milk can. The frigid entry room was the best place to leave the milk to cool, he decided. He went out to the hen house to collect the eggs, and as he poured fresh feed into the hen's feeder, the hens vacated their nest boxes. All but a couple that hadn't finished laying their eggs yet. Matt knew he would have to check the henhouse again before long. Couldn't let the eggs freeze. They might break and the chickens would begin pecking at them. Once a hen began eating eggs, he knew, the habit tended to spread through the whole flock.

When he returned to the house, Ruth was seated at the kitchen table dressed in her usual heavy sweatshirt and pants. She was sipping black coffee, the smoke from a cigarette drifting away into oblivion above her head. She looked at Matt, eyes wide and frightened, saying nothing. Matt kept his eyes on Ruth's for a long time, wordlessly telling her that he knew, that he would do everything in his power to make things alright, that he was thankful for her and loved her, lousy cigarettes and all.

Lindy had heard her grandfather latch the barn door and knew she was locked in the barn. But she wasn't concerned. She knew either Grandma or Uncle Michael would be out to check on things soon. When she had heard Grandpa come into the barn earlier, she had slunk down into the manger as far as she could get. Grandpa didn't know she was there she was sure, and he didn't know about Priscilla either. It really was just like Grandma said; *'When it comes to the cows, it's like Grandpa is blind in one eye and can't see out of the other one. He just doesn't notice things. When it comes to the chickens though, he can see things no one else can. To each his own, I guess.'*

Grandpa hadn't noticed that Zoe had gotten restless either, and was pacing around her pen. Almost the whole time he had been in there milking, Zoe had been lifting her tail and dropping bits of manure all over. Lindy decided she would clean the manure out of all three pens. She had gotten very cold sitting there and thought maybe working would help keep her warm.

With the manure fork in hand she went into Melissa's pen first. Baby Priscilla was still curled up, sound asleep, her mother's breath keeping her warm. As Lindy lifted a heavy forkful of manure, she wished, not for the first time, that she were bigger. She was more than two years older than Chris and nearly a head shorter. People always thought she was the youngest in the family. She was encouraged though, that in the two weeks she had been on the farm her weight had finally crept above 60 pounds on the bathroom scale.

Determined to get the job done, Lindy finished cleaning Melissa's pen, then went over to the first pen to clean up after Zepher. She was already feeling considerably warmer and by the time she had Zepher's pen tidy she had worked up quite a sweat.

She went through the sliding gate into the second pen. Zoe was lying down now, facing her. Talking soothingly to Zoe, Lindy began scooping up the small piles of manure and tossing them out the window. It was much easier than the other two pens had been even though there were a lot more piles to clean up. She slipped and nearly fell as she stepped on something slimy in one corner of the pen. Peering closely, she saw what looked like a big pile of egg whites spread over the straw. Then she looked over at Zoe and, alarmed, saw what looked like a big purple balloon under Zoe's tail. The balloon was getting bigger and bigger as Zoe tried to push it out. Was this a *'water bag'* that she had heard Uncle Michael mention?

Lindy bent down behind Zoe for a closer look. She wished there was more light in the barn. As Zoe pushed, Lindy thought at first she was imagining she saw a calf's foot and nose inside the balloon. Then, after a particularly long, hard push by Zoe, she knew for sure that's what she was seeing. Instinctively, she knew that something was wrong and started to run for help. At first she couldn't understand why the barn door wouldn't open, then with a sob remembered she was locked in. She pounded on the door and hollered, to no avail. Racing back to Zoe's pen, she realized that the fate of this calf was in her hands. Somehow, she had to get its nose out of that balloon so it could breathe. But how? If she broke the balloon, would it hurt Zoe? Would it maybe make her bleed to death? She decided she had to take that chance, remembering that there had been no balloon around Priscilla. Maybe it was supposed to break, but for some reason Zoe's hadn't. With nothing else to work with, Lindy pulled off a mitten and dug into the balloon with her fingernails. Zoe gave a final push and the calf's hind feet plopped out onto the straw. The balloon broke open spewing a dark yellow slime under the calf. Zoe was immediately on her feet, snuffling excitedly over her snorting, sneezing baby. Lindy wondered why the calf's face was dark yellow. Was it all right? Had she done something wrong? Then, as Zoe licked at the calf's face, she saw that the yellow was coming off and the face was white underneath as it should have been. She lifted one of the calf's rear legs as Uncle Michael had said to do to check whether the calf was a boy or a girl. Just then she heard someone unlatching the barn door, and turning with a beaming smile on her face, announced, "It's a girl!"

When Matt and Ruth had exchanged their long, silent look, Matt had set his basket of eggs on the counter and had drawn a chair close to Ruth's, grabbing her hand and squeezing it hard as he sat beside her. Ruth had pressed her other hand hard over her mouth trying, unsuccessfully, to staunch the tears welling up in her eyes and spilling down her cheeks. Matt placed his hands on either side of her face, wiping away the tears with his calloused thumbs. Pulling her face toward his, he gently kissed her forehead, then her eyelids, then the bridge of her nose. That was all Ruth needed, and taking a deep breath and swallowing hard, she quickly regained her composure. Matt had his faults, goodness knows, but his silent tenderness had always been able to sooth her in moments of crisis. Smiling wanly, she asked, "How's the calf?"

"What calf?" Matt frowned, not understanding.

"Melissa's. She had her calf shortly after one this morning."

"Oh. I didn't see any calf. But then, I really didn't know to look for one."

"You didn't look at the cows in the calving pens?"

"I looked at them, but not closely. It was pretty dark in there, you know."

"Yes, I suppose. But I wish you'd take a closer look when you go out there in the mornings."

"Were you out there when she calved?"

"Yes."

"What about Michael?"

"He was there too."

"Who was the last one out of the barn?"

"Michael stayed to clean up. Why?"

34

"Well, he's got to be a bit more responsible, that's why. He left several of the windows open then didn't latch the barn door. And he forgot to lock the back door to the house too!"

Ruth frowned. "That doesn't sound like Michael!" She looked at Matt. "Michael wouldn't *do that!*" she cried, suddenly alarmed. Leaping from her chair, mindless of her aching joints, Ruth rushed out to the entry room and quickly got into her coat and boots, Matt right behind her. Together they reached the barn door, and unlatching it and stepping inside, they were greeted by a deliriously happy Lindy, announcing, "It's a girl!"

Michael came rushing into the barn, tousled and disheveled looking, as Lindy was relating the details of the calf's birth to her grandparents.

"I knew Zoe was getting very close to calving, so I had my alarm set for five," Michael explained. "I must have turned it off then dozed off again. But I can see I wasn't needed; Lindy was here and had everything under control."

Lindy blushed charmingly at Michael's praise. "I was scared I was doing the wrong thing, but I knew I had to do *something* so the calf could breathe!"

"You did exactly the right thing," Michael told her. "If you hadn't been here, if you hadn't taken the chance of doing *something*, that calf wouldn't be alive right now."

"How is it you happened to be out here?" Ruth asked.

"I couldn't sleep, thinking about Priscilla. So I came out here to get a better look at her." Lindy paused. "When Grandpa came out to milk Felicity I didn't let him know I was here. I thought he might tell me it was too cold out here and would make me go inside."

"Well, you've had quite a start to the new year, haven't you! And here I was reluctant to let you experience an abnormal calving situation, afraid it might mark you for life. I guess you showed me that sometimes a grandma can have a lot left to learn!"

"Well, this isn't getting anything done," Matt interjected. "Everything's going to be a little harder to do and take more time now, so we better all have a little planning session together and decide who's going to do what, and when, and how, and so on. We'll have to get everything properly planned out."

"As soon as I finish the chores out here I want to get on the CB radio to see if I can contact anyone, find out what the situation is," Michael said, as Ruth and Matt nodded agreement. "But I have one request regarding the planning of who does what. I'd like to have Lindy help me in the barn, if that's okay," he added, looking fondly at his suddenly radiant little niece.

Lindy looked expectantly at her grandparents. Matt and Ruth looked at one another, then in unison at Lindy. While Ruth smilingly nodded her head, Matt said, "Good idea, Michael. Can't think of anyone more capable of handling the job."

"The cows haven't been fed yet, so I'll get started right now!" Lindy cried excitedly, picking up a stack of feed pans.

"Wait a minute! Have you thought up a name for Zoe's calf?" Ruth asked.

"Patrice."

"Some special significance to that name?"

"I have a friend named Patrice back in Edmonton."

"Your best friend?"

"Well, no, not exactly. She's not *my* best friend, but I'm *her* best friend. It's kind of hard to explain. My two best friends don't like Patrice because she's…large. She's really tall and she weighs too much, I guess, but I like her anyway. She's nice," Ruth just gave Lindy a look, saying nothing, while Lindy gazed at the new calf in the second pen, obviously uncomfortable.

"I guess she's really nicer than my other friends. I wish they liked her. Then I wouldn't feel so bad every time I hang out with *them* and ignore *her.*"

"Is there something about Zoe's calf that reminds you of your friend, Patrice?"

"Yeah, in a way. Zoe's calf is a lot bigger than Priscilla and she's, well, different because she was born all yellow. And I don't know why, but there's something about her face that kind of reminds me of Patrice."

Ruth laughed. "Remind me to tell you some day about a game I play inside my head with the cows and calves. Not right now, but some day. I'm glad you decided to name your calf after a good friend."

"My calf?"

"Yes, yours. She wouldn't be alive if it weren't for you."

"Oh." Lindy's face was a blank. "Thank you Grandma," she said politely, but without enthusiasm.

Ruth saw Lindy's eyes flick briefly toward Priscilla in the third pen. *'Oh my, it's Melissa's calf she feels the closest to, even though she saved Zoe's!'*

"So…, now that you have *two* calves, you'll be kept pretty busy."

Lindy's eyes brightened with astonishment. "*Two* calves?"

"Yes. Priscilla and Patrice. They both have special meaning for you, and they're both yours. *For keeps,* as you kids say!"

Lindy dropped the feed pans, threw her arms around her grandmother's waist and hugged her hard. Some things were just too wonderful for words!

Everyone, except Carin and Chris, was gathered around the table watching Michael eat breakfast, disappointed that he had not been able to raise anyone on the radio.

"It's a holiday and it's still early. Ten past seven," Michael said, checking his watch. "I'll try again a little later, but as soon as I'm finished here I'm going to take a quick run down to the convenience store. They're open at seven, 365 days a year. Maybe someone there will know something."

"What if there's no one there?" Rachel asked. "What then?"

Michael grinned at his sister. "Why wouldn't there be someone there? It's not as if everyone suddenly died! The only thing that died is electricity and probably everything, or almost everything, computerized."

"I'm going with you. If they're open there might be some things I should pick up."

"I'd rather you didn't pick up anything edible," Ruth interjected. "Leave whatever food there is for someone else. We have plenty."

"For right now, maybe. But what if it takes a week or more for the power to be restored?"

"We have enough food put away to last a year, more if we're careful."

Rachel looked around her, dumbfounded. "Where?"

"You and Ted are sleeping right on top of it. I'll show you later. But for God's sake don't breathe a word of that to anyone. And on second thought, *do* pick up something frivolous at the store so no one will think it's funny you went there early in the morning and then didn't buy anything. No doubt there will be a hungry person somewhere we can give it to later."

On the five- mile trip to the convenience store, Michael tried the CB radio again. Still nothing. "No truckers out and about on a holiday, I guess. Not close by, anyway."

"Are you sure it will even work?" Rachel asked.

"It should. It's not computerized like everything else."

As they approached the outskirts of town, they could see dozens of cars parked at the tiny strip mall, and people leaving the convenience store laden with heavy looking bags.

"Looks like Dow is having a good day," Michael observed.

"Dow?"

"Dow Marchant. He's been running that store along with his wife and kids for the past 8 or 9 years. I'll bet he's never had such a busy day."

"This whole thing is really starting to scare me, Mike. What if it lasts for weeks and no more food is available? What are people going to do?"

"An even bigger concern is what are they going to do for heat. There's not that many people with wood or propane stoves any more, especially in town. And even most wood or oil furnaces need electricity to operate. People are more likely to freeze to death before they starve."

"There must be something we can do to help out! Ruth cried hysterically.

"Don't panic yet. Not until we know more."

"I can't stand the thought of little kids being cold and hungry! And, what about the elderly, or people who can't get around and help themselves? What's going to happen to them?"

"I think Mom has some ideas to help as many people as possible if this blackout continues. But you've got to realize, Rachel, that if it continues for a long time, it's going to be *other people* who will be our biggest threat, not the cold or the lack of food."

Michael turned into a parking spot, just after it was vacated by another shopper. "Rachel, why don't you look around the store, buy something, anything, while I talk to Dow and maybe a few others, see if anyone knows anything. Okay?"

"Okay," Rachel said hesitantly, giving Michael a speculative look. "You don't want me talking to anyone, do you?"

"No, I don't," Michael said, unable to look Rachel in the eye. "I'm afraid you'll say the wrong thing, let something slip about the way we're fixed at the farm."

"Well, that's really flattering, little brother," Rachel said hotly. "Do you think I'm that stupid?"

"No, but I think you are kind-hearted and generous, too much so at times, and if you talk to someone with a hard-luck story you won't be able to help yourself."

Rachel looked ashamed. "Why do you make it so hard to be mad at you? You and Mom both. I want to be rip-roaring mad right now; then maybe I wouldn't feel so darn scared!"

Michael leaned over and kissed Rachel on the cheek. "I know. C'mon, let's see what we can find out."

There were no shopping carts in the little store and people were standing in two lines, arms filled with as much as they could carry. Behind the counter, Dow's wife, Marilyn, and daughter, Marissa, were adding up purchases on small calculators and making change from a cash box under the counter. His son, Drew, was putting purchases in plastic bags. Marissa was having a problem with a customer who wanted to pay with a check. No checks or credit cards could be accepted her dad had said, but the customer was getting angry and very loud. She looked pleadingly over at her father who was standing by the dairy section, finally catching his eye and silently pleading with him to intervene.

Coming over, Dow recognized the young man who wanted to pay with a check. He knew he had two little kids and no steady job. He glanced at the carton of milk, the bread, cereal, eggs, peanut butter and boxes of crackers and cookies on the counter, and almost imperceptibly nodded his head. Relieved, Marissa accepted the check and Drew packaged the items. The young man had the decency to look embarrassed. He knew his check was no good. And he suspected that Dow knew too. He'd make it up to him though as soon as he got his first paycheck from the new job he'd be starting in a few days. Meanwhile, his kids and his pregnant wife had to eat.

Michael and Rachel had watched the exchange at the counter and after the man left the store, Michael joined Dow, who had gone back over to the dairy case.

"Hey there Mike," Dow greeted him heartily. This is sure some screw-up, huh?"

"I guess you could call it that. Or something worse. Has anybody heard anything about what's going on?"

"Just one carton to a customer, please," Dow told a middle-aged woman loading her arms with three cartons. "There won't be any more milk delivered for another 3 days and a lot of people will be coming in for milk today for their kids. Thanks for your cooperation. Sorry, Mike," he said, turning to face him again. "Nobody is paying attention to my 'one to a customer' sign, so I have to stand guard over the milk. Looks like there won't be anything edible left in the store by noon. Everything's orderly though, nobody's in a panic and they probably won't be for another couple of days. The grocery stores should be open tomorrow, but their stocks are probably pretty low, like mine. Tomorrow is delivery day though for everything but the dairy stuff. If there's a delivery, that is!"

"Any idea how long this might last?" Michael asked.

Dow took a deep breath, exhaling forcibly. "I'd say we're either going to have the power back on in a matter of hours, or maybe a few days at most…or, it's going to be a very long time. Too long to even want to think about it."

"And which way do you think it will be?"

Dow looked hard at Michael, measuring his words carefully. "I think long enough that we will all have to find a new way of living. The phones and the TV and radio broadcasts being knocked out along with the power tells me this isn't something that's going to be simple to fix."

"You don't think there will be any deliveries tomorrow, do you?"

"I honestly won't know that until tomorrow."

"I've been trying to get someone on the CB radio, but so far this morning, nothing. There *must* be some truckers running even though it's a holiday, wouldn't you think?"

"Not necessarily. Not down in this end of the valley anyway. This is 'no man's land', remember, as far as everyone in Metro is concerned. We don't count down here; the politicians don't even know we exist. If there are any trucks running, they would be headed for Metro, guaranteed! The hell with the rest of the Province!"

"If this is going to be a long spell, we've got to have some kind of a plan. Lots of people are going to need help. Any chance of getting together later today to talk over some ideas?" Michael asked.

"Well, I'd have you over to my place, but it's like a refrigerator there. I should have put in a woodstove instead of building a useless fireplace for the 'atmosphere'!"

"That's okay. You can come out to the farm. We've got heat, at least. And bring the family along. The more heads the more ideas. I know my folks will want to do whatever they can to help."

"Would it be alright if I brought old Nate Taylor along? He's well into his eighties now, but he still has one of the sharpest minds around, and more common sense than anyone I've ever known. Also, he has no heat now in that little apartment he moved into, and a little time soaking up some heat from a woodstove would likely be a mighty welcome thing for the old guy."

"Oh, absolutely bring Nate along. I was even going to suggest it," Michael lied.

"Great! That's just great! I don't know what time I'll be closing up here, but by the look of things, it won't be long. Or, did you want to wait until tonight, after supper maybe?"

"Any time you want to show up will be fine. Anyway, you probably don't have a way to fix yourselves a hot meal, do you?"

41

"Oh no, Mike," Dow said, shaking his head, "We wouldn't want to impose...unless, well, we could bring something along to cook there."

"Whatever you want. I'm not sure what we have,...some turkey, I guess. I know Mom was planning a holiday dinner today and she won't mind some extra company. Not under the circumstances."

"I really appreciate it, Mike. We'll be there and I'll bring Nate along. We can try to figure out some kind of plan of action I guess, even if we never get to use it. And I hope to God we don't."

While Michael was talking to Dow, Rachel scanned the shelves in the small, crowded store looking for items that nobody seemed to be picking up. She finally selected a cake mix, icing sugar, a box of semi-sweet baking chocolate and a package of flaked coconut.

On her way to the lineup at the counter, Rachel passed a small freezer chest of expensive ice cream bars. No one seemed to be buying ice cream, so she picked up a box of 12 bars. Then, as she passed the candy display, she added a package of four chocolate bars to her purchases, hoping she had enough money with her to pay for all the calories piled in her arms. A young woman in the other line looked questioningly at the items Rachel was carrying, then, smiling shyly, she asked, "Somebody having a Birthday?"

"Oh, uh, *yes!*" Rachel said, suddenly realizing she was buying the basics for a Birthday celebration. "My little girl. She'll be eleven. No, wait a minute, twelve. They grow up so fast, don't they?"

The young woman smiled, readjusting her own purchases as she waited patiently for it to be her turn at the counter.

Michael was already in the truck waiting for her when Rachel exited the store. As she walked around to the passenger side, she noticed that the car in the next parking slot had the motor running. There were two small children in the back seat bundled in blankets and eating sandwiches, and a man and an obviously pregnant woman in front. She recognized the man as the one who had made a fuss about paying with a check.

On impulse, Rachel tapped on the driver's side window. The man turned to her and reluctantly rolled the window down a few inches.

"Would you like to have these for the kids?" Rachel asked, reaching in her bag and pulling out the package of candy bars. "I decided I don't want them," she explained. "And I don't want to stand in line to get my money back."

The young man started to refuse, but Rachel said, "Please. You'd be doing me a favor. This was an impulse buy, and I gained so much weight over the holidays that..."

"Okay," the man grinned. "Thanks." He quickly pulled the package into the car and rolled up the window again.

Rachel smiled and waved to the children in the back seat then hurriedly got into the truck.

"What was that all about?" Michael asked, starting the engine.

"Nothing. Just get out of here," Rachel said, her voice strained.

Michael looked at her curiously, but did as she asked.

"They were eating in the car, Michael," she said with a sob. "Not that that's such a strange thing, people eat in their cars all the time. But not in a parking lot, with the engine running. Oh Mike, Mike, they have no place to go to get warm and the gas tank will run out eventually." She looked at him with tear filled eyes. "What's going to happen to them? And how many more are there just like them?"

Michael kept his eyes on the road. He didn't have any answers.

CHAPTER FOUR – JANUARY 1, 2005

Ruth peeled back the aluminum foil and peeked at the nicely browning turkey. It still had a couple of hours to go, but it had to come out of the oven for a while so Rachel could bake her cake. She'd insisted, since there would be five extra people for dinner.

While Michael and Rachel were gone, Ruth had stuffed the turkey and put it in the oven to roast. She was determined to make everything just as normal as possible and that included a holiday dinner for the first day of the new year. She had set Carin and Chris to the task of removing the ornaments from the Christmas tree in the living room, while Matt and Ted were in the cellar hooking up the windmill powered generator. Lindy was out in the barn, taking her job very seriously.

When Michael and Rachel had returned from their trip to the store, Michael had stayed in the truck trying to raise someone on the CB radio. Amused by Rachel's purchase of the expensive ice-cream bars, Ruth told her there was no room for them in the freezer and just to leave them on the ledge outside the kitchen window. "They'll stay frozen out there for sure!" she had said, glancing at the outdoor thermometer that read a frigid minus 10 celcius.

Everyone, with the exception of Michael and Lindy, had gathered around the kitchen table for Matt's planning session. "It's going to take me a while to get the electricity on," he related. "I've run into a couple of glitches with the converter and need to wait for Michael to help figure things out. But even when we get the electricity going, it doesn't mean we can go back to using it like before. Power has to be reserved for the most essential things, like the freezer and refrigerator, the water pump and electric fence. We won't be able to use the electric baseboard heaters and no lights can be turned on during the day. It would be best if we used them as little as possible at night too, and rely more on the oil lamps. No using the dishwasher or clothes dryer or any small electrical appliance. No flushing toilets every time they are used. In fact, no using the toilets at all during the daytime. It will be strictly the outhouse during the day, toilets at night only.

"No daily showers and hair washing," he added, looking pointedly at Rachel and Carin. Eight people doing that every day might put an overload on the system. So that's going to be the order of the day until we know just how much power is generated. I know I should have tested everything out before now, but...I guess I really didn't think anything would happen."

"It will be *disgusting* not to take a shower and wash my hair every day," Carin pouted.

"What's disgusting," Matt retorted, "is how vain, pampered and wasteful North Americans have become in the last half century! We can't continue to do that Carin, not now!" Seeing his granddaughter's chin begin to tremble, Matt softened his voice. "You'll see that I'm right, honey. You think you need to shower and wash your hair every day because you've been conditioned to think that way. You *do* need to wash your hands frequently, but it's sponge baths for everyone for the time being."

"I won't mind," Chris said. Everyone but Carin chuckled at that.

"We've been sidetracked enough now," Matt said. There are a lot of things we have to get sorted out. First, everyone is going to be assigned certain tasks. Ted, I'm giving you one of the most important. The woodstoves and fireplaces are going to be your responsibility. You will need to haul in wood every day and keep the fires going. You'll also need to haul out the ashes." Ted nodded agreement.

"Chris, you will keep the kindling boxes full, feed the barn cats and feed the hens and collect the eggs in the afternoon. I'll do the feeding and egg gathering in the morning, along with the milking. Rachel and Carin, I'm afraid you'll have to be the broom, mop and dusting brigade. There's no wall- to- wall carpeting except out back, so we won't have to waste energy using a vacuum cleaner. Rugs can be done with the carpet sweeper or shaken outside. Grandma, here, will plan the meals and do most of the cooking since she's the one who knows what food is available and exactly where everything is located. Also, nobody is going to be anybody else's maid. We will all be responsible for picking up after ourselves, changing our own beds and sorting our own laundry. Both laundry and dishes will be team efforts and we'll all take turns. Any questions?"

45

"Doesn't Lindy have to do anything?" Carin asked sarcastically. "Where is she anyway?"

"Lindy got her assignment earlier this morning and that's where she is right now. She's going to be helping your Uncle Michael with the cattle. And, by the way, did you hear that Lindy saved a new born calf's life?"

Carin stared at her grandfather open-mouthed, but Chris piped up, "How did she do that?"

"Well, there was a sac around the calf that usually breaks when a calf is born, but this one didn't. The calf would have smothered if Lindy hadn't broken the sac."

"How did she know to do that?" Carin asked.

"She didn't. She just knew that everything wasn't all right and took a chance that she was doing the right thing by breaking the sac. That takes guts, and we're really proud of her!"

"Can I help in the barn sometimes, too?" Chris asked.

"I'd never turn down a willing hand," Matt answered. "It won't be long and there will be *two* cows to milk, so maybe you can help with that. Think you'd like to learn how to milk a cow?"

"Yeah!" The voice showed enthusiasm, but the face didn't.

"Okay," Matt continued. We're all going to have quite a bit of free time to fill with five extra hands sharing the load around here, so maybe all of you can put some thought into how we are going to fill it. Then again, we may not have any free time at all when we start doing what we can for other folks around here. In the spring and summer, of course, there will have to be a reassignment of chores."

"Oh no! We're not going to be here *that* long!" Carin moaned.

"I don't ever want to leave!" All eyes turned to Lindy as she came through the kitchen door with Michael. "I want to stay here forever," Lindy continued. "I don't want anyone to be freezing and starving, though. I want everything to be all right. I just don't want to go back home. Ever!"

"Well, we'll discuss that when the time comes," Rachel said firmly. "Were you able to get anyone on the radio, Michael?"

"I could only get hold of our vet, Ian McDonald. But he's been in contact with a trucker who works for the food distributor near Middleton. It doesn't look like there will be any food deliveries down this way tomorrow. Management is directing all supplies to the larger population areas. Something about doing the most good for the most people."

"That's a little hard to take," Matt said. "But I can understand their thinking. It's in the Metro area, Halifax, Dartmouth and Bedford where the trouble will start if there's going to be trouble."

Rachel went to the refrigerator. "Mom made a huge plate of sandwiches for lunch so everybody better dig in now. That refrigerator is losing it's cool quickly."

"As soon as we've had a bite, Michael, I need your help hooking up that generator," Matt said. "There are a couple of things I can't quite figure out with the converter."

"And I'm no help with it at all," Ted added.

Ruth gave Ted a searching look. "I've sure got something I need your help with, Ted. I'd like you to haul that Christmas tree out of the living room. Then, you and Rachel can take apart the bunk-beds up in the kids' room and haul them down to your room out back."

"How come?" Rachel asked.

"We aren't going to be using the baseboard heaters so that means there will be no heat to that room the kids are in. There are vents above the woodstoves to the other two bedrooms, but not that one. The chair in that back room of yours folds down into a small bed that should be just about right for either Chris or Lindy, so you won't have to haul that heavy twin bed down that Carin's been using."

"The couch in the living room folds out into a bed. Couldn't the girls use that instead of hauling those bunk-beds down here?" Rachel asked.

"No. Nate Taylor will be using the couch in the living room."

"Well when was that decided?" Matt asked.

"As soon as I learned he was coming over here with Dow and that he had no source of heat in his apartment. Nate doesn't know he's staying here yet. But he is. There's no way I'm letting that old man go back to a freezing cold apartment all alone." Ruth looked around the table at everyone. "And that's final!"

"I've got no argument with that," Michael said, chewing the last bite of his sandwich. "If you're ready Dad, let's get at that converter. I've made arrangements to contact Ian again in two hours. He's

47

trying to set up a CB relay so we can find out what's happening all over. Hopefully, we'll learn how widespread this is. It could be that Nova Scotia is the only place with a problem."

"Not likely, Son," Ruth said. "Remember, we couldn't get stations on the radio outside the Province that we can usually pick up."

"Let's get those bunk-beds," Chris said. "And I'll get our toothbrushes and cups and take them to the bathroom back there. And we'll need our clothes too. Carin can help with those."

"What's Lindy going to do?" Carin asked.

"Lindy's going to take a nap." Ruth said.

"Why am I going to take a nap?"

"Because you hardly got any sleep last night and you will probably be up half the night again. I expect Zepher to pop on us tonight. C'mon, you can help me open up the couch in the living room while your dad takes out the tree. You can take a nap in there."

"Why don't you join her," Matt suggested. If Zepher has her calf tonight, it won't be just Lindy out in the barn you know."

Lindy snuggled next to her grandmother on the couch, pulling the comforter up to her chin and sighing contentedly "Do you remember the summer we were here when Dad was on tour?"

"Mm hmm."

"I was only five then, but I remember how much I loved it here. I was sad for a long time after we went back home." Lindy yawned. "I wanted to still be here and I'm so glad we're back here again. I'm…" Lindy's voice trailed off and she was almost instantly sound asleep, as only a happy, exhausted child can be.

'Yes, I remember the summer you were here,' Ruth thought. It was almost six years ago. She remembered how Lindy had been fascinated by Matt's garden. Like most city kids she thought that food was just something you found in grocery stores, and never thought about how it got there. She remembered Lindy's amazement that tiny seeds pushed into the ground became little green shoots that grew and grew over the summer into recognizable food. That garden had been a revelation for her.

Smiling to herself, Ruth recalled how Lindy would head for the hen house first thing every morning to collect eggs from the nests. She loved animals and it had made her sad that chickens didn't like being held or petted. Before the summer was over, though, she had made a pet out of one young hen. It had gotten left out in the rain and was a dejected looking thing when Lindy found it. She had bundled it up in a towel and held it in her lap, gently drying it and talking to it. After that, it had followed her around everywhere.

Ruth also remembered the day she had been getting cattle ready for the local Exhibition. Lindy had been with her, brushing a calf that was going to be shown. Suddenly she had stopped brushing and a very thoughtful look had crossed her face.

"Grandma," she had asked, "If Grandpa's garden gives us vegetables, and his trees give us fruit and his chickens give us eggs, what do your cows give us?"

"Meat," Ruth had answered honestly.

:"What kind of meat do they give us?"

"Hamburger, steak, roasts; it's all called beef."

"How do they do that, Grandma?" she had asked, carefully surveying the calf she was brushing. "How do they give us beef?"

Ruth recalled how she had known that question was coming and how she had dreaded having to answer it. She had taken Lindy by the hand and had led her over to a bench under an apple tree to give herself time to think.

"Everything that people eat was once a living growing thing," she had said. "But nothing is still living when people eat it. When you pick an apple or a plum off a tree it is no longer living as soon as it is picked. It's the same with a carrot or potato pulled from the ground. Like fruits and vegetables, meat animals must no longer be living before people can eat them."

A solemn "oh," had been all Lindy said before running off to resume brushing the calf.

Later, Matt had cooked hamburgers on the grill. Ruth remembered watching with trepidation as Lindy took a bite and chewed thoughtfully.

"Grandma, was this hamburger one of your cows?"

"Yes."

"What was its name?"

"Bambi," Ruth had answered honestly, knowing that was probably the worst possible name for Lindy to hear.

Lindy had held her hamburger out in front of her, studying it critically, silently. "Hmm," she had finally said. "Thank you Bambi, you made good hamburger!" Then she had taken another bite and that had been that!

Ruth opened her eyes and looked over at the peacefully sleeping little girl. *'Would you react the same way now that you are eleven as you did when you were five?'* she wondered. Lindy stirred, then turned over on her side, drawing her knees up close to her chest. *'Yes, you probably would,'* Ruth decided. *'You are practical and wise beyond your years.'*

Ruth could hear Rachel beating something in a bowl in the kitchen and the enticing aroma of roast turkey had drifted into the living room. She decided she'd better go have a look at how that bird was coming. It would, after all, have to be fit for company.

As she walked into the kitchen, she heard the refrigerator begin to hum. *'Electricity,'* she thought. *'The whole world runs on it and no one is prepared to live without it.'*

CHAPTER FIVE – JANUARY 1, 2005

Dow looked at his watch. Almost 1:30. There was still a steady stream of people coming into the store but there was nothing much left but some junk food and ice cream.

Still lots of ice cream. It was so cold, nobody wanted to even think about ice cream, he imagined.

The store had still been fairly warm when they had opened it at 7am, but with so many people entering and leaving it now felt like a freezer. Marilyn and the kids were trying to wait on customers wearing their heavy winter parkas and gloves.

"Time to close," he called out to them as he flipped over the OPEN sign on his door and locked it. There were still a couple of customers in the store and Marilyn and Marissa totaled up their purchases while Dow wrote SOLD OUT in big block letters on a piece of cardboard and taped it to the glass on the door. He unlocked the door to let the last two customers out just as another car pulled up right in front.

"We're closed," he called out to the man as he was stepping from his car.

"I just need some cigarettes," the man said. I thought you were supposed to be open until eleven."

"Not today. We're just about sold out of everything and it's like an ice-box in here."

"I won't take a minute. Just need to get some smokes. Come on man, have a heart. There's nothing else open!"

Reluctantly, Dow opened the door wider so the man could enter. He was young, early twenties at most, unshaven, with bloodshot eyes and grimy looking clothes. Dow didn't recall ever seeing him before.

The man looked around the store. "Holy shit! You *are* just about cleaned out," he drawled. "Must have made quite a haul today, huh?"

Dow was beginning to feel apprehensive and he could see that Marilyn and the kids were wide-eyed with alarm. "What brand of cigarettes do you want?" Dow asked, trying to keep his voice steady.

"Well now, I don't see my regular brand. Must be sold out, huh? Give me a couple of packs of those," he said, pointing. "On second thought, I'll take the whole carton, along with what you have there under the counter."

Dow felt a rush of adrenalin as the man thrust his hand in his jacket pocket. *'Oh God,'* he thought. *'He's going to pull a gun on us!'*

There was a wad of bills in the man's hand as he pulled it out of his pocket, and he peeled off a fifty and two twenties and handed them to Marilyn. Wide-eyed, she handed him the carton of cigarettes, then reached under the counter for his change.

"That's okay," the man said. "Keep the change, but don't forget those two candy bars left there under the counter. I really appreciate you letting me in like this."

Dow unlocked the door, let the man out then quickly relocked it. He let out his breath forcibly, not realizing that he had been holding it. He felt light headed.

"You should have seen your face!" Marilyn exclaimed, starting to giggle.

"Me! You should have seen yours!"

Soon all four of them were laughing in relief. "Why are we laughing?" Dow howled. "We could have been robbed!"

"We could have been killed!" Drew exploded with laughter.

"We could have been *both!*" Marilyn tittered.

"I've gotta pee!" Marissa giggled, wiping at the tears streaming down her face and making a dash for the back room door.

Dow left the engine running to keep the car warm while he scurried up the shoveled walk to Nate's apartment. He was about to knock on the door when it was abruptly opened. Nate was dressed to go out somewhere and Dow was unsure now whether he should tell him about Michael's invitation.

"Come on in, Dow," Nate said. "It's about as cold in here as it is out there but at least there's no wind."

"Are you about to go somewhere?" Dow asked.

"No, just trying to keep warm. Not doing too good a job of it though."

Relieved, Dow related what he had come for. "Michael Kingsley was by the store earlier and he wants to get together to talk over some ideas on how we are all going to get through this power outage in case it lasts a long time. He says he wants you in on it. Ruth is doing up a holiday dinner and their place is warm. What do you say?"

"I say I'd be a fool to turn down an invitation like that! Are you heading over there right now?"

"We're going home to get changed. I'll be back by to pick you up in about an hour."

"I'll be ready."

Half an hour later, Nate was ready. He was dressed in his navy blue suit, French-cuffed shirt and striped necktie. The cold was playing hell with his arthritic hands and the tie had given him problems, but he finally got it right. His black wing-tip shoes had a spit-shine a General would be proud of, he thought, as he carefully slipped his feet into rubber galoshes and tucked the bottoms of his trousers smoothly inside. He put on his gray wool overcoat with the muskrat collar that could be turned up to warm his neck, then slid his black calfskin gloves over his gnarled fingers. He draped his white silk scarf around his neck then lifted his dark gray fedora out of its box and fitted it to his head. He appraised himself in the bedroom mirror, thankful that he had gotten a recent haircut. It was hard to recognize the tall, spare, gaunt featured old man staring back at him from the mirror as being himself. His mental image was of a much younger man. Concentrating on the clothes instead of the face, he said out loud, "You'll do." Then he stood near the door waiting for Dow.

.

Nate had intended to save Dow the cold walk up to his door, planning to step outside as soon as he heard the car pull up out front. But his mind must have been numbed by the cold and drifted off, his hearing too, because a sudden knock on the door startled him. When he opened it, there was Dow, smiling at him.

"All ready?"

"Ready," said Nate. He stepped stiffly out onto the small landing, closing the door behind him. Then reaching up above the doorsill he produced a key, securely locked the door, and replaced the key above the sill.

"Do you leave your key there all the time?" Dow asked, perplexed.

"All the time. That way I'm never locked out because I forgot the key. I always know where it is."

"But doesn't that make it awfully easy for a burglar to get in?"

"It never has. Burglars don't know the key is there, because they don't think anyone would do something so obvious. That's why I do it!" Nate gave Dow a lopsided grin.

"Shaking his head, Dow laughed and said, "C'mon, let's go get some roast turkey and a warm fire!"

Lindy sat on the rug in front of the woodstove in the family room, stroking Buddy's ears. Her Grandmother had just brought a wonderful looking man into the family room and invited him to sit in a lounge chair by the fire.

"Nate, I'd like you to meet my younger granddaughter, Lindy. Lindy, this is Mr. Taylor," Ruth said.

"How do you do, Mr. Taylor," Lindy replied. "I'm happy to meet you. This is Buddy," she said, patting Buddy on the head.

"It's nice to meet you too, Lindy. It's been a long time since I've met such a charming young lady. But I already know Buddy. He and I had quite an adventure together a few years ago."

"You did? What happened?" Lindy moved closer to Nate.

"You mean your Grandmother hasn't told you Buddy's story?" Nate asked, turning to Ruth with raised eyebrows.

"No. What story, Grandma?"

"Mr. Taylor is referring to the story about how Buddy came to be our dog. Actually, I wrote a story about it. Mr. Taylor is in the story because he is one of the people Buddy went to on his way to finding us. You see, he was lost for a long time, and…"

"Do you still have the story? Can I read it?"

"Do you want me to get it for you right now? Or do you think you could wait until after dinner?"

"Right now would be better," Lindy replied.

Ruth laughed. "Excuse me Nate while I find that home-made book for Lindy, *'right now'*."

Ruth passed Matt on his way into the family room bearing a tray of filled coffee mugs and fixings. On the way over, Dow had learned that what Nate had missed most all day was a hot cup of coffee and had relayed that message to Matt.

"Oh my!" Nate exclaimed. "Is that ever a welcome sight! Hot coffee is what I've missed most today. You never know how you'll miss something until you don't have it. We take so much for granted nowadays." He took a sip of coffee and closed his eyes, savoring it.

"I've been getting acquainted with your delightful granddaughter, Matt."

"Did she tell you about how she saved a calf's life this morning?" Matt asked.

"No! You saved a calf's life?" he directed at Lindy.

Matt told Nate the whole story and Nate kept glancing at Lindy throughout the tale, seeing her modestly, blushingly, dismiss it as nothing special.

"Do you think you'd like to become a veterinarian when you're older?" Nate asked Lindy.

"No," Lindy said decisively. "I want to be a farmer."

Nate sat back in his chair as though he were dumbfounded by Lindy's answer. "I've been around a lot of years," he said, "but I don't believe I have ever heard a little girl say she wanted to grow up to be a farmer! A teacher maybe, or even a doctor, but… Why do you want to be a farmer?"

"Because it's the most important job in the world," Lindy said matter-of-factly. "Nobody *needs* a teacher or doctor every day, but everybody *does* need food every day."

"What an incredible child!" Nate exclaimed, turning to Matt. "How did an old goat like you wind up with such a treasure?"

Ruth found the typewritten story she had written about Buddy in the bottom drawer of her dresser. Matt had wanted her to get it published, and she had meant to one day, but it was one of those things she had never gotten around to doing. It was just a bound manuscript now, not really a book at all. *Home At Last* she had titled it. It was written from Buddy's point of view. Now Ruth thought maybe that was a silly way to have written it, but at least Lindy might like it.

She passed the dining room and paused seeing Carin in there setting the table. Two places had to be set at one end since there would be thirteen people at a table meant for twelve. Carin was wearing a sullen look. She's probably put out, Ruth thought, because Lindy is talking with Nate and she has to do this all alone.

"Oh, Carin, what a beautiful job you've done!" Ruth exclaimed, going over to look at the table. "Everything looks perfect!"

Carin's smile showed her obvious pleasure at being praised. "I found these wine glasses in the china closet," Carin said. "Mom said we'd be serving wine with dinner and I thought these would look nice."

"They are exactly the ones I would have wanted you to use, especially with company here today," Ruth said hugging Carin.

"What's that?" Carin asked, pointing to the bound manuscript in Ruth's hand. Ruth told her about the *Buddy Book*, and that Lindy had asked to read it.

"I'd like to read it too," Carin said. "Could I read it first, then Lindy can read it when I'm through with it? Please?"

Ruth made a quick decision and handed the book to Carin. Lindy could handle being in second place far better than Carin could, she reasoned. And right now, Carin needed to feel special. Lindy had had her day in the sun. If she could think of something, she would make sure Carin had her day too.

"Thanks, Grandma," Carin beamed. "I'll read it fast so Lindy won't get *too* upset!"

"Couldn't you find the book?" Lindy asked, seeing her grandmother's empty hands.

"It seems you aren't the only one who would like to read it," Ruth said, giving Lindy a warning look. "Carin would like to read it while you are out in the barn with the cows."

Lindy quickly shrugged off her disappointment. "That's okay, I guess. Can I show Mr. Taylor his room?"

Nate looked from Lindy, to Ruth, then to Matt. No one said anything.

"What do you mean, '*show me my room*'," he asked Lindy.

"We fixed up the living room for you. That's going to be your bedroom while you're here," Lindy said.

Nate tossed his hands up in front of him. "No, no, no, no," he said. "I won't hear of it. You have a full house now and you don't need a cantankerous old man hanging around."

"But Grandma said she wasn't going to give you any choice, Mr. Taylor, and she didn't want any arguments about it, either. Besides, I want you to stay."

"We need you to stay, Nate," Ruth said. "There's going to be a whole lot of things we're going to have to figure out how to do if this power outage continues for a long time, and none of us know how to get by without electricity and supermarkets and everything else we are all used to having."

"You are the only one of us who has ever lived without those things," Matt added, "and you can tell us how things used to be when you were young, how they *can* be again if necessary. Please don't say 'no'."

Nate stood, drawing himself up to his full height. "I'll stay," he said softly.

Lindy took Nate by the hand. "Come see your room," she said, and led him into the living room.

There was a couch opened up into a bed, and across from it a delicately carved antique sofa of superb craftsmanship. On the south wall, bracketing an enormous window that began about two feet from the floor and extended nearly to the ceiling, was an exquisite antique burled walnut desk on the left and a most interesting hand painted curio cabinet on the right. At the other end of the room there was a small fireplace with a softly burning log and the half wall to the side held a wonderful array of books. A Comfortable looking wingback chair and a small round table in front of the fireplace completed the furnishings, and dominating the center of the room was an obviously authentic oriental rug. With the exception of the television on one wall, Nate could have believed that he had stepped back in time to a more gracious era. He knew he would be most comfortable in this familiar feeling room.

"Do you like it?" Lindy asked. "I think it's the most beautiful room I've ever seen. Except for the dining room. That's beautiful too."

"Yes, it's beautiful, Lindy," Nate said. "Very beautiful."

"I'll go get you some more coffee and you can have it in here by the fireplace," she said, darting away, not asking Nate if he wanted more coffee.

Nate sat in the chair in front of the fire and lowered his head, feeling embarrassed and a bit ashamed. *'Maybe there is a small bit of truth in them wanting me here because they think I can be of some help,'* he told himself. *But mostly it is because they are good people who don't want to see an old man cold and hungry. To think they would do that for me even though all these years they have been here I have treated them coldly, as though they didn't belong because they are outsiders, because they are Americans and there is only one reason why Americans came to Nova Scotia in the 60's and 70's.'* Nate lifted his chin with resolve. *'But that is over now, and I need to put that behind me, try to get around those feelings, give them the benefit of...'*

"Nate," Matt said from the doorway. "We have some time yet before dinner. I thought it might be a good idea if I drove you over to your place while it's still light out to pick up a few things you might need overnight. We can get the rest tomorrow."

"Can Mr. Taylor have more coffee first?" Lindy asked, carefully setting the tray she was carrying on the small table beside Nate. "You know what you always say, Grandpa, 'One cup of coffee is never enough; it takes two to really hit the spot.' And Mr. Taylor hasn't had a second cup yet."

"I think you're planning on spoiling me," Nate said, patting Lindy's hand.

"I'm going to try my best. I'm already pretending that you're my great-grandfather. I never had one before," Lindy said shyly. "If I did, I would want him to be just like you."

Nate had trouble getting the words past the sudden lump in his throat. "Then maybe you'd better start calling me Grandpa Nate," he said. "I wouldn't want my great-granddaughter calling me Mr. Taylor."

Lindy fairly beamed.

When Dow and his family had arrived, Dow and Drew had joined Michael in the truck to hear what news was available on the CB radio. Chris had just finished collecting eggs, and with the basket on his lap, was perched on Drew's knee in the cab of the truck. Michael had made contact with Ian who told them he was waiting for a relay message and to stand by; he didn't expect it to be that long a wait. They passed the time with small talk, each of them reluctant to discuss the situation for fear that talking about it would make it more real, or worse yet, make it a fact rather than a mere possibility.

Marilyn and Marissa were getting acquainted with Rachel in the kitchen, exchanging pleasantries and offering to help with the final preparations for the dinner. Ruth joined them, after first peeking in the dining room to see how Carin was getting along. Carin, finished with setting the table, was seated in a small fireside chair, her eyes glued to the typewritten pages of the *Buddy Book*. To Ruth's immense relief, she appeared to be completely engrossed. She didn't know why, but it was important to her that Carin, especially, liked the story.

Matt had just left with Nate to go pick up a few things and Lindy had trailed behind them, saying she was headed for the barn to check on things.

Rachel suddenly looked around her, then asked, "Has anyone seen Ted lately?"

"Who's Ted? Marilyn asked.

"My husband. If you'll excuse me, I think I'll go out back and see if he's there." Rachel was feeling a bit concerned. Ted had been acting somewhat detached all day, as though he wasn't quite all there.

"Well, there you are!" Rachel said cheerfully, seeing Ted checking the fire in the little oil stove. "We've missed you. You should come and meet the company."

Ted sat dispiritedly on the futon and sighing, looked up at Rachel. He didn't know how to put what he was feeling into words.

"You wish we weren't here, don't you Ted," Rachel stated. "Me too. But we are here and right now we just have to try to make the best of it."

"That isn't it, honey. I actually don't mind being here at all. I just feel so…useless! I don't know how to do *anything* except play musical instruments. I look at your brother, Michael, and there he is about fourteen years my junior, he has a business degree and yet he knows how to do just about anything mechanical, electrical, you name it. *He knows all the guy stuff!* While *I* barely know how to change a light bulb! I don't even feel competent hauling in wood and keeping the fires going! I'm scared to death of the cattle and I'm ashamed to admit I'm just a bit jealous of my own daughter because she feels so at ease with them. Carin is miserably unhappy and I don't know what to say or do to make things better for her." Ted stood and began pacing. "I guess the worst thing of all is the knowledge that if we weren't here being taken care of by your folks, we wouldn't survive. Because I wouldn't know how to help us do that. And I am convinced, Rachel, absolutely convinced, that if we were in Edmonton right now, that's what our situation would be! I think we are all in for a very bad time of it, for a long time, and I don't know how I can ever fit in or how I can be of any use to anyone. It's like I'll always be standing on the edge, reacting rather than acting, because I haven't a clue how to live in the kind of world this will become!"

Rachel went over to Ted and laid her head against his chest. She didn't know what she could say to make him feel better because she felt the same certainty of disaster and the same inadequacies within herself.

CHAPTER SIX – JANUARY 1, 2005

They listened to what Ian McDonald had learned, with growing apprehension. "It's already started," Michael said solemnly. How about waiting until after dinner before we tell everyone the bad news. It could very well be the last peaceful dinner we have for a long time, and there's no sense in ruining it for everyone."

Dow nodded agreement. "I'm glad now that Drew and Chris got tired of waiting and got out of the truck to stretch their legs. That wasn't something they needed to hear. That little guy," he nodded, indicating Chris, "probably wouldn't have been able to resist telling everyone." They got out of the truck.

"Uncle Michael!" Lindy called from the barn door. "I think you should come take a look at…"

"Is it Zepher?" Michael called.

"No, it's Mia."

As Michael walked toward the barn, Lindy excitedly told him what the situation was. "Grandpa hasn't been out to milk Felicity yet, and I haven't looked at the milk cows since this morning. But I just went to feed Mia so Grandpa wouldn't have to and she's in there trying to have her calf. It's too soon, isn't it? Grandpa said she was due in ten days. But there are two feet and a head sticking out of Mia and she's standing up and keeps turning around in a circle, talking to the calf and trying to reach it. Come on! Quick! I think the calf's stuck!"

When Michael and Lindy reached Mia's pen, she was standing over her squirming calf, softly talking to it and licking it clean.

"She did it all by herself!" Lindy exclaimed.

"That's the way most calves are born," Michael told her, going into the pen and lifting the calf's leg. "Well I'll be darned, we've got another girl! Got another girl name handy, Lindy?"

"I'll have to think about this one."

"Let's just leave Mia to get acquainted with her baby and go in and get cleaned up for dinner. I swear I can smell that turkey all the way out here in the barn. How about you?"

61

"It's all right to leave her?" Lindy asked, ignoring the question.

Michael tweaked Lindy's nose. "Lindy, you're going to wear yourself out over these cows! Most of them have their calves all by themselves and they take care of them and feed them all by themselves. You don't need to watch them *all* the time."

"I like watching them."

"I know, and I really appreciate that you do, but…"

"Pitty-Pat."

"What?"

"Pitty-Pat. That's the new calf's name," Lindy said. "It just came to me that's what her name should be. She *looks* like a Pitty-Pat."

"And *you* look like somebody I could beat in a race to the house!" Michael said, poking Lindy in the stomach and starting to run.

"Hey, no fair, Uncle Michael; you had a head start!" Lindy hollered, in hot pursuit.

Everyone ate as though there were no tomorrow. Stuffed and sluggish, they pushed their chairs back from the table groaning with satisfaction.

"We sure look like an energetic group, don't we!" Dow chuckled.

"I haven't had a meal like this for more than eighteen years," Nate said. "Not since I lost Helen. My compliments and thanks to all you ladies. I would stand and offer a toast to you if I could move!"

"Well, I guess I have to move whether I can or not," Matt said, looking at his watch. "It's past five already and cows tend to get a bit testy if they are late being milked."

"Do you have to milk Mia now too, Grandpa?" Lindy asked.

"Her calf will take care of most of the milking for the first couple of days," Matt said. "Then I'll have to start milking her regularly. But I'll be letting Felicity dry up soon to get ready for her next calf, so I'll only have two to milk for a week or two right now."

"Can I go out to the barn with you? I have an awful lot to learn if I'm going to be a farmer."

"You can, unless your Mom or Grandma have other ideas," Matt said.

"If you mean the dishes, I don't expect the kids to help tonight. We'll all be getting in one another's way as it is," Ruth said.

"I'm washing," Marilyn offered. "And Rachel and Ted can dry."

"What am I supposed to do?" Ruth asked.

"Relax!" several voices said in unison.

"I guess I won't argue about that," Ruth said, looking questioningly at Michael. He looked nervous all of a sudden and kept glancing at the kids. "Carin," she said, "Why don't you and Chris take Marissa and Drew into the family room along with your 3D puzzle. I bet they'd like to help you with it."

"Sure," Carin said, happy for the reprieve from kitchen chores. "This thing is really great," she told Marissa as she picked up one side of the plywood board on which the puzzle was being assembled, while Marissa picked up the other end. Carefully they eased it through the door into the family room. Drew was only too happy to follow. From the moment he had first set eyes on Carin he was smitten. That first eye contact between them felt like a bolt of lightning to Drew.

"What is it Michael?" Ruth asked as soon as the children were out of earshot.

"It isn't good Mom," Michael said sadly. "You know, we talked about having a few days before panic set in, but Ian has been getting reports on his relay network all day from truckers, and it's already bedlam in Halifax. A lot of the grocery stores have been broken into and looted, but the worst of it is the fires. People are setting fire to anything they can find to get warm. It's crazy! It's only been, what, about 16 hours since the power went off! There have been power outages much longer than that and no one set fires and started looting!"

"This is different, Michael, and people know it," Ruth said, her voice quavering. "They *know!* And right now they are more cold and angry than anything. But by tomorrow they will be downright scared and the fear that people in the city will be feeling is what we in the country have to fear the most."

Dow looked pensive. "Want to take a ride into town with me, Michael?" He asked. "We could take a quick look to see if there are any signs of hysteria here and be back by the time your dad is done milking. If we're going to be sitting up half the night trying to hatch some kind of plan, it might be good to know what kind of eggs we're sitting on."

Michael nodded. "Let's go," he said, not wasting any time thinking about it.

"Can I get you some coffee, Nate?" Ruth asked. "Or sherry, perhaps?"

"No, Ruth. Thanks, but I'm fine," Nate said absently.

"What are you thinking, Nate," she asked softly.

Nate was having trouble meeting Ruth's eyes. "This is not easy for me to say, Ruth. I'm feeling horribly ashamed and I have a great need to apologize to you and Matt." Nate was speaking slowly, measuring each word before it was spoken.

Ruth frowned. "I don't understand."

"I've had no business feeling the way I have about the two of you for all the years you've been here. I should have tried to understand, should have realized that times are different now, the way people think is different. I'm not trying to make any excuses for myself, but I guess that being a Second World War Veteran made me feel that anyone who won't stand up and fight for the principles his country believes in is a coward and isn't worthy of respect or of being thought of as a friend or neighbor. I have never been a friend or neighbor to you, Ruth," Nate said, finally looking her in the face. "But you have been a friend and neighbor to me, even though I am undeserving."

Ruth moved from her place at the table and sat down next to Nate. "Nate," she said, placing her hand on top of his, "You haven't said specifically what has bothered you about us all these years, but I guess I know. It's about Vietnam, isn't it?"

Nate nodded, looking ashamed.

Ruth laughed softly. "I don't know how the rumor was started, but we've been aware of its existence from time to time, and even after all these years it hasn't stopped. Maybe the rumor got started because people here couldn't believe that anyone would want to move to Nova Scotia for any reason other than to escape involvement in a war. Nova Scotia isn't exactly a 'happening place', but that's precisely why we moved here. We wanted to live a life vastly different from our life in Boston. For six years we came here every summer so we knew for sure this was where we wanted to be."

Nate gave Ruth a searching look as she continued. "We finally moved here in the summer of 1978, four years *after* the U.S. pulled out of Vietnam. We were always amused that people thought Matt was a draft-dodger and that no one stopped to think about the discrepancy in time or that the U.S. had been drafting 19 and 20 year old kids, not family men pushing 40! Matt had served two years in the Army right after high school. That was between Korea and Vietnam. Then he went to University. He's had a long- term career as a structural engineer and I was the head of nursing services at a medium sized hospital. We gave up financial security and retirement pensions to come here and live on a farm so we could raise our young son in a more wholesome environment. Rachel was seventeen then, and was attending Acadia University. Very few people around here even knew we had a daughter, especially one that was eleven years older than Michael. Now you know our story, Nate," she said, squeezing his hand.

"And now I have reason to be doubly ashamed," Nate said.

"No you don't. If Matt had been younger, the rumor could have been fact. If there had been any danger of him being sent to Vietnam, he would have done just about anything to avoid it, I'm sure. He thought of it as an immoral war."

Nate was shaking his head. "There's no apology I could give you that would be adequate. I..."

"No apology is necessary at all. We have thought of you as a friend ever since you took care of Buddy when he was lost. Whether you know it or not, that's when we became friends of yours too. And now it's simply our turn to do something for you. That's what friends are for."

For the second time in a few hours, Nate felt a lump in his throat. Only this time it was bigger and he couldn't get any words around it.

Dow and Michael returned from their trip to town just a few minutes after Matt and Lindy came in from the barn. Lindy joined the other youngsters who were all sitting on the rug in front of the woodstove in the family room, with Buddy the center of attention. They had given up working on the puzzle. "There's not enough light from these oil lamps," Carin had said. So she was telling Marissa and Drew the story about Buddy when Lindy walked in.

Lindy clapped her hands over her ears. "I don't want to hear it!" she said. "I want to read it for myself." But bits and snatches kept coming through, intriguing her, and gradually she lifted her hands from her ears, totally engrossed in the story. Drew was watching Carin's face as she talked, watching her lips forming words, the soft glow from the oil lamps creating a halo-effect around her head giving her an unearthly radiance in Drew's eyes. She took his breath away. If he had been asked to, he couldn't have repeated a word Carin said.

"Annapolis looks like a ghost town," Dow told everyone after they had all assembled around the dining room table, mugs of fresh coffee steaming in front of them. "There's not a light to be seen anywhere, though a few houses have smoke coming out of the chimney."

"We didn't see anyone," Michael added. "No people on the streets and no cars other than ours. Both grocery stores look intact and so does Dow's store. So at least the panic hasn't set in down our way yet."

"No, it would start in the city," Matt said. "If it starts at all."

"It already has," Dow replied bleakly. Then he and Michael related all they had learned from Ian about the situation in Halifax. There were a couple of things they hadn't related to Ruth and Nate previously, saving the worst of the news for the time when everyone was present.

"Several men tried to hijack a truck when the driver pulled over to the curb to relay a message to Ian. The driver got scared and took off pretty fast. He says he felt a couple of bumps and is pretty sure he saw a large object flying sideways, probably a body, but he didn't stop to find out. That trucker thinks he killed someone and he's pretty shaken up," Dow told them.

"We got Ian on the radio again on the way back from town," Michael said. "The panic is spreading like wildfire through Dartmouth and up into Bedford, too. It's just a matter of time before outlying areas get hit."

"My God, that's not even two hours from here!" Marilyn wailed. "What are we going to do?"

"Pray for snow," Nate said. "It will take a while for roads to be cleared, if they get cleared at all, and snow will buy us some time."

"But surely the government is doing something," Rachel said. "Isn't there some kind of emergency measures plan they will be implementing?"

"*They*," Nate boomed, "aren't likely to be doing anything right now except saving their own skins! You say yours was the only car on the road in Annapolis," he said pointedly to Michael and Dow. "So where were the town police? Snug under a down comforter in their beds with the police cars parked in their driveways, I'll warrant!"

Michael and Dow nodded. "There aren't enough police to be everywhere in Metro," Nate continued, "so I'd be willing to bet they aren't visible anywhere. Can't say that I blame them, either. The politicians in the past 30 or so years have made a mess of things for everyone. There doesn't seem to be one whole brain among the lot of them! Can we realistically have any faith in leaders who are little more than a self-serving bunch of egotists who, over the past 30 years, have given themselves raises of over 800%, pandered to big business and all but wiped out agriculture and the fishery here?"

Everyone was silent after Nate's outburst, and he took that as a license to continue. "I remember how it was here before the government decided that farmers and fishermen had to 'get big or get out'. Everyone used to be able to make a decent living when everything was on a small scale. And that includes taxes. No farmer had to have an off-farm job to support the farm the way they do today. Everyone who lived out in the country produced something to sell year round. There was milk, eggs, butter, cheese, beef, chicken, pork, lamb and every kind of fruit or vegetable that could be grown here. The people who lived in town were the farmers' customers. And the farmers, in turn, were customers of the town merchants. It was the same with the fishermen. Nobody got rich, but it was an economy that worked. People weren't on welfare and there was no such thing as a food bank. Unemployment? No such thing for anyone who wanted to work. Or for anyone who wanted to eat. Two or more generations lived under the same roof and mostly got along. Child - care was something done by families, not strangers. And government didn't tell us how to live, didn't pass laws that made us buckle up or wear helmets or take our kids away if we warmed their backsides when they deserved it!"

Nate looked at everyone sitting around the table. "I'm sorry," he said. "Please excuse an old man for getting up on his soapbox and having his say. I guess I needed to do that because I'm feeling a little scared about what's happening. But I'm stepping down now, because nothing I've said is going to solve the problem we're faced with."

"Don't be so sure of that," Ruth said. "We have an immediate problem of survival that we need to concentrate on first of all, but the image you just gave us of how small communities used to work may be the ideal solution for the long term…if there is a long term."

"The immediate need is for heat and food," Matt said, rising and beginning to pace. "We have to concentrate on solving that problem for as many people as possible."

"And protection," Dow interjected. "Anyone who has heat and food will be prey for anyone who doesn't. That means we have to have boundaries, almost an enclosed group, because let's face it, we aren't going to be able to organize a very large area."

"No, not immediately," said Michael. "But if we establish a focal point, say right here, then spread out in both directions, we can develop a sort of survival colony, like Ian's relay with truckers."

"We'll need an inventory of people and houses with a heat source first of all," Matt said excitedly, searching in the sideboard for paper and pen. "Now, immediately to the east of us are the Turners. They have a fireplace and at least one woodstove. The Elliotts across the road from them have an oil furnace that's probably electrically fired so it's a pretty safe bet they have no heat. Then there's that young couple that recently moved into the old Stewart place and I don't know what kind of heat they have, do you Ruth?"

Before Ruth could answer, Nate put up his hand for attention. "This won't work on paper," he said. "You are forgetting that this is a very neighborly place. Most people without heat have probably already been invited into a neighbor's home where there's a source of heat. Just like you invited me into your home here. Our job is to get out there tomorrow morning and contact the closest neighbors. Then get *them* running a relay in both directions. Most people will be inclined to help their next -door neighbor, if they aren't already. What we need on your paper there, Matt, is a list of all the resources in the area; the few farms that still exist and what they produce on a daily basis like milk and eggs, and food that might be stored in large quantities like potatoes and apples. Then there are the stores and what they have that people might need for cooking; gas barbecues and camp-stoves, things like that. Besides a complete inventory of things that might be needed, we'll need to turn the grocery stores into food banks."

"Nate," Dow interrupted, "What if the people who need things can't pay for them?"

"Nobody is going to be paying for anything," Nate said. "Dairy farmers have to milk their cows twice a day and if there are no milk trucks picking up the milk, what are they going to do with it? Dump it?"

"Are you suggesting that farmers and store owners should just give everything away to whoever needs it? They'll never go for that!" Dow said adamantly.

"Well, unless someone can come up with a better idea, they will have to be convinced that it's necessary." Nate said. "What should we do, let only people with money survive and everyone else be damned?"

"What about barter?" Marilyn suggested. "Someone could get milk from a dairy farmer and in return give the dairy farmer something he needs."

"But that would still leave out anyone who has nothing to trade," Nate objected. "And what if the dairy farmer didn't want or need what was being offered?"

Michael had been deep in thought. "What I think we will need," he said, "is a system of debits and credits. There is very little actual money in circulation anymore, you know. Most monetary transactions are nothing more than an electronic transfer of debits and credits to personal or business accounts. If we can think up some simple way of implementing such a system…"

"That still leaves out people who have nothing to start with because they would have no means of obtaining credit," Nate pointed out.

"Couldn't labor or services be their credit?" Marilyn asked. "Does it have to be goods?"

"This is giving me a headache," Matt said, grimacing. "It's obviously going to take a lot of working out. How about if for right now we concentrate on making an inventory of farms and all the things that might be available in local stores that could be urgently needed. The sooner we do that and make contact with those farmers and merchants the less chance there will be of any looting getting started. Because if that happens, things are going to get out of control fast!"

"If you're going to be doing an inventory, now's a good time for me to go check on things in the barn," Michael said.

"Oh, I saw Lindy go out about 15 or 20 minutes ago," Ruth informed him.

"Why am I not surprised?" Michael laughed. "But checking the cows shouldn't have taken her that long. So, maybe I better go check on *Lindy!"*

"Since I don't know any of the farmers, or anything else, I'd better go re-load woodstoves and fireplaces," Ted said. "Wouldn't want to get fired from my job!" he said a little too heartily.

Rachel gave him one of her annoyed looks then turning to Matt, asked, "Dad, do you want me to play secretary?"

Ted didn't wait around to hear the answer. He'd get all the damn fires going good, he decided, and the one in the little stove out back would be the last one he checked. After that he was hitting the sack. '*No one will miss me,*' he told himself. '*I'm not needed.*'

Michael heard the back door of the barn squeak shut just as he came in the front door. Shining his flashlight in that direction, he saw Lindy trying to coax Lady into the fourth calving pen.

"What's going on?" Michael asked, giving Lindy a hand.

70

"I thought Lady ought to come in," Lindy said. "She's all soft around the tail-head."

Michael felt around the sides of Lady's tail, and surprised, said, "She sure is!" He went out to look at a chart hanging on the wall in the center of the barn. "Hmph. She's due in six days. Looks like she's going to be a little early."

"That's okay, isn't it? Lindy asked. "Mia was ten days early and it was okay."

"Oh yeah, six days isn't much too early. I'm just wondering why they all seem to be calving early though."

"Zepher's not. I looked at the chart and she's due today. I don't think she's going to make it today though."

Michael checked Zepher and had to agree with Lindy. There would be no calf out of Zepher tonight. "Everything else okay outside?" Michael asked.

"I think so. You might want to check for yourself, though."

"I don't need to if you already did. Come on, let's go back to the house. We won't need to come back out for a couple of hours."

"Hey Uncle Michael, bet I can beat you to the house!" Lindy called as she began running.

"No fair, Lindy!" Michael hollered. "You had a head start!"

Rachel had a list of all the farmers in the area and was working on the list of store- owners when Michael and Lindy came in from the barn.

"Look what I found on the window ledge outside," Michael said, holding a box of ice cream bars aloft. "Funny how you can eat a big meal and swear you won't need to eat again for a week, but about four hours later you feel you could use a snack."

No one seated around the table refused one of the expensive ice cream bars. Before taking hers, Rachel checked to make sure there were five left for the kids. *'Twelve bars and thirteen people,'* she thought. *'Who is left out?'* Then it came to her. Ted. Ted was the odd man out. Rachel helped herself to an ice cream bar.

Ted was stretched out in the middle of the futon in the back room, still fully dressed except for his shoes. He heard Michael and Lindy come in from the barn, laughing and making enough of a racket to wake the dead. He could hear the wind beginning to pick up outside, occasional gusts whistling around the corner of the house. Listening to the wind, he was lulled to sleep.

He awoke slowly a couple of hours later, a dream still fresh in his mind. He concentrated hard on recalling the details and his mind sorted them out rapidly, like reading a sheet of music. Suddenly he smiled to himself in the dark. "That's the answer," Ted said out loud. *'It's going to take using some of that precious stored energy,'* he thought. *'But the wind will take care of that.'*

He feigned sleep when he heard Rachel and the kids come in to get ready for bed, Rachel sighing and tossing a comforter over him. He lay there awake developing his plan until he could be certain everyone else was asleep. Then he would get busy.

CHAPTER SEVEN – JANUARY 1, 2005

Tom Bricker was colder than he could ever remember being in his life. His one thin blanket had been enough in the drafty little apartment when the heat was on and he was fully clothed. But he felt if he didn't do something soon he would freeze to death right there in his bed. With the blanket wrapped around him, he got out of bed and groped around the dark room, locating the bottle on the cluttered table. He knew he had emptied it hours ago, but still he upended it to his shaking mouth, trying to squeeze out a few more drops.

The apartment was about one-quarter of a one- story house that had been built on the edge of the town marsh in the early 40's. It was set off by itself, exposed to the wind in every direction. The rest of the house, separated from Tom's quarters by a thin wall, was occupied by a couple who were in their 70's, living as best they could on an inadequate old-age pension. Tom, at 42, was an unemployed farm worker existing on welfare.

Earlier, just before it had been fully dark, Tom had seen a pick-up truck go past on its way into the downtown area, then go past again on its way out of town. It had been the only vehicle he had seen in more than two hours, and there had been none since.

Although not especially bright, Tom had always been a hardworking man who prided himself on giving an honest day's work for an honest day's pay. Until there was no longer any work, that is. So, what he knew he was about to do went against his nature, but he felt he really had no choice in the matter.

Folding the blanket in half, he wrapped it around his shoulders over his threadbare coat and secured it with a large safety pin. He pulled his knitted wool cap down over his ears and drew on his thin wool mittens. Scrabbling his way blindly across the room, he located the one tool he owned; a heavy duty flat-head screwdriver. He paused at the door, nearly losing his nerve. Then, with a shiver of resolve, he stepped out into the freezing night air.

His target was the building supply store a quarter of a mile down the road. A sudden gust of wind whipped at his back, lifting the trailing ends of the blanket and flipping them over his head. Grasping frantically at the ends of the blanket, he held them tightly against his thighs and, slightly bent forward, he loped off toward the store.

Tom grasped the sturdy padlock on the back door of the building center's warehouse, cursing as his cold numbed fingers lost their grip on the screwdriver and it fell clattering to the ground. He searched around the pitch black ground with his feet, brushing them around in a semi-circle to the front and sides of him. Tears were streaming from his eyes, turning to rivulets of ice on his face and he screamed in frustration just before his foot struck a small object and sent it skittering. On his hands and knees, Tom felt around and finally his hand enclosed a round tapered handle. His fingers told him he had located his screwdriver.

He pounded at the padlock for several minutes, willing the screwdriver to become a hammer, and succeeded only in breaking off a tiny chip on the head of the screwdriver. He was about to pitch the offensive tool as far as he could throw it, when he decided to try using it as a pry bar under the hasp. The wood in the cheap hollow-core door splintered almost immediately, the screws popping out effortlessly. Gasping with relief, Tom entered the dark interior, closing the door behind him.

He had been in both the store and the warehouse section many times before, but didn't remember where to find what he was looking for. He needed light. Locating the connecting door into the store, he got his bearings and headed to the section where he thought the flashlights and batteries were displayed. Tom decided that if he was going to steal he might as well steal the best. Selecting an expensive lantern, he ripped open the container and installed a heavy- duty six-volt battery. Turning away from the front display window he hunkered down and depressed the button on the lantern then quickly depressed it again. It worked. He picked up two more of the large square batteries, a D-Cell flashlight and several packs of D-Cell batteries. He was tired of living in the dark.

Feeling his way back to the door leading to the warehouse, Tom went in and shut the door behind him. There were no windows in the warehouse, so no one could see in. He turned on the lantern. He was

74

looking for one of those propane barbecues. There was one left, still in the box, and he pulled it out into the aisle. Disgusted, he saw that the tank was not included. "Like buying a car with the engine sold separately," *he muttered. He found two propane tanks, but they were empty. With growing dismay, Tom realized the propane barbecue would be of no use to him.*

'But what about the other kind that uses briquettes?' *he thought. Foraging again, Tom found one in a box that was almost three feet wide, and there were bags of briquettes and starter fluid right along side. Hauling his prizes into the aisle, he went back and got a large wheelbarrow he had passed earlier. Four bags of briquettes and two cans of lighter fluid, plus the flashlights and batteries filled the bottom of the wheelbarrow with the barbecue resting on top, extending over the sides. As he was turning to go, he saw the butane barbecue lighters. Slapping himself on the forehead with the heel of his palm, he gasped then giggled nervously, grabbing several of the lighters and shoving them under the barbecue. Here he had found himself something for heat, but never thought about needing matches.* 'Lucky I saw these lighters,' *he told himself.* 'Damn lucky!'

He was headed toward the back door when he passed a stairway leading to the loft. 'That's where the guys that work here eat their lunch,' *he thought. As long as he was there, he'd have a look at the place. Shining his lantern around the windowless room, he saw a large table, several chairs, an old-fashioned refrigerator, a counter with cupboards underneath and two vending machines. The refrigerator held nothing of interest, but the cupboard disclosed a real find. There was a half bottle of rye and nearly a full bottle of rum. Tom set the bottles on the table then turned his attention to the vending machines. Taking the chipped screwdriver from his coat pocket, he kissed it then easily pried open the coin box on one machine then the other. Toonies and Loonies, thirty- four dollars in all. It took a bit of work prying the backs of the vending machines open, but he really wanted that cola to go with the rum. And the bars of candy and bags of chips and snacks in the other machine were treats he hadn't been able to afford for a long time. Locating a small cardboard box, he filled it with candy and snacks and a few cans of pop then slipped the bottles of rye and rum into his coat pockets.*

He tripped on something, and shining his light on the floor saw that it was the turned up corner of a carpet remnant that was about 8 feet long and 4 feet wide. It was a thick, dark blue plush with foam backing. On impulse, Tom rolled it up lengthwise then staggered clumsily out the door with the rug, box and lantern. He reassembled everything on the wheelbarrow then found he couldn't get it through the back door of the warehouse. He unloaded it, cursing all the while then reloaded everything once he was outside.

The short walk back to the apartment seemed to take an eternity. The wind was directly in his face, nearly blinding him all the way home. More times than he cared to count, he had to stop and readjust the load to keep everything from toppling.

His doorway was too narrow for the wheelbarrow so he had to unload everything out in the wind. He would dispose of the wheelbarrow later, he decided, after he got some heat in the place.

Tom decided it would be easiest to heat the bathroom since it was the smallest of the three rooms. He drew the curtains closed on the little bathroom window then turned on the lantern and tackled the box with the barbecue. There were legs that were supposed to be attached, but he saw that he needed a Phillips head screwdriver and he didn't have one. So he placed the bowl of the barbecue on his bath mat, emptied nearly a full bag of briquettes into it then liberally soaked them with the lighter fluid. Using the butane lighter, he touched the small flame to the nearest briquette and the entire thing immediately exploded into flames four feet high.

Tom's heart was pounding. As the flames died back, he was thankful that he hadn't been able to install the legs. If he had, his ceiling most likely would have caught fire. Already feeling warmer, he brought the rug into the bathroom and unfolded it then set the pillow from his bed against the wall. He shut the bathroom door, drank some of the cola from a can then filled the can to the brim with rum. There was a draft coming in under the bathroom door and around the small window, so he wedged towels under the door and up against the window- sill.

Sighing contentedly, Tom sat on the soft rug, braced the pillow behind his back and covered his legs with the blanket. He opened a bag of peanuts and poured some into his mouth followed by a long drink of rum and cola. The warmth, inside and out, was making him drowsy. He'd try one of those candy bars next, he decided.

Tom was dead from the toxic fumes and smoke before the smoldering bath mat leaped into flames, burning him and the elderly couple in the other side of the house beyond recognition. No one came to the rescue. No one even saw the fire. And Tom never got to eat a candy bar.

In the building supply store, in the dark, Tom had passed a row of portable kerosene heaters and stacked cans of kerosene. And in less than eight hours, Dow would be in town knocking on doors. But at three minutes before midnight, on the first day of the new- year, Tom Bricker and Meredith and John Hampton were dead. Because Tom was colder than he had ever been before in his life.

CHAPTER EIGHT – JANUARY 2, 2005

Ruth had convinced the Marchants they should spend the night rather than going back to their cold house. They had a fireplace in their living room and plenty of dry wood, but they had had no time to get a fire going all day.

Dow and Marilyn were snug on an inflated mattress in the dining room in front of the fireplace, while Marissa and Drew slept in the recliners in the family room.

Ruth had told Michael to get some rest. She would check on Lady's progress around midnight and Michael could set his alarm for 2 am. If it weren't necessary for him to get up, she would simply turn off his alarm clock and let him sleep. She regretted that she had promised Lindy she would wake her when Lady was about to have her calf.

It was a quarter to twelve when Ruth went out to the barn, buffeted along by a frigid northeast wind all the way. Shining her lantern into the fourth pen, she saw two small hooves protruding from Lady as she pushed, then retreat back inside again as Lady relaxed. Ruth went into the pen and waited for the next contraction. She had to make sure those were front feet before she went to wake Lindy. There was only a minute to wait until Lady arched her back and pushed again. Sure enough, those were front feet.

Ruth was facing into the wind on her way back to the house and was gasping for breath by the time she reached the back door. She went through the laundry room leaving her lantern on the washer and opened the door to the back room, tiptoeing over to the lower bunk to wake Lindy. Lindy was instantly awake and as Ruth whispered that she would wait for her in the laundry room while she got dressed, she marveled at the resiliency of the young. Waiting, Ruth lit a cigarette and inhaled deeply.

"I wish you wouldn't do that, Grandma," Lindy whispered, coming up behind her.

"So do I," Ruth whispered back, stubbing out the cigarette in the ashtray. Lindy smiled.

Ruth and Lindy both carried lanterns and Ruth hung on to Lindy all the way to the barn. She was afraid she would be blown away by the gale- force wind. Lady was laying down now, intent on giving birth. The calf's head and shoulders were out now, nostrils twitching and eyes blinking. Lady gave another big push as she simultaneously got up on her feet, and the rest of the calf plopped out onto the straw. She immediately got busy tending her baby. Lifting the calf's leg, Ruth announced, "It's a boy."

While Lindy watched Lady clean her calf, Ruth checked on the other three calves and their mamas then made Zepher stand so she could feel around her tail-head. "I'm going out to check in the free-stalls," she called to Lindy. She braced herself for the onslaught of the wind as she stepped out into the corral, but found that it was not unpleasant at all. The ten foot high windbreak fence that Matt and Michael had installed around the perimeter of the corral was surprisingly effective. Although Ruth had always wanted a windbreak for the cattle, the intent of the fence now was more to keep people out than to protect the cattle from the wind. The corral was like a fortress.

All the cows were in their free-stall beds, some asleep, some chewing their cuds. Ruth went down the line, shining her lantern on the rear quarters of each cow in turn. Brandi, as usual, began groaning when Ruth reached her stall. She had been a pet ever since she was born and she always had to let Ruth know how tough it was to be pregnant.

As she reached the last of the stalls, Ruth heard Lindy calling. She hurried back out to the corral as Lindy hollered from the barn door, "Lady's having another calf!"

"Damn," Ruth muttered, rushing to the door. She never liked to see one of her cows have twins; it took too much out of a cow to raise them.

Lady had the second calf halfway out, and this one was backwards. Ruth could already see, thankfully, that it was another bull. If it had been a heifer, it most likely would turn out to be sterile. Lady was standing, but before Ruth could grab the calf's hind feet, Lady pushed and swung around at the same time, and the calf flew out with a thump onto the straw.

Lindy was alarmed. "Is it hurt?"

"No," Ruth laughed. "But it sure is wide awake after that thump!"

Side by side they watched Lady tending her second calf, every once in a while turning back to the first calf and licking its face.

"Look," Lindy laughed. "Just like a boy. He doesn't like having his face washed!"

"Stick your thumb in that first calf's mouth, Lindy, and see if he's ready to suck," Ruth instructed.

"He sure is," Lindy sang back. "He's just about sucking my thumb off!"

Ruth went to the barn cupboard and took a three- liter bottle and calf nipple out of the plastic bag in which it was stored. Then she went to Mia's stall and milked the bottle full of colostrums. The little Jersey was surprisingly cooperative for a first calf heifer, for which Ruth was thankful. She was feeling much too tired to have to evade kicks from a first calf heifer that had yet to learn the ropes about milking.

She fed half the bottle to the first calf then the other half to its twin. By the time the second calf had finished his bottle, the first one was greedily nursing Lady.

"We can call it a night now, Lindy," Ruth said. "They are both fed and that second calf will get up and nurse when he's ready. There will be plenty left for him."

Reluctantly, Lindy let herself be led out of the barn and Ruth made her walk back to the house hanging on to the back of her coat, blocking her from the wind as much as possible. She kissed Lindy on the top of her head, told her to wash her hands and think up a couple of good boy names for the twins.

Ruth checked her watch. It was almost ten to two. She went into Michael's room and pushed the OFF button on his alarm clock, wondering how she was going to record the birth date of the twins. One had been born before midnight, the other after midnight. Two different days!

Ted had been awake when Ruth came and woke Lindy. He had been lying there, composing in his head the letter he would write explaining everything. When Lindy came back in from the barn, he went over everything once more, refining the details, until he could hear Lindy's even breathing, signifying that she was asleep.

Quietly, he crept out of the back room and into the office. The small oil stove was set low, and the room was just a few degrees above freezing. Ted turned up the heat; he'd be there a long time.

He felt his way across the room to the computer desk, sat in the chair then took a deep breath before turning the computer on. The screen sprang to life, making Ted blink from the sudden brightness. He knew exactly what program he was looking for. This was one time when his ability on the piano and sax came in handy; his dexterity could be transferred to a keyboard as well. He chose the graphics he wanted for the finishing touch then, pleased with the results, printed out a copy.

He turned on the photocopier, inserted his printed sheet and set the machine for 99 copies, the most it would copy in one setting. He checked to see that the right size paper tray was full then pressed the START button. "Great," Ted said under his breath. It was a good, clean, quiet copier.

While the machine was doing its work, he went back to the computer and began writing his letter. Though he had had it so carefully composed in his head, he found himself having a bit of trouble with it, repositioning some sentences and changing or eliminating others, simplifying it. The copier stopped several times, needing a reset or an addition of paper to the tray. There were a little over 2000 copies when he ran out of the 11 X 17 paper he was using.

The letter finished to his satisfaction, he printed out a copy then photocopied 99 more on letter size paper. He had no idea how many he would need, but decided to just keep copying until it looked like he had enough.

He lit an oil lamp before turning off the computer. Placing it on the large office desk, he let the glass chimney warm up before turning the wick up brighter. He laid the stack of 11 X 17 photocopies on the desk then adjusting the paper- cutter, neatly cut the copies down the center lengthwise in stacks of about 50 at a time. When that task was completed, Ted thought, '*Now comes the tedious part.*'

Searching through the desk drawers, Ted couldn't find what he needed. '*Matt is such a meticulous old cuss,*' he was thinking, '*surely he has them around here someplace!*'

He finally found what he was looking for in the bottom cabinet of the computer desk. There were three of them; that should be enough, he hoped.

Ted checked his watch. Ten minutes to four. He didn't know if he would have time to finish before Matt went out to milk the cow, but he would give it his best shot!

Matt's first thought on rising was that computers had accomplished in the blink of an eye what had taken Ruth 40 years to accomplish. He was finally cured of turning on bright lights before dawn!

He lit an oil lamp in the kitchen then went through his usual morning routine of stoking up the kitchen stove, boiling water and making coffee. Since he didn't know how to go about making toast without using the toaster, he settled for a small bowl of cornflakes instead.

Ruth had everything scrubbed and waiting for him on the freezer in the entry room; the milk pail, milk can, filter, bottles and udder wash. The wind was still howling out there, so Matt wrapped a wool scarf around his neck and the lower half of his face in addition to his regular garb. He noted with satisfaction that the door was locked. As he picked up the milk pail, udder wash and lantern, and stepped out into the wind, he muttered, "I'm getting too old for this."

When Ted heard Matt come out to the entry room, he quickly extinguished the oil lamp. He listened as Matt shuffled around getting into his overalls, coat and boots then heard him mutter something to himself as he went out the door. He saw the light from the lantern and Matt's illuminated silhouette go past the office window and tried to estimate how many steps it took to get to the barn, pacing them off in his head. When he was sure Matt wouldn't see the light, he lit the oil lamp again and continued with his work. *'How long will Matt be in the barn?'* he wondered. *'Half an hour? No, he has two cows to milk now, doesn't he? An hour, maybe?'* Ted didn't think he could be finished in an hour. This was taking much longer than he had thought it would. He was slowing down now, and his thumb was numb, too.

He needed a cup of coffee; that would get him going again. He slipped into the kitchen and poured himself a cup, adding three heaping spoons full of sugar for energy. As he stirred the coffee, Buddy padded past him, yawning, and stood waiting at the kitchen door.

"No, damn it!" Ted whispered hoarsely. "Go back!" he pointed. Buddy ignored him, staring intently at the door- knob. Muttering obscenities under his breath, Ted let Buddy out, telling him to hurry up. Not wanting to waste any more time, he went back into the office again.

Intent on his work, he forgot all about Buddy until he heard a single, imperative *'Woof!* at the back door. Moving swiftly, he opened the door just as Buddy was preparing to woof again. "Shhhh!" Ted hissed as Buddy stepped inside. Buddy gave him a disdainful look, shook himself then stared at the doorknob that would let him back into the kitchen. Angrily, Ted opened the door and Buddy slipped inside then turned and stared at the box of dog biscuits sitting on the counter just inside the door. "Oh for the love of...," Ted muttered through his teeth as he fished in the box and pulled out a treat for Buddy. Buddy took it as his due, and trotted with it in his mouth to the family room. Now in a panic over the time he'd lost, Ted resumed his work in the office.

Matt remembered that Ruth had been angry with him yesterday for not checking on the cows in the calving pens a little closer. He decided he would do that first thing before milking Felicity so he wouldn't forget. He shined his lantern into the first pen.

"You're alright," he said aloud. In the next two pens, mothers and babies were dozing. Shining his light into the fourth pen, Matt exclaimed, "Well, what have we here!" One twin was standing, looking at him curiously; the other was curled up asleep. "That's a fine looking pair, uh…, Lady is it?" Matt decided he'd give those twins some of Mia's colostrums since her calf couldn't take it all, and he'd just as soon do that as freeze it in case another calf needed it. But, he'd have to milk Felicity first, take that milk in the house and strain it, then come back out and tend to Mia.

It took no more than ten minutes to milk Felicity, then Matt braved the wind in his face back to the house, his lantern lighting the way. He stomped onto the deck and went into the entry room. The milk was strained and poured into the bottles when Matt saw the clean nursing bottle on the freezer.

"Well shit!" he exclaimed. "Why didn't I see that before? I could have saved myself a trip back out there!"

When Matt left again, Ted let out his breath. *'Why didn't Matt see the light?'* he thought. He had moved quickly when he heard Matt stomp on the deck, but still. It was starting to get light out, Ted reasoned, so maybe that made the light inside the office less visible. At any rate, he'd have to take the chance. He couldn't stop now, not when he was so close to being done.

But he'd grab another cup of coffee first, while the coast was clear!

Matt had been gone almost half an hour when Ted heard him stomp on the deck again, and he quickly doused the light. Matt went right back out again, this time to the hen house. *'I'm glad he's a stomper,'* Ted thought. *'At least he gives me warning!'* He realized suddenly that it was getting light enough now for him to see what he was doing without the aid of the oil lamp. If only Matt had no reason to come into the office, he'd be finished by the time everyone else was up.

Matt remembered that he hadn't let Buddy out yet and figured the poor old guy must be ready to burst. Sticking his head in through the family room doorway he called Buddy softly so as not to waken Marissa and Drew. Buddy groaned and rolled over onto his back on the couch, all four feet in the air, looking ridiculous. Clearly, he was not interested in going out. Perplexed, Matt lifted the pot on the stove to pour himself another cup of coffee. It felt strangely light- weight and less than half a cup of coffee dribbled into his mug.

Knowing he had made the usual four cups of coffee just as he did every morning, Matt thought maybe Ruth was already up. But there was no empty mug on the table or in the sink. Thinking she may have taken her cup of coffee with her out to the laundry room to have a cigarette, he checked. But there was no sign that Ruth had been there. He went upstairs and saw that she was still sleeping soundly. Scratching his head in bewilderment, he decided that he must have left the pot in too hot a spot on the stove and the coffee had simply steamed away. There was no other explanation for it! Shrugging, he made a full pot of fresh coffee.

Michael wandered into the kitchen, followed shortly by Ruth. After coffee to wake up and news about the twin calves, Michael headed out to the barn to feed the cattle. Ruth put sausages in a big iron skillet and set it on the stove. As the sausages began to sizzle, she asked Matt to mix up a big batch of his special pancake batter, while she fixed herself her usual breakfast. No pancakes and sausage for her! She scooped a generous helping of cottage cheese into a bowl and covered it with crushed pineapple. Then, going to the potted feverfew plant on the windowsill, she picked off a leaf and snipped it into small pieces on top of the pineapple. She mixed everything in together then dug in with relish.

Matt shivered with distaste. He couldn't see why anyone would want to eat something like that when they could have sausages and pancakes instead. But that mess was Ruth's favorite breakfast and her favorite dessert too. There was no accounting for taste.

Matt missed having the radio on, but he knew Ruth didn't. The only way she liked the radio was off. He liked country music and some pop, and she liked classical instrumentals, although she never got tired of hearing Celine Dion or Barbra Streisand. He liked plants and gardening and she liked tending animals. *'How different we are,'* Matt thought. *'Don't know if our marriage has worked because of that, or in spite of it!'*

Everyone began gravitating to the kitchen, one by one, and Ruth was kept busy flipping pancakes on the grill. Ted, finished with his project, had put everything in a cardboard box then, finding an appropriate moment, had slipped into the bathroom off the back room. He tried, unsuccessfully, to wash the indelible red ink from his hands. He hoped he had been able to scrub enough of it off though so no one would notice.

After everyone had eaten, Matt said they should leave the dishes and all come into the dining room. It was almost 7:30 and there were still a lot of things to discuss before they could put any plan into action. Ted slipped out the kitchen door and returned a few seconds later with his cardboard box. Carrying it into the dining room, he placed it at the head of the table in front of Matt.

"What's that?" Matt asked irritably, not wanting any interruptions.

"The answer to what you were trying to figure out last night, but couldn't," Ted said.

Matt looked at Ted doubtfully. "I don't understand," he said.

"Here, read the letter first," Ted said, handing a copy to everyone, including all the kids. "That will save us a lot of time." He waited nervously while everyone read, suddenly unsure of his plan or how it might be accepted.

Finished reading, Matt reached in the box and picked up one of the long strips of paper, read what was printed on it then turned it over and looked at the 7 red thumbprints evenly spaced along the back of the sheet. He looked up at Ted with growing amazement then at all the jubilant faces around the table.

Nate stood, and slapping the letter with the back of his hand said, "Hallelujah! We are saved!"

"Well, not *everything* may work without a few glitches," Ted said nervously, feeling exhilarated.

"Nothing ever could," Nate said, "because there will always be people who want more than their share or who will do less than others. But even if we'd had a month to develop a plan, I don't think we could have come up with a better one."

Ted was beyond speech as everyone thanked and congratulated him. He was aware, especially, of the look of respect and pride on the faces of his wife and children. That meant more to him than anyone could ever know.

Ruth and Lindy were the only ones left on the farm. Everyone else had been dispatched to specific locations in the four available vehicles. Michael, Nate and Rachel would be in Bridgetown with the pickup, handing out letters at every sixth house with the request that it be passed along to neighbors on either side. Dow and Drew were in Annapolis Royal doing the same, and Ted, Marilyn, Marissa and Carin were contacting random houses along the 18- mile stretch between the two towns on the north side of the river. When they finished, they would do the same on the south side of the river. Matt and Chris would be contacting people in the village of Granville Ferry and all the way down to Victoria Beach. It was going to be a long, cold day they knew, but they had set out with enthusiasm and a will to succeed.

They were certain there would be other people as well out doing what they could to help one another. Because if there was one thing that could be said about small towns in Nova Scotia, it was that people took care of one another. That was the main asset they had to work with.

Before she tackled the massive cleaning up in the kitchen, Ruth sat down and re-read Ted's letter.

Carol Kern

Re: **Survival Plan**

Dear Neighbor,

We are all going to help one another through the most difficult time we will, hopefully, ever know. The most urgent, immediate needs are for heat, water and food, in that order. A plan has been developed to insure all of us of these basic needs. It is essential that everyone, without exception, cooperate to that end.

Requirements of the plan are:

Heat: *Everyone with a source of heat in their homes must take in neighbors or others who have no source of heat.* **No one can be left out!**

Water: *Everyone with a source of clean water must make water available to whoever needs it*

Food: Farmers *will be expected to make any foods produced on a daily basis, (milk, eggs, etc.) available at* no cost *to a central food distribution center*

Farmers with stored winter vegetables and fruits, (potatoes, apples, cabbage, squash, carrots, etc.) will be expected to make these foods available for distribution to whoever needs it, at no cost.

Farmers with meat animals, (beef, pork, lamb and poultry), will be expected to make these foods available for distribution as need arises at no cost.

Grocery Stores will be expected to act as food banks and distribution centers, for both food and water, utilizing their present stocks and all foods brought in by farmers, at no cost.

Fishermen will be expected to make their catches of fish and shellfish available for distribution at no cost.

House Guests: Everyone who has moved into a house with heat must contribute every item of food in their possession to the food supply of the host homeowner.

Anyone *with food put by for the winter will be expected to use that food before relying on the food bank/distribution center.*

<u>Woodlot owners</u> with reserves of dry firewood will be expected to make this source of fuel available to whoever needs it at <u>no cost.</u>

*Every man, woman and child will be issued seven (7) **Trade Bucks** for a week's supply of food, water and fuel for heat as needed. Farmers supplying food daily will automatically receive a day's ration of these necessities, if needed, for every member of their household. Farmers supplying food occasionally, (meat), will receive a pro-rated supply of food, (1 to 7 days worth) based on the amount supplied, (1 steer = 7 days) for every member of their household. <u>All others</u> will be required to perform a service, (8 hours a day in exchange for 1 day's supply of food, water and heat. (If incapable of doing so, for any valid reason such as age, disability, illness, etc., other members of the household will be expected to perform additional services).*

This service can be assisting farmers, helping at the food bank, making deliveries, teaching, doctoring, nursing, cutting and splitting wood, shoveling snow, or whatever needs to be done.

<u>Definition of Household:</u> All persons living under the same roof, whether related or not.

There will be a meeting in the Legion Halls in both Bridgetown and Annapolis Royal tomorrow, January 3, at 1 pm. <u>One member only from each household should attend.</u> Locate other households in your area and car pool to save gas. Leadership is needed, so please keep that in mind when selecting the household member who will attend. All of the above will have to be organized within neighborhood committees.

Copy all information from this letter that you feel you will need to remember, then take the letter to your neighbors on either side, (two or three on each side) and make sure they do the same. <u>No one can be left out!</u>

We have been dealt a blow we were not prepared for, but with everyone working together we will all survive. May God bless and keep us all.

Sincerely,

A Neighbor

'*Yes,*' Ruth thought, '*It will work!*' She knew it would work because everyone would be scared and would want to band together for mutual benefit. She also knew there would be people who would object and refuse to cooperate. There were bound to be some of those. But there would be others who would make up for it.

She was amazed at the amount of thought and detail Ted had put into their sketchy plan and the way he got around the problem of money, or lack thereof. Everyone was equal, wealth and power were meaningless, and no one had to "work" for his daily bread. "Provide a service" was a much more palatable term. And putting his thumbprint in red ink on the back of the Trade Bucks was a stroke of pure genius. No one would be able to duplicate the Trade Bucks for their own benefit because no one had Ted's thumb print but Ted!

A letter was something they hadn't thought of; it would make contacting everyone so much easier and so much faster. '*This idea will spread,*' she thought. '*And I know there will be more letters needed.*'

She went out to the office and saw that the original letter was still in the copier. Turning it on, she set it for 99 copies, filled the paper tray and pushed the start button.

More Trade Bucks would be needed too, but a search told her they were all out of the 11 X 17 paper. They would simply have to find some. What they couldn't find though was another thumbprint exactly like Ted's. Poor Ted. He was going to need a new thumb before they were through!

When the 99 copies were done, Ruth turned off the machine and wondered if Lindy would ever tire of being out in the barn. She was out there now, mucking out the stalls so Michael could attend to more important matters. '*What a Godsend she is,*' Ruth thought. '*Lindy and her Dad, both!*'

Sighing, she went back into the kitchen and tackled all those dishes.

CHAPTER NINE – JANUARY 2, 2005

The first thing Dow and Drew saw when they turned into Annapolis Royal was the charred ruin of the tacky little duplex on the edge of the town marsh. That smoldering mess was to have been their first stop.

Driving past slowly, Dow saw that there was nothing he could do. If Tom and the elderly couple hadn't gotten out in time, there was nothing that could be done for them. They would be buried under the smoldering rubble.

"That must have happened very early this morning," Dow soberly told his son. *'While we were all snug, warm, well fed and blissfully asleep,'* he added to himself.

Feeling like a hit and run driver must feel leaving the scene of an accident, Dow quickly accelerated, anxious to leave behind the appalling scene and the feeling of defeat and the odor that accompanied it. He drove past the grocery stores, building supply and hardware stores and the liquor commission to the first block of houses.

"Every sixth house," he reminded Drew. "But the exception to that is any house with smoke coming out of the chimney. We want to personally contact every one of those. Those are the key houses."

The town felt deserted. There were no other cars on the street, no people outside. It was still early, but there should have been a lot of people out and about by now. As they made their way down that first long block of houses, he and Drew quietly handing a letter to whoever opened the door, then retreating quickly, Dow felt a growing sense of disquiet. Would anyone pay attention to the letter? Were they on a fool's errand? As Dow turned the corner onto the first side street, Drew shouted, "Look Dad!" Dow looked back and saw several people bundled in parkas and boots, scurrying across yards to the house next door. He and Drew looked at one another and grinned. "Let's go get 'em tiger!" Dow whooped, slapping Drew on the knee.

The first stop for Michael, Nate and Rachel was the big dairy farm on the edge of Bridgetown. Ray and Mel Webber, the owners, could be difficult at times so it was felt that all three of them should approach the brothers. Their cooperation was critical. Dairy farmers, they knew, were very protective of their industry. They, along with egg and poultry producers, were the only supply managed commodities. That meant they were among the few farmers who received a price for their product based on the average cost of production plus a fair wage for their labor.

Michael handed Ray Webber the letter and paced nervously while he read it. When he had finished with it, he called his brother and his two grown sons away from their tasks in the barn to read the letter.

Ray looked grimly at Michael, then Nate, and finally Rachel as though he were sizing them up. "Are the three of you going to be passing these out all over town?" he asked.

"We are!" Nate replied, vehemently.

"Well, not if we can help it," Ray said. "That's too much for just the three of you to do." They had piled into two cars, barn overalls, rubber boots and all, and following Michael's directions for the distribution of the letters, they cut the amount of time it would have taken to cover Bridgetown by two-thirds.

Michael found out later that the brothers and their sons had already made plans to start delivering milk to people in town, especially those they knew had children. And their house, with a big wood furnace, was already filled with less fortunate neighbors.

'*You never know where heroes are going to turn up!*' Michael thought.

The team of Ted, Marilyn, Marissa and Carin was watching their supply of letters disappear at an alarming rate. Houses were so spread out in the rural area that they often had to leave a letter at almost every house. They had nearly covered the ten miles from Bridgetown back to the Kingsley farm when Ted decided they would have to take the time to stop in and run off more copies of the letter.

When he drove up the lane to the farm he could see a pickup truck he didn't recognize parked in the farm- yard. Alarm bells started ringing in his head and looking at the others in the car he could see that they were feeling the same way. Cautiously, they got out of the car and approached the back door of the house. They could hear voices, male voices, but they couldn't catch what they were saying.

Ted broke out in a cold sweat. They never should have left Ruth and Lindy alone! God only knew what..., then they heard Ruth laugh.

Ted opened the back door and saw two rough-looking men standing there. They each had a stack of letters in their hands and were preparing to leave. Ruth came out of the office bearing more letters and handed half to each man.

"Ted!" she exclaimed. "You're back early!"

"We've run short of letters," he said, eyeing the two men warily.

"Another batch of 99 is being copied right now. You can take those. This is Dave and Harold Franklin," she introduced the two men. "The letter was passed along to them from a neighbor and they want to help."

"We're going to pass these letters out all along the shore road," one of the brothers said. "And there are a lot of little side roads too. We'll be recruiting more people to help out. It's going to take a lot of people helping out to reach everyone!"

Dismayed, Ted went into the office to wait for the copier to finish its run. *'This is going to be a whole lot bigger than I ever envisioned,'* he thought. He could see the plan as workable, manageable on a small scale, but...Shaking his head, Ted picked up the copies of the letter, warm from the copier. "Better run off another batch," he said aloud, resigned to the fact that his survival plan was spreading way out of the intended area. He took a look at his red-stained thumb, remembering the tedious hours of stamping the backs of the Trade Bucks. "Maybe that idea is going to turn out to be the dumb move of the century," he said dispiritedly.

Dow and Drew had reached their own neighborhood and Dow decided to get a fire going in his living room fireplace while Drew delivered more letters. They would be coming back here tonight so it would be a good idea to warm things up a bit. Once the fire was going, he went out to the patio and hauled the propane barbecue in through the kitchen and into the living room. It was all they had to cook on and it would add a little more welcome heat. There was an extra tank of propane too, so he wouldn't have to worry about that for a while yet. He closed off all the doors to the living room and moved a lounge chair closer to the fire. About to sit down and wait for Drew, he decided he'd better check on old Mrs. Henderson next door instead. He really didn't expect her to be there; someone surely would have seen to her by now. But he'd better make certain.

Dow knocked on Mrs. Henderson's door and waited. He knew she didn't move very fast unless she wanted to. He knocked again and waited some more. As he turned to leave, satisfied that she wasn't there, he saw her pull aside a curtain at the window and peer out at him. She opened the door slowly, wrapped from head to toe in a thick down comforter. Wasting no time, Dow scooped the slight old woman up in his arms saying, 'I'm taking you to my place."

He was halfway across the yard when Mrs. Henderson began to wail, "Emily! Emily!"

"Who's Emily?" Dow asked, stopping in his tracks.

"My little cat!" she cried plaintively.

Turning back, Dow carried Mrs. Henderson back to her house and waited while she found Emily. She instructed Dow to lock her door, showing him that she had her purse with the key inside so she could get back in when she wanted. Then she stood, enshrouded in the comforter, holding onto her purse and cat, waiting for Dow to pick her up again. Once settled in his arms, she instructed Dow to jiggle the doorknob to make certain the door was securely closed and locked. He shifted the load in his arms slightly to do as she requested.

"Do you have soup?" Mrs. Henderson asked before Dow had taken ten steps. "Emily and I are both quite hungry."

'*Oh boy!*' Dow thought to himself, already puffing from exertion.

He settled her into the lounge chair near the fireplace then gave her a copy of the letter to read while he lit the barbecue and foraged in the kitchen for a can of soup. '*What kind would she like?*' he thought then decided not to ask. She was probably intending to feed some of the soup to the cat, so he thought the chicken and rice would be a good choice. He poured the contents of the can into a small saucepan then found a bottle of water in the refrigerator and added a can of water to the pan.

Mrs. Henderson was squinting at the letter when Dow set the pan of soup on the barbecue to heat. "It's no use!" she said testily. "It's such small print and I can't read it without my glasses and I must have left them at home. Why is it such small print?"

"So that it would all fit on one page. Here, I'll read it to you," Dow offered. He wasn't about to carry her back over to her house so she could retrieve her glasses!

He was nearly finished with the letter when the soup boiled over, sending a smoky stench throughout the room. Dow removed the pan and turned off the barbecue then went to the kitchen and poured the soup into a large bowl, found a box of vegetable crackers, some butter and a lunch-box size container of apple juice. He put everything on a tray, added a knife and spoon, and carried it into the living room and placed it on Mrs. Henderson's lap. Drew was standing in the living room doorway with his mouth open.

Mrs. Henderson looked all around her tray, lifted the plate of crackers and butter, moved her knife, searching. "Where's the napkin?" she asked.

"Napkin!" Dow exclaimed, snapping his fingers and heading swiftly toward the kitchen. He brought her back a paper napkin, neatly folded, and placed it on her tray. With a look of disdain and a sigh of resignation, she grudgingly accepted it.

Dow put another log on the fire then said, "We have a lot more letters to circulate, Mrs. Henderson, but we should be back before dark. You should be fine 'til then."

"Perhaps you should call me '*Bea*' Mrs. Henderson said, since I am a member of the household now."

"A member of the household now?" Drew protested, once they were back in the car. "Dad!"

"She's a very sweet little old lady," Dow told Drew, unconvincingly. "She's just a bit set in her ways, that's all." *'She's an imperious old bat!'* he said inside his head.

■■■

Richard Martin had no idea what he was going to do. It was surprising how fast the food could disappear when it was freezing cold and there was nothing to do. The small box of cereal and liter of milk had been polished off by the four of them this morning, and the whole loaf of bread had gone for peanut butter sandwiches for lunch and fried egg sandwiches for dinner yesterday. The kids had eaten the cookies and they had all had one of the candy bars that lady had shoved through the window of the car. All that was left was a quarter of a jar of peanut butter, 6 eggs and a few crackers.

They had depended on the food bank for the past several weeks, but now it was closed. So were the two grocery stores and even the convenience store where he had paid for the little food they'd had with a bad check. The Christmas food basket from the Salvation Army was long gone. They had all been forced to eat sparingly for too long to be able to ration food when they had it.

The Martins lived in one side of a two family house. The owner, a bachelor in his mid-thirties, lived on the other side. The money from what little bit of work Richard had been able to find for the past several months had gone for rent. There was no money left over for food. He was to have started a full time job right after new years and he was sure he could have talked his employer into paying him daily for the first few days so he could feed his family. Now there would be no job, unless the electricity came back on.

The landlord had gone to Halifax to be with some friends over the holidays. Richard didn't know when he would be back, but, after trying to stay warm in the car yesterday morning, he decided to risk breaking into his landlord's garage to see if there was anything there he could use for heat. All he could find was a 2-burner propane camp stove, with a small amount of fuel left in the cylinder. They had used up all the fuel the night before frying eggs, and even though they had closed themselves off from the rest of the house in one of the bedrooms, it hadn't been enough to make any difference in the temperature of the room for more than a few minutes.

Mickey, Richard's 3 year- old son, had a cough, but there was no fever so Richard wasn't too concerned. It was 5 year -old Cassie that bothered him. She was eating all right, but like an automaton, and had been too quiet the past few days. It was as though she had lost her spirit. Both kids were covered up to their chins in bed, one on either side of their mother, Doreen, who was reading to them from a book they had read a hundred times. Mickey was interested in the story but Cassie just lay there staring into space.

Richard heard a car outside and pushed aside a corner of the heavy drapes to look out. The car stopped, and Richard saw that the man who got out was the owner of the convenience store. He had some kind of paper in his hand and he was headed for their front door. *'He's after me for that bad check!'* was Richard's only thought. He put his finger to his lips, looking warningly at Mickey as Dow knocked on the door. Mickey, grinning widely at the game being played, pulled the covers over his head as Dow knocked again. Doreen looked down at the bedcovers, ashamed and embarrassed, but Cassie just continued to stare into space.

Richard heard Dow walk across the porch to the other side of the house and knock on the door. Getting no answer, he walked back past Richard's door and looked around the side of the house. Then he went back to his car, the paper still in his hand, and drove off. Richard was glad he'd driven his car into the landlord's garage the day before. He thought now that it must have been providence that made him do that.

"I'm going out!" he suddenly announced. Doreen gave him a frightened look, but said nothing. She put her arms around her children and Mickey snuggled in close but Cassie did not respond. Richard stood looking at the three people he loved most in the world. He was sobbing inside over his failure to take care of them and knew if he didn't leave soon he would collapse in a blubbering heap. He couldn't do that to them; he had to leave them some hope.

Stepping out onto his back porch, he let out a harsh sob as his eyes filled with tears. He didn't know what he was going to do. He just stood there with his gloveless hands shoved deep into the pockets of his jacket, wracked with sobs, feeling weak and useless.

Finally gaining control of himself, Richard found he had been staring at his landlord's back door. He walked slowly across the porch and grasped the handle of the storm door. It was locked. Wrenching his teeth in sudden anger, he pressed down on the cheap aluminum handle with both hands until he heard something snap. He released the handle and the storm door gapped open. The doorknob on the inner door turned smoothly, and Richard stepped into his landlord's kitchen.

His first thought was for food. Opening the refrigerator he found 5 bottles of beer, a couple of half empty bottles of wine, an unopened bottle of apple juice, a slimy, rotting head of lettuce, a rancid looking square of margarine on a dish, mustard, 2 grayish-green hotdogs and something brownish-gray in a bowl. He took the 5 bottles of beer and the apple juice and set them on the table then closed the refrigerator. Changing his mind, he took out the two bottles of wine too.

The contents of the cupboard were more promising; two unopened bags of potato chips, a can of sardines, a can of flaked ham, a whole box of saltines and, oh joy, two big cans of sliced peaches. A few seasonings and spices was all that remained.

Richard set the food on the table then walked into the living room. It held the expected bachelor clutter of sound system, tapes, CD's videos and girlie magazines. The air in the room was acrid from cigarette butt filled ashtrays on practically every surface. He went down the hall and looked in the bathroom. It was so filthy it turned his stomach, so he continued on to the first bedroom. It was set up as an office with a computer, fax, filing cabinet and littered desk. The other bedroom was dominated by a king-size waterbed that was fast turning into a bed of ice. Richard searched through the dresser drawers then the closet. There was nothing of interest. He almost missed the little nightstand, dwarfed as it was by the huge bed. The top drawer held a porno book, condoms, antacids and reading glasses, in addition to a number of crumbled candy wrappers and something that resembled a hardened white crayon. The bottom drawer had, of all things, a Gideon Bible resting on top of a wool scarf. And under the scarf was a gun.

Hesitantly, Richard reached into the drawer and picked up the small pistol. He could see that it was loaded. He slipped the gun into his jacket pocket then picked up the scarf to see if there were more bullets in the drawer. There were none. He unfolded the scarf and placed it around his neck then, as an afterthought, picked up the Bible and closed the drawer.

Searching around the kitchen for some kind of container to cart his loot next door, he opened a broom closet and found a large plastic bucket filled with cleaning supplies that had obviously never been used. He emptied the bucket than lifted it out of the closet, revealing a propane cylinder identical to the one on the camp stove. "Please God!" He said aloud, picking it up. It was full.

Richard set the filled bucket on the floor in his kitchen and draped the scarf over the back of a chair. Taking the Bible, a bag of chips and the apple juice with him, he went into the bedroom. "A snack for you," he said cheerfully, "And something new to read aloud." His look told Doreen not to ask him to explain. He would surprise them later with the propane cylinder and they would have a hot meal of scrambled eggs and ham topped off with a dish of sliced peaches before it was dark.

The propane couldn't be used for heat. It had to be saved for cooking. They would be warm enough in bed together, the kids sandwiched between him and Doreen. He patted the gun in his pocket. He would feed his family after all. First thing in the morning he was going hunting.

∎▪▪▪∎

Michael had contacted Ian on the CB radio and had arranged to meet him at the gas station on the far side of Bridgetown at one o'clock. Ian was there waiting for him when Michael pulled up. The survival plan was something Ian wanted to circulate in his area and he had a team of over 50 volunteers ready to get started. It was critical to get things moving before the hysteria in the city spread too far. It was having a ripple effect that was spreading out more and more by the hour. They needed to create their own ripple that would spread out and stop the threat from the Metro area dead in its tracks.

Ian read the letter through carefully. "I can see some potential problems with this," he said. "But I think overall it's going to create some optimism, and most importantly, some hope."

"What do you think the biggest problem will be?" Michael asked.

"People with money and position," was Ian's immediate reply. "They will want to buy themselves an advantage and they're going to object to being on the same level with everyone else."

Michael nodded agreement. "It might help a lot though if those people were asked to be the organizers and record keepers. You know, sweat equity without the sweat. After all, it's not like we're trying to create a communist society here, just a temporary means of survival for everyone. Equally!"

"One thing, I guess, that really surprises me is the way that every farmer I've talked to will be behind this 100%," Ian said. "Some of them, as you probably well know, can be real pricks to deal with when it comes to certain issues, but they are going to turn out to be the main supporters of any plan to get food, free of charge, to everyone who needs it."

"I've never seriously doubted the farmers," Michael said. "But the store owners might be a different matter. It's not going to be easy to convince most grocery, hardware, pharmacy, etc., store- owners to just give their stock away to anyone who needs it. Some of that information isn't in the letter, such as people who require prescription medications not having to pay for them, and propane dealers supplying fuel at no cost. Those are going to be the tough people to deal with and we're going to have to come up with some solutions before the town meetings tomorrow."

Shaking his head, Ian said, "You know, I am a big fan of technology and use it a lot, but when I think of all the work ahead, all the hardships, I find myself wishing that computers had never been invented. They are the cause of all this."

Michael grinned sardonically. "You and my Mom would certainly be in agreement on that point. She's been saying for years now that some day computers would prove to be the curse of the universe! It looks like that day has arrived."

Ian had been going to drive down to the Kingsley farm to get Ruth to run off some copies of the letter for him, but he was saved the trouble. As he was pulling out of the gas station lot, a pickup truck came barreling down the road, the driver leaning on the horn. Ian recognized the Franklin truck.

Harold Franklin rolled down the window, leaned out and handed Ian a sheet of paper. "Read that," he commanded, "and let me know if you'll help spread these around."

"I've seen it. "I'm on my way now to the Kingsley's to get Ruth to run some copies off for me," Ian said "I'll be running them up around Middleton."

"Got some here for you. This is the second load I've picked up today," Harold said, handing Ian several hundred copies. "There won't be any more. Ruth ran copies on every scrap of paper she could find."

Ian nodded his thanks and climbed into his truck. Looking at his gas gauge then over at the useless gas pumps, he said to himself, *'Wonder where I can find a criminal who'd know how to get the gas out of those tanks. When we run out of gas, everything else stops too!'*

Lindy popped breathlessly in the back door just as Ruth finished putting on her overalls. "How's Zepher?" Ruth asked.

"Fine!" Lindy chimed.

"Fine. Then why did you come rushing in?"

"Oh! I wanted to tell you I thought up names for the twins. I know you never name the bulls *real* names like you do the heifers, but I hope you won't think the names are too silly," Lindy said with an impish grin. "Since this is the "P" year, how about Pete and Repeat."

"Suits me just fine," Ruth said. She saw that Lindy was still wearing a grin. "Do you have something else you want to tell me?"

"Yeeessssss," Lindy said importantly, drawing the word out. "Zepher had a bull too, and I named him Patriot."

"Zepher had her calf? When? Why didn't you come get me?"

"The answers are 'Yes', 'about an hour ago' and 'because you were busy photocopying and Zepher didn't need any help.' Patriot is a smart calf, too. He's already nursed and his belly looks like he swallowed a ball!"

"Well, then…," Ruth said, taking off her overalls.

"Don't you want to go out and check on things?"

"Maybe later. I imagine you have everything under control. It's about time for me to get the spaghetti sauce started anyway. I like to cook it slowly for a long time on the back of the stove."

"Can I help? I should learn how to cook, too."

"Sure. Would you like to chop some onions and garlic?"

"No, I probably won't *like* to, but I will do it anyway!" Lindy said, her impish grin back again.

"You're too much!" Ruth said, hugging Lindy tight. "Did I ever tell you how much I love you?"

Lindy assumed a serious look. "No Grandma, I don't think you ever did!" she said, her eyes twinkling mischievously.

Michael, Nate and Rachel arrived back at the farm a few minutes before four. Lindy took Nate by the hand and led him in his stocking feet to the lounge chair in front of the woodstove then brought him his slippers and a cup of coffee. He was too tired to do more than smile at her weakly, but registered his appreciation by stroking the back of her head when she drew up a stool and sat beside him. He closed his eyes for just a second then drifted off, his hand falling to the side of the chair. Lindy gently lifted Nate's arm and placed it in his lap then covered him with a blanket.

"Poor Grandpa Nate," she said, coming out to the kitchen. "He shouldn't be doing so much at his age. He's exhausted!"

"Lindy," Rachel said, fondly, "You were a little old lady when you were born, you know that?"

Lindy couldn't figure out what her Mother meant, so, shrugging, changed the subject and told Michael about Zepher's calf.

"You took care of it all alone?" Michael asked.

"No, Zepher did. Most cows have their calves all by themselves, you know," she said, eyes twinkling.

Michael burst out laughing, he and Lindy the only ones who knew why.

Ted, Marilyn, Marissa and Carin drifted in at ten past four followed just a few minutes later by Dow and Drew. Ruth wanted the Marchants to stay and eat, but Dow declined.

"We have another member of our household now." Dow said. He told everyone of his experience with old Mrs. Henderson and soon found himself laughing. *'Many things in life aren't so funny when they are happening,'* he told himself. *'But recalling them can often be hilarious!'*

"If you won't stay, then you'll take some spaghetti with you," Ruth informed Dow. "I made more than enough for everyone. Besides, you're going to have to get beds down to the living room and you've already put in a full day. You don't want to have to figure out what you're going to eat on top of everything else." She filled a large insulated casserole dish with spaghetti and another with salad. Then, discovering that the Marchants had no oil lamps, she insisted that they take two along with them. It would be dark from 5:30 pm to 5:30 am, and twelve hours in the dark was too long a time, Ruth insisted.

Ruth had finished milking the two Jerseys, again splitting a bottle between the twin calves then milking out another bottle full to save in the freezer in case there was a calf that needed it. Mia's udder was still pretty full, but her own calf hadn't nursed yet.

While she tended to the chores, Ruth went and looked out the barn door several times to see if Matt's car was there with the others. Nagged with worry, she was short-tempered and impatient with the twins when they butted the bottle, with the mama cows when they didn't clean up their feed fast enough, and with the manure fork that had suddenly seemed to grow too big for the manure windows, hitting the edge and dumping the manure back in the pen rather than out the window.

Michael had finished feeding and checking on all the cattle in the corral and heifer barn, the lights from the tractor enabling him to see what he was doing. As Ruth finished cleaning and re-bedding the last pen, Michael ushered two more cows into the remaining calving pens.

"Mandy and Emerald look like they need to be in," Michael said, taking the heavy milk bucket from his mother while giving her a searching look. "I'm going to go look for them," he said softly, reassuringly. "Dad probably just ran out of gas or something. You know that old car of his is a real gas-hog."

"Take Ted with you," Ruth urged, trying to keep the fright she felt out of her voice and her eyes.

Michael drove slowly through Granville Ferry, checking on the left of the narrow road for a sign of Matt's car, while Ted checked on the right. The winding road followed the shoreline, turning inland at intervals then back out to hug the water's edge. There were no other cars on the road. Snow had drifted deep in places, creating barriers across the road like speed bumps made of mounded sand. They could see by the tracks that there had been cars along the road earlier. Michael straddled the centerline as they wound their way slowly past cottages, farm- houses, tourist shops and open fields.

They were nearing the end of the road at Victoria Beach when they finally spotted Matt's car in the middle of the road, facing them, with it's nose pointing curiously down.

"I told you your Dad and Michael would come looking for us," Matt told Chris, relief sounding in his voice. "There was no need to worry about that."

"I wasn't worried," Chris exclaimed. "I'm just hungry! Can I tell them what happened?"

"Well, we'll see...," Matt started to say as he rolled down the window when he saw Michael and Ted approaching the car.

"We got shot at, Dad!" Chris cried excitedly.

"What! Are you all right?" Ted asked anxiously.
"You better let me explain what happened," Matt told Chris. "A shot was fired, but we weren't shot at, exactly. I'll tell you the whole thing on the way home." They decided to leave Matt's car where it was rather than try to tow it home with 2 flat tires. "If it's in someone's

way, they can just push the old thing into the bay for all I care," Matt said.

On the way home, Matt told them that most of the day had been uneventful. Chris had gotten bored rather quickly delivering the letters until, at one house, an elderly woman praised him and gave him a candy bar. From then on he had been able to pretend he was going Trick or Treat and what had been a chore, suddenly became fun.

Then, at around 3:30 that afternoon, they had been getting close to Victoria Beach when they turned in to make a stop at a house that was about 150 feet back from the road. They had driven just a few feet up the driveway when both of the front tires blew. Matt had gotten out to see what had caused it and discovered a long board studded with hundreds of long nails stretched across the driveway. The board was frozen in place and had been covered with snow.

Matt had jumped over the barrier and was walking up the driveway to deliver the letter when a man came out of the house carrying a shotgun.

"You're trespassing! Get off my property!" the man had yelled. Matt had explained he was on an important mission and started telling the man about the survival plan as he walked toward him. The man had fired a shot into the air.

"That was a warning." He had bellowed. "The next shot won't be. I don't want to hear about your survival plan; I've got my own."

Matt had backed his car out of the driveway and had turned back toward Granville Ferry. He would have kept going until those tires were nothing but ribbons if it hadn't been for getting stuck in a deep drift across the road. There were no other houses close by and Matt had decided he didn't want to bother anyone, anyway. People had enough problems without him adding to them. So, he and Chris had climbed into the back seat of the car, covered themselves with the blanket that Ruth made him keep in the car, had lit one of the candles that Ruth made him keep in the glove compartment, and had waited for Michael to come to the rescue.

"That house back there," Matt had added, "had smoke coming out of the chimney and there was a windmill in the yard. It looks like someone other than Ruth was prepared for something to happen."

CHAPTER TEN – JANUARY 3, 2005

Richard crept out of bed tucking the still warm blankets around Mickey who had been sleeping curled up next to him. He closed the bedroom door softly behind him and pushed his feet into his boots. It was like stepping into blocks of ice. His jacket was where he had left it, draped over the back of a kitchen chair on top of the wool scarf. He draped the scarf over his head, crossing it under his chin then again around the back of his neck, and tucked the ends inside the collar of the jacket. He had slept in his clothes to keep them warm, but already his jeans were stiffening from the cold.

Shining his flashlight around in the garage, he picked out the hose he had seen there before. With his pocket- knife he sawed through the rubber hose freeing an eight-foot section. He stowed it on the floor of his car in front of the passenger seat then added a five- gallon gas can and a big insulated picnic jug. *'Water,'* he thought. *'Got to find some water.'* Finding nothing else in the garage that might be useful, Richard opened the garage door, backed his car out without turning on the lights then closed the garage door again. He drove away in the pre-dawn with the lights off.

On a side street he found two cars parked next to the curb, one behind the other. Neither car was locked, *'Thanks to good old small town trust,'* Richard thought. Shining his light in the first car he saw that the gas gauge read close to empty. The second car, though, was a gold mine. It had over three-quarters of a tank full. And, wonder of wonders, there was half a roll of peppermints and almost four dollars in change in the open ashtray. They went in his jeans pocket.

He removed the gas cap and inserted about four feet of the hose into the tank, positioning the gas can against the fender of the car, at the ready. Taking a deep breath, he braced himself and sucked hard on the hose then released the end into the can. Nothing happened. It had looked so easy when he saw it being done in a movie, once. He tried again and kept sucking until the oily liquid rushed into his mouth, gagging him. Quickly, he pushed the end of the hose into the can. When the can was full and the gas kept flowing, he bent the end of the hose over and wedged it into the top of the gas tank. He carried the full can of gas over to his own car across the street, poured in the gas then repeated the process two more times. He decided that would have to do. The taste of the gas in his mouth was making him retch.

Leaving the hose in the tank, he went over to the snow- covered yard, punched through the icy crust and lifted a handful of snow to his mouth. He scrubbed his lips and chin with the snow, then reached for another handful and shoved the snow in his mouth, chewing it, dissolving it and swishing it around in his mouth then spitting it out. That was a little better. He reached in his jeans pocket for a mint and swished it around inside his mouth. That was a lot better. It burned like hell, but at least one part of him was warm.

He replaced his gas cap, stowed the can in the trunk then patted the gun in his jacket pocket. He was going hunting and he knew where. About five miles out on the road to Bridgetown he had seen deer several times entering and leaving a thick stand of alders near the road. Alongside was a farm lane that wound up the hill to an isolated farm- house with an orchard in front, cascading down the hillside.

Richard had never shot a deer before. He had never even fired a gun before. But he was sure he could do it. He had seen it done often enough in the movies. Just pull the hammer back, aim and *squeeze* the trigger, don't pull. He was determined to bring meat back for his family.

Once he got past the houses in town, he turned on his headlights. That made everything seem more normal. Driving along with the taste of gas still in his mouth, it occurred to him that next time he had to siphon gas he'd take the rest of that hose in the garage, pull his car up alongside and he's just drain the whole tank into his car all at once. He had driven along for several minutes, shivering from the cold, before he remembered to turn on the heater. Then, basking in the warmth, he missed the place he was looking for and had to turn around and go back. There was a turnoff on the side of the road opposite the stand of alders. It was a dirt track that led down to the river and he followed it for several yards until his car was out of sight from anyone traveling on the road.

Richard got out of the car, walked back down the dirt track and huddled next to some bushes growing near the side of the road, his hand cradling the gun in his pocket. When it was light enough, he would have a clear view of the woods and the orchard in front of the farmhouse. He would be able to see if deer were feeding in the orchard, but knew he'd have to get closer to shoot one.

Richard was startled by a light that suddenly appeared up at the farmhouse; then, ghostlike, moved across the yard reflecting rhythmically off something shiny until it disappeared at the barn door. *'Someone carrying a light of some kind, going to the barn,'* he reasoned.

It was beginning to get light when he saw the man return to the house with a lantern and a pail. *'Of course!'* he said to himself. *'That's what the shiny thing was, a pail. A farmer out milking the cow. Milk. Maybe he could get some milk for the kids too.'*

Richard was freezing and cramped waiting to catch sight of a deer. He decided to turn his car around, facing the woods, and sit in it for a few minutes with the heater on. He pulled into a spot where he would still be hidden from the road yet could see the woods and the end of the lane. He couldn't see the farmhouse on the hill or the orchard but it would only be a few minutes before he was back crouching by the bushes, he told himself as the warmth from the car's heater began to envelope him.

It was light out when Richard came to with a start, hearing the honk of a car's horn. A pickup truck with two men and a woman in the cab was pulling out of the lane across the road, heading toward Bridgetown. A car was close behind the truck, with two men in front and two kids in back, headed toward Annapolis Royal. He turned off his engine, noting with alarm that the fuel level was down to about a third of a tank. *'Damn you for a fool!'* he swore at himself.

Unsure of what to do, Richard got out of his car and sprinted across the road, going a few yards up the lane. The brush was thick and impenetrable alongside the lane but as he walked further he saw an opening where the packed snow underneath was well trodden and deer tracks were clearly visible. They led out of the woods and straight up the lane, obliterated in spots by tire tracks, but easy to follow just the same.

Richard kept his hand curled around the handle of the gun, expecting to see a deer leap out in front of him at any moment. The tracks led up the hill and around in back of the farmhouse, then simply vanished. There were tire tracks, boot tracks and dog tracks everywhere, but he couldn't find a trace of the deer tracks.

Suddenly realizing that he could easily be seen from the house, Richard crouched down beneath a window and cautiously raised his head to peer inside. He could only see part of the room, but there was something about it that made him feel there was no one there. *'There were, what...seven people that left here a while ago. Could be there's no one home.'*

He tried the door at the back of the house and found it locked. Going across the yard and around to the side of the house, he was about to step onto the deck when he heard a cow bawling out in the barn. He remembered the farmer and the milk pail, how he wanted milk for the kids. *'Milk and meat,'* he reminded himself. *'Cows have milk and cows* are *meat.'* With a gleam of determination in his eyes, Richard strode purposefully toward the barn.

He waited a few moments for his eyes to adjust to the dark interior, pinching his nostrils as he was assaulted by the various barn odors. Breathing through his mouth, he surveyed the pens on his left then went over for a closer look. At his approach, the cows in the first two pens got swiftly to their feet and snorted at him warningly. "Son of a bitchin' *big* mothers," Richard mumbled aloud. Then he noticed the calves. "Protectin' your babies, huh?" The cow in the third pen paid no attention to him, but her calf put it's head through the slats of the gate and nosed his pant leg, leaving a smear of milky slime. The cow in the fourth pen acted like the first two cows, only worse. She had her head down and was pawing at the straw, glaring at him. He skirted past the cows in the last two pens. They looked absolutely massive laying there, eyeing him balefully as they chewed on something in their massive jaws.

Richard went over to the back door and cautiously peeked outside. There were cows milling around everywhere, inside what looked like a fort from an old western movie. One was headed for him and he quickly slammed the door.

He made up his mind. He would take the calf in the third pen.

Stealthily opening the gate, he placed his hand on the calf's rump and pushed it out of the pen, quickly closing the gate again in case that mama cow got concerned and came after her baby. He scooped the calf up in his arms, grunting. It was a lot heavier than it looked. He decided he's have to drape it around the back of his neck in order to carry it back to his car and was trying to figure out the easiest way to do that when he heard the sound of running feet. Turning swiftly toward the sound, with the calf in his arms, he saw a little girl running for the barn door.

"Hey!' Richard called loudly. But she was gone. He ran with the calf to the barn door and tried to push it open. "Damn kid!" he roared, kicking at the door. "She locked me in!" *'She's gone to get someone!'* he thought, in a panic. He looked around. There was no way out, nowhere to hide that he could see. *'Where was that kid hiding?'*

He backed away from the door and over to the third pen. Setting the calf down on its feet, he kept his left arm around its front legs and reached into his jacket pocket for the gun. With the gun in his right hand, he wrapped his arm around the calf's hind legs and lifted it up in front of him again. Then with the gun pointed toward the barn door, Richard was prepared for a standoff.

Lindy burst into the kitchen screaming for her grandmother. Ruth came rushing into the kitchen from the family room where she had just finished putting a log in the stove. Lindy was crying so hard Ruth couldn't understand what she was trying to say. She bent down and took the child's face in her hands.

"Take a deep breath, honey," she said soothingly. "Now tell me, slowly."

"He's taking Priscilla!" Lindy sobbed.

"Who? What do you mean, *'he's taking Priscilla?'"*

"The man in the barn! He picked up Priscilla and he's going to take her away! Don't let him, Grandma. Please!" Lindy wailed.

"Is he still in the barn, do you know?"

"I locked him in."

"If you locked him in, he's still there. There's no way he can get out of there without getting a terrific electric shock."

All the while Ruth was talking she was getting into her overalls, coat and boots. Lindy was impatient with how long she was taking.

"Hurry Grandma!" she pleaded, tears staining her cheeks.

110

"There's no hurry if he's locked in. Do you know if he saw you?"

"Yes. He yelled '*Hey!*'"

"You stay here. I don't know exactly what I'm going to run into out there and I don't want you in any danger. Stay inside and lock the door."

"Aren't you going to take a gun or something?" Lindy asked incredulously.

"No," Ruth answered after a moment's thought. "I think I will be safer if I'm an unarmed Grandma rather than a pistol-packin' mama." She touched Lindy's cheek. "It will be all right. Mind me now, and I mean it!"

Resolutely, Ruth walked to the barn. There was no halting, no break in her stride, belying the terror she felt and her urge to run and hide.

Richard tensed as the barn door opened. He had waited for this moment to draw back the hammer on the gun so whoever came in would hear it and know he was armed.

"Hello!" Ruth said heartily, stepping inside and closing the door behind her. "Oh! Lindy didn't tell me you had a gun. You don't need it. I'm not armed, and there's no one here but a little girl and her grandma. Me."

"I'm taking this calf, lady, and you're not going to stop me!" Richard said defiantly.

"What do you want with that calf?"

"I've got hungry kids and no food. I'll be wanting some milk too," he added, trying to sound like the tough gangsters he'd heard in the movies when he was a kid.

"You plan to eat that calf?"

"That's right."

Ruth shook her head. "That's a lot of trouble for such a little bit of meat."

"Feels like 70, 80 pounds to me," Richard said. "It'll go a long way."

"Actually, Priscilla weighs 70 pounds," Ruth said, taking a seat on a bale of straw. "Priscilla, that's the calf's name. She's a special pet of my granddaughter's. She was there when the calf was born and she named it after a doll she used to…

111

"Just can it lady! Richard yelled. "This ain't a social call!"

…have," Ruth continued. "That calf feels heavy, but all you'll get is 7 or 8 pounds of meat off it. A newborn calf is mostly bone, and after you cut off the head and feet and bleed it and pull off the hide, why…"

"Just shut up! Shut your face up!" Richard bellowed, feeling sick to his stomach.

"Set the calf down," Ruth said softly. "It's too heavy to hold like that. Look at you, you're shaking from the exertion."

"Just let me past," Richard said, jaw jutting forward, "and you won't get hurt."

"No," Ruth said. "Taking that particular calf will break a little girl's heart. I can't let that happen. Take another calf instead. Take one of the twins."

Richard considered. He felt bad enough about what he was doing without being responsible for breaking a little kid's heart too. "All right," he said. "But you'll have to get it. That cow won't let me near."

Ruth nodded and went into the fourth pen. "You live in Annapolis Royal, don't you?" she asked nonchalantly.

"It's none of your business where I live."

"No, of course not, but I'm just wondering how Dow could have missed you. Dow Marchant, you probably know who he is, has that convenience store just this side of town?"

"What do you mean you don't know how he missed me?"

"Dow and his son, Drew, were taking a letter around to everyone in town. It's a survival plan where everyone gets taken into homes where there's heat and everyone is sure of having enough to eat. I don't know how he could have missed you."

Richard stared at Ruth as what she said sank in. He felt suddenly weak and his arms and legs began to tremble. He could feel himself slowly wilting as he gulped back the tears that sprang to his eyes. "He didn't miss me," he said softly, hollow-eyed. "I didn't answer the door. I thought he was there because the check I wrote him bounced. I…" Richard sank to his knees, the calf landing on all four feet. "Go back to your mama, baby," he said, tears rolling down his cheeks. "And don't get me another calf," he said turning to Ruth. "I couldn't kill it. Not now. Probably never could have."

Ruth put Priscilla back in the pen with Melissa then approached Richard and squeezed his shoulder. "Your family is going to be all right," she told him reassuringly. "Now, how about releasing the hammer on that pistol before someone gets hurt accidentally."

Richard looked at the gun in his hand, his index finger stiffly against the trigger. His hand was numb and it took all the concentration he could muster to move his finger back from the trigger. He realized he didn't know how to release the hammer. "I don't know how," he said apologetically.

Ruth gently took the gun from Richard's hand, released the hammer then handed the gun back to him. He looked at it in horror. "No, I don't want it!" he muttered incoherently.

As she slipped the gun into her own pocket, Ruth looked frankly at Richard and made up her mind. "I want you to bring your family here," she said. "We have heat, we have food enough, and we'll make room."

Richard glanced sharply up at Ruth, not quite believing what he was hearing. "You want us to stay here with you?"

Ruth nodded.

"After what I just tried to do to you here?"

Ruth nodded again.

"But,…"I'm black and…"

"I can see that." Then, misunderstanding, Ruth said, "Oh, if staying here would make you uncomfortable because we're not, um, black too, we could try to find…"

"No, I didn't mean that," Richard stammered. "It's just that…, well, you know…" he said with pleading eyes.

"What color you are doesn't matter to me if it doesn't matter to you," Ruth said softly, looking Richard in the eye. She didn't see hesitation there; she saw a look of relief.

"All right," he said, suddenly shy. "I'll get to my car and go get Doreen and the kids."

"You'll come in the house first and get that shakiness under control before you get behind the wheel and drive anywhere," Ruth commanded in her no-nonsense voice. "Besides, there's a very upset little girl in there who needs assurance from you that you aren't going to take her calf or harm it.

Richard followed Ruth to the house, his legs feeling as though the bones had turned to rubber. Ruth was surprised at how calm she had felt, even with a gun pointed at her belly, and wondered when her own reaction would set in.

When Lindy was certain it was her grandma knocking on the door she opened it hurriedly then gasped and recoiled as she saw Richard standing there too. "It's okay," Ruth quickly reassured her. "And Priscilla is back in the pen with her mama, unharmed."

Lindy eyed Richard warily. "You were going to take my calf," she accused. "Why?"

Richard looked at her apologetically. "I have two hungry little kids and a wife who's going to have a baby soon. I was scared. I didn't know what was going to happen to us. I'm sorry."

"Were you going to eat her?"

Humble and acutely embarrassed, Richard just nodded his head.

"But that isn't going to happen now," Ruth interjected. "He's going to bring his family here to stay with us," she added, carefully watching for Lindy's reaction to that news. Richard watched too, aware that for some reason this child's acceptance was more important to him than just about anything he could ever remember.

"You look cold," Lindy finally said, blinking her eyes rapidly. "You could probably use a hot cup of coffee."

Richard clapped a hand over his mouth, scrubbing at his quivering lips and jaw. The tears that sprang so unselfconsciously to his eyes were the same as the tears when he saw the birth of his children. They were tears of joy.

After an exchange of names, Ruth settled Richard at the kitchen table with a cup of coffee, a plate of freshly baked cinnamon buns and a copy of the survival plan letter, while Lindy went back out to the barn. Ruth sat in silence until Richard finished reading the letter.

"I'd like to hear how you got to this point in your life if you'd care to tell me," Ruth said, matter-of-factly.

"We moved here from Dartmouth about six months ago," Richard began slowly. "I got a job cooking on a fishing boat here but it didn't work out so good. I got seasick a lot," he said sheepishly. "So, I got another job, just temporary, as a replacement cook in a restaurant over in Digby while the regular cook had gall-bladder surgery. That lasted three weeks. After that I could just find relief work, two days a week. I was supposed to start a full time job today as the cook for that new place opening up in Bridgetown. But it looks like they won't be opening now, at least for a while. The last couple of months I could just about keep a roof over our heads is all, and most of what little food we had came from the food bank."

"Why didn't you apply for social assistance?"

Richard shook his head. "I spent most of my life on the dole and I promised myself I would never go back on it. It's a trap, more than a help."

"What did you do in Dartmouth before you moved down here? Ruth asked.

"I had a good job for over four years as a short-order cook in a little place until the owner decided it was time for him to retire. I got some unemployment money but still used up the little bit of savings we had, just to live. I finally took a job at McDonalds as a shift supervisor, just to be working, but was only there a couple of months. I got talked into taking another job that I thought was going to be the best thing I ever did. Only, it turned out to be the worst. That job really screwed me up. McDonalds wouldn't let me come back to work for them because I had quit without notice, and I wasn't eligible for unemployment after that."

"Why is that?"

"I got fired. And they won't give you unemployment if you get fired. I got fired," Richard explained, anticipating Ruth's question, "because I couldn't do the job."

"What kind of job was it?"

"It was telemarketing at one of those fancy new call centers. I got paid minimum wage but was told I'd make a lot of money with bonuses after a certain number of orders. But I never had enough orders to qualify for a bonus, or even enough to cover the wage they were paying me, so they fired me. That was the worst job I ever had and I was led to believe it would be so great!"

"I know what you mean," Ruth said, squeezing Richard's hand. "I had to take that kind of job once myself, back about 40 years ago."

Richard's look of surprised skepticism led her to explain. "Oh yes, those jobs existed back then as well. Only we weren't called telemarketers and we didn't work with a computer in front of us in a fancy high-rise office building. We were called telephone solicitors and we worked in a back room with a dial phone and a telephone book. No matter how you try to dress it up though, it's still the same low paying, sleazy, dead-end job it's always been!"

Richard laughed humorlessly. "I wish I'd known. Why does the government act like that kind of job is the greatest thing since sliced bread, even giving those companies millions of dollars to set up shop?"

Ruth repeated the humorless laugh. "Did you ever wonder if maybe politicians lived in a complete void somewhere all their lives before they emerged one day as politicians? Or is it just that they are so in awe of computers that any job that involves a computer has got to be great? They don't just throw millions at companies to create lousy jobs, they also throw millions more into centers where everyone can go to access the internet. They call this the 'age of information' but as far as I'm concerned the internet has made it the age of *mis*information! Any yahoo and his dog can put whatever he wants on the internet. Does anyone really need such a wealth of garbage in their lives?"

Richard sighed, shaking his head. "I guess if nothing else, we're all going to get a break from it, for a while at least."

"Well," Ruth laughed, "This isn't getting your family here. And your wife is probably feeling pretty anxious by now."

"You're sure this is going to be okay?" Richard asked. "It's not like when your family gets home it's going to be a 'guess who's coming to dinner' kind of thing?"

"It's going to be more like 'guess who's *cooking* dinner," Ruth smiled mischievously. "I'm the designated cook around here, and cooking is something I've always hated. So I guess you might say I have an ulterior motive for wanting you here."

Richard's eyes held a glint of warmth as he turned at the door to look at Ruth. "You didn't know I could cook when you asked me to bring my family here. I'll be happy...no, more than happy to do all the cooking. And that's a promise," he added sincerely.

After Richard left, Ruth went up to Michael's room and began emptying his dresser drawers and transferring his things to the empty dresser in the now unused spare bedroom. She emptied his closet as well and removed nearly all his mementos and personal belongings. These she took down to the office. Returning to the bedroom, she put fresh sheets on Michael's double bed then hauled the inflatable mattress into the room. "It'll be a bit cramped," she surmised as she worked the foot pedal, inflating the mattress. "It's really a shame that other bedroom can't be used right now." '*In the spring,*' she thought. '*Oh God, surely it won't be that long!*'

Richard arrived with his family shortly before eleven. After Ruth showed them their room, they all assembled in the kitchen. Richard insisted on serving everyone the homemade turkey noodle soup Ruth had made.

While he busied himself, Ruth got acquainted with Doreen. She was a lovely young woman, quiet and shy, with a soft melodious voice and a dimpled smile. Ruth learned that the baby was due in about six weeks and that Doreen had had very little prenatal care. She immediately fished around in a kitchen cupboard, found the two bottles she was looking for and placed them on the table. "Vitamins," she said. "Take one every day, you too Richard, starting right now. And these," she said, indicating the second bottle, "are chewable vitamins for the kids." Ruth dispensed them, watching with satisfaction as the vitamins were obediently swallowed.

She turned her attention to the children as they ate their soup. Mickey was an adorable little imp, with his mother's dimples and his father's bright expressive eyes. He was perched on his knees on the chair, eating ravenously. Cassie was eating her soup mechanically, seemingly in her own little world, her delicate features exhibiting no emotion or even awareness of the other people around her. Ruth noted that Lindy was watching Cassie closely, and when the children were finished eating, Lindy took them in the family room and read them a story.

117

"Cassie?" Ruth asked, looking pointedly at Doreen once the children were out of earshot.

Doreen shook her head, sadly. "She was like any other little girl until about six months ago, about the time we moved here. Then she started to get very quiet and didn't smile much anymore. Sometimes I would find her just sitting alone, crying quietly, not making a sound just with tears streaming down her face. And she couldn't tell me what was wrong. She said she didn't know. She was always a good little kid, very obedient and eager to please. But now she's *too* good. And she hasn't spoken a word since the lights went out."

"It breaks my heart to see her like this," Richard said. "We've had her to the doctor and he says she's maybe a little malnourished, a little too thin, but otherwise healthy and bright. Shy, he said. She's just shy, being in a new place and all."

Ruth listened sadly to the two young parents who were obviously very concerned about their older child. She wished she had some answer for them, or at least some words of encouragement. But for once, she was at a loss for words.

CHAPTER ELEVEN – JANUARY 3, 2005

The Legion Hall was set up with rows of chairs facing the stage. Chris and Drew had set them up in ever widening semicircles, with aisles down the sides only. They put two long tables in front of the stage and arranged the stacks of notebooks and pens in neat rows across both tables. There was a table and four chairs up on the stage, along with the box of Trade Bucks with Ted's red thumbprint on the back. Dow, Matt, Ted and Marilyn would be on the stage, while Carin, Marissa, Drew and Chris would be on hand to pass out notebooks and pens.

Everyone except Drew and Chris had spent the morning contacting store- owners and compiling an inventory of the items available to help see everybody through the crisis. The two boys, besides having the responsibility of setting up the hall, had what was to them the unsavory task of jogging over to Drew's house twice that morning to tend to old Mrs. Henderson and keep the fire going in the fireplace.

Drew and Chris were ordered about as though Bea considered them her personal servants with no other purpose in life other than to carry out her wishes. They were sent on several missions to her cold dark house to fetch things she needed, with the admonishment not to touch any of her things or snoop around.

"I'm not going to be able to stand having her around all the time," Drew confided to Chris on their way back to the Legion. "We all have to be in the same room and she snores all night like a drunken sailor then says she didn't get a wink of sleep."

"Mmph!" Chris responded in sympathy. He was bursting with pride that an older guy of fifteen had been treating him as an equal all day. He was having the best day of his life, except for that old lady of course.

"She wouldn't eat the spaghetti your grandma sent home with us," Drew continued. "Said it was too spicy and she'd have indigestion all night. Just wanted soup she said, then complained later that all she'd had to eat all day was soup! Really ragged my dad out for being gone so long, leaving her there alone in the dark, freezing, with the fire burned too low. Didn't like the rollaway bed she had to sleep on and even wanted mom to put on different sheets because she didn't like the *color* for cripes sake. '*I never use anything but white linen,*' Drew mimicked in a falsetto, making Chris laugh.

By the time they were back at the Legion, Chris was feeling considerably more mature and was fairly strutting.

People began arriving at the Legion Hall by 12:30. Dow, Matt and the others finished wolfing down the sandwiches they had brought with them, eating them in a back room out of sight in case there were people there who had had nothing to eat. They couldn't help feeling a bit guilty and sneaky doing that, and none of them took any pleasure in eating.

By one O'clock the hall was filled even though only one member of each household was supposed to be there. The four adults took their places at the table on the stage, with Matt as the designated speaker. As he searched the crowd of anxiously silent people he could read a wide array of emotions on the faces turned up toward him. There was fear, bewilderment, resentment and outright anger on those faces. It was with a fair amount of trepidation that Matt arose and addressed the audience.

"Folks," he began, raising his hand for attention. "This is an informal gathering to figure out how everyone is going to survive the unfortunate situation we are in. Those of us up here on the stage are an ad hoc group and our intention is to present a survival plan to you that you can either accept or reject, in whole or in part. We think it is a plan that will work, but one or many of you here may have a better idea. I'm not here to make a speech, but I'd like you to listen to what I have to say before you start asking questions or presenting other ideas. It's just possible that when I finish talking your question will have been answered.

"There probably couldn't be a worse time of year for this disaster to have happened. Our survival means that everyone, without exception, will need shelter with a source of heat. That's why everyone was asked to check out the situation of his immediate neighbors. I sincerely hope everyone has done that and that no one has been forgotten. But there may not be enough homes with a source of heat to accommodate everyone. So we have made up an inventory of heat sources that are available in local stores. There's also an inventory of camp stoves and propane barbecues that can be used for both cooking and heat. Also, we've identified all the sources of light; lanterns, batteries, oil lamps, candles, etc., as well as equipment for communication; CB radios, Ham radios and walkie-talkies.

"I'm telling you all this so you'll know there are lots of things available in the immediate area to help us all get through this, for however long it takes. The last thing we want is for anyone to be left out because that is going to cause panic.

"I know that next to your immediate concerns for survival you are all wondering how widespread the problem is and how long it will last. How long it will last is something we don't know yet. But we've had a relay of CB radios getting messages around the Province ever since dawn on New Year's Day. And there's a ham radio network now across the country. I'm afraid the news isn't good. As far as we have been able to determine, power is gone all across Canada and everywhere in the U.S. that we've heard from. It looks like all computerized systems have been shut down, and since all generation of electricity and communication systems such as satellite broadcasts and phones are operated by computers, well,...But technicians are busy working on the problems and we are assured that everything will be fixed in due time, and will be up and running again. Meanwhile, we all have to get through this together. And what I'm going to tell you next should really drive home the point that we can't afford to have any panic here.

"There is panic in the Metro area. It started early New Year's Day and it's been escalating ever since. There is a high incidence of looting, fires, house break-ins, you name it, in Metro. People are cramming into the hospitals because they have back-up generators and the emergency measures people have set up hostels in school gymnasiums. So something is being done, but there's not nearly enough places available to accommodate everyone. No one ever envisioned a disaster of this magnitude, with absolutely everyone affected, the emergency measures people included!

121

"We're a little more fortunate living here in small towns and rural areas. For one thing, there are a lot more woodstoves here than in the city. There are also still several farms in the area that will be a continuing source of food and water. But it's not going to be an easy time for anyone and it's best that everyone realize that right now. It's not going to be 'business as usual' for anyone.

"For starters, I'm going to hit you with what we see as the part of the plan that is going to be hardest for some of you to accept. For the things that we need to survive, heat, food and water, your money is no good. No one is going to be able to pay for those things. And that also includes anything that is necessary for warmth such as outdoor clothing, blankets, sleeping bags and so on.

"I hear a lot of murmuring out there and I can tell you I already know that a lot of store owners don't like this idea. They feel they have a lot of money tied up in inventory and they can't afford to just give it away. But the farmers in the area have all said they will be giving away the food they produce so no one goes hungry, and I'm betting the store- owners will want to give away whatever they have that is needed so that it goes to the people who need it rather than having their stores broken into and having everything stolen. Because, mark my words, that's what will happen. It's happening right now in Metro.

"We've all got to be concerned right now with living, not *making* a living. And the giving and providing for everyone isn't going to be just on the shoulders of farmers and store- owners. Everyone has to contribute with either goods or services. I actually hate to use that terminology because every time I do I think of the most hated tax ever conceived by our government, but unfortunately those are the most fitting words. Goods that are needed or services that are needed. One day of teaching school is worth one day of food, water and heat. One day of doing *anything* that needs doing is worth food, water and heat.

"There needs to be someone designated to be in charge of every area of 50 to 60 people. Select whomever you want. That person will be the record keeper who keeps track of the Trade Bucks and sees to it that services are carried out. These people will be fulfilling a service that way.

"Before I go any further, I'm going to ask if there are any questions about anything so far. Yes, Jim!" Matt said, pointing to a man in the front row.

"I want to know why, if someone needs a heater or a carton of milk or anything else and he can afford to pay for it why a store owner or farmer has to *give* it to him instead!"

"Because there is too great a risk that only those with money will wind up getting what they need," Matt replied. "Store owners and farmers would be tempted to hold out for cash from a favored few, and those few would get more than their fair share and there'd be nothing left for those who can't afford to pay. That's why no one can pay for those essentials." Matt paused, looking for raised hands. "Yes, the lady over there on the end. I'm sorry, I don't know your name ma'am."

"It's Judy Belamy. I'm wondering about this 'service' thing. I understand that everyone should contribute what he or she can in exchange for food and heat. Those are basic needs for everyone, so that's only fair. But how does that apply to children or the elderly or the handicapped?"

"Good question, Judy. That's certainly something I slipped right over. I guess I can tell you what *our* thinking is about that, but maybe there are other ideas out there. We don't think that anyone under the age of twelve should be required to perform any service outside of their own household. Their main job is to play, grow, learn and bring a little joy and hope for the future into their households. Teenagers who are still in school have a full- time job learning, but they could make themselves useful on weekends, especially older teens. The elderly? It depends on what they can do. Can they teach someone to play checkers? Can they watch younger children or knit a pair of wool socks? Can they play a fiddle? There are probably hundreds of things that can be done by the elderly and the handicapped too that will add immeasurably to the enjoyment of life for everyone. Does that answer your question?"

"Yes, it certainly does. That sounds good to me!" Judy said.

"Okay, Bob, you've been waving frantically there. What's your question?" Matt asked.

Bob Graham was an aspiring politician, a pompous little man who was noted primarily for being full of himself. He smiled affably, making certain as many people as possible had focused their attention on him. "I have a comment followed by a question, actually," he said. "I would like to say that I think this survival plan is not only workable, it will probably be the only way we will all live to tell about it. My question is, who is the genius who came up with the idea, or was it a collaborative effort by the four of you up there?"

Matt looked over at Dow and Marilyn seated to his right then to Ted on his left. Ted softly said *'No!'* without moving his lips. Matt turned and looked directly at Bob Graham. "Bob," he said, "There are many people involved, too many to name anyone in particular. You might say the whole idea is the result of knowing what people are like here, knowing what they would want to see done because of how they react in times of trouble. If someone's barn burns down the whole community pitches in to rebuild it; if someone has an accident the community stages a benefit. People here have always taken care of one another. They may not always get along when times are good, but you can always count on your neighbor here when times are bad."

A deep voice from the back of the hall rang out. "Siddown Bob! Ya been upstaged!" followed by laughter and a smattering of applause. Then the applause grew and turned into whistles and shouts of *'Here! Here!'* and everyone knew they were applauding themselves.

"There's still a lot of ground to cover," Matt yelled, breaking up the applause. "Instead of answering more questions, we're going to divide into groups so we can get every area organized. But first, whoever is designated an area leader will need to have the use of a pickup truck or a minivan. And right after we finish here, get that vehicle over to the Irving station in Granville Ferry. Keith will have a generator going there and he'll fill your gas tanks, but *only* the tanks of the designated leaders for now. You'll learn why within your groups. Second, anyone who hasn't had a decent meal today, or no way to cook, after you leave here get over to the Samson Restaurant. Bill has been keeping warm in his kitchen slaving over his propane stove all morning baking that wonderful bread of his and cooking up huge pots of soup. He'll dish it up in big family size containers for you to take home! And hold the applause and cheering, okay? We've got work to do!

"All right now. Everyone who lives north or west of the traffic lights in Annapolis Royal, pick up notepads and pens up here and take your chair to the back of the hall on the right. Those who live south or east of the lights, go to the back on the left side. Lequille and out highway 201, front of the hall on the right; Granville Ferry to Victoria Beach, front left. Granville Center, Belle Isle and Parker Mountain Road, center of the hall. Everyone else, up here by the stage. One of us will be coming around to each group to show you how we think you should proceed, but start by writing down the name of every person in every household, with each household on a separate page. Let's go folks!" Matt finished, clapping his hands together loudly.

Dow came over and slapped Matt on the back. "Round one is over and we're not down for the count!" he exclaimed.

"It's a good thing too!" Matt declared, "or I would have embarrassed all of us. I've never had to pee so bad in my life!"

As Matt ran off the stage, Dow called after him, "Great exit line!"

CHAPTER TWELVE – JANUARY 3, 2005

"Something's been bothering you all day, Ted. Care to talk about it?" Matt asked on the way home.

"I've been a little nervous about leaving Ruth and Lindy alone all day again," Ted said seriously. "It really shook me up yesterday when I went back for more photocopies and there were a couple of guys there I didn't know. Of course, I don't really know anyone here, but that's beside the point. Do you really think it's safe leaving them alone?"

"I guess I never really thought about it. Ruth is alone a lot of the time, but the situation is different now, isn't it. We have to go back first thing in the morning to meet with the group leaders though and help get the food allocation organized. And then there's the latrine situation to iron out. We can't have people getting sick because of unsanitary conditions. We'll see what Ruth has to say, okay? You may be worrying for nothing."

'*What's the use,*' Ted thought. Matt would see that the whole world was taken care of and neglect to take care of his own family in the meantime.

"Wanna hear something funny?" Chris called out from the back seat. "That Mrs. Henderson that's staying at Drew's complained that she had nothing to eat yesterday but soup. And guess what? She's getting soup again tonight! I hope we aren't having soup. I'm so hungry I could eat a bear. *Two* bears, even!…or."

"Shut up Chris!" Carin complained. "Sometimes you sound so juvenile!"

Chris tried to think of a cutting remark he could lash back at Carin. But instead, he found himself wondering if Drew thought he was juvenile. '*Oh man, leave it up to Carin to make me feel like a dumb little kid,*' Chris thought, fighting back the lump in his throat. In the dark of the back seat, he stuck out his tongue in Carin's direction then crossed his eyes. That would show her!

Carin was seething. All afternoon she had watched Drew treating Chris like they were the same age, but he wouldn't even talk to *her*. Ever since that first night he had been at the farm she had been aware of Drew looking at her. But when she turned to look back at him he would look away, frowning. He'd been doing that all afternoon, too. And Marissa! That big cow of a girl telling her '*do this*' and '*do that!*' Like she was some kind of pea-brain! It hadn't helped a bit to learn that Marissa thought she was eleven or twelve years old. 'You're *almost fourteen?*' Marissa had bellowed. '*You sure don't look it!*' Just because she wasn't a big fat cow like *someone* she could name. Carin decided she didn't like Drew or Marissa very much. She wondered if she could just stay home tomorrow, except…, she liked the excitement of helping to organize everything. Abruptly, her focus shifted to what she could do to make herself look older.

Ruth was in the office, nervously listening for Matt's car. It would be easier to hear his arrival from there. She wanted to intercept him before he walked in and found Richard Martin and his family all moved in and sharing their home. Although she had glibly assured Richard there would be no problem, she wasn't sure. Not sure at all. It wasn't that the Martin's were black; she knew *that* wouldn't matter. It was the idea of anyone else moving in at all! The office was cramped with the twin bed that had been moved down from the spare bedroom and the old chest of drawers that now held Michael's clothes. Ruth didn't think Michael would mind giving up his room temporarily; he pretty much always took things in stride. But Matt was a very private person. And there were already six more people in the house than he was used to. Four more might be more than he could handle. Ruth braced herself when she finally heard the car, and went out to the entry room, waiting just inside the door.

Ted felt his heart leap into his throat when he saw the strange car parked in the yard. He was out of the car and running for the house almost before the car stopped. Throwing open the door, Ted saw Ruth recoil and heard her gasp, eyes wide with fright. "What's wrong?" they yelled at one another, simultaneously. "Are you all right?" they barked in unison.

"Let's start over," Ruth said, holding up one hand, the other over her heart. "Why did you come rushing in here?"

"That car out there." Ted panted. "I thought maybe you were in trouble."

"No trouble. We have company."

"Company?"

"I'll explain,…to all of you at once," Ruth said as Matt, Carin and Chris came bustling through the door. "Come into the office, everyone."

"What's all this doing in here?" Matt asked, indicating the bed and chest. "And all Michael's stuff."

"Michael is going to be using the office as a bedroom because I've moved a young family into his room," Ruth stated matter-of-factly. "They had nowhere else to go and we *do* have the room in this big old house."

"How did they happen to come here?" Ted asked.

"That's not important," Ruth said offhandedly. "All that matters is that they're here and they'll be staying. Please, all of you, make them feel welcome. They've had a pretty hard time of it and they really need for us to accept them."

Matt had just stood there, eyes hard, chewing on the inside of his bottom lip while Ruth talked. When she finished, he bowed his head, exhaling forcibly. "I guess *we* should do what we have been telling everyone else *they* should do," he said. "It's only right."

Relieved, Ruth said hesitantly, "There's something else you should know before you go in to meet them; they're black." She looked at everyone for a reaction, and was surprised when all Matt said was, "I'd better get changed and go do the milking."

"It's done," Ruth said.

Matt gave Ruth a searching look. "You shouldn't be doing the milking along with all the heavy work with the cattle and the house and cooking and…"

"You forget. I have Lindy here to help with the cattle, and the newest member of the household is a cook, by profession. *He's* fixing dinner, and wants to do all the cooking while he's here. And you *know* I won't object to that!"

Michael, Nate and Rachel arrived home about 20 minutes later than Matt and his crew. The five children were seated at the kitchen table being waited on by Richard and Doreen.

Rachel and Richard looked at one another, frowning, knowing they had seen one another recently, but not able to remember when or where. Recognition came to Rachel first; the pregnant wife and two small children jogging her memory. She pointed at Richard. "Now I remember where I saw you! You're the man I gave the candy bars to in front of the convenience store!"

"Right!" Richard exclaimed, recognition dawning. "I was trying to figure out where I'd seen you before! Hey, thanks! We really appreciated that. Well...hey..., it's a small world, huh?" Richard said, following an awkward pause.

Rachel smiled her agreement. She assumed, as did Michael and Nate, that Matt had asked the family to come stay at the farm. She was pleased to see that Carin was taking an obvious interest in the little girl. She was an exquisite looking child, but seemed to be very shy. It probably wouldn't be long though before she would lose that shyness and the peace and quiet that went along with it, Rachel decided.

After dinner, Matt usurped the dining room for a comparison session of what took place in Annapolis Royal verses Bridgetown. Although Bridgetown had twice the population of Annapolis, there was only one grocery store there compared to two in Annapolis. Both towns had hardware and building supply stores, but there were six restaurants in Annapolis and none, yet, in Bridgetown. Both towns had a bakery.

The biggest difference between the two towns was the number of people prepared for the power outage in Bridgetown. Five years previously, at the time of the Y2K scare, a good portion of the people in the Bridgetown area had installed solar panels on their roofs along with banks of storage batteries and converters. Others had purchased heavy -duty generators and storage tanks for diesel fuel. And for the past five years, those same people had gotten used to the idea of having a good supply of non-perishable food on hand too.

"We should be thankful there are people who were prepared for this," Nate said. "Even if some of them don't want to take part in a survival plan, at least they won't be a drain on the available resources."

"In my mind that's pure selfishness," Matt chided.

"We were planning to be selfish too, you know," Ruth stated. "Or at least I was. My only concern was for my own family, their survival and safety. I'm still not sure how or why that changed. But maybe some of those 'prepared' people in Bridgetown will change their thinking too."

"There are still concerns from a lot of people, especially from store owners who are already existing on a tight margin," Nate said. "They're concerned about what will happen if and when the banks are back functioning. They figure the banks will be calling in a lot of loans. I told them I didn't think they had to worry about that. There would be too many loans to call in so my bet is they wouldn't call in any."

"I think the worries people have are going to change," Ted said. "Instead of worrying about what the banks are going to do or what the state of their businesses will be when the power comes back on, I think they are going to be worrying about how to protect themselves from outsiders. Because, I think there's going to be a lot to worry about on that score."

Everyone silently digested Ted's words, their minds busy imagining scenarios that filled them with dread. Ted had dared to say what was in the back of everyone's mind; that thing that lay there suppressed because no one wanted to think about it. The possibility of strangers descending on them with evil intent was terrifying.

"How did you happen to bring Richard and his family here, Dad?" Michael asked.

"I didn't have anything to do with it," Matt responded. He was here when we got home."

All eyes turned to Ruth. She knew she would have to give them some kind of answer and it would have to be the truth, as far as it went. "He came here looking for food. This is a farm and I suppose he thought we might have some food here that we could spare." Ruth took a deep breath then continued. "When Dow knocked on his door in town yesterday with the letter, Richard thought he was there because he had written a bad check the day before and somehow Dow had found out and had come to collect. So he didn't answer the door. And his landlord who lives on the other side of the house *couldn't* answer his door because he had gone to Halifax. So, Richard didn't know about the survival plan. He was missed. And that makes me wonder how many more people may have been missed!" Ruth exclaimed, cagily directing the focus away from Richard.

That possibility had been discussed at the meetings in both towns and was resolved by dividing the areas into small sections. No one would be missed, unless they wanted to be.

The discussion turned to the problems that would have to be tackled the next day, especially sanitation, since the sewers could not be used.

"Holy shit!" Michael yelped, suddenly leaping out of his chair. "I forgot all about feeding the cattle!"

"Relax," Ruth said, reaching for Michael. "They've already been fed, long ago, while it was still light out."

"How? You can't drive that tractor."

"No, but Richard can. I instructed him on what to do. He's afraid of the cattle, though, so he just put the hay in the feeder and Lindy and I did the rest. By the way, I think Lindy has a little surprise for you. She's probably waiting for you out in the barn right now."

"I really don't like Lindy going out to the barn at all hours, all alone," Ted said. I know she's not afraid of the cattle and you've got me pretty well convinced she's sensible around them, but I still wish there was always someone with her out there. Those two men up here yesterday, and then Richard today, well, that has me pretty edgy. Maybe *they* meant no harm, but what about the next person?"

Michael noticed a strange look cross his mother's face; sudden alarm? Fear? He decided he had read the look right when she said, "You're right Ted. She shouldn't be out there alone. Michael, you better go out now and when you come back in bring Lindy with you."

As Michael walked out to the barn, he knew he would have to drag out of his mother, somehow, the reason for that sudden look of fear. He was convinced there was something she wasn't telling them.

Lindy was in the barn all right, sitting on the edge of the manger in the third pen, playing with Priscilla. "Go look in the last two pens, Uncle Michael," she called out as she saw him approach. "They're both girls, but they haven't been named yet."

"Lindy," Michael said, sitting down next to her, "Grandma doesn't think you should be coming out to the barn alone anymore." Seeing that Lindy had a crestfallen look at that pronouncement rather than the perplexed or indignant look that he would have expected, Michael surmised that *both* Lindy and his mother were hiding something.

"What happened today, Lindy? What happened that made your Grandma afraid for you to be out here alone?"

"Richard came in the barn," Lindy said softly, her head lowered. "He didn't see me because I was sitting over there in the straw petting Mia's baby, Pitty Pat. She drank too much milk and had a tummy ache, so Grandma gave her…"

"Never mind that," Michael interrupted. "Just go on about Richard."

"Well, he looked in all the pens and he looked out in the corral then he came back to Melissa's pen because she was the only cow that wasn't trying to protect her baby. He took Priscilla out of her pen. He was going to take her because his kids were hungry," Lindy said, her voice breaking.

Michael put his arm around her shoulders. "What happened then?"

"I ran out of here fast and latched the door behind me. Then I went and got Grandma."

"Did you come back out here with her?"

"No. She wouldn't let me. She made me stay in the house and lock the door. It seemed like Grandma was out in the barn for a long time, and when she came back to the house, Richard was with her."

"Were his wife and kids here too?"

"No, he had to go get them."

"Didn't either you or Grandma hear his car come up here? Didn't Buddy bark?"

"He didn't have his car here. He was parked across the road in that dirt track that goes down to the river."

"Hmmph," was Michael's only response. The rest of the story had been filled in by his mother earlier, but she certainly had left out the details. He wondered how many more details there were, that Lindy didn't know about. Like what took place in the barn between Richard and his mom. Well, he was going to find out!

Richard and Doreen had insisted on doing the dishes and cleaning up the kitchen after dinner. When they finished, they joined the five children in the family room. Carin was reading aloud, some story about a dog, and Chris interrupted to explain to Richard and Doreen that it was the story of their Grandma's dog, Buddy.

Buddy was on the couch, flanked on either side by Carin and Cassie, while Chris was helping Mickey build a car with Lego. Richard and Doreen sat at the table where the 3D puzzle sat partially constructed, looking at it with amazement. They both found themselves getting interested in the story as Carin read aloud. She read with a lot of animation but it didn't have that phony sound that most adults affected when reading to children.

In the dim light, Richard was searching for a piece of the puzzle when Doreen placed her hand on his arm. Their eyes met and Doreen rolled hers toward the couch, wanting Richard to look. What he saw brought a prickling of tears behind his eyes.

Cassie was petting the dog's head, a faint smile playing at the corners of her mouth. Then, looking up at Carin, the smile grew and turned into a brief giggle.

Richard grasped Doreen's hand, squeezing hard. His eyes shining in the lamplight, he whispered, "Lord God A'mighty thank you for bringin' me here!"

Carin was waiting for the opportunity to talk to her mother. She had her chance soon after Michael went outside. Her mother and grandmother had come out to the kitchen to make hot chocolate for everyone. "Better use up some of that milk before it spoils," she heard her grandmother say.

"That's enough of the story for now," Carin told Cassie. "I'll read you some more tomorrow night." Leaving Cassie on the couch, petting Buddy, she went out to the kitchen.

Carin had never been one for beating around the bush. When she had something to say she said it, damn the consequences. But she was a bit hesitant now about the request she was going to make, certain the answer would be 'no' and that an argument would ensue.

"Mom, I think I'm old enough to start wearing makeup," Carin declared. "I'm small for my age and I have to do something to make myself look a little older so people won't think I'm only twelve. I think makeup is the answer."

Rachel looked at her daughter, mouth agape, wondering where that had come from all of a sudden, while Ruth stirred the hot chocolate on the stove, trying to hide her smile.

"A little makeup is not out of the question, I guess," Rachel said, surprising Carin.

"Really?"

"Sure. I think I started wearing lipstick when I was fourteen and you're just a couple of months away from that age."

"Great! Could you show me how to use it?"

"There are other things you can do to make yourself appear older in addition to a bit of makeup," Ruth said. "Your mom was even smaller at fourteen than you are, and we worked out a few tricks to make her look more like her age. How about serving everyone some hot chocolate while I go upstairs and get a few things. Then, we three 'girls' will go out back and see if we can add a couple of years to your age."

"Makeup first," Rachel said. She applied a rose colored lipstick to Carin's lips, outlining their fullness with care. Next came a dark brown waterproof mascara applied sparingly, followed by a light dusting of blush on her cheeks.

"Mmm, just right!" Rachel said, pleased with her handiwork. "Now for the hair. Grandma's good at that."

"First we get rid of this low-slung pony tail," Ruth said, loosening Carin's thick honey-blonde hair. She parted Carin's hair down the middle then brushed the hair on one side into a handful behind her ear and began braiding it.

"Pigtails!" Carin exclaimed. "That will make me look even younger!"

"Hold still!" Ruth commanded.

"Some things never change," Rachel laughed. "I had exactly the same reaction when your Grandma did the same thing to me."

Carin endured the braiding then was surprised when the braids were fastened to the top of her head with a small gold clasp. The curling ends fell naturally in place on top of her head, adding a full inch of height.

"Are you ready?" Ruth asked. She flipped on the light switch in the bathroom, using some of the precious electricity for the debut of her precious grown up granddaughter.

Carin was stunned. "Is that me? Wow, I look at least...fifteen, don't you think? Can I go show Dad?"

"Just one finishing touch," Ruth said, producing a new pair of black boots. "Go ahead, put them on," she urged as Carin looked at them in disbelief.

"Those are the new boots you got for Christmas!" Carin exclaimed.

"Yes, and they have a platform sole and two inch heels and they are completely unsuitable for an old woman but just exactly right for a young lady who looks fifteen," Ruth said, all in one breath. "And aren't we lucky our feet are the same size! Now these boots won't go to waste."

"Thank you Grandma," Carin said, eyes sparkling. "And you too Mom. I never knew you guys were so cool!" She slipped on the boots, spun a circle of delight then went to show her Dad the new Carin.

"Do you think she has any idea how lovely she is?" Ruth asked Rachel. "Did you have any idea when you were her age? Because you were you know. So fresh looking, so perfect, when you stopped

135

being a child and became a young woman." Ruth's eyes had filled with tears and she brushed them away with a grimace. "My, I'm getting maudlin in my old age!" she exclaimed.

Rachel wrapped her arms around her mother, whispering, "I love you Mom."

It seemed like everyone converged in the entry room at the same time. Ruth and Rachel were coming in from the back room, Carin was coming out from the kitchen, and Michael and Lindy were coming in from the barn.

"Wow Carin, you look great!" Lindy gushed.

"Mom, can I talk to you for a minute?" Michael asked.

"What did your Dad say about your new look?" Rachel asked Carin.

"Come on in here," Ruth said, ushering Michael into the office. "May as well light a lamp in here while we're at it. As you can see, this is going to be your room for now. I've, uh, moved the Martins into your room."

"It's the Martins I want to talk about," Michael said. "I want to know what took place in the barn between you and Richard!"

"I guess you've been talking with Lindy about that. Should have known you would."

"So tell me the rest of it. *All* the rest."

Ruth sat on Michael's bed. "When I went into the barn, Richard was holding Priscilla in his arms and..., Ruth paused to clear her throat,...and, he had a gun in his hand pointed right at me."

Michael blanched. "A gun? Does he still have it?"

"No, I have it. Richard doesn't even know how to use a gun and he was scared to death and shaking. I was very calm for some strange reason. I think now it's because I knew instinctively he wouldn't use the gun. It's like it was nothing more than a stage prop and we were just acting out a scene together that had to be gotten through so we could get to the important part of the play. It's hard to explain Michael, but I knew I was in no danger. He's a good man, I'd stake my life on that. But he was a desperate man. Think about it. Two little kids, one obviously needing some kind of help, a pregnant wife. What would you have done in his place?"

"I don't know," Michael said, running his hands through his hair. "This is some god damn mess isn't it!"

Ruth was about to redress Michael for swearing, but decided she'd let it pass this time. "There's still so much for everyone to do to get things organized, and I may as well tell you I'm going to feel a whole lot safer with Richard and Doreen here with me all day."

"Were you not feeling safe?"

"I don't think I really admitted it to myself, but I've been awfully jumpy being here with just Lindy. Ted made me realize what a good part of the tension is all about. I've been very nervous every time Lindy was out in the barn by herself. The fact that Richard could gain access to the barn *unseen…*"

"You're sure you'll feel safer with Richard here?"

"I felt immeasurably safer all afternoon!"

Michael paced, repeatedly running his hands through his hair. It was a habit long familiar to Ruth, a sign that Michael was trying to work out a problem. "What did you do with the gun, Mom?" he suddenly asked.

"I took the bullets out and put them in a cartridge box then put the gun up high in a kitchen cupboard."

"Show me. I'm going to bring the gun out here and keep the office door locked."

As Ruth and Michael came into the kitchen, Buddy came trotting in from the family room, heading for the back door. "Buddy has to go out," Ruth said. "The gun's in that cupboard, top shelf on the right," she whispered, pointing.

Michael reached for the gun, looked it over carefully then tucked it into his waistband under his shirt.

Neither Michael nor Ruth saw Cassie standing in the shadowed doorway to the family room. Nor did they see her happy, sparkling eyes widen in terror momentarily then cloud over and become dull with defeat.

CHAPTER THIRTEEN – JANUARY 4, 2005

Dow turned the metal storage shed in his back yard into an outhouse. Using a welding torch, he thawed the dirt floor in the back of the shed a layer at a time, digging down until he had a sizeable hole. He removed the bottom of a small wooden crate, placed the crate over the hole then cut a hole in the top and installed the toilet seat from his downstairs bathroom over the hole. It was crude, but it would serve the purpose.

Bea was livid. She saw no reason why Drew couldn't keep buckets of melted snow handy to fill the water tank so the toilet could be flushed whenever she needed to use it. No amount of explaining about water freezing and pipes and bowls cracking got through to her. She demanded that the seat from the upstairs bathroom be installed downstairs immediately, if not sooner. Then she made it known, in no uncertain terms, that there was absolutely no way she was going to trek out to that shed in the cold, nor would she use a bucket as a chamber pot!

To Bea, nothing was as it should be. Her tea was never steeped long enough, or much too long. It was not sweetened enough or was too sweet and was always too hot or too cold. And they absolutely *must* do something about making toast for her in the morning! The lounge chair should be moved closer to the window during the day so she could see to read better and to look outside. Then it should be moved back nearer the fireplace if she felt a chill. She was left alone too much, and God only knew what would become of her!

"You have lived alone and done everything for yourself for years now," Marilyn pointed out to her. "Why do you suddenly need to have everything done for you?"

"It's different, not being in my own home with all my own things that I'm used to," Bea said airily. "Now make yourself useful and brush my hair back before you take off for the day and leave me here alone to freeze. And fetch me that lap robe for my knees," Bea ordered Marissa.

Dow had had enough. He calmly detailed the rules of the house to Bea and informed her that she would adhere to every one of them. Bea countered with an objection to every stated rule, her voice a rising crescendo of indignation.

'She sure has some voice for such a fragile looking old bird,' Marilyn thought.

"You leave me no choice," Dow said ominously, taking his penknife from his pocket and opening out the blade. "I'm going to have to go cut me a switch!"

Out in the yard, Dow examined several small branches on a tree then made his selection. After trimming off a few twigs, he brought the switch down in a swift arc, testing its strength and heft. *'This always worked with the kids,'* he told himself. *'Just seeing me cut the switch was enough; I never had to actually use it. But what if the old girl calls your bluff you dumb ass! What are you going to do then? Huh?'*

Inside the house, Bea was watching out the window, muttering to herself. "You wouldn't,...you couldn't,...oh, that's preposterous!" She recoiled in disbelief as she saw Dow test the weight of the switch, an alarmed "Oh!" escaping her as she fled from the window.

When Dow came back in the house, he saw Bea in coat and overshoes making a hasty beeline for the makeshift outhouse in the back yard.

Drew and Marissa could hardly contain their mirth. Hands clasped firmly over their mouths, they rushed past Dow out into the front yard and threw themselves into a snow-bank and rolled around accompanied by peals of laughter.

"You were lucky," Marilyn told Dow, smiling widely.

"Wasn't I though!" Dow conceded, sheepishly letting out his breath. "Think I'll keep it handy. It might be a good thing for her to see it once in a while."

Nate had developed a bad cold traipsing around in the frigid wind the past two days, and Lindy insisted he stay home, preferably in bed. Ruth seconded that motion.

Nate didn't put up much of an argument, except to say that someone would have to take his place at the meeting in Bridgetown.

It was decided that Ted and Chris would go over to Bridgetown with Michael and Rachel. Chris was put out by the idea until Matt told him it would give him a break from old Mrs. Henderson. He could see the advantage in that, especially since it would be Carin who would become the victim of her sharp tongue.

Matt drove the pickup since it would be just Carin and himself going into Annapolis. He glanced over at Carin several times, wondering why she looked so grown up all of a sudden. It seemed like just yesterday that she was a little girl, and now…

"We haven't had much of a chance to talk since you've been here," Matt said, making conversation. "Things have been so hectic. There's a lot to do again today, and there will be people coming in to the Legion, I'm sure. And then there's Mrs. Henderson to look in on for Dow. I think you and Drew should tend to that end of things, if that's all right with you."

"It's okay with me," Carin said, "but I don't know about Drew. I don't think he likes me very much, Grandpa. He won't even talk to me. So, he probably isn't going to be too delighted to have to spend the day with me."

Matt drove along, thinking, and didn't say anything more until he pulled into the Legion parking lot. "You say you don't think Drew likes you?" Matt asked.

"Uh huh."

"Hmm. Do you ever catch him looking at you and then when you look back at him he turns away real fast?"

"All the time. And then he frowns."

"And he won't talk to you?"

"No! Every time I try to talk to him he just mumbles something and looks away. Is there something wrong with me Grandpa? I mean, it doesn't matter to me if Drew doesn't want to be my friend, but at least I'd like to know why!"

"Sweetheart," Matt said, "the problem isn't yours. It's Drew's. He has all the symptoms of having a crush on you and he obviously doesn't know how to handle it."

"Why would he have a crush on me? He doesn't even know me!"

"Because he'd have to be blind not to."

"Are you putting me on, Grandpa?" Carin asked suspiciously. "I'm small for my age, I'm too skinny, I don't have any…" she said, looking despondently down at her chest,…"You know. My mouth is too big, my *teeth* are too big…"

"You better take another look at yourself in the mirror," Matt said chuckling. "Because, what I see is a slender, petite young woman with a dazzling smile, incredibly beautiful eyes and a spitfire personality."

"Really?"

"Really! I would defy any red-blooded fifteen- year old boy to *not* have a crush on you. Didn't you have boys after you in Edmonton?"

"No. There were a couple of them though that acted a lot like Drew is acting. I've just never paid much attention to boys, so I never cared if any of them liked me or not. Do you really think Drew likes me?"

"I'm sure of it. Now get out of the truck and let me be on my way. I'll be back to pick you up at four. You're going to have mostly fishermen coming in today to register. But most of that will be handled by a couple of the boat owners so you and Drew will just be here to answer some general questions. You both know how everything is organized since you've been in on it from the beginning."

"Do you think the fishermen are going to accept directions from a couple of kids?"

"I honestly don't know, honey. But I think they won't be so inclined to give a couple of kids a hard time." Matt took off his cap, looked at it critically then put it back on his head. "I wish there were more of us that had been in on the original planning. Right now it seems like we need to be in about six places at once. But the most important thing today is getting those food allocations sorted out so that rations can be picked up by area leaders. That, and developing a sanitation plan."

"I almost hate to get out of this truck," Carin said ruefully. "I'm soaking up as much heat as I can because it's so-oo-oo cold in that Legion!"

"That's why you need to get over to Drew's house every hour or two, besides checking on Mrs. Henderson. I'll see you around four," Matt said, kissing Carin on the cheek. "Now scoot, so I can get out of here!"

Drew was walking across the Legion parking lot when he saw Carin unlocking the door to the hall. His steps faltered as he looked around for Chris. He'd been eager to tell the story of the switch and Mrs. Henderson but that wasn't something he could tell Carin about. Hell, he got tongue-tied if he even *thought* about talking to her, let alone trying to tell her a funny story!

Carin turned and smiled at Drew as he approached. "Are you ready for another numbing cold day?" she called out.

"Mmph," Drew answered, feeling his face suddenly turn warm. *'Damnit, I'm blushing!'* he chided himself. *'Maybe she'll think my face is red from the cold. She* can't *think I'm blushing!'*

'He's blushing,' Carin thought. *'Maybe Grandpa is right and Drew has a crush on me.'* Carin felt herself blushing at the thought.

Drew busied himself setting up tables and chairs, equipping each of them with notebooks and pens, while Carin talked with Dwight Chambers and Sam Connolly, the two fishing boat owners who would be briefing the fishermen.

"Fish is going to be a very important part of the survival plan," Carin was telling the two men. "Fish was kind of a last minute item mentioned because my Dad didn't think about it at first. We're from Alberta, and there's no fishing industry there."

"Your dad came up with that plan?" Dwight asked. It's all his idea?"

"Oh no. Nate Taylor and Dow Marchant were up at my grandparent's farm on New Years Day and they were talking about the things that would have to be done to help everyone get through this, especially if it lasted a long while. My Uncle Michael had talked to somebody on the CB radio and found out that people were going crazy in Halifax and they didn't want that to happen here. My Dad just sort of put everybody's ideas together and came up with a plan. But, like I said, fish was one of the last things he thought of."

"There's going to be a lot of fishermen coming in here today expecting to sell their fish, not give it away. And that includes me, too. Fishing is hard work, and there's boats to pay for, fuel, wages for the men...we can't afford to give our fish away!" Sam nodded agreement.

"Farmers work just as hard as you do," Carin said. "Maybe even harder. They can't afford to give away the food they produce either, but that's what they're doing. And what about the grocery store owners? They had to pay for all the food in their stores and they can't afford to give it away either. But they are. And the two of you and your families are some of the people the farmers and store owners will be giving food to!"

"But if we get paid for our fish no one will have to give us food, we can pay for it!" Sam countered.

"Who do you expect to pay for the fish?" Carin demanded. "The store- owners? So they can give it to all the people who can't pay for it in the first place? No one has any money. And what good is money going to be to you? You can't buy food. Your fair share will be *given* to you. You can't buy gas to run your boat or fuel to heat your house because it will be *given* to you. You don't have to pay your help because *their* payment for services will be food, water and heat. And you pay for your food, water and heat with your *fish!"*

Dwight and Sam looked at one another then back at Carin, each lost in his own thoughts, weighing what that little bit of a girl had said. Carin took their silence to mean they needed more convincing. "Nate Taylor said that what we have to fear most is people who are cold and hungry. They will be desperate and desperate people will kill to get food and heat. If only people who can afford to pay for it get to eat and stay warm, there will be a lot of desperate people trying to take it from them. That's why it's important to see that everyone has what they need, and why no one can pay for anything."

"Nate said that, huh?" Dwight said. "He's a pretty smart old codger. I'd like to have a talk with him. You know where he's staying?"

"At our place. He's come down with a bad cold so we made him stay in bed today."

"How did he happen to wind up at your place?" Sam wanted to know.

"My Grandma heard he had no heat in his apartment so she had him brought out to the farm to stay with us. There's a man there with his wife and two little kids, too. His name is Richard Martin."

"Black fella?" Sam asked.

"Yes. He's a cook, and a pretty good one, too."

"Yeah, I know who he is. He was doing some cooking on one of the fishing boats but the guy never could get his sea legs. Spent most of the time with his head hangin' over the side of the boat."

"How come you folks took them in?" Dwight asked.

"As my Grandma said, 'we have heat, we have the room and we have food.'"

"Drew!" Dwight called, motioning him over. "This young lady here has been telling us…"

"I heard." Drew said. "Everything she has told you, you can rely on." For the first time, he looked directly at Carin and smiled at her. Listening to her talking to the two men, he had come to the conclusion that Carin was so far above him she was unattainable. That knowledge set him free to be himself in her presence. "The situation in Metro is a lot worse than she let on though. It started just after dawn on New Years Day with looting, some fires being set, house break-ins and hi-jacking. The emergency measures people are doing what they can, but there is still a lot of panic. That's what this plan hopes to avoid. And so far it's working. But if the fishermen don't want to be part of it, it could all be a waste of effort. And the fishermen could wind up being the biggest threat to the rest of us, because they have to eat too. And they need more than just fish."

"Nothing can be the way it was," Carin added, "because everything has changed. We just went back in time about a hundred years in the blink of an eye, and no one was prepared for that to happen. So now we have to do whatever it takes to get all of us through it. Either we *all* make it, or maybe none of us do."

"We'll do our part," Dwight assured the two solemn young people. "It won't be easy convincing some of the guys, but…"

"But there's always a way to make an attitude adjustment," Sam said, slamming his beefy right fist into the palm of his left hand.

Carin picked up the tote bag she had brought from home containing the lunch Richard had fixed for her, Drew and Bea Henderson. On the way out the door, a gust of wind blew the hood of her parka back. She had forgotten to tie it after loosening the hood in the Legion Hall. "Drew, could you fix this for me please?" she asked, grimacing from the cold.

Drew reached over with one hand and hauled the hood back over her head. "No. Tie it," Carin said. It will just blow off again if it isn't tied."

Drew had to face Carin to tie the cord under her chin. Fumbling nervously, his hand brushed her cheek, sending a jolt from his hand down to his feet and back up to his head, turning his face scarlet. Carin kept her eyes on his face as Drew tied a neat bow then lifted his eyes meeting hers, where they lingered a second. His lips parted and he swallowed hard. "I'll take this for you," he said, reaching for the tote bag. Carin slipped her gloved hand into his. "Let's run!" she cried playfully. "We'll be where it's warm quicker that way."

Drew would swear later that his feet never touched the ground all the way home.

Bea had kept the fire going in the fireplace instead of letting it die back as usual. She had also tidied up the room that seemed to be left in a jumble every morning.

Carin introduced herself, wondering if this could possibly be the waspish old woman Chris complained about. She liked Bea immediately, and the feeling seemed to be mutual. "I've brought you something special," Carin said beaming. "But first, I'm afraid it's soup again for lunch!"

"Oh, I don't mind soup, my dear," Bea assured her. "Why, I practically live on soup. I don't have to chew it, you see," she tittered. Drew stood there with his mouth open. "Don't just stand there with your mouth open," Bea chided sweetly. "How about getting us some bowls."

"Oh lovely!" Bea gushed when the bowl of hot soup was set in front of her. "It's homemade and absolutely delicious. So much better than canned."

"Do you have one of those big black skillets?" Carin asked Drew.

"Mmph," Drew answered, as he went to fetch the skillet. *'Good God, I'm right back where I was!'* he thought dejectedly. *'Blub, blub, blub, duh!'* he muttered, flipping his bottom lip with a finger. *'Why does she have to be so perfect?'* he thought. *'Why can't she belch after eating soup, or something? Why can't I even think when I'm in the same room with her? Why does she want this friggin' 20 pound frying pan?'*

"Thanks Drew," Carin said, looking him directly in the eye.

Drew looked away, cursing himself for blushing again.

With the fireplace poker, Carin lowered the cooking grate over the andirons and set the frying pan on it to heat. Then she laid three thick slices of bread in the pan, leaving them until they had turned crusty and brown. She flipped them over and spread something spicy smelling on the browned surface then when it was melted, added more. Using an oven mitt, she lifted the pan from the grate and set it on the hearth.

Serving a slice to Bea, Carin said, "It's butter, honey and cinnamon and it's so good! I made some last night for Mr. Taylor."

"Mr. Taylor?" Bea asked nonchalantly.

"Yes. Nate Taylor. He's staying with us at the farm. You must know him. Everybody knows everybody else around here."

"Yes, I'm acquainted with Mr. Taylor." Bea paused, "Did he suggest you make this delicious treat for me?"

"No, he didn't know I'd be coming here today. But we all had to change places because Mr. Taylor is sick in bed today."

"Nothing serious I hope!" Bea said, alarmed.

"I don't think so. It's just a cold."

"Even a cold can be serious when you get to be his age. Take good care of him, will you dear?"

"My sister Lindy is taking good care of him. In fact, she's probably mothering him to death right now." Carin looked at Drew. "We'd probably better get a move on, don't you think?"

"Mmph," Drew answered.

"Drew," Bea said, waggling her finger at him as Carin took the frying pan and dishes out to the kitchen. "I like your young lady. You hang on to her."

"My young lady? I'm not even sure she knows I'm alive," Drew said dispiritedly.

"Nonsense! That girl has a crush on you. It's written all over her!"

"You think so?" Drew asked, perking up.

"And why not? A handsome young man like you? Shh, here she comes," Bea whispered.

Carin and Drew were already out the door when Drew exclaimed, "I'll be right back. I forgot something." He rushed back into the living room and gave a very surprised old woman a kiss on the cheek, saying, "Thanks!"

'Nate Taylor,' Bea mused. *'How old will I have to be before I get over him?'* She had been in love with Nate ever since she was fifteen. She remembered how handsome he had looked in his army uniform, going off to save the world, and how frightened she had been for his safety, how much she had missed him. Bea's eyes clouded over at the memory of her parents convincing her of Nate's unsuitability, how she would be wasting herself with a man who was socially beneath her, and how they had introduced her to a young doctor and had her safely married at seventeen, just before Nate's return from the war.

Nate had married her best friend, Helen. Helen had been so wildly in love with Nate that she never knew Bea was in love with him, too. Until the day she died, she never knew. But Carl did. His dying words to her had been *'Now you are free to be with the man you have loved all these years.'* She had never told him, yet he knew, perhaps had always known. Carl had loved her; she knew that beyond a doubt. But they had both settled for something less than perfect. Nate and Helen? No, not perfect either. They had never had children though they both desperately wanted them. She and Carl had no children either. They hadn't wanted them. But she would have wanted children with Nate, she knew.

"Oh Nate!" Bea sighed his name aloud.

Dwight Chambers and Sam Connolly were arguing with a burly fisherman when Drew and Carin returned to the Legion. They stayed out of sight, listening, remembering Sam's suggestion for an attitude adjustment.

"...the word of a god damn, yellow, draft dodging American!' they heard the man say. "Look who you're trusting! And how do you know there's anything going on in Halifax? Because *he* said so?"

"It's more than just Matt. Dow Marchant has heard for himself what's happening in Halifax and so has Nate Taylor," Dwight shouted.

"Oh, so now we're listening to doddering old fools and Jew shopkeepers who can't even keep track of their own wives, are we?"

"Now what's that supposed to mean, Earl?"

"Well, now, you know exactly what that's supposed to mean, don't you Dwight?"

"Listen, you slimy scumbag. I don't know what you *think* you know, but you're wrong. And so is your attitude about Matt, Dow and Nate. They're trying to do something to save the lives of people around here and..."

"They're getting somethin' outa this, you mark my words. Did you ever meet an American or a Jew you could trust? Those guys are commies! It's as plain as the nose on your face!"

Carin had heard enough. She came charging out of the back room, walked up to the offensive man named Earl, placed her fists on her hips and yelled up into the man's face, "That's my grandfather you're talking about!"

"Well more's the pity for you. I feel sorry for ya, girlie. Now why don't ya..."

"*You're* the one you should feel sorry for! Because you're the one who is going to be left out! No one is going to buy your fish. We don't need you or your fish, you know. But *you* are going to need *us!*.

"Why don't you go play with your dollies like a good little girl and leave us three men to our man talk!"

Carin turned and looked at Dwight and Sam then back at Earl. "Three men?" she asked. "I only see *two!*" She turned and walked away then halfway to the door turned to face the man again. "*Two* men and, what was it Mr. Chambers called you? Oh yeah, one *scumbag!"*

"You're some piece 'o work, kid!" Earl yelled after her.

"Ain't she though!" Dwight exclaimed. "I wish she was *my* kid! I'm that proud of her for standing up to the likes of you."

Mustering up the nerve, Drew breezed past Carin and planted his feet directly in front of the big man. "I want to know what you meant when you said my father couldn't keep track of his wife!" Drew demanded.

Earl gave Dwight a menacing look. "How many *more* kids ya got stashed in the woodwork, huh? Maybe ya oughta ask Dwight here that question, kid," he said looking at Drew and snickering.

"I'm asking you. You're the one who said it!"

"All right kid, ya wanna know? Your mama spent the night with Dwight here a couple a years ago, and who knows how many times since!"

"You liar!" Drew bellowed.

"I oughta take my belt and learn you kids a little respect!" Earl said menacingly.

Dwight held up his hand. "You'll not lay a hand on him, Earl Drummond. You're getting all the respect you deserve!" Looking Drew in the eye, he said, "Your mom was over on the shore at one of those home shopping parties women have, a couple of years ago. It started snowing hard and the wind came up, so your mom left the party early and tried to beat the storm home. She slid onto the shoulder of the road and got stuck in a big drift with that little car of hers, practically in front of my place. She came knocking on my door for help, but my truck was in the shop. There was nothin' to do but have her stay there 'til morning, and she called your dad and let him know. Earl here was picking me up early to go fishing, and he seen your mom there and her car parked in front of my place. He never would believe the truth because some men can't think any way but dirty and mean. And Earl here is the all-time champion of dirty and mean," Dwight said, shifting a glance toward Earl. "He never misses a chance to say something bad about his neighbors, truth be damned!"

"You owe me an apology," Drew told Earl. Carin too, and…"

"That'll be the day, I apologize to a couple a snot-nosed kids!"

"...my mom and dad, and Carin's grandpa," continued Drew. "And Dwight here, and..."

"See ya around!" Earl hollered over his shoulder as he tramped heavily across the floor. "You ain't heard the last 'a me, you can bet on it!"

"The sad part is, that's probably true," Dwight said, to no one in particular.

"I thought you were going to use that for an attitude adjustment," Drew said to Sam, pointing at his fist.

Sam held his fist up in front of him. "That would work on some people, but not Earl Drummond. My fist wouldn't make a dent in a head that thick!"

"I feel sorry for his wife and his two boys," Dwight said sadly. "They don't deserve the kind of trouble he's going to bring them when he gets back home."

Carin and Drew walked somberly, side by side, to Drew's house. The confrontation with Earl Drummond had broken the ice between them, giving them a common bond. But there was no lightheartedness, no playfulness now in their awareness of one another.

"What's draft dodging mean, Drew?" Carin asked. "That horrible man said my grandpa was a g d yellow draft dodging American. That made me mad because it doesn't sound nice, but I don't know what it means."

"A draft dodger is someone who wouldn't go into the army and came to Canada so he wouldn't have to."

"But my grandpa was in the army. There's a picture of him in his army uniform in my grandparent's bedroom."

"Are you sure?"

"Of course I'm sure. He was a lot younger looking then, but it's him all right. Why would you ask me if I'm sure, like you didn't believe it?"

Drew hesitated before answering. "I've always heard that Matt Kingsley came to Canada so he wouldn't have to go to Vietnam."

Carin grabbed Drew by the arm, stopping him in his tracks. Facing him, she looked up at his face trying to read the look she saw there. "Does everyone here believe that?" she asked, incredulous.

Drew nodded his head. "But I don't think it matters to most people. It doesn't matter to my Dad, I know."

"It matters if it's a lie!" Carin said hotly. "When my Grandpa picks me up at four, will you come back to the Legion with me so we can tell him what people are believing about him?"

"Sure, but…, what if it's true?"

"It's not," Carin said adamantly. "You'll see."

Drew clasped Carin by the shoulders. "Dwight said he was proud of you. I want you to know that I am too."

"Me too, you," Carin said, smiling.

"It took guts to stand up to that…scumbag!"

"I've never used language like that before; it embarrassed me to say it."

"You didn't look embarrassed. You looked like you were full of fire!"

"Funny you should say that. My Grandpa called me a 'spitfire' this morning."

"Spitfire," Drew said, trying the term out. "I think that's what I'll call you from now on."

"Okay," Carin laughed. "Then what can I call you?"

"Will you be my girl?" Drew blurted.

"That's too long; think of something shorter," Carin gasped in reply.

"If you'll be my girl you can call me lucky."

Carin looked down at her feet, saying nothing. Gently lifting her chin so she was looking at him again, Drew's eyes repeated the question as he whispered, "Spitfire?"

"What…Lucky?" Carin whispered back, a hint of a smile creasing the corners of her mouth.

Drew pressed his lips softly against Carin's, tenderly sealing the pact. She tasted like cinnamon and honey and made the cold and anger and shyness melt away as he hugged her close to him. His girl!

The after dinner meetings were becoming a ritual, a time to exchange information and recap everyone's day. Carin's news of the incident with Earl Drummond was disturbing for everyone.

"That man has always been a troublemaker," Matt said sourly. "And he treats his wife and kids abominably. I've never heard about any physical abuse, but he seems to get a real kick out of humiliating them publicly. As far as the story about me being a draft dodger is concerned, well, it's something that comes up from time to time. As I told you and Drew this afternoon, Carin, I don't pay any attention to it anymore. Some people are always going to believe what they want to believe, and there's nothing that would convince them otherwise."

"I'm glad we didn't have to contend with any fishermen in Bridgetown," Michael said. "But we're sure going to need to have some fish hauled up there. There's so little to work with in that town with just one grocery store. The bakery has a big supply of flour, so that's good for now. But it won't last long. "I'm afraid the people in Bridgetown aren't going to fare as well as those in Annapolis, and that could be dangerous."

"We'll have to see to it that they do fare as well," Matt said evenly. "I don't exactly know how yet, but we'll figure out something."

"You've been awfully quiet, Mom," Michael said. "Is everything okay here?"

"Other than being a little tired, everything's fine, I guess. Cassie being so good and so quiet drains my energy far more then her rambunctious little brother. I wish I knew what to do for her."

"I'm going to go read her some more of the Buddy Book now," Carin decided. "She really seemed to like it. It made her laugh last night."

"That's what Doreen said. But by bedtime she had the saddest look again and her eyes were filled with tears. If only she could tell us why," Ruth sighed. "Oh, before I forget Matt, could you call on Doctor Sanders and arrange a time for him to see Doreen? She's past due for a checkup."

"Among the hundred other things I have to do, I suppose I can try to fit that in," Matt said testily.

"There's no need for you to get snarky about it. It's not as though I can pick up a phone and make an appointment, you know. If I could, I would, and wouldn't have to bother you, seeing as you have a 'hundred' other things to do!"

"Well I do!" Matt retorted. "There's the…"

"Oh spare me the shopping list! The 'hundred' things you have to do are all self-imposed. You could be delegating other people to do almost everything! You don't have to do it all yourself. This whole thing is a team effort, Matt. How about letting someone else carry the ball once in a while?"

Furious, Matt got up from the table, telling Ted, "Come on. You and your thumb have work to do!"

"Wait a minute," Ruth commanded. "That's something else that's gotten out of hand. When Ted devised this idea, he was only thinking about the immediate area, not the whole valley and beyond! You need to simplify this! There are already area leaders in place with responsibility for 50 to 60 people in 8 or 10 households, right? Let *them* take care of the Trade Bucks for everyone in their area. And each area leader from now on can use his own thumb- print. There's already a place on those Bucks for name, age, occupation and household, so it should be a simple matter for area leaders to set up a file for each household and keep track of who does what in the way of services. The way you have things set up is way too complicated and time consuming."

"Any more criticisms?" Matt asked sarcastically.

"I agree with Ruth," Ted said. "I think she's got the best idea yet. Give those area leaders the responsibility for everything in their area of 8 to 10 households; the acquisition of food, water and fuel and its distribution. Also, seeing to it that everyone in their area who is capable of contributing does so. Additionally, they will handle all the Trade Bucks for their area."

"How would you see that working?" Matt asked with growing interest.

"How about two file boxes," Ruth interjected. "The first box is divided by households and the seven Trade Bucks for every member of that household is in the file. Every day, one Trade Buck for each person is transferred to the second file, which is set up in the same way. At the end of the day, everyone who has performed a service to earn their daily bread and heat will have their Buck removed from the second file and put back in the first one. The idea is, at the end of every week, all the Bucks are back in that first file. If there are any left in that second file, the area leader will know who hasn't done his or her fair share. Simple, easy to keep track of, and the area leader will have an easier time of assigning things that need to be done."

Matt stood looking at Ruth while he digested the idea. "I think you just lifted a huge weight off my shoulders," he said haltingly. "I don't know why I didn't see that it could work that way."

"You didn't, because you're a man, and men think everything has to be big and complicated to work. Women are used to simplifying because they've *always* had to manage a hundred things at once."

"Well, that may solve one problem, but it doesn't solve the problem of sanitation or organizing the fishermen."

"Yes it does! Area leaders and everyone in their area can look after their own latrine facilities. Fishermen can organize themselves. All it takes is determining how many fish are needed and taking turns. It's the same for farmers with meat animals. Leaders can determine how many pounds a week are needed in each area, and farmers can take turns providing it. Just let each group be responsible for itself."

"We'd have to have a general meeting to let everyone know how things will be organized."

"So have it!" Ruth exclaimed. "And in two days, at the most, everything should be in place."

"And what am I going to do after that? I'm not an area leader."

"Important stuff. Like seeing that the people who live under this roof stay safe rather than subjecting your little granddaughter to a face-off with the likes of Earl Drummond. Like getting through this whole thing alive, without a stroke or heart- attack. Like learning to just *be*. We may be in for a long haul, but if we get through the winter everything is going to look a lot different."

"Why is it you always seem to wind up putting me in my place?" Matt asked sarcastically.

"Because you always seem to need it!" Ruth answered flippantly.

CHAPTER FOURTEEN – JANUARY 5, 2005

Carin had told her Grandfather he was right about Drew, and that they were now 'going' together.   Since Matt never missed an opportunity to have a bit of fun, he decided to have a bit of sport with Drew.

Drew was visibly upset the next morning when Carin didn't come into town with her grandfather. *'You blew it! It was all too fast for her and she doesn't even like you'* he was thinking, fidgeting nervously.

"Was there some special reason you needed Carin here today?" Matt asked solicitously.

"Uh, no!   Well, yeah, kinda," Drew stammered.   "Uh, Mrs. Henderson was looking forward to seeing her today."

"Oh, I see. Well, she wanted to come and…"

"She did?" Drew asked eagerly.

"She sure did. And she was furious that her grandma wouldn't let her after what happened yesterday."

"She told you what happened yesterday?" Drew asked, coloring.

"Yes. And let me tell you young man it upset all of us to hear about it!"

"I, I'm sorry Mr. Kingsley, I just…"

"Well, what's done is done. I just hope nothing comes of it."

"You do?" Drew asked faintly.

"Of course!" Matt answered brusquely.   There was an extended pause. "That Earl Drummond could prove to be a dangerous man!"

Confused momentarily, Drew responded, "Uh, you're talking about Earl Drummond?"

"Of course! What did you think I was talking about?"   Matt demanded.

"I,…eeee," Drew said, gesturing with his hands and shrugging. "I dunno! I think I must've blanked all that out, you know, and it just came back to me," he declared, snapping his fingers, "just like that

155

when you mentioned his name! Oh yeah, that was…, it really was…bad!" *'whew!'*

"I think Carin was looking forward to seeing Mrs. Henderson again and that's why she was so upset at not being allowed to come back today," Matt said seriously. "Do you suppose Bea might like to take a drive out to the farm for a visit? I think I can spare the gas for that. I could pick her up about eleven then she can have lunch there and you won't have to worry about fixing anything for her."

"Oh, well…yeah, I can ask her if she wants to do that. I'm kinda responsible for her though, you know."

"Then why don't you come along?" Matt asked, biting the inside of his bottom lip.

"I guess I could do that," Drew said offhandedly. "Yeah, that would be okay. I, uh, sort of missed seeing Chris yesterday."

"So, I'll be at your place at eleven," Matt said, turning and walking back to his car. *'Got out of there just in time!'* he said to himself, grinning. *'Couldn't have kept a straight face for another second!'*

"Wow, Cassie! How did you do that?" Carin exclaimed. "I've been looking and looking for that piece and you come along and pick it up,…just like that!" she said, snapping her fingers. "The box says this puzzle is for age twelve and over. Are you secretly a grown-up passing yourself off as a five-year-old?" Carin asked, playfully poking Cassie in the ribs. Cassie, eyes twinkling, picked up another piece of the puzzle and set it in place. "I don't believe this!" Carin exclaimed again, now truly dumbfounded. "Okay," she said, "now find the piece that goes here." Cassie looked where Carin pointed then at the pieces of the puzzle spread out on the board. She focused in on a piece and without hesitation, picked it up and set it in place.

Carin went to find Richard and Doreen to come witness the marvel. But Richard was up in the attic with Grandma and Doreen was giving Mickey a sponge bath after he spilled apple juice all over himself. She found Michael coming out of the office and he reluctantly agreed to come see what a whiz Cassie was with that complicated puzzle.

Cassie's eyes lost their sparkle instantly when she saw Michael come into the room. She stared at the pieces of puzzle on the table and didn't respond when Carin asked her to find the piece for a certain place.

Puzzled, Carin frowned up at Michael who returned a questioning look with raised eyebrows. "Gotta go," Michael said. "Maybe next time Cassie will have something to show me." At his words, Cassie stiffened, raising her eyes to Michael's belt buckle, with fear in her eyes. Michael didn't notice, but Carin did. She wondered why Cassie would be afraid of Uncle Michael. It didn't make sense.

Cassie retreated inside herself, seeing the room and hearing the softly spoken words. 'Come here Cassie. I have something to show you. And you have something to show me, don't you!' Then the hand over her mouth and the hurting, oh so bad; must be quiet, can't cry because then the gun will make Mommy and Daddy and Mickey dead, they will all have the lights go out. Never tell! Never tell! Must be quiet and the hurting will never stop, never stop, because then they will be dead!

Huge tears were streaming soundlessly down Cassie's face. Carin picked her up and carried her to the lounge chair in front of the stove, snuggling her close on her lap, stroking the back of her head and whispering, "It's all right. Whatever it is, it's going to be all right. Can't you tell me what's wrong, Cassie, so I can help?"

'Never tell. Never, never tell. There will always be a Michael with a gun!'

"I'm going to put the puzzle in the dining room," Ruth said, breezing into the family room and lifting the board with the puzzle. "Put that down on the table in here," she called out to Richard.

Richard carried in two big, heavy looking squares of plywood, one resting on top of the other and connected by a swivel caster. The top board could be rotated in a complete circle, and Mickey, following at his dad's heels, couldn't resist giving it a spin.

"What's that for?" Carin asked, lifting her cheek from the top of Cassie's head.

"It's a base for the dollhouse we're going to build. Is something the matter with Cassie?" Ruth asked, seeing her tear-stained face.

"She just started crying. I don't know why," Carin shrugged helplessly.

"Tell me what happened just before she started crying, step by step. There must be a clue somewhere as to why this happens."

"We were working on the puzzle, and, Grandma you wouldn't believe it but Cassie can pick up the right pieces and put them in one after the other. I wanted to show someone what she could do so I got Uncle Michael to come in here. But then she wouldn't do it. She just stared at the puzzle. Then Uncle Michael said he had to get going and Cassie looked at him like she was scared. Then when he left, she started crying."

Cassie was beginning to look upset while Carin related what had taken place and when she finished, Ruth's question terrified her.

"Are you afraid of Michael, Cassie?"

Cassie violently shook her head no, her eyes, her face terror stricken.

'Never tell! Never! Or Mommy, Daddy and Mickey will be dead!'

Matt arrived with Drew and Bea Henderson at about a quarter past eleven. Ted, Rachel and Chris, who had gone over to Bridgetown with more copied off Trade Bucks, were due back at noon. Everyone had promised Ruth they would devote just half a day today to the survival plan, and take the rest of the day off. Michael hadn't gone anywhere at all. He had relieved Ruth of the cattle chores and photocopied more Trade Bucks.

When Bea learned she would be going to the Kingsley farm for lunch, she made Drew accompany her next door to her house so she could fix her hair properly and slip into a special dark blue cashmere dress and stockings. Shivering from the cold, she applied a light touch of makeup and sprayed cologne in the air over her head so it would drift down, settling lightly over her hair. Last, she put on her good winter boots with the fur cuffs and her long mink coat. Nothing on her head, she decided. It would muss her hair. She surveyed herself critically in the mirror, carefully avoiding looking directly at her face. Seeing all those wrinkles at once was too much to bear.

Drew smiled at Bea's transformation as she descended the stairs. She looked like the wealthy old lady she was, rather than the frowzy, frumpy old lady she had become ever since Drew had known her. She had taken so long to dress for the occasion though, that Drew had to rush to make himself presentable by eleven.

Nate had come out of his room around eleven, dressed nattily in dark brown slacks and tweed jacket. He spotted the large box with a picture of a dollhouse on the front almost immediately. "What's this?" he asked, sounding delighted.

"It's a dollhouse kit I bought almost twelve years ago. I had planned to build it for my granddaughters, but it's one of those things I never got around to doing. Now I'm glad I didn't. It will be a good project for everyone, don't you think? Look, there are furniture sets to build for every room, scale-size wallpaper, rugs, pictures, you name it! Everything right down to the dishes and pans for the kitchen cupboards and toys for the nursery. I've been collecting them for years."

Nate looked at the picture of the three-story dollhouse that, when completed, would stand 4 feet high, 3 feet wide, and 2 feet deep. It was a beautiful old Victorian style house and Nate could hardly wait to begin working on it. He missed the carpentry work that had been his lifelong occupation. This dollhouse would give him something to do with his hands and his mind. It was a welcome sight.

So was Bea Henderson when she arrived a few minutes later. He hadn't seen Helen's long time best friend in months and it was good to see her. He had never stopped missing Helen, not for a day. Bea's presence brought back fond memories of times that he and Helen, Bea and Carl had spent together.

Bea was astonished when Richard and Doreen took their places at the dining room table along with the other adults. Their place was in the kitchen, she felt, but no one else seemed to think it was out of the ordinary that the help ate with the family and company. Things were certainly different nowadays, she decided, and she wasn't so sure she liked it. That little girl of theirs, too. She appeared to be retarded or something. And the little boy. A rambunctious nuisance as far as she could see; into something every minute. She wondered how Nate tolerated living under the same roof with them.

Nate. Bea turned her attention to him as though the two of them were the only ones there. "I heard you've been ill Nate, and I was so worried about you," Bea said solicitously. "Are you sure you're up to having company?"

"I'm fine now," Nate informed her. "I had a slight cold and Lindy made me stay in bed and fed me some capsules that Rachel had brought with her from Alberta. The cold symptoms just seemed to disappear."

"It's Echinacea," Rachel explained to Bea. "I really believe in the stuff. My whole family takes it at the first sign of a cold or the flu, and it seems to make the virus ineffective. Of course, most doctors will say there is no evidence that it works, but it's enough for me that it does. Doctors don't know everything."

Bea was incensed by what Rachel said. Carl had been a doctor, and a good one too, with a very lucrative practice. To him, herbal medicines and such things as homeopathy had been outright quackery! Out of deference to her hosts, however, she would let it pass without a retort. Surely Nate would not be in agreement with the use of herbal remedies and he was, after all, the only one who mattered. He probably hadn't had a cold at all.

"It's gratifying to me that you are well, Nate," Bea said, patting his hand, "whatever the reason."

Ruth listened to Bea with growing amusement as she coquettishly plied Nate with questions and compliments, monopolizing him during the entire meal. *'Why the old bat is flirting!'* Ruth laughingly told herself.

Out in the kitchen, Chris was vying for Drew's attention and generally making a pest of himself. "Hey Drew, watch this!" Chris said, throwing a carrot stick in the air and catching it in his mouth.

"Ey Dew, otchis!" Mickey mimicked, tossing up a carrot stick that landed in his eye and set him howling. Carin comforted him with a kiss to make it better.

"Watch this, Drew!" Chris repeated, hitting the tines of his fork with his index finger, sending it flipping in the air then catching it. "Pretty neat, huh?"

"Otchis Dew!" Mickey called out, hitting his fork and sending it flying into Cassie's glass of milk, spilling it.

"That's about enough, Chris!" Carin said hotly between gritted teeth.

"Me!" Chris protested. "I'm not the one who spilled the milk!"

"You're the cause of it. Why don't you stop acting like a three year old and eat your lunch!"

Sullenly, Chris kicked Carin in the shins under the table. Carin's sudden gasp of pain as she reached for her leg angered Drew. He knew what Chris had done.

"Why don't you act your age!" he spat venomously at Chris. "I thought you were an okay kid before. I guess I was mistaken!"

Chris pushed away from the table, sending another glass of milk toppling. Mickey quickly followed his hero into the family room where they both sat on the couch with Buddy, arms folded, sulking. *'I'll show her!'* Chris vowed to himself. Carin was always the source of trouble for him, but he'd get even with her. He would for sure. He'd just have to think of a way.

It had begun snowing lightly before they all sat down to lunch, but by the time they were finished the light snowfall had become a squall. "Maybe it will blow itself out before long," Matt surmised. "I've seen that happen before, plenty of times. I really miss getting weather reports. How did they ever use to cope without knowing what the weather was going to be?"

"Seems to me we never knew what the weather was going to be even *with* weather reports," Nate laughed. "How about if we go take a look at that dollhouse now."

They all piled into the family room to watch as Nate began working on the dollhouse. Everyone was taken with the box of tiny replicas of household items that Ruth had collected over the years; the miniature books and folded newspaper, the sewing basket with knitting needles and scissors, the broom and dustpan and especially the dollhouse family made of fine grained kidskin with bendable arms and legs.

Carin and Drew soon tired of the dollhouse and went back to the dining room to work on the puzzle. Cassie followed them. "Will you show Drew what a whiz you are at this puzzle?" Carin asked. She half hoped that Cassie would refuse and leave the two of them alone. But, Cassie picked up a piece of the puzzle and set it in place. After only a few seconds hesitation, she set a second piece in place, then a third.

"How do you do that, Cassie!" Drew raved. "When I tried to work on this puzzle a few days ago I would have to look for an hour before I found the right piece. You must be some kind of a genius," he said, playfully mussing Cassie's hair. Cassie didn't smile, but her eyes were shining with pleasure. In a matter of seconds, she again selected a puzzle piece and set it in place, Carin and Drew pretended to work on the puzzle as they talked to one another, occasionally praising Cassie and watching as a faint smile crept over her face, little by little. They were simply enjoying one another's company, and found they didn't mind having Cassie there at all. Centering their attention on her to cover embarrassing lapses in conversation, she made the perfect foil for their budding romance.

By three in the afternoon it was apparent that it would be impossible to get Bea and Drew back home. "Even if I plow the snow out of the lane, the road into town will be impassable," Matt said. "They won't be out plowing the road until the snow stops, probably not until tomorrow morning."

"I won't mind sleeping in the lounge chair again," Drew said, "but there's no way to get word to my folks where we are."

"Oh, don't worry about that," Matt said. "I saw your dad today and told him you and Mrs. Henderson were coming here for lunch. He'll know you couldn't get back because of the snow. We'll have to try to get into town tomorrow afternoon though because Doreen has an appointment to see the doctor at two."

"I'll take the other lounge chair," Michael said. "Mrs. Henderson can have my bed in the office."

"You're sleeping in the office?" Bea asked. "Don't you have your own room?"

"Yes, but the Martins are using it while they're here. Actually, I like being downstairs. I often have to make trips out to the barn in the middle of the night, and sleeping down here is a lot more convenient. I've spent many nights in a lounge chair by choice!"

"Why on earth do you have to go out to the barn in the middle of the night?" Bea asked.

"We're kind of running a bovine maternity ward out there right now. A maternity ward for cows, that is," he added, in case Bea didn't know what a bovine was. "Sometimes they decide to have their calves in the middle of the night. Lindy here has been helping out with the calving," Michael said, looking fondly at his niece. "And of course Mom. Actually, she probably delivers as many calves as I do."

"Good heavens!" Bea exclaimed. "Ruth, you don't actually play midwife to cows, do you? And allow this little child to see that?"

"Why yes. It's just a natural part of farm life," Ruth said. '*You're darn tootin' you insufferable old windbag!*' Ruth thought. She was becoming increasingly annoyed with Bea as the day wore on.

"Speaking of natural parts of farm life," Matt said, "it's about time to tend to a few chores. Richard, you and Ruth take a well- deserved break today. Michael, the two kids and I will do them."

Carin, Drew and Cassie continued with the puzzle while Nate and Ted played a game of chess at the other end of the dining room table. Nate had reluctantly abandoned the dollhouse construction because the glue had to set before he could continue. The game of chess was a diversion to get rid of Bea for a while. Her clinging and cloying sweetness was wearing on his nerves. *'She's enough to give a man sugar diabetes!'* he thought.

Bea, perturbed at being usurped by a stupid game that required her silence, turned her attention to Cassie and the puzzle. She found that the little girl's ability was indeed amazing. "Why, the child is a…, oh dear, I can't think of the correct term for it, but you know, when the kind of child Cassie is can do something extraordinary?"

'If you're referring to the term "idiot savant" you bloody well better not remember and blurt it out!' Ruth said to herself. She took Bea by the arm, and with a gesture of her head let Bea know she wanted to talk to her out in the kitchen. Bea went along, perplexed.

"I know what you're referring to," Ruth said quickly, "but you're wrong about that. She's not autistic, she's likely had a trauma of some sort that she can't or won't tell us about. Cassie was a completely normal little girl up until about six months ago when she started to change. Then, when the lights went out she stopped talking. Every once in a while she gets a faraway look in her eyes then she starts crying. There's never any sound when she cries, just tears. It's the most heartbreaking thing I've ever seen!"

Richard and Doreen, who were in the kitchen preparing dinner, heard Ruth explain about Cassie to Bea. Hearing Ruth say it, they were certain now more than ever that Cassie had experienced something that had caused her to close in on herself. What that something could be, or when it might have happened, they could not imagine.

"Is there any insanity in the family?" Bea asked obtusely, as though Cassie's parents were either deaf or ignorant. Richard and Doreen both flashed an incredulous look at Bea, and Doreen quickly put a restraining hand on Richard's arm to stop him from making the derisive retort she saw forming in his eyes. She let Ruth do it for them.

"That's the most insulting thing I've ever heard anyone ask!" Ruth said hotly.

"It's a perfectly logical question, and no insult was intended," Bea said testily. "Bad genes will always surface somewhere. Carl used to

164

say that all the time, and he was usually right about things. It's likely something genetic with the child and you're all wasting your time looking for some external cause. Tell me, what trauma would make a child a…, ah, I have it now! An idiot savant! That's genetic!"

"Cassie has never seen a puzzle before like the one in there," Ruth gestured. "She could very well have a superior intelligence in many areas that we don't know about!"

"That may be the case, but it wouldn't prove that she *doesn't* have a genetic aberration. It may actually prove that she *does!*"

Ruth patted Bea's hand. "We'll see about that," she said as condescendingly as she could muster through her anger.

In a huff, Bea trounced back into the dining room. Ruth looked at the sad faces of Richard and Doreen and went and wrapped her arms around both of them. "If you could have heard all the four-letter words that were in my head when I was listening to that woman, you'd wash my mouth out with soap!" she told them.

The dinner conversation was strained and as Ruth helped Richard remove the dishes she told him, "You go sit down. I'll get the dessert."

Richard had prepared rhubarb crisp using rhubarb that Ruth had cut in small pieces and frozen the previous summer. It had been made in Bea's honor, when he learned it was her favorite dessert. After filling the dishes with the crisp, Ruth brought in a large container of vanilla ice cream from the freezer in the entry room. She put a scoop of ice cream on top of the dessert in one bowl then placed it in the warming oven. Lindy gave her a puzzled look, and Ruth put her index finger to her lips and winked. Lindy's eyes glittered, knowing her grandma was up to some mischief.

Ruth topped all the desserts with a scoop of ice cream, serving them around first to the children then placing the rest of them on a large tray. She put the ice cream back in the freezer before she removed the last dish from the warming oven. '*Good,*' she thought, '*it's nicely softened.*' Carrying the tray into the dining room, Ruth sang out, "Rhubarb crisp, Bea. Especially for you!" She took the dish that had been in the warming oven, winked at Richard then dumped the contents of the dish over Bea's head.

Bea's cries of outrage were wonderful to hear. The looks of astonishment, then mirth on everyone's face was even more gratifying. But the best of all, Ruth thought, was the way a big blob of still frozen ice cream found it's way down the back of Bea's scrawny neck, sliding down inside the gaping neckline and coming to rest at her belted waistband. She was an extraordinarily wonderful mess!

"Oh how clumsy of me!" Ruth exclaimed in wide-eyed innocence. "Here, let me help you," she said, wiping at Bea's head with a paper napkin, managing to grind in the sticky rhubarb and firmly attach the napkin to the top of Bea's head. "I think you better go take a shower," Ruth said, trying to keep her voice from shaking with laughter.

She marched a howling Bea out to the back room past an astonished group of youngsters, showed her where the towels were and said she'd bring her something to change into. Then she went back to the dining room, took her place at the table, and began to eat her dessert without a glance at, or a word to, anyone. She didn't know who snickered first, but it came from Nate's direction. Infectious laughter spread around the table, bringing the children piling in from the kitchen, all except for Cassie.

"You did that on purpose, didn't you?" Nate asked.

"Yes I did!" Ruth declared, smiling winningly.

"And your grandpa called *you* a spitfire," Drew said to Carin. "I guess we all know who you take after!" Drew decided this was a good time to tell everyone about his dad cutting a switch and threatening Bea, and the laughter renewed, imagining Bea trying to deal with a situation in which she didn't have the upper hand.

"That's really awful, treating an old woman like that," Rachel said, trying to keep a straight face.

"I certainly hope so!" Ruth said with enthusiasm.

As Richard cleared away the dessert dishes, he bent down and kissed Ruth on the cheek. "Thanks," he murmured softly.

Nate decided that since there wasn't enough light to work on the dollhouse, he would teach Cassie to play chess. He told her how each piece moved and the object of the game, then had her watch a game between Ted and himself. She watched avidly, concentrating on the moves, something that would have bored most children her age. If there was enough time for another game before her bedtime, Nate decided, he would let Cassie decide the moves.

Bea didn't want Nate to see her without makeup and with her hair hanging damp and stringy around her face. She climbed into Michael's bed with a book, thinking she would read for a while. She couldn't get comfortable. The pillow behind her back didn't feel right no matter how often she adjusted it. Her feet were cold. She was used to sleeping with wool socks on her feet and she felt strangely loose and naked without them.

Telling herself Michael wouldn't mind, and it was just too bad if he did, she rummaged in his top drawer for a pair of socks. As she lifted a pair of heavy gray wool socks that would reach almost to her knees, Bea uncovered a gun. Staring at it, she wondered why Michael would want to sleep with a gun close at hand, in the office, where he could hear every footfall outside on the deck.

"Oh my!" she exclaimed softly, hurriedly putting on the socks then extinguishing the oil lamp. She lay shivering, listening wide-eyed to the creaks and groans of the old house as it dealt with the wind and the icy cold, prepared to not get a wink of sleep that night.

Her last thought before drifting off was of danger lurking outside, and no one knowing when or where it would strike.

CHAPTER FIFTEEN – JANUARY 6, 2005

The snow had stopped sometime during the night Matt saw, looking out the bedroom window. He hurried with his usual morning routine, knowing he had several hours of snow removal ahead of him, an unwelcome chore at any time. *'If only there was a cab on the tractor, it wouldn't be so bad,'* he thought for the hundredth time.

He had just finished making a pot of coffee when Ruth appeared downstairs, grouchy as usual in the morning before she'd had coffee. Matt knew better than to talk to her, though he wondered why she was up so early.

After her first couple of sips of black coffee, Ruth said, "I'm going to do the milking this morning. You've got enough to do clearing snow. I'd appreciate it though if you'd clear a path to the barn before I go out so I'm not wading in snow up to my hips."

Matt, dressed for battle with the snow, unlocked the back door and looked out at the pristine beauty of the unblemished snow covering the yard and trees. Even in the gray beginning of dawn it was a breathtaking sight. Then he looked along the deck that ran past the office. "Well shit!" he muttered, seeing the trampled snow, dirty in spots with stains of manure picked up by barn boots. Michael had obviously been out, several times by the looks of it. Grumbling, Matt grabbed the snow shovel that stood inside the back door. "Can't anybody else use this thing?" he mumbled. "Am I the only one who knows how to shovel snow? Packed down like this it's harder to shovel. Damn Michael anyway. I ought to get him up and make him come do this!"

"I see you can shovel better when you grouch about it," he heard behind him. Turning, he saw Ruth at the door, letting Buddy out. Trotting up behind Matt, Buddy sat down, waiting. Matt leaned on the shovel. "If you're waiting for me to shovel a path for you out to all your check-spots, forget it old boy," he told Buddy. "It's not gonna happen!" Buddy stood, lifted his leg against the banked snow on the deck and created a golden runnel. He sat back down again and waited.

"Why can't Michael shovel some of this snow when he goes out to the barn?" Matt asked.

"Oh stop griping," Ruth admonished. "I guess Michael and I could ask why you never have your sleep disturbed with barn checks! It all evens out, you know."

"Was there a calf born during the night?"

"Yes. And some of those tracks are mine, and Lindy's. Bella had a bull. First bull she's ever had."

"Get back inside before you catch your death," Matt barked, noticing that Ruth was still in her bathrobe.

"Keep it down! You'll wake Bea," Ruth said in a half-whisper.

"I don't give a rat's ass!" Matt grumbled after Ruth had shut the door.

Bea lay awake wondering how many more sleep interruptions there would be before morning. How inconsiderate these Kingsley's were! The first time Michael went out, she had been awakened by the sound of someone crunching along the deck in the snow. She had reached into the still open drawer next to the bed before realizing it was Michael. He had come into the entry room and was talking to Ruth.

With all her wakefulness, thanks to all the coming and going to the barn, she had had plenty of time to decide what she would say to Nate. Surely he could not like having to live here and would be grateful for the proposition she was prepared to make. They were old friends, after all, sharing memories of happier days. Visualizing herself dancing in Nate's arms while an orchestra played 'Stardust' in the background, Bea began drifting off again when the sound of a tractor clearing snow right next to the office brought her fully awake. Grumbling, she pulled the covers over her head to help shut out the noise.

Nate worked on the dollhouse right after breakfast until he reached a point where he had to wait for the glue to dry again before continuing. Bea had let him know she wanted to talk to him, privately if that was possible in this house. He was determined to put her off as long as possible.

He was relieved when Lindy, Cassie in tow, asked him to teach her how to play chess too. Taking the two little girls into the dining room, he set up the chess- board with an aggrieved looking Bea at the other end of the table. She was dressed in a multi-colored nylon wind-suit that belonged to Rachel and which was suitable for a woman half her age, which Rachel was. On Bea, the outfit looked ridiculous, especially with her hair done up in a formal looking French roll and wearing a pair of men's heavy gray work socks on her feet. Bea obviously thought she looked charming though, girlishly fussing over him and flitting about like a giddy adolescent. *'How tiresome she still is,'* Nate thought.

Lindy soon tired of learning to play chess, saying she would rather watch Nate and Cassie play. She draped an arm across Nate's shoulders, leaning her head close to his.

"Child, don't hang on Mr. Taylor that way!" Bea admonished. Seeing Lindy's abashed look as she pulled away, Nate said, "How about me hanging on to you, then!" as he wrapped an arm around Lindy's waist and drew her close again. Still slightly embarrassed, Lindy said she thought she'd work on the puzzle awhile, and Nate reluctantly removed his arm from around her waist.

He was acutely aware that in just a few short days Lindy had become the most important person in the world to him. She was both the child and the grandchild he would never have, she was the child he imagined his beloved Helen had been at that age, and she was just Lindy too. Just Lindy, in the here and now, and that was enough for her to be. She filled a great void he hadn't known existed.

Cassie couldn't help herself. When it was Nate's move at chess, she would glance over at Lindy fruitlessly searching for the next piece of the puzzle. After a quick scan of the board, she would point to a puzzle piece then Lindy would pick it up and set it in place. "That is so amazing, Cassie!" Lindy enthused every time. I wish I knew how you did that!"

"Our Cassie seems to have a real knack for seeing things in three dimensions," Nate said. "She's going to be very good at Chess too, if I can get across yet another dimension. Chess is almost like seeing into the future, knowing what the consequences of an action will be before the action is taken. That's what makes chess the world's most challenging game. This situation we're in…"

"I think the children would like to work on their puzzle, Nate," Bea interrupted. "So why don't the two of us go into the living room where we can have a private chat."

Seeing no reasonable way out of it, Nate nodded agreement. *'May as well get it over with,'* he thought. He knew from experience that Bea was capable of a relentless tenacity when she zeroed in on an objective. And he knew without a doubt that he was the objective and always had been.

"Now, I don't want you to say anything until you hear me out, Nate," Bea began. "I want you to move into my house in town. We can get one of those kerosene heaters from the building supply store and make a nice cozy little nest out of the living room. I have a wonderful library you know, and you could read to your heart's content without anyone around to disturb you. We have been very close friends all our adult years and there are oh, so many memories we share, you and I. The most natural thing in the world would be to share our golden years together as well. What do you say, Nate? You are the dearest person in the world to me, you know."

Nate was sitting in the wing-backed chair with his head bowed listening to Bea. When she finished speaking, he raised his head, looked directly at her and said, "The answer is no, Bea. I don't want to move in with you. I'm quite content right here."

"Surely not, Nate! There are so many people in this house there's hardly room to move, let alone have any privacy. And that child, that Lindy, monopolizes you; she…"

"Lindy," Nate said loudly, "is the light of my life. I didn't know I had the capacity to love anyone anymore the way I loved Helen, but I couldn't love Lindy more if she were my own child. I *want* to be around her, can't you see that? She has a sweetness, a kindness, a loving and generous heart that is so rare it's…"

"You foolish old man! You're using a child to replace your memory of Helen! I would be a much better replacement. I was Helen's best friend! And I have always been so very fond of you. You might even say I've been a bit in love with you all these years."

"You've never been even a little bit in love with me, Bea, though you've deluded yourself with that idea for as long as I've known you. No, now you hear *me* out!" Nate said, holding his hand up, palm out, as Bea attempted to interrupt. "I was never the least bit interested in you, and that made me unattainable. As a result, you have spent most of your life trying to seduce me and I knew long ago that I should have let you before I fell so deeply in love with Helen. And why should I have let you? Because we all would have been spared years of heartache, Carl and Helen especially, watching you constantly pursuing me. We all knew, if you could have had me, you wouldn't have wanted me. There was no way you would ever have been content married to a lowly carpenter."

"You're wrong, Nate. I've always wanted you, yes, because I've always been in love with you!"

"You wanted me because you never could understand why I would choose Helen over you. I was in love with Helen before I went overseas. I was delighted to come back and find you married because you were no longer an obstacle. I had hoped never to have to tell you this, Bea, but I abided you only because you were Helen's friend. I've always thought of you as a silly, vain, frivolous opportunist. I felt sorry for Carl until the day he died and I am not, under any circumstances, going to move into your house with you."

Bea looked at Nate with hate filled eyes, nostrils flaring. "How dare you feel sorry for Carl!" she spat. Carl loved me!"

"Yes, he loved you. Even though you didn't deserve that love."

"He thought I was beautiful, vivacious, fun, beguiling! But you couldn't see that. You settled for a plain Jane who grew fat and gave you no children. I would have given you children, Nate, I…"

"Stop it, Bea! Enough!" Nate barked harshly. "Have you no pride at all? What is it going to take for you to realize that I want nothing to do with you? What?"

"I don't believe you really mean that, Nate," Bea said, her chin jutting out. "You will come to your senses once you've thought it over."

"I'll come to my senses right now!" Nate shouted, getting to his feet. "I'm not going to waste another moment of my life in your presence!" At that, he stalked out of the room.

After lunch, which Nate said he preferred to eat out in the kitchen with the youngsters for a change, Matt asked Nate and Ted if they would like to take a run up to Bridgetown with him to see how things were going. "The plow was headed that way when I was about halfway done with our lane and I just saw it going back toward Annapolis. It should be pretty clear sailing in both directions," Matt said. "Oh, don't forget Doreen, you're to see the doctor at two. Whoever drives you into Annapolis can take Mrs. Henderson and Drew back."

"I'll drive you in, Doreen," Ruth said. "There's something special I want to try to find in town and I've been cooped up here for days. It'll be good to get out."

"Uh, Ruth? Richard asked. "Can I talk to you a minute in the kitchen?"   Ruth followed Richard and raised her eyebrows questioningly when he turned to look at her. "I was wondering when you would be getting more staples, you know. We are running out of things pretty fast with all the mouths being fed and company and everything," Richard said almost apologetically.

"Oh for heavens sake!" Ruth exclaimed. "I completely forgot to show you where the food is stored in the cellar! You have put together some wonderful meals though with the little you've had to work with."

"I saw the potatoes and apples, and I guess some squash, onions and carrots down there. I've been using some of that. But flour, sugar, coffee, stuff like that…"

"Come on, I'll show you," Ruth said. "You can get what you need, whenever you need it." Puzzled, Richard followed her out to the back room and watched as she pulled aside a rug, revealing a trap door. As he descended into the stone tunnel, his mouth dropped open in amazement. "Holy shit!" he exclaimed. "You've got your own grocery store down here!"

"It was a place to hide what may be the most valuable thing in the days to come," Ruth said seriously. "It was intended to be only for us, no outsiders. But somehow that changed, and I'm not sorry it did."

"I came here with a gun," Richard said, with his head bowed. "I would have stolen from you to feed my family. Yet, you are entrusting me with the knowledge of this place. Why?"

"Because I can. This is your survival now too," Ruth said simply, gesturing toward the stockpile of food. "It may look like a lot, but believe me it will go fast. There's probably enough food here for all of us for a year if we're careful and use it wisely. But there won't be any to share with anyone else. We don't dare do that because we don't have enough for *everyone*. You can't tell anyone about this, you know. But it's yours to share along with the rest of us."

"That still doesn't answer why."

"The 'why' is because I saw a good person trying to provide for his family the only way he knew how. And I saw that he wasn't very comfortable having to do it. I was never afraid of you, Richard, not even when the gun was cocked and pointing at me. I'm not sure why. But you *did* make me remember that I should be afraid of other people coming around here and I'm grateful for that. It's something we all need to remember."

Chris decided he wanted to go into Bridgetown with the men, so they all piled into the pickup and headed down the road. "We need to contact Ian again," Matt said, switching on the CB radio. "There's been too little news the past couple of days for my comfort."

Doreen put Mickey and Cassie down for a nap then got herself ready to go to the doctor. "I'm going to have the doctor see that everything's all right with the baby," Doreen explained. "I won't be gone long, and your daddy will be here." Cassie, who had been looking anxious, was reassured when she learned that her daddy wouldn't be going along.

Rachel wanted to go into Annapolis too, just to get out for a while. And Carin, of course, wanted to be with Drew as long as possible. So there were six of them piled into the Kingsley car headed for Annapolis Royal.

Richard watched them leave, then nervously approached Michael as he saw him coming in from the barn, followed by Lindy. "I need to take my car and go into Annapolis too. Is that all right? The kids are down for a nap."

Michael looked at Richard speculatively. He obviously had some urgent reason why he wanted to go into town, but...

"We didn't bring enough of the kid's clothes when we came out here because we didn't know for sure if,..., and I forgot to tell Doreen to stop and get them."

"Okay, sure," Michael said. "If the kids wake up before you're back I'll take them out to the barn with me and Lindy. They might get to see a calf born!"

"Great," Richard said, putting on his jacket. "I'll be back quick as I can."

Richard wanted to get everything out of his apartment that belonged to his landlord, Michael Cooper. That bastard, Richard knew, would have him thrown in jail for theft as soon as look at him. He could never wait for his rent money even though he knew Richard didn't have enough money left over to feed his kids. As he drove, he tried to remember what he had taken; the camp stove, and the fuel canister from the kitchen. He'd have to put the empty one back on the stove. The piece of hose he couldn't put back even if he had it and the food, he wouldn't worry about that; there was no way to trace what had happened with food. The beer and wine would have to go back, though. The Bible! That was still in his apartment. He had to put it back. And the scarf. No. No, not the scarf. He'd had it over his head; there could be some of his hair on it. DNA, they could catch anybody now. The gun. He didn't know what Ruth had done with the gun. Doesn't matter. They'll think someone broke in and stole food and a gun. Understandable, under the circumstances. But there wouldn't be a trace of anything in his apartment, he'd see to that. There'd be nothing to link him to the thefts. Then a new worry assailed him. What if Michael had somehow gotten back and had already found his things in Richard's apartment? Richard drove as fast as he dared on the still snow slick road into Annapolis.

Lindy peeked into the bedroom and saw that Cassie and Mickey were both sound asleep. "They're asleep," she reported to Michael. "So can we go back out to the barn now?"

"Don't you think you should stay in here with them?" Michael asked.

"But they're asleep!" Lindy said pleadingly.

"I guess they'll be okay," Michael said, with some reservation. "I sure wish Julie would lay down and get it over with. She's always such a pain when she's calving. With every pain she stands up and looks around for her calf."

"I have a friend named Julie," Lindy said while getting into her coat. "Sometimes she can be a pain too."

"Hey, you know what!" Michael exclaimed as they walked together to the barn. "When Cassie wakes up I'm going to see if I can find my old Rubics cube for her."

"What's a Rubics cube?"

"It's a kind of puzzle that was popular with all the kids back when I was about your age. I still have it somewhere. It was always in my dresser drawer so maybe your grandma put it in that old chest of drawers when she moved my stuff down to the office. I'll bet Cassie would really like it!"

"She's sure taking her old sweet time," Michael said. "I can't even grab those feet to help her along because they slide back in every time she stands up."

"You'd think she'd get tired of laying down, standing up; laying down, standing up every few minutes," Lindy said.

"Eventually, she lays down and has it, when *she's* ready, and not before." Michael paused. "We've been out here a good twenty minutes. I think we should go back in and check on the kids. I wouldn't want them to wake up and get scared because there was no one there."

"I can stay here with Julie," Lindy said. "I know Grandma doesn't like me being in the barn alone anymore, but the *little* kids are in the house all alone! And we haven't been able to tell yet if those are front feet or back feet we're seeing. *Someone* should keep watch!"

"Okay," Michael conceded. But if I'm not back out here in a few minutes it means the kids are awake and I want you to come in. Check?"

"Check," Lindy said, saluting.

Cassie walked from the family room into the kitchen as Michael came in the kitchen door. Wild-eyed, she looked around the room.

"Your daddy went into town to get more of your clothes at your house," Michael said.

Cassie lowered her head, breathing fast and swallowing the cries that threatened to escape from her throat. Then she heard the words she knew were coming.

"Come with me, Cassie. I have something to show you." *'And you have something to show me,'* she finished for him, in her head.

It was going to happen again like it always did when mommy went to the doctor, and she had to let it. Or else Mommy and Daddy and Mickey would be dead from the gun. Placidly, Cassie followed Michael out through the entry room and into the office. He led her over to the chest of drawers by the bed saying, "I think it's in here," as he opened the top drawer. Cassie saw the gun before Michael shoved socks on top of it.

With tears seeping from the corners of her eyes, Cassie pushed off her sneakers and reached up under her dress, pulled down her underpants and stepped out of them. Then she climbed onto the bed, laying on her back with her legs pressed close together, locked at the ankles. Waiting.

"Ah, here it is!" Michael exclaimed, turning and seeing Cassie stretched out on the bed. "Still a little sleepy, huh? Hey, what are the tears for? Come on now, no need to cry."

'Can't cry! Have to be quiet!' "I be quiet," Cassie said in a sobbing whisper. "I won't tell." She pulled her dress up around her waist, making pathetic little mewling sounds in the back of her throat, stifling her cries with a sobbed "Oh!"

Michael sat on the edge of the bed, stunned and shaken. "Oh my God," he whispered. "Oh God, no!" He pulled Cassie's dress down, covering her. He looked at Cassie's pathetic little face, the eyes swollen with tears, staring back at him; the quivering mouth hiccupping back the fear that distorted her features. His first impulse was to grab her up and hold her close, protecting her so that no one could ever hurt her again. But he could see she was terrified of him, of what he might do to her, *thought* he would do to her.

"Someone hurt you, Cassie, but *I* won't hurt you," he said soothingly. "I would never, ever hurt you." Cassie swallowed hard, eyes staring at Michael, unbelieving.

"Whoever hurt you was a very bad man," Michael continued. "Who was it Cassie?"

'Never tell! Never!' Cassie shook her head, fresh tears coursing down the sides of her face.

"You need to tell me Cassie so I can lock that man away so he can never, ever hurt you again." Cassie shook her head again, eyes fearful. "Did he tell you something very bad would happen if you told?"

She quickly nodded her head, her face a grimace as she pressed her lips together suppressing a wail. "What did he say would happen?" Michael pressed. Cassie took a deep breath. "Mommy and

Daddy and Mickey would be dead," she whispered between sobs. "With the gun," she added, pointing to the dresser drawer.

"What is the man's name, Cassie?" She put her hand over her mouth, shaking her head. "Your mommy and daddy and Mickey are safe here. The man can't find them here, honey. And you're safe too. That man is never going to hurt any of you again. I won't let him. Tell me his name, Cassie," Michael sad gently.

"Michael," she whispered.

Shaking, Michael closed his eyes, releasing the tears that flowed down the sides of his nose. When he opened them again, Cassie was staring at him in wonderment. He picked her tiny underpants up from the floor, slipped her feet into them and together he and Cassie pulled them up where they belonged. Then he put her sneakers back on her feet.

"I'm going to pick you up and carry you into the house, Cassie," Michael said softly, lifting her off the bed. "Then I'm going to hold you on my lap in front of the stove and I want you to tell me all about what the man named Michael did to you."

Cassie reached up and touched a tear on Michael's cheek as he carried her into the house and sat with her on his lap. He wrapped his arms around her, holding her close, rocking her.

"Michael is a bad man. Say it, Cassie," Michael urged.

"Michael is a bad man," she whispered.

"Say it out loud. You're mad at him for what he did to you! *I'm* mad at him for what he did to you!" Michael said, his voice rising. "You don't have to be quiet! Say it as loud as you want!"

"He's a bad man!" Cassie said, her voice quavering.

"He hurt you! He did a very bad thing!"

"He hurted me ba aaad!" Cassie wailed. "I hate that bad Michael! He, he put the gun here," she gasped convulsively, touching the left side of her head. "An' his hand on my mouf, hard. An' he hurted me here so baaaad!" she wailed again, placing her hand between her legs in remembered agony.

"Did he do this to you more than once?" Michael choked out. Cassie nodded.

"Lots of times?" She nodded again. "When Mommy went to the doctor an' I an' Mickey was takin' a nap."

'*That's enough,*' Michael thought. He couldn't bear to hear any more and Cassie was crying so hard she could barely talk. Deep wrenching wails wracked her tiny body as Michael held her close, tenderly kissing the top of her head and telling her to cry, as long and as hard and as loud as she wanted. He told her she was okay now. He'd never let anyone hurt her again.

Lindy suddenly appeared in the doorway, wide-eyed and breathless with alarm. She had heard Cassie's cries when she was halfway to the house from the barn and had run the rest of the way, not even stopping to remove her boots. "What happened to Cassie?" she asked.

"I just found out what's been the matter with her," Michael said softly. And that's all he would say.

Cassie fell into an exhausted sleep, punctuated by the convulsive sobs of a child who has wept long and hard. She was still cradled in Michael's lap and Lindy was holding a somber Mickey on hers, his thumb in his mouth, when Richard returned.

He knew at once that something had happened; the tension in the air was almost palpable.
"Take Mickey into the dining room," Michael said softly to Lindy. Although she wanted to hear what Michael had to say, she did as he asked without a word. When the two of them left, Michael asked Richard to sit down.

"I found out what's been the matter with Cassie for the past several months," Michael said, without preamble. "Is there someone who lives near you named Michael?"

"My landlord, Michael Cooper," Richard replied, frowning. "Why?"

"Did he sometimes baby sit for the kids when Doreen went to the doctor?"

"He looked in on them while they were taking a nap, yes."

"Would you happen to know if he kept a gun in a drawer by his bed?"

"Yes," Richard said hesitantly. "But it's not there now. I took it. Are you trying to tell me Michael did something to my little girl?"

Michael nodded, looking down at the sleeping child in his arms. "He raped her, Richard," Michael said so softly it was barely more than a whisper. "He raped her repeatedly, every time Doreen went to the doctor. He held a gun to her head and told her if she made any noise or ever told anyone he would kill her mommy, daddy and Mickey."

Richard threw his hands over his eyes, taking deep gasps of air. "Oh God. Oh God, no," he moaned. The idea that his baby endured what she did, repeatedly, thinking she was protecting him and her mom and little brother was almost more than he could bear. *'What kind of a no-good father am I, anyway! I can't even take care of my own little girl! She was taking care of me!'*

He looked at Cassie as she slept in Michael's arms and he longed to take her from him, to hold her, protect her, never let anyone touch her again. But he didn't deserve that. He had let her down; he didn't deserve to hold her anymore, he didn't deserve her love.

"How did she happen to tell you about it," Richard suddenly asked, "when she would never say a word about it to anyone before?"

Michael told him what had transpired out in the office, leaving out no details. "I'm sure she saw the gun in the drawer. It's the gun you took from your landlord. Mom unloaded it and had me put it away for safe keeping. And in Cassie's mind, I was another Michael with a gun in the drawer, and I was going to hurt her."

The skin around Richard's mouth had turned pale with fury as he listened to Michael. "I'm going to kill the son of a bitch," he said through clenched teeth. But I want to make him suffer first. I want him to hurt the way Cassie hurt, over and over, and I want him to be afraid, just the way Cassie was."

"Do you know where he is?"

"Halifax. Said he was going to Halifax to spend the holidays with friends."

"If he's lucky, someone has already blown his head off in the rioting there. And if he's not lucky, I'll be there to help you with however you want to deal with him when the time comes."

CHAPTER SIXTEEN – JANUARY 6, 2005

"As they say in the funny papers, 'I've got good news and bad news.' Which would you like to hear first?" Matt said, almost as soon as he, Nate, Ted and Chris trooped into the house.

"What's going on here?" Nate asked, seeing all the somber faces in the family room. Everyone had reddened, puffy looking eyes and the sniffles.

"We have some good news and some bad news too," Ruth said. "The good news is that Cassie is talking again and the bad news is the reason why she stopped in the first place."

Cassie was reluctant to let Michael out of her sight, and it took a great deal of persuasion to get her to stay in the family room with the other kids while the grownups retired to the dining room to talk. She adored Carin though, and her promise to read more of the Buddy Book was the compelling incentive.

Michael, repeating the story for the third time, found his anger toward Michael Cooper increasing with each telling. For Richard, it meant telling everyone about the gun and how it wound up in the dresser drawer in the office. For Ruth, it meant confessing that she hadn't told the whole story about Richard, which brought everything full circle again to Michael who did know the whole story.

Ruth noted that Matt just sat there listening, his face increasingly grim at each new revelation. She was waiting for the bomb to fall, and when it didn't, she felt compelled to corner Matt on his way out to the barn to do the milking. "You didn't have anything to say about all the deceptions around here, Matt, and I'm wondering why. That isn't like you."

"After hearing what had happened to Cassie," Matt said, haltingly, "nothing else was important enough to make a fuss about. And when you piece everything together, I guess all the deceptions were for a good cause. They led to the discovery of what was wrong with Cassie. Now, as I see it, there are two things to do. First, help Cassie get over this and second, make Michael Cooper wish he had never been born!"

"Vengeance Matt? That's not like you either."

"Not when a wrong has been done to me personally, no. I don't believe in personal vengeance. But Michael Cooper has committed the most despicable crime it is possible for a human being to commit, short of murder. I'm not talking about the rape, although that certainly is horrible, especially for a small child. I'm talking about his enslavement of another person's body and mind over a long period of time for his own perverted use, without regard or remorse for the pain and mental anguish he inflicted."

"You can't take the law into your own hands, Matt, although I agree with you that watching that man squirm would be a pleasure."

"I know just how I'm going to make him squirm too, if I get the chance."

"How's that?"

"I'm not telling," Matt said somberly. "That's going to be my little secret for now. But what I'm hoping I'll get the chance to do is something Michael Cooper will never forget, believe me!"

Ruth was about to try prying the devilish plan Matt had for Michael Cooper out of him when they were interrupted by Michael, hand in hand with Lindy and Cassie. "Looks like I have two girls for barn help now!" he said, raising their entwined hands as high as he could without lifting the girls off the ground. "Cassie wants to feed the barn cats and she might even want to try giving a bottle to the twins!"

"Michael is going to be a very important part of Cassie's recovery," Ruth observed as she watched the trio enter the barn. "He's her hero now."

"Your 'good news, bad news' got upstaged earlier," Ruth said to Matt after dinner. "But it will have to wait a bit longer because Rachel and I are helping with the cleanup so that Richard and Doreen can be a part of our after dinner discussion group.

They have really been left out of things and to some extent, so have the three older kids. I'd like everybody together in the dining room, Cassie and Mickey, too."

"That's either going to be boring for the kids or a pain for the adults...or both," Matt said. "Probably both!"

"You don't give your grandchildren enough credit. Kids today have a lot more savvy than they did a generation ago and everything happening now affects them in some way. That gives them the right to be a part of any decisions that are made."

"What if I have some things to relate that they would be better off not hearing?"

"Could anything be worse than what they already heard today?"

"They don't fully understand what happened to Cassie!" Matt protested.

"If you don't think so, then go ask Chris what his understanding is of what happened to Cassie. He would be the least likely of the three to understand."

Matt took Chris out to the office for a man-to-man chat while the dishes were being washed. When the two of them came back out of the office, Matt looked sheepishly at Ruth. "Don't you get tired of being right?" he asked. "Okay, the kids are in. 'Nuff said."

"I'll start with the bad news," Matt began. "I'd just as soon get it over with so I can get to the good stuff. Ian's network doesn't have much news from the Halifax area because there are no truckers going in there. There's too much snow, it's too risky and there's too little gas. But we found out that some of the farms in the Musquodoboit Valley and on up into Truro have been hit. Actually, there are isolated incidents all over, up as far as Kentville. But there's no pattern as to the type of farm being hit. It might be a dairy farm in one place, a sheep farm in another and a potato farmer in a third. It's random, or so it appears. There's not a lot..."

"Is there any shooting?" Chris interrupted.

"I was about to say, there's not a lot of violence taking place at the farms. Most farmers are giving people something to eat. But when they run out of something to give, that's when the real trouble will start. If there's been any shooting, I haven't heard about it."

"Do you think we might wind up having to defend this place?" Rachel asked.

"That's always a possibility. We're prepared for defense, but not with guns." Matt said, looking pointedly at Chris. "The entire perimeter of the farmyard has six strands of electric wire fencing. It completely encloses the barns, outbuildings, house, garden area, the whole farm- yard, with one exception. That exception is the end of the lane as it turns around in back of the house. Ruth wanted something constructed there, but it's about a thirty foot span and we didn't quite know how to tackle the problem without it being too inconvenient to get in and out of here with the cars. Richard knows about that hole in the perimeter; he walked right through it!"

"Let me take a look at it tomorrow," Nate said. "Maybe I can come up with a solution that doesn't involve driving posts in the ground. Won't be able to do that with the ground frozen."

"How about a wall?" Chris asked.

"It would take materials we don't have. Let's let Nate take a look at it tomorrow. Maybe you can give him a hand and come up with some ideas," Matt added, after seeing the dejected look on Chris's face. "Those six strands of wire on the perimeter are set a foot apart. No one can climb through them or crawl under them without getting zapped. And unless someone brought along a pole vault or an Olympic athlete, they wont get *over* those fences either. Right now they are powered by a solar battery with an intermittent current. Anyone touching a wire will get stung pretty good, but not really hurt. If it's absolutely necessary, and I do mean *absolutely*, the fence can be hooked up to the house current and changed from intermittent to constant. If it is though, anyone who touches it is toast."

"The cows know to stay away from wires," Lindy said, "but the calves haven't learned that yet. That electric fence won't kill the calves, will it?"

"There's not any electric wires *inside* the corral," Michael explained. "They're all on the outside of the windbreak, so none of the cows or calves would be hurt." The relief on Lindy's face was evident.

"We will be keeping in close contact with Ian," Matt continued. "But one of the things that bothers me is the lack of word of any kind from Yarmouth. The threat could come from that direction too, you know."

"You said we're not prepared to defend ourselves with guns," Richard said. "Does that mean there are none or you don't plan to use them?"

"Actually, both. There are just a couple of .22 rifles and a shotgun, not a lot of firepower and we wouldn't want to use it anyway. Our defense is going to consist almost entirely of making it hard for people to get in, so they go away and leave us alone."

"Couldn't we booby-trap the lane the way that guy did that shot at us?" Chris asked.

"We sure could, Chris, if it gets to the point of not being able to leave here. But we wouldn't want to risk being victims of our own booby-traps."

"In any case," Ruth said, "I think we need to put a sign at the end of the lane with a warning that the electric fence is on regular current, not intermittent. The intent is not to kill anyone, just keep them away."

"'An keep that bad Michael away!" Cassie piped in.

"*Especially* keep that bad Michael away!" Michael agreed, squeezing Cassie's hand.

"This is awfully depressing stuff we've been talking about," Carin said. "I thought you said there was some good news, Grandpa."

"There is. I'm the bad news guy and I'm done now. Your dad's going to tell you the good news and when he's done I have some *more* good news."

"You'll have to excuse me for a few minutes," Ruth said. "I'm going to make us some coffee and hot chocolate but I'll be listening to most of what you say from the doorway. Uh, I was wondering if you would help me, Doreen?"

Doreen went out to the kitchen with Ruth, saying nothing as she left the table.

"We're going to talk, you and I, after this meeting is over," Ruth said to Doreen, once they were out of earshot of the others. Doreen said nothing, mechanically setting out mugs on a large tray while Ruth made the coffee and hot chocolate. "We'll go out to the office where we won't be disturbed." Ruth added.

"Is that an order, ma'am?" Doreen asked, her back turned to Ruth.

"Yes, that's an order, Doreen."

"So you blame me too," Doreen stated.

Ruth went over to Doreen, turned her by the shoulders so they were face to face, and gently said, "No, I don't blame you. But you obviously blame yourself and that's what we have to talk about."

"The good news is brief, but it's really good news," Ted said. "Food is going to be delivered down here tomorrow from the distributor outside of Middleton. It's mostly flour, fats, cereal and canned vegetables, but add that to what's coming in fresh from the farmers and everyone will probably be eating healthier than they have in years."

"That *is* good news!" Rachel exclaimed. "I've been feeling a little guilty eating so well when I know there are a lot of other people with very little, or with very limited choices."

"It's good news for us, even though we don't need any of the food coming in. A lot of people are aware now that we must have a good supply of food here since we aren't scheduled to receive any. Not even milk," Matt said. "So if there weren't some food deliveries, our own supply would be very hard to hang on to."

"Is all the food coming in being donated?" Michael asked.

"Some, but not all," Ted answered. "The food stored at the warehouse is being donated by the distributor, but the flour and canned vegetables are coming from up in the New Minas area and that food has to be paid for. The towns and the county are picking up the tab. All they're going to do is write a check that can't be cashed until the banks are open."

"Couldn't everybody have done that all along instead of having these Trade Bucks?" Lindy asked.

Matt shook his head. "There are too many people here who's only income is a check that comes in the mail in a brown envelope; government employees, teachers, doctors, pensioners, the unemployed and those on social assistance. Even though they may have that money *due* them, there's no guarantee they'll ever get it."

"Well, that's all I have to report," Ted said. "Now let's hear *your* good news, Matt. You must have been keeping it a secret because I've no idea what it could be."

"The power will be back on in a couple of days," Matt said, smiling.

Everyone started talking at once and Matt gave them all a few minutes to get the excitement out of their systems before he held up his hand and hollered for attention.

"There's a flip side to the power being restored. It's only going to be back on in a part of Annapolis County, not the whole Province or anything close to it! We've been capable of getting the power on in this area ever since it went off," Matt disclosed, "because of the tidal power plant here."

"Then why wasn't it turned back on right away?" Ted demanded.

"It only generates enough electricity to service about 2000 homes at the most, when power is being used at normal levels. In order to service the greatest number of people, it was essential to have everything unplugged in every house that isn't occupied. In those that are occupied, if the main source of heat is electricity, the thermostats, unfortunately, will have to be turned off. Dow has that situation at his house, for instance, so he's going to have to continue living in the one room that has a fireplace. He can't turn on the electric heat. Electrically fired oil furnaces can be used, however. Everyone has to be notified, and every house checked, and that all takes time. The rules for the use of electricity will be almost exactly the same as they are right here; no lights on during the day and as little as possible at night; outhouse for daytime use, etcetera. The power is to be used for water, cooking and food preservation. Refrigerators are one of the big power users, so they are one of the reasons why people can't move back to their own homes. Three or four families, all under one roof, sharing the same refrigerator, will help make the power stretch to 3 or

4 times what it normally would. That would result in power for 5 to 6 thousand homes. That's the target, at any rate."

"The Henderson house has an oil furnace. I wonder if Bea will be inviting Dow and his family to move in there," Nate mused.

"Nate, from what I could see while she was here, she'll probably be asking *you* to move in with her," Rachel said.

"She already has, without knowing there would be heat."

"You're not going to leave here, are you?" Lindy asked.

"Not if it means moving in with Bea! That's about the last place I'd ever want to live!"

Matt sighed, shaking his head. "None of you seem to have caught the real significance of this news," he said. The people here in this part of Annapolis County are going to be the only ones in the Province to have electricity, running water and an organized food supply system, as far as I know. That's going to make us a target for everyone who doesn't have those things. We are talking about close to a million people."

There was silence around the table as everyone digested Matt's news.

Doreen followed Ruth into the office. There was already an oil lamp lit in the room, casting a golden glow that was more appealingly intimate than the light created by electricity could ever be. It set exactly the right mood for a heart to heart talk.

"It's my fault," Doreen said. "Five times I left my little girl in the care of that animal. Five times I made her endure something unspeakable because I didn't want to have to take my children with me when I went to see the doctor."

"I see," Ruth said seriously. "So you knew all along that Michael was abusing Cassie and you just..."

"No, of course not! If I'd had any idea I would *never* have left the kids with him!"

"Then how is it your fault if you had no inkling it was happening?"

"I should have known! Cassie blames me. She's blamed me from the start. She was putting out all kinds of signals but I never picked up on them."

"Wait a minute now. If you never picked up any signals, how do you know there *were* any signals?"

"I *misinterpreted* the signals. They started right after we moved here. That's when Richard and I found out we were going to have another baby, and we told the kids. Cassie seemed to want to distance herself from me more and more as the months passed. I thought she resented me for wanting to have another baby; she was very jealous of Mickey when he was born. But now I know that wasn't it at all. It wasn't a growing resentment, it was a growing hatred for a mother who was supposed to love her and take care of her, yet could leave her with a man who hurt and terrified her."

"You didn't know, Doreen. You have to forgive yourself for not knowing!"

"Forgiving myself isn't going to make Cassie forgive me! And it isn't going to bring her back to me! You're probably wondering why I haven't shed a tear over this and I probably wouldn't have believed such a thing could be possible before all this happened. But now I know its true. Some things really *do* hurt too much to cry!"

CHAPTER SEVENTEEN – JANUARY 7, 2005

Nate was out at first light, taking measurements and assessing the materials on hand. The lane was fifteen feet wide and there was a nine- foot span from the lane to the back of the house. On the other side of the lane, it was exactly eight feet to the side of the chicken coop. *'Thirty two feet of vulnerable territory,'* Nate thought. *'Big enough to drive a tank through!'* The ground was level on the side by the chicken coop, but on the house side, the ground sloped up toward the foundation. *'No wonder they didn't do anything about protecting this area,'* he told himself.

He surveyed the available materials inside the workshop. There was a lot of rough-sawn lumber stacked on one side, some good 2 x 10 planks and bags of cement. In back of the workshop, Nate found what appeared to be another stack of lumber completely hidden by snow. Brushing it off, he saw that it was a pile of old, used railroad ties. As he looked at them, an idea began to take shape in his head.

As Nate headed back to the house, he met Matt on his way in from the milking. "Think of any way to protect that area?" Matt asked.

"Yup! I think so!" Nate answered. "We can build a free-standing wall on either side of the lane, held in place by its own weight. Not a rock wall, though. It would take too long to build and it's too easy to tear apart."

"What, then?"

"A stacked railroad tie wall. I'm going to need some of those big rough-sawn planks, a bale or two of straw, bags of cement, the biggest galvanized spikes you have, some rocks, two strong young men and a boy thrown in for good measure!"

"That's quite an assortment!" Matt laughed. "What about the lane itself, though."

"I've got something else in mind for that. It will have to be a fake so we can get in and out of here, but I think it can be made to look real enough to fool most people."

After the snow had been removed from the two areas where the walls would be constructed, Nate laid flakes of straw on the ground, one layer thick on the level side of the lane, and in staggered layers on the sloping side until a railroad tie would sit on it level. He poured water over the straw until it was thoroughly soaked then instructed Richard and Ted to place the railroad tie on top of the straw, broad side down. He spread a thin layer of water soaked straw on top of each tie before another was laid on top of it. "In the winter, water soaked straw is almost as good as glue or cement for sticking things together," he said.

By mid morning the two walls were six feet high. Before the work crew went in for coffee and a bit of warmth, they poured buckets of water all over the walls. "We'll let mother nature work out here a while, while *we* take a break!" Nate said.

When they returned to the job, planks were nailed to the railroad ties, covering all the seams, then firmly attached to the sides of the chicken coop and the house. Chris was kept busy hauling rocks on his toboggan, "Nothing bigger than your head," Nate told him, while Nate framed out a lightweight gate.

"We're going to build some dummy posts on the ends of these walls, eight feet high, and fill them with cement," Nate said. "It's too cold for the cement to cure, but the cement will add weight to the ends of the walls and it will look like cement posts in the ground that nobody took the wood frames off of. The slurry from cleaning out the wheelbarrows can be poured around the bottom of the posts; every little bit of camouflage helps."

The loads of rocks Chris collected were placed on top of the walls, adding another 300 pounds or more to the weight of each wall. "Getting there!" Nate exclaimed, obviously enjoying the project. "We'll get this finished up right after lunch. Shows what can be done with a little ingenuity and a lot of good help!"

"Won't somebody be able to just climb over the wall?" Chris asked.

"I figure they won't want to with a couple of electric wires to go over," Nate said, winking at Chris. "You'll see, after lunch."

The six foot high gate was attached to the dummy post with six strap hinges. It worked so smoothly and was so well balanced, it could be opened with one finger. The gate closure was a series of large screw eyes, with those on the gate resting on top of another set in the other dummy post. The gate could then be securely closed by inserting a heavy-duty rebar down through the screw eyes. About a foot from the top of the gate a heavy-duty hook and eye closure was installed for extra security. The gate could now only be opened by someone from inside the enclosure.

The finishing touch was the phony electric wire that raised the height of the gate and walls by another two feet. Additional wire was attached to the gate to make the entire structure appear to be electrified.

More water was dumped over the rocks on the walls. "Those walls will freeze solid overnight," Nate said. "And tomorrow morning we'll bank some straw and snow on both sides. That will keep the ground frozen there well past the time the frost is out of the ground in the spring."

Ruth marveled at the structure when she went out to see it later that afternoon. It looked sturdy enough to her to withstand the force of a speeding locomotive. Scanning the fortress that now completely surrounded and enclosed them, she couldn't help but wonder if, in their attempt to protect themselves from other people, they might actually be creating their own prison.

Before going back in the house, Ruth opened the trunk of the car and took out the shopping bags and boxes she had stowed there the day before. The manager of the variety store in town had accepted her IOU for the puzzles, educational games and art supplies, but not for the two small snowsuits and pairs of boots. "Little kids being able to get outside to play is essential for the survival of their parents' sanity," he had joked. "That makes kids' snowsuits a survival item. You could probably consider the other things you got survival items too, but…"

Ruth smiled, remembering. It had been a long time since the years in Boston when she hadn't had to look at price tags before buying something. Both Cassie and Mickey had been wearing the winter jackets and boots they'd had the year before. Everything was too small, and not warm enough for them to enjoy being outdoors for more than a few minutes. She planned to sneak the new clothes in to Doreen now that both the little ones were napping. They were to be a present from Doreen to her kids.

'Doreen.' Ruth had no idea what she could say or do to help. It was as though, when the light went on for Cassie, it went off for Doreen. Now *she* was the silent one, going about her daily routine like a robot, hollow-eyed and emotionless. She spent every minute she could off by herself, assembling the tiny furniture for the dollhouse and trying out various wallpaper prints and carpeting for each room. And she still hadn't shed a tear.

Ruth saw a dramatic change in Cassie. She was talking, laughing, playing like any other little girl. Yet, she was still reserved toward her parents, especially her mother. In fact, she was acting no differently toward her mother than she had ever since they had arrived at the farm; silent and unsmiling. She knew both Doreen and Richard took that to mean Cassie was blaming them for what had happened to her, and that most of the blame was Doreen's, because it was Doreen who had left her in the care of Michael Cooper.

But there was something that didn't add up to Ruth, and it nagged at the back of her mind like an itch too deep to scratch. The idea that Cassie resented her parents having another baby kept surfacing in her thoughts, and no matter how often she dismissed it as being an illogical reason for Cassie's continued coolness toward her parents, it was a constant thought.

Setting her armload of bags and boxes on top of the freezer in the entry room, Ruth went into the laundry room and took her cigarettes and ashtray out of the cupboard. She lit a cigarette and inhaled deeply. Smoking helped her to think, and she had to think through this problem between Cassie and her parents. She knew that confronting Cassie directly for an answer was out of the question. At the same time, she didn't want Doreen and Richard to feel she was meddling in something that was none of her business. *'But I may as well admit to myself that I'm an inveterate meddler,'* Ruth thought, *'because I know I'm not going to be able to let go of this.'*

Lindy came in the back door and, smelling the smoke, looked in the open door of the laundry room. "Looks like you caught me," Ruth said. Lindy, her face a blank, scooped up the pack of cigarettes and the lighter, taking them with her out to the entry room. She removed her coat and boots then came back into the laundry room with a lit cigarette held between the first two fingers of her right hand.

"What do you think you're doing?" Ruth demanded.

"I'm almost twelve and that's the age most girls start smoking," Lindy said. She took a puff of the cigarette and coughed.

"Give me that!" Ruth exclaimed, taking the cigarette from Lindy and stubbing it out in the ashtray. "You are not going to start smoking!"

"Tell you what, Grandma. I promise I won't start if you promise me you'll quit!"

"Oh, cute move snooks! But it's not going to work. I'm not going to let you smoke and you're not going to manipulate me into quitting."

"I just want to be like you, Grandma! But I also want to have you around for a long time. I don't want you to kill yourself with those," Lindy said, pointing to the cigarette in Ruth's fingers.

"I have to want to quit for myself," Ruth explained, stubbing out her half finished cigarette. Lindy looked at the cigarette in the ashtray, smiling.

"And don't look so smug! I put it out because…I've had enough, for now. It's not because of anything you said or did!"

"Oh, of course not!"

"It isn't!"

"I'm agreeing with you!"

"Here, help me carry all this stuff inside," Ruth said, grabbing a bag off the freezer.

"You did quit smoking for almost two years, Grandma. You could just not start again."

"Well, look at all the weight I gained doing that! That's as bad for my health as smoking!"

"You look exactly like a grandma ought to look!" Lindy said. "And now you have a nice soft lap to sit on, which you didn't have before!"

"You're too much for me!" Ruth exclaimed. "Did I ever tell you how much I love you?"

"No Grandma, I don't think you ever did!" Lindy replied, playing the game. "What is all this stuff, anyway?" she asked, indicating the bags.

"It's sanity survival stuff for grownups."

"Coloring books and crayons?" Lindy asked, looking in a bag. "Ohhh, I getcha!"

"Doreen glanced disinterestedly at the boots and snowsuits, busy attaching miniscule drawer pulls to a tiny chest of drawers she had just completed for the dollhouse. "Please try, Doreen!" Ruth begged, sitting down next to her. "Don't give up! I've been giving it a lot of thought, and I think maybe you were right all along. I think the reason for Cassie's continued coolness toward you has nothing to do with what happened to her. Haven't you noticed she's almost as cool toward Richard as she is toward you? I could be wrong, but I have a gut feeling that the *real* reason is that she resents you and Richard for having another baby!"

Doreen looked searchingly at Ruth. '*If only that were true!*' she thought. Leaning back in her chair, she stared off into space.

"How did Cassie act when you would come back home from visiting the doctor?" Ruth prodded.

Doreen frowned, trying to remember. "She was…clingy, hanging all over me like she couldn't stop touching," she said, a faraway sound in her voice.

"And what was your reaction to that?"

"I,…pushed her away, brushed her off,…got irritated, told her to let me be. It was a long walk to the doctor's office and I would be tired, especially as I got further along."

"Was she clingy every time you came back from the doctor?"

"Only the first couple of times, I guess. But,…she was clingy without touching, you know? She had to be wherever I was and she would look at my feet or my middle. It was like she couldn't take her eyes off me or I'd disappear or something."

"She wouldn't look at your face?"

"No, and I thought that was strange at the time. Strange, and annoying, too. I remember thinking that. Because, before we moved to Annapolis she used to climb in my lap all the time and put her hands on the sides of my face and press on my cheeks. 'I'm makin' you a kissy mouf,' she would say, and look me in the eye and giggle. She hasn't done that for months now."

Ruth momentarily pondered what Doreen said, then asked, "Do you think it's possible that Cassie thought if she looked at your face she wouldn't be able to resist telling you what Michael Cooper was doing to her; thinking if she told, he would kill you?"

Doreen lowered her head, shaking it back and forth slowly. "I don't know. I only know that I am carrying around a guilt I don't know how to deal with."

"Do you want your little girl back? The one who climbed in your lap and made you have a kissy mouth?"

"I don't deserve to have her back, but, oh yes,…I want her!"

"Then act like you do! You've been treating her as though she doesn't deserve to have *you* back! And before you get all hot under the collar and defensive," Ruth said, seeing Doreen's sudden look of outrage, "just think how things might look to Cassie. It's been about 24 hours since we all learned what happened to her, and you were the only dry-eyed person in the room! You haven't talked to her, smiled at her, touched her, nothing! Don't you think she might take that as a sign you don't care what happened to her because you don't love her anymore?"

"Cassie is rejecting *me*, Ruth! I want to hold her close and never let her go, but…I just don't…"

"Then do it! I might really piss you off saying this, but I'm wondering which one of you is the child! Who is it that was hurt, Doreen? It wasn't you! Stop acting like it was! Cassie needs you now more than she ever has before. You and Richard, both. He's acting as though he's half afraid of her too!"

"She doesn't seem to want anyone but Michael," Doreen said sadly.

"She thinks of Michael as the one who rescued her and comforted her. That makes him special in her eyes. But she's also becoming very attached to Carin and Lindy. As important as they are to her, though, they are a poor replacement for her parents.

"What if I try and she rejects me?"

"Then you try again. And again, and again, and again if necessary. Never give up. Having your little girl back is worth the effort, isn't it?"

Matt had seen Dow's car pull into the lane, and he opened the newly constructed gate so he could drive right through. Drew was with him, and the two of them were amazed to see the new walls extending from the buildings.

"It would certainly deter me!" Dow exclaimed to Matt. "I'm glad you got something figured out for this space. I know it was bothering you having this unprotected area, ever since Richard just walked through undetected. Never could figure out why Buddy didn't raise the alarm, though."

"Buddy likes everybody," Matt explained. "Someone on foot wouldn't faze him, and he never barks at a car that's been here before. He can remember the sound of every car that's ever been here, and he only barks if it's a strange car. Nate came up with the idea for the wall and gate. We started on it first thing this morning."

"This morning!" Dow exclaimed. You built this in less than a day?"

"We all worked on it," Chris said as he came out of the chicken coop with his basket of eggs. "All the guys, I mean. Not the women."

"Is Carin inside?" Drew asked, impatient to see her.

"Yeah," Chris scowled. "But I've got something to show you. Look what Grandma got for me in town yesterday!" Eagerly, he pulled a slingshot out of his jacket pocket. "I'm gonna set up some cans and try it out as soon as I take these eggs in the house. You wanna…"

"I'll take them in for you." Drew said, taking the basket from Chris and walking toward the back door. Chris stared icy daggers at Drew's back until he disappeared around the corner of the house. '*Carin,*' he thought. '*She's really getting to be a pain!*'

Chris fished six pop cans out of the recycling bin in the workshop and set them up by the hay barn on a board supported by two sawhorses. He knew there were some small rocks to be found in the gravel pile at the far end of the hay barn. Pulling back the tarp that covered the gravel, he selected about a dozen small pebbles and stuffed them into his jacket pocket.

Chris took the slingshot out of his pocket, admiring it. It was a real one, not a toy, and Grandma had said she thought he was old enough and responsible enough to handle it wisely. He could never aim it at a person or an animal, Grandma had said, because it could kill almost as easily as a gun. It was for target practice only.

One of Chris's favorite pastimes was lining up his plastic toy soldiers and shooting them down with rubber bands from about a dozen feet away. He was a dead aim with a rubber band, so he figured he would be with the slingshot too. But he found it wasn't that easy. He had finished off all the rocks in his pocket and hadn't hit one single can! He retrieved as many of the rocks as he could find then went back to the gravel pile for more, determined to master the darn thing. In a way, he was glad Drew wasn't there to witness his failure.

Dow and Matt went into the workshop to talk. There had been a great deal accomplished in the past two days, and Dow was eager to give Matt all the details.

The power would be on tomorrow, and every household was now equipped with a makeshift latrine, patterned after the one Dow had constructed for himself. The food delivery that morning had gone very well and most of the flour had gone to the bakeries to make bread. "Funny, you know," Dow said, "but it's bread people miss the most. Kind of tasteless stuff compared to most other food, but for some reason it's the most satisfying. Must have something to do with the smell or the texture. Or maybe it's that 'give us this day our daily bread' thing."

School would be back in session in two days. All the old-time rural schools that had been converted to community halls would again become one -room schoolhouses. Kids would be walking to school, and there would be lots of parents to help out. A hot meal could be prepared at the schools every day, because they had all had kitchens installed when they were converted to community halls.

Every greenhouse in the county was being set up to grow vegetables and would be heated by propane shop heaters and huge outdoor wood furnaces. Even the tennis court by the high school in town was being turned into a greenhouse, and the 'townies' would be learning how to grow food, how to cook basic unprocessed food and how to preserve it by canning, freezing and drying. Older kids would learn how to care for babies, small children and the elderly. They would also learn about nutrition, first aid, basic carpentry, how to use tools that didn't have to be plugged in and how to make useful items from trash. They would learn about teamwork, be physically active through outdoor sports, and creative through music and art.

"What about basic subjects?" Matt asked. "Are they just going to be ignored for now?"

"They'll be included too, of course," Dow assured him. "But the teachers are going to have a lot of help with everything. It looks like we'll wind up with one teacher for every 3 or 4 kids. Most won't be licensed teachers, but the kids will sure be getting a lot of personal attention!"

"Where do we fit in all of this?" Matt asked.

"You and Nate are needed for carpentry and helping out with the planting and growing of food; Rachel and Ted for teaching child care and music, and we'd really like to have Richard at the high school to teach some basic cooking skills."

Matt was happy about the prospect of getting involved with organizational things again. That was where he felt most useful and fulfilled. He'd happily leave the bulk of the farm work to Michael and Ruth; they enjoyed it, while he never had.

"That's all the good news," Dow said. "But there have been some other developments that I'm not too happy with."

Mayors had come out of the woodwork and were acting like they were personally responsible for everything positive that was happening. One had even been in contact by ham radio with some of the bigwigs in Halifax. "That burns my ass!" Dow exclaimed. "If those pompous jerks learn we have power here, they'll either try to move down here and take over, or worse yet, try to divert the power to Halifax. I don't think that's possible, but if it was they'd do it!"

Matt listened to all Dow had to tell him, patiently waiting for him to finish. Not that he wasn't interested in the news; he definitely was. But he had his own agenda to discuss too, and he broke into the conversation at the first lull.

"Do you know Michael Cooper, Dow? Richard's landlord?"

"Yeah, I know him. He's not around right now. Didn't Richard say he had gone to Halifax?"

"Yes. I just wanted to know if you knew him, maybe could tell me something about him, your impression of him, who he hangs out with, that kind of thing."

"I don't know much. He runs some king of a business out of a home office. He's only lived here about a year, bought that two family house and I think Richard and his family were the only tenants he ever had. I wouldn't know who his friends are or if he even has any here. He impresses me as,...I don't know, 'oily' is the only word that comes to mind. The way he talks, the way he moves, a little too smooth and slippery. You know what I mean?"

"I think I do," Matt said.

"Why do you want to know about Cooper?"

"Brace yourself," Matt said then paused. "He raped little Cassie Martin five times and told her he would kill her parents and her little brother if she ever told anyone," Matt said grimly.

Dow was speechless, sitting perched on a sawhorse with his mouth hanging open. Matt related the series of events the previous afternoon and the way Michael had learned what had been wrong with Cassie. He ended by saying he wanted to know the minute Cooper returned to his place, *if* he returned at all.

"Why Matt? What are you planning to do?"

"If I don't tell you, you won't be an accomplice," Matt said. "But if I tell you, you'll be as responsible as I am in the eyes of the law. Which way do you want it to be?"

"I want to know."

"So you can stop me,...or help me?"

"I'll help," Dow said softly.

"Really? What about human rights?"

"Human rights be damned! Where are Cassie's human rights? I don't have any faith in the justice system doing any more than telling him he was a bad boy!"

Matt had a mischievous smirk on his face. "Okay," he said. "Here's the plan."

Chris was growing discouraged. He hadn't hit the mark once and was getting tired of retrieving rocks that were hard to find, even though the yard around the hay barn had been plowed out. He decided maybe he needed bigger rocks, and went back over to the gravel pile and pried out several rocks the size of small eggs.

Out of the corner of his eye, he saw that Carin and Drew had come outside and were making their way through the drifts toward the heifer barn. When he saw Drew reach out and grasp Carin's hand, he was overcome with a sudden fury. He fitted a smooth round rock into the slingshot, and drew back the heavy rubber band as far as he could while aiming at Carin's back. After a moment's hesitation, he released the rock. '*I can't hit anything, anyway,*' he told himself, justifying the action. But it felt good just to see a rock flying in Carin's direction.

Drew turned to say something to Carin when she plunged facedown into the snow. At first he thought she was playing, but when she didn't move he quickly turned her over. When he did, the rock that had struck her at the base of the skull fell from the scarf wound around her neck, and buried itself in the snow. Drew could see that Carin was breathing, but was obviously unconscious.

"What in the...?" he murmured. "Carin?" he said softly, shaking her gently. "Carin!" he said loudly, shaking her harder. "Dad! Dad!" he hollered frantically.

Dow and Matt came on the run out of the workshop. "What happened?" Matt yelled, seeing Carin stretched out in the snow, not moving, with Drew leaning over her.

"I don't know!" Drew said frantically, as Dow and Matt reached Carin's side. "She just all of a sudden pitched over in the snow, head first, and she's out like a light!" Matt loosened the scarf around Carin's neck, and pulled her head back, frowning. "It's almost like she just fainted," Drew said shakily. "Like she just blacked out instantly!" Matt took a handful of snow and rubbed it around Carin's neck then lightly slapped her cheek. She stirred, moaning slightly then opened her eyes. "What happened?" she asked weakly.

"We don't know," Matt answered. "We were hoping you could tell us!"

"Everything just went black," Carin faltered. "I don't know why."

"Let's get you in the house," Dow said, picking Carin up in his arms. A very concerned Drew followed on his father's heels then ran ahead to open doors. Matt looked around, perplexed. He saw the board with the pop cans way over by the hay barn, but there was no sign of Chris. He'd have to remind that boy to put things away when he was done with them he told himself as he scurried after Dow.

When Chris saw Carin fall, he ran around the gravel pile, crouching down behind it. White-faced and shaking, he tried mentally to erase the moment he released the rock, to make it so it never happened. Huge tears escaped as he accused himself; '*You killed Carin!*' "I didn't mean to," he sobbed softly. "I didn't think the rock would hit you, Carin. I didn't mean to!"

He saw Dow carrying Carin into the house, with Drew hanging on to her. Then Grandpa followed them around the corner of the house. Chris sat in the snow, huddled in misery. He would just walk up into the woods and lose himself, he decided. His mom and dad would never forgive him; they wouldn't want him around anymore. That thought brought fresh tears as he visualized himself alone, lost, cold and hungry, the way Buddy has been in the story. But he wouldn't be found and saved and brought home to a family that loved him and missed him. He would be stiff and dead when they finally found him, if they bothered to look at all.

Chris saw his dad carrying Carin out to the car, with his mom, Dow and Drew right behind them. Then, wonder of wonders, he heard Carin's voice protesting that she could walk, she didn't need to be carried, and didn't need to see the doctor either.

He sat up tall and alert, craning his neck to see her. She wasn't dead! Maybe she wasn't even hurt bad! Chris was jubilant at first, thinking that now he wouldn't have to run away. But Carin would tell everyone that she had been hit with a rock from his slingshot and get him in trouble. Grandma would take the slingshot away from him and he would never be able to figure out what he had done that made him hit the mark. But the worst part would be the look of disappointment grandma would give him. He thought of other possible consequences too, remembering the story Drew told about his dad cutting a switch. That would be something he hadn't experienced before, and though he didn't relish finding out what it would be like, he didn't exactly fear it either.

Chris stayed by the gravel pile until he could see the two cars pull out of the farm lane and onto the road into town. Lugubriously, he collected the pop cans and put them back in the recycling bin then went to the house for whatever punishment awaited him.

He nearly ran into his Grandpa coming out the door with the milk pail. "There you are!" Matt exclaimed. "Where have you been?"

"I…Uh, was at the gravel pile," Chris said haltingly, not looking at his grandfather.

"Well, put those cans back where they belong."

"I just did."

"Good. How's the slingshot work?"

"I couldn't hit the cans, so I went to see if I could find some bigger rocks and…"

"What size rocks were you trying to hit the cans with?" Chris fished in his pocket and pulled out a pebble. "Well no wonder you couldn't hit anything. You need to use bigger rocks because you have to be able to hold on to them with the ends of your fingers," Matt said. "Don't look so miserable! You'll be able to do it. Just need bigger rocks." Matt patted Chris on the head then continued on his way to the barn.

Grandma asked him how he had made out with the slingshot too, then told him to go get cleaned up for supper. Carin mustn't have told anyone something had struck her in the head from behind. If she had, Grandma would know it had been him with his slingshot. Was it possible that Carin didn't know that something had hit her? Was he going to get away with it after all? If so, why did he still feel so rotten!

Ruth knew what had happened, but she also knew there were times to interfere and times to let kids learn their lessons on their own. This, she decided, was one of those times, because the vision she'd had of Chris with a slingshot hadn't been fully played out yet.

After supper, while Michael, Lindy and Cassie were in the barn and everyone else was in the dining room waiting for them before starting their meeting, Chris went into the family room where Carin was stretched out in a lounge chair. The doctor couldn't determine why she might have fainted, but said she should rest as much as possible for a few days. Chris eyed Carin warily, wanting to be certain she was really okay.

"Why did you have to use such a big rock?" Carin asked, with her eyes still closed.

"What?" Chris was startled. "What do you mean?"

"You know perfectly well what I mean," she said, opening her eyes.

"If you knew, er, *thought* I hit you with a rock, why didn't you tell anyone?"

Carin sighed. "I don't know. I guess I didn't understand why you would want to hurt me like that and, well, I didn't want to get you in trouble."

"Why not?"

"I don't know that either. Except I don't especially like seeing you get in trouble because you do things without thinking. And everybody already has *enough* problems. We don't need any more."

"I didn't mean it, Carin," Chris said, a sudden lump in his throat.

205

"You were mad at me about something, so you meant it all right. What were you mad about?" Chris shrugged. "It has something to do with Drew, doesn't it?"

"He was *my* friend until you came along!" Chris said sullenly.

"Ahhhh!" Carin said softly, understanding. "Drew is a cool older guy and you liked having him take an interest in you, right?"

"Right! And you ruined everything!"

"Chris, I'm going to tell you something I haven't told anyone else, except Grandpa. Drew asked me to be his girlfriend, and...he even kissed me. He still likes *you* the same way, as a friend. But he likes me in a different way. If you want him to still be your friend, you can't do dumb things to get his attention. And you especially can't do anything to try to get back at me. That will make Drew hate you."

"You're his girlfriend?" Chris asked. How did that happen?"

"I'm not sure. It just did. Some day *you* will meet a girl you want to be around a lot. Then you'll understand."

"Well, I already understand *that!* I liked being around Holly Brennan back home. She was *my* girlfriend."

"I didn't know you had a girlfriend! That's great, Chris!"

"I didn't kiss her yet or anything," Chris said, looking embarrassed. "But I like her, a lot!"

"Then maybe you can understand what Drew is feeling. Even if the girl he likes is your own dumb sister."

"Hey," Chris said, changing the subject in case the conversation was about to get mushy. "Do you think maybe Mickey kinda thinks I'm a cool guy the way I think Drew is?"

"That's obvious, isn't it? He tries to do everything you do and go wherever you go. You have a lot of power over him right now. You can show him how to be a dork or you can show him how to be a cool guy. I don't think he's old enough to tell the difference yet, but you are."

"I'm sorry, Carin," Chris said softly. "I was mad at you, but I didn't really want to hurt you. When you fell, I thought I killed you. I wanted to go away somewhere and die too. It felt awful," Chris rambled, tears springing to his eyes.

"There are going to be lots of times it feels awful growing up," Carin said. "But if you always stop and think what the consequences might be, there will be a lot of dumb things you will never do. That's the main thing everyone has to learn about growing up."

CHAPTER EIGHTEEN – JANUARY 8, 2005

The yeasty aroma of rising bread greeted Matt as he came downstairs. He inhaled appreciatively, remembering what Dow had said the day before. "The staff of life," he mumbled out loud. "The only thing that smells better than bread rising is bread baking." Richard, or maybe Ruth, must have been up late, Matt figured. Who made the bread didn't matter. Having a nice thick heel hot from the oven to slice off and slather with butter when he came in from milking is what mattered!

Matt found himself adapting fairly well to the intrusion of so many people in his house. As long as he had his quiet time alone in the barn, he would be okay with everything. He thought Ruth was going to be a different matter, though. He could already see the signs. She had always been an impatient person; when she wanted something done, she wanted it done yesterday. And problems should be solved immediately, if not sooner. But the problem between Cassie and her parents, especially her mother, was going to take some time. He would bet on that!

Matt saw that the back door was unlocked. "Well shit!" he muttered, realizing he wasn't going to have his time alone in the barn after all. The cold assailed him as he stepped outside, and he peered at the thermometer next to the back door. Minus 30 celcius, it read. "Holy shit!" he exclaimed. "The milk will probably freeze before it hits the pail!" The icy air made his nostrils feel pinched together, and he pulled his scarf up over his nose before making his way to the barn.

Lindy was in the first calving pen drying off a newborn calf's ears and tail with an old towel. "I thought you weren't supposed to be out in the barn alone," Matt said brusquely.

"I thought it would be okay now that there's a gate to close so no one can get in here," Lindy explained. "Heidi didn't dry her calf off very well and it's too cold to be wet. I wish I could use the hair dryer," she said, looking at her grandfather pleadingly. "It would dry her and warm her at the same time."

Matt considered. "I suppose it will be all right to use it, but only on the ears and tail, okay? Wouldn't want them to freeze off. I've seen that happen and they wind up pretty silly looking cows. Not to mention, they've got nothing to work with to help shoo away flies in summer!"

"I think Brandi will have her calf today too. If she does, and it's still real cold, can I use the hairdryer on her calf too? Just the ears and tail, of course," she quickly added.

"We have to watch how much electricity we use," Matt replied. "But…, I suppose it might be necessary to use it today." He started over to the other side of the barn to do the milking then suddenly turned back. "Who's making the bread in the house, do you know?"

"Uh, Grandma," came the distracted reply as Lindy hauled the hair dryer and an extension cord out of the cupboard.

"Grandma, huh? I suppose she was up all night."

"Not *all* night. She went to bed a couple of hours ago."

'Oh great,' Matt thought, *'that ought to put her in a good mood for the day.'*

Breakfast was the usual bedlam, with Mickey demanding and whiney, managing to spill either milk or juice every morning. Matt took his coffee and hot buttered heel of bread into the dining room and was surprised to see Ruth up after only a couple of hours of sleep. She was eating another one of her strange concoctions, although Matt had to admit it looked pretty good and smelled even better. She had spread butter on both sides of a thick slice of bread, grilled it until it was brown on both sides then spread a big spoonful of sour cream over it and topped it with maple syrup.

"That looks good!" Matt said cheerfully. Ruth gave him a baleful look. *'You can be cheerful in the morning,'* she thought. *'You get ten hours of sleep every night! As soon as it's dark outside, you're done for the day! And you better not even think to ask me to…'*

"Do you suppose you could fix me one of those?"

Ruth got up from the table, went through the kitchen and out to the laundry room for a cigarette without a word to anyone. Matt waited expectantly, sipping his coffee, anticipating the breakfast treat Ruth was preparing for him.

He had a long wait.

It was extremely cold out, but Ruth could see it would be clear and sunny. The sun helped. That bright shining orb made everything seem warmer than it was.

Lindy was spreading fresh straw in the pen where Heidi had given birth to her calf. "Open the windows and let the sun in," Ruth told her. "That sun is good for them. Vitamin D. They don't get nearly enough of it in the winter here, so we need to take advantage of every sunny day." She went into the second pen to check on Brandi. "Still a few hours yet," she said, patting the cow on the head. Brandi groaned. "Cassie hasn't seen a calf born yet, has she?" Ruth asked Lindy as she came out of the last pen.

"No. She's usually in bed by the time the cows calve."

"I'd like her to see Brandi have her calf. I've got a hunch it would be good for her to experience that, and Brandi would be an especially good one to see."

"Why would Brandi be especially good?"

"She moans and groans all through labor, but when the calf is ready to emerge she calms down and pushes it out without making a sound. And you never saw a cow get so excited over a calf! Brandi could almost make you believe that she is the only cow in the world that can perform such a wonderful feat as giving birth. I just have a feeling it would be good for Cassie to see that," she repeated.

"I think the kids are pretty excited about the idea of getting back to school tomorrow," Rachel said. "And I have to admit I'm looking forward to it too."

"Amen to that! Ted exclaimed. I've been feeling like a fifth wheel around here and I can't wait to get my hands on those musical instruments and fertile young minds. I just hope I'm up for the challenge!"

"I'm not sure any of us are," Rachel laughed, "but it certainly should be interesting. I've always thought I would like teaching, but I never figured I'd have the chance to find out."

Ted chuckled. "Me too. Wouldn't the school board and the teacher's union just love to find out what the curriculum is going to be and that,…, horrors, most of the teachers aren't teachers!"

Ruth left Cassie and Lindy alone in the barn, looking after Brandi. Lindy knew she could always get her grandmother or Uncle Michael if any help was needed.

'Truthfully answer any question Cassie might ask you,' Grandma had said. *'If you don't know the answer, tell her you don't know; don't make anything up.'* Lindy was pleased that she had been entrusted with the responsibility for both Brandi and Cassie. Her confidence with the cattle had never wavered since the day she was locked in the barn and saved the life of Zoe's calf. And all she had to do with Cassie was be her self.

Brandi was laying flat on her side, moaning.

"Why is she doing that?" Cassie asked.

"Because her baby is trying to come out and it hurts her," Lindy answered, matter-of-factly.

"Where does the baby come out?"

Lindy pointed to Brandi's vulva. "Right there. It stretches big enough for the calf to come through, and that's part of what hurts."

Brandi groaned, and pushed with another contraction. The tip of one small hoof could be seen briefly then disappeared as the pain subsided.

"She will hate her baby for hurting her," Cassie stated emphatically.

"No she won't. She will be so happy to see her baby she will forget all about the hurt."

Cassie scowled. "I would hate the baby!"

"Not when it's your own baby, you wouldn't. All you would feel is love for the baby once it stops hurting."

Still scowling, Cassie looked at Lindy. "Will it hurt my Mommy?"

"Yes. It always hurts. But I think maybe the first baby hurts the most. Your mommy is going to have her third baby so it probably won't hurt so bad."

Cassie frowned, counting on her fingers. "It's Mommy's second baby, not the third!"

"No, it's the third," Lindy said, sounding positive. "You were the first baby, and Mickey was the second one. So the baby inside your Mommy right now is the third!"

"I'm not the first baby! I wasn't inside Mommy's tummy!" Cassie said vehemently. "I never did that!"

"Silly," Lindy chuckled. Everybody in the whole world was inside their Mommy's tummy before they were born! But nobody remembers it. See that cow in the next pen? That's Heidi. She had her baby early this morning and already the baby doesn't remember being inside its mama. And, want to know something else? Heidi is Brandi's baby! She was a little bitty calf herself just a few years ago, but now she's a mama too. That's her fifth baby. That's five babies she's had," Lindy said, holding up her hand and waggling her fingers. "And every one of them grew inside her tummy, one at a time."

"I was a little baby inside Mommy's tummy too?" Cassie asked pensively.

"You sure were!"

Cassie was silent for a few moments, digesting the idea that she had actually been inside her mother. Then, "What did I do in there all day?"

"I don't exactly know, because I don't remember being in my mom's tummy either. But I don't think a baby does much of anything inside its mama except sleep and grow until it's big enough to be born."

"Does it hurt to be borned?"

"I don't know. But I think it might, a little. A baby gets squeezed pretty tight coming out."

"And I hurt my Mommy when I was borned?"

"Yes, I'm sure you did."

"Was I all yucky?" Cassie asked, seeing the wet, slimy feet of Brandi's calf emerge.

"It's always messy getting born. But you haven't seen anything yet! It gets yuckier, and then it gets really nice when you see how much the mama loves the yucky, messy baby."

Cassie watched, spellbound, as the calf's legs emerged further and further. When the pink nose could be seen, Brandi stopped groaning, rolled over onto her chest and began to push in earnest.

"It doesn't hurt her anymore!" Cassie said, delightedly.

"Oh, it hurts the most right now," Lindy said. "But Brandi knows her baby is almost born so she doesn't care how much it hurts now. She's just anxious to see her baby!"

Brandi turned to look at her rear end, making soft mooing sounds. "What's she doing now?" Cassie asked.

"She's talking to her baby already."

"What's she saying?"

"I don't understand cow talk, but I think she's telling her baby everything is all right, it's almost over. And she's probably telling it how glad she is to see it and that she loves it."

Once the calf's head had fully emerged, a few more strong pushes from Brandi expelled the calf. The calf shook its head, snorting, and Brandi immediately got to her feet, talking to her baby all the while she tended to it with her rough tongue.

"She loves her baby!" Cassie said, in hushed wonder.

Heidi put her head over the gate into Brandi's stall, looking at the newborn calf and making soft mooing sounds. Brandi stopped licking her calf, and, reaching over to Heidi, swiped her tongue over the side of Heidi's face then resumed licking her baby.

"She loves Heidi, too!" Cassie exclaimed, gleefully.

"Well sure! Heidi is her baby too, even if she's all grown up now. I'd better check to see if it's a boy or a girl," Lindy said, lifting the calf's leg. "It's a girl," she announced. "Now we have to think up a name for her that starts with a 'P'."

Cassie squinted at the calf like she was thinking very hard. "Hmmm," she said. "I don't think I know how to do that."

"Think of the 'P' sound," Lindy said, "then think of a girl's name with that sound. Puh, Puh, Puh," she prodded.

"Puh, Puh, Puh," Cassie repeated, concentrating hard. Then, a sudden look of elation spread across her face. "Pammy," she shouted. "My friend at school is named Pammy. That's a 'P' name, isn't it?"

"Yes!' Lindy said, delighted by the name. "It's perfect! We can even spell it with an 'I' at the end, like both Brandi and Heidi are spelled!"

"Cassie nodded her head vigorously, smiling. "Hi baby Pammi!" she sang to Brandi's calf in a high, piping voice.

Ruth appeared to be sleeping in the lounge chair in front of the woodstove. But she was far from being asleep. Her mind was centered on the two little girls in the barn, wondering what was taking place and whether or not it would make any difference. Her stomach felt tied in knots and every nerve in her body felt ready to explode with tension as she waited, outwardly calm to all appearances.

Doreen was seated in the other lounge chair, quietly stitching a tiny patchwork quilt for the dollhouse. Nate and Carin were in the dining room playing chess, Mickey was asleep upstairs, Michael and Richard were removing manure in the barnyard and everyone else had gone into town to see what they could do to help set up the schools.

Ruth felt a shot of adrenalin shoot down her spine as she heard Cassie and Lindy come into the kitchen. '*Do the right thing, Doreen!*' she prayed, opening her eyes to a barely perceptible slit. '*Please!*'

Cassie appeared in the family room doorway, smiling serenely, her eyes on her mother's face. Doreen quickly put aside her needlework, returning Cassie's smile and extending her arms in invitation. Her breath caught in her throat as Cassie climbed into her lap, straddling her, never taking her eyes off her face. When she felt the little hands on her cheeks, the dam broke inside Doreen. "I'm so sorry, baby," she whispered, as tears cascaded down her face. "I'm so sorry I left you with that bad man. I didn't know he would hurt you."

214

"I know you didn't, Mommy," Cassie said, puzzled by Doreen's tears. "I couldn't tell you! Why are you crying? He won't hurt me any more."

"Because I thought you blamed me for letting that man hurt you," Doreen sobbed. "But I'm crying mostly because I am so happy to have my little girl back in my arms. Oh how I've missed holding you, sweetheart!"

"I missed you too, Mommy. I didn't know I was a little baby inside your tummy, like Mickey, and like this baby," Cassie said, patting her mother's stomach, "before I was borned. I didn't remember that."

"Nobody remembers that. But I remember how happy I was when I would feel you kicking inside me, and how much I wanted you. Do you want me to tell you about it?" Doreen asked, wiping at the tears on her face. Cassie nodded gravely.

"Your daddy was with me when you were born, and…"

"Daddy was there too?"

"Yes. And he was so happy too! When the doctor put you in my arms, your daddy and I were crying with happiness, like I'm doing now. We couldn't stop looking at you, you were so perfect, so wonderful!"

"Was I all wet and yucky?"

"Uh huh," Doreen said laughingly. "And you were slippery, too! But we didn't care. You were the baby girl we had dreamed about and you made us so happy!"

"Did it hurt you Mommy when I was borned?"

"Yes, but it was worth it. And it will be worth it with this baby too, because I have enough love for all my babies," Doreen said, touching her stomach.

"I an' Mickey will love the baby too," Cassie said solemnly, "'cuz we was in your tummy already an' now *we're* already borned! I didn't know before," she frowned apologetically.

"It seems there were things we both didn't know," Doreen said, fresh tears flowing.

"I saw a calf get borned, Mommy," Cassie said, leaning forward and laying her head on her mother's breast. "It was all wet and yucky and its mama loved it too. It's a girl, an' we named her Pammi with a

'I' on the end. Baby Pammi," she murmured sleepily. Then, "I love you, Mommy," she said, in a whispered sigh as she buried her face in Doreen's neck.

When Nate left Lindy and Carin to play a game of chess together while he glued the tiny shingles to the nearly completed dollhouse, he found a scene in the family room that greatly pleased him. Ruth and Doreen were both sound asleep with tear-stained faces, and Cassie was snuggled asleep in her mother's arms. *'They've set everything to rights,'* he said to himself. *'I guess it's time for me to set a few things to rights too.'* He went past them into the living room, stretched out on top of his bed and thought about what he needed to do. He wasn't concerned about falling asleep. Ever since his first day there, Lindy had kept him too full of coffee to be able to sleep during the day. *'Lindy; how I will miss her!'*

CHAPTER NINETEEN – JANUARY 9, 2005

"Nothing can be wasted," Richard began his lecture to the group of 20 teenagers. "What you have always thought of as garbage is mostly edible and there has to be a plan for its use. Perishable foods such as fresh vegetables and fruit should be eaten first, before it...perishes," he said, eliciting a spattering of laughter. "Non-perishables such as rice, beans, anything in a can or in a dry package can be reserved for the time when there is nothing fresh to eat. And that time will come when the winter fruits and vegetables run out before more are ready in the summer. We can't count on any more food being delivered so we have to use whatever is available. And we have to make it last.

"What you see on the table here has been donated by a farmer. It will make a nice meal for about 6 to 8 people. But we are going to turn it into a nourishing feast for twenty. You are the fortunate twenty today; tomorrow twenty other students will be the fortunate ones.

"This is about a 2 pound chicken. It goes in this big pot of water. There's one small cabbage, 3 onions, 6 carrots, 6 potatoes, a cup of brown rice, 3 cups of flour and 2 cups of milk. There's also a real bonanza here of 10 apples.

"All the vegetables will be chopped and will go in the pot with the chicken after it is cooked enough to remove from the bone. The cup of rice goes in the pot too. We'll be making dumplings out of the flour and milk and will add them to the soup pot when the soup is almost done. We'll make applesauce out of the apples and I'll be showing you how to peel both potatoes and apples so that the skins can be baked, seasoned and eaten.

"We're having chicken/vegetable/rice soup with a dumpling in every bowl and applesauce for dessert. And we'll have spicy baked potato skins and apple skins as an appetizer while we're waiting for the soup to cook.

"So, chop- chop," Richard said, clapping his hands together. "Let's get busy and...chop-chop!"

Ted sat at the piano in the basement music room of the middle school. He had been assigned to grades 4 through 8, which meant he had all 3 of his own kids as students.

Only a small percentage of the students would be learning to play instruments. The remainder would be in choral groups according to their grade. Ted would also be able to select the best voices from among all the students for a performance group.

The boys and girls in grade 4 filed into the room looking apprehensively at the new teacher, unsure of how they were going to like the new curriculum. Chris was new to them too, and they were all aware that the teacher was his father.

Ted had arranged the chairs in three semi-circular rows facing the piano, and he swiveled on the piano stool and looked over his students, smiling. "Good morning!" he said enthusiastically. "My name is Ted Pendelton and I'm not a teacher. I'm a professional musician who can play almost any instrument, some better than others, and I play regularly with a country rock group you've never heard of and a jazz / blues group you've never heard of either. I'm not famous, but I make a decent living and love what I do. I'm from Edmonton, Alberta. I was here for the holidays when the lights went out, and now I can't get back home. But I honestly can't say I'm sorry about that. I think I'm going to enjoy playing at being a teacher, and I'm hoping this is going to be a fun class for you too.

"We're going to warm up our voices with a wonderful old classic song I'm sure you all know…Row, row, row your boat," he said slowly and solemnly to groans and titters from the students. "Following that will be everyone's favorite, Doe a deer." He divided them into 3 sections, and after playing a flamboyant introduction on the piano, began tapping out the accompaniment to row, row, row your boat with one finger, to the delight of the enthusiastic singers.

Rachel was in the high school gymnasium with a dozen pre-school toddlers and a dozen grade twelve students. Tumbling mats covered the floor at one end of the gym and each of the young adults was busy trying to teach his or her young charge how to turn a somersault.

Mickey was thoroughly enjoying his first taste of school. After many unsuccessful tries, he finally placed his head in the correct position, rolled head over heels then sat up with a look of wide-eyed amazement. The big girl who was coaching him clapped and cheered, urging him to do it again. He did so, over and over, as though he couldn't get enough of this fun activity. School was great fun!

After tumbling, Rachel read a story that the older students had to act out together to the delight of the toddlers then the story was repeated and the little ones acted out the story with the help of their new, older friends. A snack of graham crackers and milk was followed by a quiet time of the students getting to know their young charges, one on one.

The trust had already been established through play and Mickey obviously enjoyed the personal attention, as did the other children. They were all still at an age where they could relate to, and share with, an older person better than they could with another child their own age. But they would learn to interact with other children, and the students would learn that little kids could be fun and interesting rather than a source of irritation.

Rachel was pleased with the way things were going. There would be times of frustration and irritation she knew, but that's what they were there for. The young people were going to learn what caring for a child was all about, so they would be better prepared to be parents themselves one day. Or, be prepared to *never* be parents!

Tables, sawhorses and sheets of plywood had been hauled over from the farmers market and set up inside the newly constructed greenhouse on the tennis court next to the high school. Matt had an assembly line going, with several students filling bedding trays with potting soil, others planting lettuce, broccoli, cauliflower and tomato seeds, still others labeling, watering and placing the trays on tables.

Nate was busy constructing enclosures where some of the seedlings could be transplanted and grown to full size long before it was warm enough to put them outside. They would run the entire length of both sides of the tennis court, five feet wide. The transplant beds would be layered first with fine gravel, then compost, and finally topped with peat moss. Fresh vegetables were going to be needed as soon as possible. It was estimated there was no more than three weeks of food left at the food bank, and that might be stretching it. After that, there would be meat, milk, eggs, fish and vitamin tablets.

'*Thank God for the farmers and fishermen,*' Nate thought as he nailed a board in place. '*The rest of us aren't carrying a fair share of the load and I don't know how we can ever repay them. They're going to be the ones who are preyed upon by everyone else too, when the food runs out. Life isn't fair. It just damn well isn't fair!*'

Bea spent the day visiting the principals of the high school, middle school and grade school. She had their unanimous approval for a special project during school hours and was almost beside herself with excitement. She felt young again as she walked back to her house with a brisker step than she'd had in years. There were people out all along the route, shoveling snow or spreading ashes on sidewalks. They greeted one another cordially, remarking about the weather and asking about one another's health. She had almost forgotten how friendly people were and how beautiful Annapolis Royal was in the winter as she walked past one stately mansion after another on St. George street, before turning up the walk to her own.

Dow and his family would be moving into her house that evening and she found she was actually looking forward to it. Her cat, Emily, greeted her at the door as she entered, rubbing herself against Bea's legs as she removed her boots and put on embroidered carpet slippers. "You're happy to be back in your own house, aren't you Emily," she cooed to the cat as she picked her up and carried her to the back of the house.

She and Carl had had a Florida room built onto the south side of the house the year before he died. It was her favorite room and she regretted that Carl hadn't lived to enjoy it. They had both eschewed the idea of using their government old-age pension check for a trip to Florida for the winter the way most of their acquaintances did, preferring instead to spend that money in the local area. Bea had never regretted it.

But she had become somewhat of a recluse over the past few winters, and now that was going to change. She would find a way, too, to convince Nate to share her house and her life with her, if it was the last thing she ever did.

She didn't know that Nate had already made a final decision in that regard, complete with a well worked out set of stipulations. Life was definitely going to change for both of them!

Ruth and Doreen found themselves thoroughly enjoying the space and the quiet of the big house with everyone gone for the day. Michael had been in for lunch, but otherwise had been out in the barn tending to the myriad winter chores with the cattle, leaving the two women to their own devices.

"How did you know?" Doreen asked Ruth as the two of them sat at the kitchen table with steaming mugs of coffee in front of them.

"I didn't," Ruth replied. "And quite frankly I have to admit that I was a nervous wreck sitting there yesterday wondering what was taking place in the barn. It could just as easily have been the wrong thing to do, you know. But it was a risk that paid off, thankfully."

"Well I thank you for daring to take that risk. I couldn't have done that; wouldn't have even thought of it!"

"Don't thank me, please! In case you haven't noticed by now, I'm a very impatient person who has to have everything resolved or else I'm not fit to live with. I don't cope with problems very well and tend to walk away from them if I can. But in this case, there was no walking away. So, something had to be done because I couldn't bear the sad faces around here. I was also worried about what it might be doing to you, keeping everything bottled up inside the way you were."

"I'm so glad it's over! With all Cassie has been through, I wouldn't have believed it was something as simple as not remembering she was a baby inside me that was bothering her the most!"

"What's simple to us maybe isn't so simple to a small child. I didn't know what was at the root of Cassie's attitude toward you, and toward Richard too, but I thought it couldn't be that she blamed you for what happened to her. Little kids are all- forgiving. They can be treated horribly by their parents and bounce right back; partly because they know how to love unconditionally, and partly because their dependence on parents and the need for their love is so great. I figured it had to be something more fundamental that was eating at Cassie to the point she couldn't deal with it."

"She didn't think she was a part of us the way Mickey and this baby are," Doreen said, sorrowfully shaking her head. "Where did she think she came from, I wonder? A cabbage patch?"

"Who knows what kids can get in their heads!" Ruth laughed. "I don't know what Lindy said to her out in the barn, but it must have been exactly the right thing. Kids are good at saying the right thing. They don't try to psychoanalyze a situation and measure what they say or how they say it like adults do…Do you think Cassie's coping all right in school today? That maybe it wasn't too soon for her to go back?"

"I'm not nearly as concerned about her today as I was on her first day of school back in September," Doreen said. "She was always a little shy around strangers and she was scared about me leaving her. But as soon as we walked into her classroom, this little blue-eyed, blonde mite of a girl came and took Cassie by the hand and said, '*My name's Pammy and you're going to be my best friend.*' Cassie went with her and never looked back."

Ruth laughed. "God bless all the self-assured little Pammy's in this world!" she said. "What would all the mere mortals do without them!"

It was close to five-thirty and already dark out when everyone arrived home. Ruth and Michael had finished up all the chores while Doreen tended the big pot of soup and baked cornbread.

"Mm! Smells good in here!" Matt said, rubbing his hands together. "We're all starved from a long hard day and I can't tell you how good it feels to come home to a hot meal and smiling faces!"

"You didn't see any smiling faces today?" Ruth asked.

"Oh yeah, lots of them!" Matt enthused. "Everybody's spirits are pretty high. Things are happening and there's change in the air that's a little exciting for everyone. There's nothing like a crisis to pull people together and get them cooperating instead of competing."

"And how was *your* day?" Ruth smilingly asked all five children as a group.

"Good!" Mickey volunteered. "I did a su, su, uh...this!" he exclaimed, turning a somersault in the middle of the kitchen floor.

"Wow!" "Good going, Mickey!" "That's a neat trick!" everyone said at once, and Mickey grinned widely at being the center of attention. Richard picked him up and planted a big noisy kiss on the side of his neck before Mickey was encouraged to demonstrate his skill again.

"Pammy got a Barbie doll for Christmas an' she bringed it to school today an' let me play with it!" Cassie said happily.

"Would you like to take my Barbie to school tomorrow?" Lindy asked. "You can play with her any time you want."

"Can I?" Cassie beamed. "Then I an' Pammy can play Barbies together!"

"I was really too busy getting used to everything to get to meet anyone yet," Carin said. "I wish I went to the same school as Drew."

"I got to meet lots of kids," Chris said proudly. "That's because the whole class went to the music room first thing this morning, and all the kids like Dad a lot!"

"That's good to hear," Ted said. "Because I found myself having more fun than I've had in years! That's a great bunch of kids in that school."

Lindy didn't say anything about her day. She asked Michael about the calves then took Cassie by the hand to go find her Barbie doll.

"Lindy okay?" Ruth asked everyone in general. "She seems a bit subdued for Lindy."

"I'm afraid I did a pretty dumb thing today," Ted confessed. "I learned she was tone-deaf, and so did she, right in front of her whole class! I was having everyone sing the scales, individually, in order to select some kids for a choral group. Lindy can't sing the scales..., at all! I embarrassed her. How can she be almost twelve years old and I don't know she can't carry a tune?"

"Did anyone laugh at her?"

"Yes," Ted said dejectedly. "The whole class did!"

"What did she do?"

"She handled it really well. She said, 'I'll bet there's no one in the class who can sing worse than me!'"

"Sounds like she'll get over it," Ruth said.

"It still hurt; I could tell. I owe her an apology," Ted said, going to look for her.

"Do you think there's ever going to be a day when everything is okay with everyone?" Ruth gloomily remarked.

"Can I talk to you a minute, honey?" Ted asked Lindy.

"Sure," Lindy said, not looking at her dad. "Why don't you take the Barbie and all her clothes and show your mom," she said to Cassie.

"I'm sorry for what happened today," Ted said softly.

"So am I," Lindy said, looking at the floor.

"I didn't mean to embarrass you that way. I should have known, and I didn't."

"I wasn't embarrassed," Lindy shrugged. "I'm like that girl in that video we saw, you remember, when she had to sing in a karaoke bar and she was so awful! I don't mind not being able to sing. I'm just sorry I was such a disappointment. I think it was me that embarrassed you!"

"You could never disappoint me, Lindy," Ted said sincerely. "You have so many good qualities, I could never be disappointed that you can't sing. You know, I was beginning to think you were just about perfect. I think maybe I'm glad to find something you can't do!"

"Really?"

"Really. Perfect people can be perfectly boring!"

"I'm lousy at sports, too. That should make you *really* happy!" Lindy said impishly.

Ted laughed, giving her a hug. "I need someone to turn the pages in the music book for me. Interested in the job?"

Everyone's day was recapped at the after dinner meeting. "There's only a couple of bits of news to relate," Matt said. The first is that roadblocks have been set up at the county lines, so we are going to be all that much more protected from outsiders. That's really good news; those roadblocks will be manned 24 hours a day, too. The second bit of news is funny in a way, but at the same time not funny at all. You know that the three town cops are taking turns guarding the food bank at night. Well, Dow says everything was inventoried before the food distribution started, and was re-inventoried today, which it will be every week. It seems there are quite a few small bags of chips missing, and a whole whack of candy bars! The three cops have been helping themselves to snacks every night, figuring it's only junk food so it doesn't count! Dow impressed on them the fact that food is food, junk or not, and when the food runs out those missing chips and candy bars will be felt. I guess the cops are pretty embarrassed."

"What do we need, guards to guard the guards?" Rachel asked. "If you can't trust the police, who *can* you trust?"

"The temptation was a little too much for them," Matt said. "Maybe they learned something from this about human nature."

"Yeah," Ruth said. "That people are basically for themselves no matter who they are. When has it ever been any different?"

CHAPTER TWENTY – JANUARY 10, 2005

Connor Putnam flipped the 'off' switch on his ham radio and turned in his swivel chair to face Michael Cooper. "We're going to Annapolis Royal," he said. "They've got the electricity back on there and they're doling out all available food,…free!"

A slow grin spread over Michael's face. "Now maybe you won't think it was the dumb move of the century buying a house there. Especially with a tenant on one side making the whole mortgage payment for me. Like I've been telling you, that town is the perfect place for a drop-ship Internet business."

"We'll take my Cherokee," Connor said. "We're going to have to take the old back highway because we know none of the Trans-Canada highways will be plowed out."

"Probably none of the others have been either," Michael pointed out.

"No, but at least on those back roads you're never far from a house. The Jeep should get us through a lot of the roads even if they aren't plowed. And there will be farms, with food and maybe even fuel, if we're lucky." Connor winked at Michael.

"How is the fuel situation?"

"Filled the tank New Years eve," Connor boasted. "And we can siphon what's left in your tank into a couple of gas cans. That means no smoking in the car," he added, eyeing the lit cigarette between Michael's fingers.

"Hey man, the only thing keeping me going are the smokes! We should've gone looting like everyone else seems to have done. There's not a god-damn bit of food left anywhere!"

"Not so! You can get a looted bag of chips or a candy bar on just about any corner for twenty bucks a pop! Yesterday, they were fifteen bucks, tomorrow they'll be twenty-five. Time to get the hell out of here!"

"I need to find some cigarettes before we go. I'm almost out."

"What for? I told you, you can't smoke in the Jeep with filled gas cans there!"

"I figured maybe we'd stop somewhere for something to eat and I would have a smoke then," Michael whined.

"The reality of the situation hasn't sunk in yet, has it! You probably won't be eating *or* smoking until we get to Annapolis! Any stops we make will probably be to shovel some snow when we get stuck, which is likely to happen."

Connor looked disgustedly at Michael. He was sitting on the couch, legs folded in front of him, completely shrouded in several layers of blankets, puffing on a cigarette. "Look at yourself," he chided. "You're sitting there like some god damn ancient Indian chief, wrapped in your blanket and smoking your peace pipe, wondering what the hell happened while the village burns down around you!...Get up off your sorry ass, chief, and help me load the radio into the back of the Jeep. We're heading out of here before it's full light out and people start crawling out from under the covers. The fewer people we run into, the better."

The old Highway # 1 would take them all the way to Annapolis Royal. The trip started out badly, with an old clunker of a car stuck in a drift and completely blocking the road.

"Let's get out and see if we can push it far enough to get by," Connor said.

"Why don't you just push it out of the way with the Jeep?" Michael asked, finally beginning to warm up from the car's heater.

"It's a new car!" Connor exploded. "I'm not shoving that piece of junk out of the way with my new car! Now c'mon!"

Michael landed face down twice, as his feet slipped out from under him while he pushed as hard as he could. "The hell with this shit!" he exclaimed, getting back in the Jeep, scowling. He watched Connor violently kick a rear tire on the old car then pound his gloved fist down on the hood. "That oughta teach it to not get out of the way!" Michael told Connor sarcastically as he got back behind the wheel.

Connor shifted the Jeep into 4-wheel drive and slowly eased it up to the other car until the bumpers touched. He pressed down on the accelerator and felt the Cherokee's tires spin in the snow. The other car hadn't budged. Cursing, he got out and looked at his front bumper then peered in the side window of the heavy old sedan. The hand brake was on and the doors were locked. Rummaging in the back of the Jeep, he found the tire iron and viciously smashed the side window of the old car, unlocked the door and released the brake. The car moved just enough on the second push for Connor to back up and drive around it.

"Trying to push a car with the brake on, were we?" Michael taunted.

"Shut up, Mike!" Connor warned.

"Road rage! Hey, it's all the rage today!" Michael said in a falsetto voice, laughing at his own pun.

"Shut up! And see if there's anything in the glove compartment. I sometimes have a roll of mints or a pack of gum in there. Check, willya!" he ordered when Michael didn't move immediately.

Michael sifted through an array of small tools, maps, a service manual, insurance forms, registration, and uncovered a pair of men's red bikini briefs and a couple of condoms. "These are the closest to anything edible in there," he said, holding up the condoms. "Might be a little too chewy though, wouldn't you think?"

"Put 'em back," Connor said sourly.

"I thought you might keep a gun in there."

"I don't own a gun. Don't like them."

"That's probably a good thing. You don't have the temper that goes with owning a gun."

"You have one?"

"No," Michael lied. "Never had a reason to own one."

Connor swore as the Jeep slid sideways and stalled. He had taken it out of 4-wheel drive to save on gas after pushing the old car aside. Restarting the engine, he shifted once again into 4-wheel drive and easily pulled out of the drift on the side of the road. When he hit a clear patch of road he slipped it back to two- wheel and almost immediately stalled out again. He'd have to leave it in 4-wheel drive, he decided, or they'd never make it. Of course, if they ran out of gas, they'd never make it either! He slammed his hand on the steering wheel and bared his teeth as he stepped on the accelerator. Michael eyed him apprehensively.

Connor had changed in the past year. They had known one another almost six years, both working out of a Halifax office for a large pharmaceutical firm. Although they both had been on the road a lot, they saw one another fairly often. Everything changed for Connor about a year ago when he got back from a two- week trip to Newfoundland and Carla told him she wanted a divorce. She'd been playing around on him and got serious about some damn architect and the bastard had just picked Carla and the kids up and whisked them off to Toronto. Michael figured it hadn't helped when he left the company to set up his own business in Annapolis Royal. But hell, he was tired of traveling and hated the job anyway. He had it easy now, was making more money than he ever had as a detail man, and his business was fun. Selling adult movies on the Internet was a lucrative business that just seemed to get better and better all the time. Lots of repeat business, and he didn't have to wait in any more doctor's offices with snot-nosed kids spreading their germs around and funky smelling old people making their weekly visits because they had nothing better to do. He was glad to be out of it!

Michael was abruptly pulled out of his reverie as Connor plunged the Jeep into a high drift spanning the road, the tires spinning ineffectively.

"Grab a shovel," Connor ordered. They both piled out of the Jeep and began shoveling through the drift that blocked their passage. Michael took the opportunity to light a cigarette, puffing on it out of the corner of his mouth while he continued shoveling. The smoke drifted up, stinging his eyes and making them water. *'Shit!'* he thought. *'Never could get the hang of doing that. Must be some kind of trick to it that I don't know!'* Coughing, he continued to puff and shovel.

They could see a pickup coming toward them along a straight stretch of road once they were underway again. The truck straddled the middle of the road, barreling along with no indication it would relinquish its position and allow Connor to pass. He pulled over to the right as far as he could, muttering oaths under his breath. The driver of the pickup pulled up alongside the Jeep, rolled down his window and motioned Connor to do the same.

"Where you headed?" he asked.

"What're you, the Gestapo?" Connor barked.

"Not us. But you'll run into an armed roadblock about halfway through Kings County. They're not letting anyone through. Thought I'd let you know that so you don't waste time and gas getting nowhere."

"We live in Annapolis," Michael informed the two men. "You mean they aren't going to let us get back to our wives and kids?"

"The word we have is that nobody gets through," the driver said. "If what you say is true, I hope you can show proof. You're going to need it."

"You the advance guard?" Connor asked.

"Maybe," the man answered laconically, narrowing his eyes at Connor. "What's that in the back of the Jeep?"

"My ham radio." Connor volunteered no further information.

"That how you learned the valley was the place to be?"

Seeing that Connor was about to lose his temper and say something they would both regret, Michael leaned forward and called out his name, address and phone number to the man, adding, "My wife's name is Doreen and my kids are Cassie and Mickey, age 5 and 3. My wife is expecting out third baby in a few weeks and she's probably frantic. We had to go to Halifax on business and got stuck there when the lights went out. I need to get home, let them know I'm still alive!" Michael ended frantically.

"Better have some ID to show at the roadblock," the man said, gunning his engine and moving ahead slowly. Connor eased the Jeep back into the center of the road and continued heading west.

He glanced over at Michael. "Where'd you learn to lie so convincingly?" he asked.

"Natural talent," Michael boasted. "It comes in handy no matter what you're trying to sell!" An idea occurred to him. "Hey, how about trying out that line at the next farm house we come to? Farmers have food and someone might be willing to feed us with a good hard-luck story. Whatta ya say?"

"I say it's worth a try," Connor said. "My head is pounding, my gut is shrieking, and my butt is numb! It's taken over four hours to get from Halifax to Windsor, a trip that usually takes about half an hour. We're only a quarter of the way and we've gone through half a tank of gas. We're getting nowhere fast, and I'm getting pissed!"

"There's smoke coming out of a chimney over there," Michael said, pointing. As they got closer they could see a couple of half-grown kids and a dog at the side of the house. The farm lane hadn't been plowed out, but the house was only a few yards from the road. Parking the Jeep as close as he dared to the shoulder of the road, Connor instructed Michael to make sure the door on his side was locked.

"With the amount of traffic we've seen, we can expect someone to drive by in another 8 hours, easily!" Michael jested. "Yup, better lock up!"

Connor gave Michael a dark look and let him blaze the trail up to the back door of the farm- house. The kids and dog had run inside when they saw the two men get out of the Jeep, and the farmer was waiting for them on his back stoop, with a shotgun aimed in their direction.

"What do you want here?" the farmer bellowed. "Go on, get off my place!"

Michael stopped short. "We're not armed," he said, holding his arms out at his sides. "And we mean you no harm. We got stuck in Halifax when the lights went out and I'm trying to get back to my wife and kids in Annapolis Royal. My wife is expecting soon, and…"

"Took your sweet time trying to get back, didn't you?" the farmer asked menacingly.

Michael thought quickly. "Couldn't get out of there any sooner. People have gone crazy in the city. They're killing one another over scraps of food and a few matches. Cars and overturned trucks are blocking the roads everywhere. We've been holed up in a hotel room with nothing to eat for the last four days, today makes five, and we were hoping you might be able to spare…some food and water." Michael managed a little catch in his voice that sounded like a sob when he mentioned food. "We'll pay whatever we can."

"Let 'em in, Frank," a woman said, suddenly appearing behind the farmer. "I couldn't live with myself if someone came to the door hungry and we turned 'em away. It's just beans," she said a little louder. "That's all we've got left."

The tears that sprang to Michael's eyes were real; he didn't have to fake those. "Thank you," he said softly, sniffling and taking a deep breath. The farmer lowered his shotgun and motioned for Michael and Connor to precede him into the house.

The heat from the wood stove in the kitchen was welcome, but not as welcome as the smell of the beans cooking in the pot on the back of the old wood cook- stove. The woman ladled beans into large soup bowls and placed them in front of Michael and Connor. "Don't eat too fast," she warned, "if it's been several days since you've eaten. Would you drink milk instead of water? Milk is easier to come by."

They both nodded and smiled their appreciation, chewing avidly. After the initial hungry mouthfuls, Michael and Connor began to notice their surroundings. The refrigerator was missing, and in its place was a fold-up bed neatly folded into the alcove between two long counters. There was a similar bed folded up against a row of cabinets, and a double inflatable mattress standing against the wall behind the kitchen table. The refrigerator was behind a door that led to another room. Its door had been removed, they saw, when the woman opened the door to get a pitcher of milk. The refrigerator was jammed snugly across the doorway with the door to the other room used as access to the refrigerator's contents. '*Ingenious,*' Connor thought. '*Food stays cold but just enough heat escapes through the door to keep it from freezing.*'

"It's raw milk," the woman said, gently rotating the plastic pitcher to blend in the cream, "so it's going to taste a little different than you're used to." She poured out two tall glasses and Michael and Connor drank greedily. They didn't know which was worse, the hunger or the thirst.

They were aware of a sweet spicy odor in the kitchen that began to overpower the smell of the cooking beans. It smelled like muffins baking. They saw the woman nervously look at her husband then shift her eyes to the oven and back to her husband again.

"About finished?" the farmer asked. "Then I'd appreciate it if you'd be on your way. We get a little nervous nowadays having strangers around."

"I can understand that," Michael said, extracting a $50 bill from his wallet and laying it on the table.

"We don't want your money," the woman said quickly. "It's just beans and milk."

"I thought maybe we could pay you for a piece of whatever you've got baking in the oven, if you can spare it," Michael said shyly. "If not, that's okay. I want you to keep the money. We appreciate your kindness and generosity more than we could ever tell you."

Reluctantly, the woman opened the oven door and drew out a large pan of muffins. "They would of burnt in a few minutes," she said, avoiding looking at her husband. "I can give you each one." She loosened the muffins from the pan and deposited them in a small bag.

"To take with you," she said, pointedly.

Back on the road, their resolve to save the muffins for later was broken by the enticing odor emanating from the bag. "They're best when they're still warm," Michael said. Biting into the top of his muffin, he rolled his eyes and uttered a long drawn out 'Mmmmm,' sighing after he swallowed. "I don't know if these are good muffins or not, but right now they are the best I've ever eaten!"

Connor picked up a couple of crumbs that had fallen on his lap, then licked his fingers. "You better look for some ID," he told Michael. "The guy that stopped us told us the roadblock was around the middle of Kings County so we could come across it any time now.

Michael looked through his wallet. "I've got plenty of ID," he said. Drivers license, credit cards, bank card,..."

"Anything that gives your address in Annapolis Royal?"

"No. My driver's license isn't due for renewal until August. It still has my address in Halifax. Shit! My car insurance has my address in Annapolis on it, but it's back in Halifax in the glove compartment of my car!"

"If they don't let us through, we're shit out of luck!" Connor said grimly. "There's not enough gas left to get back to Halifax!"

"There's nothing to go back for anyway," Michael pointed out. "We'll just have to convince them to let us through. The pregnant wife and two little kids story has gotten us this far, and fed us too.

We'll just stick to that story and if there's any opposition, I'll become an actor the likes of which you've never seen!"

Connor slowed for the roadblock just a few kilometers west of Kentville. A stout, ruddy-faced man in a bright orange snowmobile suit peered in the side window at Connor then looked past him at Michael. He motioned Connor to roll down his window.

"I'm afraid you'll have to go back where you came from," he said, not unkindly. "We can't let anyone into the western end of the valley."

"Is there some kind of trouble there?" Connor asked innocently.

"No, and we want to keep it that way."

"I live in Annapolis Royal and I have to get back there," Michael explained, grabbing the steering wheel and leaning in front of Connor. "We got stuck in Halifax when the lights went out and it's taken us all this time to get out of there safely. I've got a pregnant wife and two little kids in Annapolis, and I've just got to get back to them!" he said, with a catch in his voice.

"Can you show me some ID?" the man asked.

Michael handed over his driver's license and credit cards, saying nothing.

"Your drivers license gives a Halifax address," the man said accusingly.

"The license doesn't expire until my birthday in august so it still shows my old address. I've lived in Annapolis a little over a year now." Michael gave the man his address and phone number. "Look," he pleaded, "I don't have any other identification on me. Isn't there some way you can check on this?...I know! I know! He said, suddenly excited. "A phone book! Look it up in a phone book!"

"Turn off your engine and give me the keys," the man instructed Connor. "This is going to take a few minutes and there's no need to waste gas."

Michael and Connor watched nervously as the man walked over to two other men bearing rifles. They saw him talking and gesticulating, showing the other men the piece of paper on which he had written Michael's name, address and phone number. One of the

234

other men took the paper and began trotting toward a house about a hundred yards from the road.

"I'm in the book," Michael said in a singsong falsetto. "I wanted an unlisted number but didn't want to pay the extra charge. Now I'm glad I'm so cheap, cheap, cheap!"

After what seemed an inordinate amount of time, they finally saw the man trotting back. "Either he can't read or he took a leak while he had the opportunity," Connor growled. It had grown cold in the Jeep with the engine off.

"We've verified that you live in Annapolis," the man said, looking across at Michael. Then he looked at Connor. "What about you?"

"He's the only wheels I've got," Michael explained. "My car was stolen in Halifax, but it never could have gotten through those roads anyway." Then inspiration struck him. "He lives in Halifax, sure. But he's family. He's my wife's brother, the only uncle my kids have and he's their designated guardian if anything happens to me, or my wife. Oh! And he's a pharmaceutical representative too. Show him your ID, Connor. He's got a whole box of samples back here of prescription drugs that might be needed," Michael said, leaning over the back seat and pulling sample boxes out of a large cardboard carton for the man to see. A favorable decision could plainly be seen on the man's face before he said a word.

"Got enough gas to get to Annapolis?" he asked solicitously.

"I'm not sure," Connor choked out, suddenly overcome with emotion when he realized they were both going to be allowed through. "I have another 10 gallons in the back there, in the cans."

"Open your gas tank. I'll put it in for you." When he had emptied the cans and returned them to the back of the Jeep, he reached in to shake hands with Connor, then Michael. "Take it out of 4-wheel drive," he instructed. "The roads are clear the rest of the way so you won't need it. Save on gas."

He handed Connor a business size card printed with the words **Valley Pass**, followed by a signature. "There's another roadblock at the Annapolis County line. Just hand them this pass and they'll let you through. God speed!" He nodded, motioning the armed men to move the barrier blocking the road.

They began to see the occasional vehicle on the road in Annapolis County, always either a small van or pickup truck. The drivers of these vehicles honked, saluted or waved at Connor and Michael in recognition of a camaraderie, or common purpose.

"This is amazing!" Connor exclaimed. "Look! There's a woman out walking a dog!" He waved and smiled, the woman returning the gesture. They passed a school, slowing down to watch a group of youngsters playing a game in the snow. They had tamped out a large circle, bisecting it with two crosses that divided the circle into four sections, with a large tamped down circle in the center. "We used to play that when I was a kid," Connor remarked. Can't remember what the game is called. I didn't know kids played that kind of game anymore! And look! There's another group playing a game I remember! It's called 'Red Rover' and the object is…"

He was distracted by a teacher coming out onto the steps, ringing an old-fashioned hand bell. "Wow!" he said. "It's like seeing things the way they were a hundred years ago, except for the cars. It's like everything is back to normal here, except we're in a whole different era. How did they manage to do this in just 10 days?"

Michael responded noncommittally, immersed in his own thoughts. He was half afraid to be coming back home. *'What if the kid said something! No, she wouldn't. She was too scared,'* Michael decided. But what if his being away for 10 days made her lose that fear? It would still be just her word against his. He had no prior record, there was no reason for anyone to suspect that he would ever do anything like abuse a little kid. It was those videos that got him all worked up. And she was there, available, with a face and skin so soft and beautiful it made him ache. She was the only one. No other little kid interested him, not even the pretty little blonde that sometimes came to play with Cassie. So he wasn't one of those, a pedophile, who could only get his kicks from little kids. But what if she told someone. What if…

"Look at that!" Connor exclaimed. They were driving through Bridgetown and there were people out and about everywhere, building snow families on front lawns, appearing to be having a great time. They all stopped what they were doing to smile and wave as Connor and Michael drove past.

"I'll be damned!" Connor said, grinning. He slowed down to get a better look. "They're putting clothes on the snowmen. Must be some kind of community contest or something. Want to stop and ask?"

"No!" Michael responded sharply. "No, we better keep moving. We have to get the Jeep unloaded and see about getting some food. Hope you can cook! I'm used to eating in restaurants all the time, and..."

"Something bothering you, Mike?" Connor asked, narrowing his eyes.

"Yes," Michael replied. "I'm going to greatly embarrass myself with what I'm about to tell you, but it has to be done. You will find out soon enough, anyway." Michael paused. "It's the beans. They've hit bottom and I can no longer control the inevitable. So, roll down your window and prepare for an onslaught of lethal gas!"

Connor threw his head back, laughing. "I can feel the stirrings myself," he chuckled. "We'll be playing a duet, probably all night long!"

About halfway between Bridgetown and Annapolis Royal they passed a farm on the right with a prominently displayed warning sign that said the property was protected by an electric fence. Both men looked up the long lane to the farmyard as they drove past. Less than a kilometer down the road there was another warning sign at the entry to another farm on the left.

"Looks like farmers down here want to keep everyone out," Connor commented. "They have food and they aren't about to share it!"

"Sure looks that way," Michael agreed. "Selfish bastards! Don't care about anyone else as long as they get theirs!"

Annapolis Royal had the same feel to it as Bridgetown, with people out walking and waving friendly greetings. As Connor pulled into Michael's driveway, he commented, "Looks pretty quiet here."

"Think I'll check on my tenants first thing," Michael said. He knocked on Richard's door, waited then knocked again. Getting no answer, he pulled a ring of keys out of his pocket and let himself in. It felt colder to Michael inside than it had outside, and he could sense that there had been no one there for some time. In the bedrooms, the beds were stripped and the closets and dresser drawers were empty. There was no food in the kitchen cupboards or the dark refrigerator. "I thought the electricity was back on," he muttered to himself. He flipped the light switch and the overhead light came on in the kitchen. "It *is* on," he said, flipping the switch again.

"Nobody here," he told Connor, coming out onto the porch and locking the door behind him. His own side of the house was as cold as the other side. Frowning, he checked his thermostat. It was in the 'off' position. Puzzled, Michael turned the dial to 70 degrees, and in a few seconds heard the tic-tic-tic sound of the baseboard heaters. His refrigerator was also dark, and checking behind it he saw it was unplugged.

"Somebody's been in here," he told Connor, ominously. He went into the room where he kept his computer and saw that it was unplugged too. So was the TV, stereo and all the lamps. "Shit!" Michael exclaimed. "I'll bet the damn waterbed is unplugged too! It'll take a week to thaw before I can use it!"

"Check to see what's unplugged in the living room, will you?" Michael asked Connor as he went into his bedroom. He plugged in the waterbed, groaning at the feel of the rock hard bed. Then he checked the bottom drawer of his bedside stand. The Bible was there, but the gun and the scarf that covered it were gone. Alarm spread through Michael making him momentarily light-headed. He nearly called out to Connor that his gun had been stolen before he remembered telling him he didn't have a gun.

"Let's unload the Jeep then go see about getting some food while this ice-box heats up," Michael said nervously, meeting Connor coming down the hallway.

"Sounds like a plan," Connor remarked. "You know, it's almost two o'clock. Took us seven hours to make what's usually a two hour trip!"

There were half a dozen pickups and a couple of vans in the grocery store parking lot. Connor pulled the Jeep in beside a pickup loaded with boxes that had names printed on the tops. The driver of the pickup gave them a curious look before driving away.

"Well now, that's the first unfriendly person we've seen in Annapolis County," Connor remarked. "No 'howdy neighbor' wave, no big fat grin plastered on his face, nothing! What's the world coming to!"

Everything looked different inside the store. Long tables were set up behind the usual checkout lanes, blocking access to the rest of the store. Behind the tables were clerks who were being handed lists they would check against a roster, and others who were putting food in labeled boxes then handing them over to customers.

When it was their turn, Michael explained his situation to a middle-aged woman he had seen before a number of times, but he couldn't remember where. Marilyn Marchant said she didn't exactly know how to handle the situation, but would get someone who did.

A man approached, looking puzzled. Michael recognized him. He was the guy who owned the convenience store near the edge of town. Smiling in recognition, Michael held out his hand.

Dow pretended not to see the extended hand. "Well, Michael Cooper, isn't it? Where did you come from?"

"Halifax. We got here about an hour ago and am I ever glad to be back! You wouldn't believe what it's like in the city."

"Have you been to your house yet?" Dow asked.

"Yes, we just unloaded the Jeep and turned on the heat. Say, you wouldn't know who might have been in my place, would you?"

"I know that someone had to go to every vacant house and make sure everything electrical was turned off before the power was turned back on," Dow said. "The amount of electricity being generated is limited so it has to be used only for essentials.

"How did anybody get in?"

"That I couldn't tell you. You have electric baseboard heat in your place, don't you?"

"That's right."

"Then I'm afraid you won't be able to stay there. Everyone with an electric heating system has had to move into a house with oil or wood heat. You can stay there tonight, but tomorrow you'll have to find another place."

"Is that what happened to my tenant, Richard Martin and his family?"

"I couldn't tell you. There was no one at all at your place the day after new years."

"Hmmm. I don't think they have any family around here. I believe they're from Dartmouth. Could be they went to stay with some relatives there. Anyway, they're sure not here!" Michael exclaimed, trying to keep the relief he felt out of his voice.

"I'm not sure what to do about groceries for you right now," Dow said, trying to sound apologetic. "We have everything pretty well planned out and there's nothing in reserve for any extra mouths that have to be fed."

"Hey, come on man!" Michael pleaded. "We're starving! There must be *something!*"

"I can give you a fish, an onion, a couple of potatoes and some milk. You can make yourselves some chowder."

"That's it?"

"For now, I'm afraid that's it. Tell you what, though. I'll be by your place later tonight with a couple other guys and we'll help you figure out where you're gonna go. You won't have to be worried about food after tonight."

CHAPTER TWENTY-ONE - JANUARY 10, 2005

"He's back!"

Dow had walked over to the greenhouse where he knew he'd find Matt to give him the news. "He's back, and he has a friend with him. They came looking for food and I told them they could stay at Cooper's house for now, but a committee would be there tonight to organize a move. Eight 0'clock okay? Pick me up on your way."

Matt nodded, grim-faced. "We'll be there. Everything we'll need is packed and ready."

"Is Nate in on this too?" Dow asked.

"No. I wasn't sure how he'd feel about what we plan to do, so he doesn't know anything about it."

"Probably just as well. The fewer people who know, the better. See you at eight."

"You're sure you still want to be a part of it, Dow?"

"Wouldn't miss it, Matt. Wouldn't miss it for the world!"

It took a long time for the house to warm up, but it was reasonably comfortable by the time Connor had the fish chowder ready.

"Need bread, something solid to go with it," Michael complained. "Lousy bastards. There was bread being loaded into all those boxes for everyone else, but was there any for us? No way!"

"They weren't expecting us," Connor pointed out. "We were probably lucky to get anything at all on such short notice. So just shut up and eat. It's not my idea of good chowder, but it sure hits the spot just the same."

"Better than beans, I guess," Michael admitted. "At least the chowder covers up some of the smell of second hand beans. It was beginning to smell like we were living in an outhouse!"

"This place stank when we got here! Stale cigarette butts everywhere and a bathroom so filthy a dog wouldn't take a piss in there!"

241

"Hey, that's what you get when there's no woman around to clean up the mess," Michael said blithely.

"Ever think about cleaning up after yourself?"

"Never happen!" Michael assured Connor. "Not for as long as I live!"

Richard stayed out of sight on the porch while Matt, Michael and Dow were let into Michael Cooper's side of the house. His hand enclosed the gun in his jacket pocket where it had been once before. Only this time it felt comfortable there. The canvas satchel with the things they would need, lay at his feet. Ten minutes, Matt had said. Give them ten minutes then come in the front door.

Connor and Michael Cooper took seats on the couch together, while Matt and Dow sat in chairs opposite them. Michael remained standing.

"Any of you men smoke?" Cooper asked. His question was answered with tacit denials. "Too bad. This is my last cigarette," he said, brandishing the pack and extracting the one remaining cigarette. "When this one is gone, I won't be fit to live with!"

"What's that smell in here?" Dow asked, wrinkling his nose. "Smells like something died in here!"

"Whoever broke into my house used the bathroom and didn't flush," Michael lied. "I hope none of you have to use the facilities. It's still too cold in here to air it out."

Connor looked at Michael in amazement. The lies rolled off that man's tongue as slick as snot off a greased palm!

"I'm going to get right to the point, Cooper," Matt said. "You aren't going to be able to stay here."

"I already know that. On account of the electricity."

"No, on account of we don't want any rapists here, especially not child rapists."

"What are you talking about?" Michael Cooper and Connor both asked at once, after a moment of stunned silence.

Matt addressed Connor. "Your friend here raped a five year old kid."

"That's a bald-faced lie!" Cooper yelled, standing up abruptly.

"Sit down!" Dow ordered, to which Cooper complied sullenly.

"Five times he raped that little kid," Matt continued. "Five times."

"She's lying!" Cooper whined, before he had realized his mistake.

"She? Who said anything about a she?" Matt asked. "If you didn't do it, how do you know we're talking about raping a little girl?"

"I assumed you were talking about a girl," Cooper said nervously. "I mean, it wouldn't be a boy that was raped, right. Boys aren't raped, are they? Just girls!" He looked at Connor for corroboration.

"Who was raped?" Connor asked Matt, softly.

"The five year old daughter of Cooper's tenant," Matt replied.

"Cassie?" Cooper yelped. "Cassie was raped and said I did it? That's preposterous! I wouldn't rape any little kid, let alone a *black* kid!"

"You held a gun to her head while you raped her, and told her you would kill her parents and little brother if she ever told."

"I don't have a gun!" Cooper exclaimed. "If somebody raped Cassie and held a gun to her head, it couldn't have been me! I don't know why she would say it was!"

"Because it's the truth," Richard said, walking in through the front door.

Cooper blanched when he saw Richard; his reaction noted by Connor and the other three men.

"Richard, so help me God, I never laid a hand on Cassie! Look, if she was even raped at all, wouldn't you or Doreen have noticed? I mean, wouldn't she have been torn and bleeding or something? A little kid like that? You couldn't have missed seeing that if she had actually been raped! Kids make things up all the time, you know that!"

"They can't make up something they don't even know is possible," Matt said calmly. "And Cassie says you washed her off afterward then you used something that looked like a white crayon on

243

her to stop the bleeding. She says it stung like a bee. Must have been that styptic pencil in the top drawer of your nightstand."

"And this was in the bottom drawer," Richard said, removing the gun from his pocket. "Underneath a scarf and a Gideon Bible!"

"I've never seen that gun before!" Cooper protested. "Are you trying to frame me for some reason, Richard? Sure you didn't rape your own kid, if she was even raped at all?"

Richard's nostrils dilated from anger and a tic played around his left cheekbone. "You son of a bitch!" he growled between clenched teeth. "You're going to pay for what you did to Cassie. But not with this," he said, gesturing with the gun. "Unless I decide to shove it up your ass and pull the trigger!"

"Did you say there's a Gideon Bible?" Connor asked, a faraway look in his eyes. "Mind if I take a look at it?"

"I'll get it," Dow said, a puzzled look on his face.

"Leave my Bible alone!" Cooper said in a panic "That's private, personal property and you have no right to touch it!"

"Why do you want to see the Bible?" Matt asked Connor, as Dow brought it out of the bedroom and handed it to him.

"I just remembered that once when Mike had a real snoot full he told me he wrote the names of all his conquests in the margins of the Book of Job. In a Gideon Bible he stole from a Holiday Inn. This is probably the one."

All eyes were on Connor as he thumbed through the book looking for the right section. He found it and began turning the pages, reading the inscriptions in the margins written in Michael Coopers neat penmanship. He turned a page and all of a sudden there it was; 'Cassie Martin' my sweet taste of chocolate. Her name was repeated four more times, each successive descriptive phrase more lewd and suggestive.

Connor had not read the names aloud. A black rage was boiling inside him as he closed the Bible over his left index finger. He turned to face Cooper who was nervously running his hand through his hair and over his face, eyes frantically searching for the lie that would be his escape.

"Stupid, Mike. Really stupid," Connor said past the gorge he felt rising in his throat. Before he could stop himself, his right fist

244

hammered full force into Michael Cooper's soft belly. "Do whatever you want to him," Connor said, looking up at Richard. "Whatever you do, he's got it coming. I've got two little girls of my own; four and seven." He knew no further explanation was necessary.

Michael Cooper still had his arms wrapped around his middle trying to stifle the pain when Michael and Dow each grabbed him by an arm and dragged him, howling, into his bedroom. They tossed him unceremoniously onto his still frozen bed while he begged forgiveness, vowing never to harm another child.

"Of course you'll never harm another child," Matt said calmly. "We're going to see to it that you'll never be able to. You caused Cassie a whole lot of pain and fear, and took something from her that she can never have back. Now *you* are going to experience the same thing, and you are going to lose something that you can never have back. The punishment is going to fit the crime."

As Michael and Dow used lengths of rope to tie his wrists securely to the headboard of the bed, Michael warned him that the knots were the kind that would tighten if he struggled. They tied the same kind of knots around his ankles, spreading his legs apart and tying his feet to the footboard. All the while, Richard held the gun pointed at Cooper's nose.

Michael Cooper became hysterical, alternately whooping and wailing, bucking and straining.

"Put a sock in it!" Dow shouted.

"Do something, Connor!" Cooper pleaded.

"Sure thing!" Connor said, as he pulled off one of Cooper's socks and forcefully shoved it in his mouth. "I'll put a sock in it for you!"

Matt unbuckled Cooper's belt and freed it from the loops. Then he unbuttoned his jeans and pulled them down along with Cooper's underwear as far as they would go. Exposed now, Cooper screamed as loud as he could through the sock in his mouth.

"You think I'm going to cut off your penis?" Matt asked solicitously. "I'm not going to do that, so don't be such a big baby. I'll bet little Cassie was a lot braver than you are."

Cooper relaxed slightly, until Matt added, "You're just going to be castrated, that's all. And you're even going to get to choose the method. But first," he said, tearing a strip off a roll of duct tape, "we have to get that troublesome penis out of the way."

He slipped the tape, sticky side up, under Cooper's penis, then bent it back over his lower belly and taped it firmly in place. "That's so, if we scare the piss out of you, no one but you will be in the line of fire," Matt said.

Reaching into the canvas bag at the foot of the bed, he pulled out what resembled a short handled set of blacksmith tongs or thick wire cutters. "This little baby is appropriately called an emasculator," Matt intoned, sounding as though he was delivering a lecture to veterinarian students. "It crushes the cord to the testicles, one at a time, and has to be held in place for a couple of minutes on each side to make sure the job is done right. Of course we'd have to be careful not to get it placed too high because we could crush the urethra as well and then you'd never pee again. The urine would build up in your bladder until it burst and then you'd die of uremic poisoning. Not a nice way to go. But if it gets placed too low, it could pinch a chunk of the testicle and I bet that would hurt like a bitch! I know how to use one of these on a little bull calf, and generally they just keep right on nursing their mamas and don't even know anything happened. Not much feeling there yet, probably. But I've never used one on a grown man before, so I could easily make a mistake." Matt paused. "What are you sweating for, Cooper? It's not hot in here at all! Imagine that," he said, grinning at the other men. "Laying on a bed of ice, sweating!"

Cooper made mewling sounds in the back of his throat as tears coursed down the sides of his face.

"He sounds just like Cassie did, telling me what this scum bastard did to her," Michael observed.

"Come on! Buck up, Cooper," Dow urged. "Be a man! After all, you aren't going to get to be one much longer!"

Matt drew a surgical scalpel out of the bag. "Now this has the advantage of being quick," he said, "but it's awfully bloody. First you slit the sac, then pull out the testicles one at a time and cut through the cords. It has to be cauterized though or you'd bleed to

246

death. I don't think a styptic pencil would do the trick, so I brought this along to cauterize you, in case this is the castration method you choose," Matt said, hauling a propane torch out of the bag.

It was plain to see that Cooper was almost delirious with fear and was having difficulty breathing.

"Better take the sock out of his mouth," Matt said. "His nose is so full of snot from bawling that he can't breathe."

Cooper gasped, taking deep breaths when the sock was pulled out of his mouth, and immediately began railing at his persecutors. "You'll never get away with this! There are laws against what you are planning to do and I'll see to it that you all pay for this!"

"There are laws against raping little girls and threatening to kill their families, but that didn't seem to deter you!" Matt pointed out. "And we aren't deterred by the law either!"

"You'll pay for this!" Cooper screamed.

"Do we have to put the sock back in your mouth so you can choke to death on your own snot or are you going to shut up and pay attention?" Matt asked. "The choice is yours."

Cooper shut his mouth tightly as Dow brandished the sock in front of his face.

"That's better," Matt said. "Now, this little number is called an elastrator." He held up a strange looking object that appeared to be a miniature dog –catcher's noose attached to a pistol grip with a ratchet device. "This elastic noose is pulled up over the testicles and is pulled tight around the neck of the scrotum with the ratchet, cutting off the blood supply. Then the trigger is pulled, and the ends of the elastic are clamped together. Your balls will ache for a while, then they'll get numb so you won't feel it as your testicles shrink and atrophy."

"How long does that take?" Cooper croaked in a hoarse whisper.

"Oh, a month, maybe two."

"How will you stop me from taking it off? Keep me tied to this bed for two months?"

"Oh no. As soon as we're finished with you, one of us will drive you out of the county and deposit you at the hospital in Kentville. Someone there will take the elastic off, but when they do you'll wish it were back on again. Because when the blood starts flowing again, your balls are going to swell and throb, and you'll swear someone is beating them with a baseball bat. They may give you morphine though, so you might not have to suffer too long."

"Don't you think you've made me suffer enough already?" Cooper sobbed.

"Good lord no!" Matt exclaimed. "You haven't felt so much as a pin stick yet, and whichever way you choose to be castrated is only going to be done once. Cassie had to go through her ordeal five times! You're getting off easy."

"Easy? This mental torture and anticipation of agony you're putting me through is easy?"

"You've had less than half an hour of it. How does that even begin to compare with five months of the same kind of terror for a five- year old child? Huh? If I could stomach it, I'd make you endure it for as long as she had to! You aren't sorry for what you did to that baby, you're only sorry about what's going to be done to you. And that makes you the sorriest piece of shit that ever existed! Now let's get on with it. Do you choose door # 1, door # 2 or door # 3? You have 30 seconds to decide," Matt said, checking his watch. "After that, Richard gets to make the choice. Twenty seconds...Fifteen seconds...Ten seconds...Five..."

"The elastic thing!" Cooper sobbed pathetically.

"Good choice. Richard gets to do the honors and that will be the easiest for him since he has absolutely no experience with castrations."

"What do you mean, Richard? I thought you were going to do it. You know how, I want *you* to do it!" Cooper pleaded.

"Well, you're not exactly in any bargaining position. Besides, I promised Richard he could be the one. It's his little girl you abused so it's his right. Don't worry; I'll coach him through it."

Cooper watched apprehensively as Matt instructed Richard on the correct operation of the elastrator. "I think I've got it," Richard finally said. "But do you have any rubber gloves in that bag?" Matt produced a couple of long plastic gloves that covered Richard's arms up to his shoulders. "Good," he said. "I don't want to come in contact with any part of this slime bag. I get sick to my stomach every time I think about what he did to my baby and that his rotten

248

body actually invaded hers. I get really worked up thinking about that!"

Cooper sobbed shakily when he felt Richard's gloved hand grasp his scrotum and slip the elastic loop up to where it connected to his groin. The look of contemptuous distaste on Richard's face was almost as frightening as what he was about to do. Richard worked the ratchet, tightening the elastic millimeter by millimeter until Cooper screamed, "It's tight! It's tight! Oh God it pinches!"

"A little tighter yet," Matt said to Richard. "It has to be tight enough to cut off all blood flow!"

"Aaiiiiiiiiii!" Cooper screeched in a girlish falsetto. "Stop please. It's tight!"

"You are such a baby," Matt said, disgusted. "There isn't even any tension on that elastic yet! Just keep going Richard until I tell you to stop."

"Oh god it hurts!" Cooper wailed as the elastic was finally clamped off.

"Not for long," Matt assured him. "It will start to go numb quickly."

Dow chuckled. "I've always wanted to call someone 'numb nuts' and have it be true. Now I can!"

"Well, let's get you put back together now," Matt said. "Lift your butt so I can haul on your drawers. Whoops, almost forgot," he said, tearing off the duct tape and innumerable pubic hairs along with it. Cooper's bellow of rage filled the room, but was nearly drowned out by the laughter of the five men who had witnessed his humiliating emasculation.

"You'll have to stay tied up there until we get the Jeep loaded with your stuff," Matt told Cooper. "Then you and your friend are going on a one way trip."

"We'll get your gas tank filled," Dow told Connor, as he helped him load the ham radio back in the Cherokee. "Then you will have an escort up to the roadblock in Kings County. We'll be waiting for you when you make the return trip and will make arrangements for you to stay someplace."

"I can't tell you how much I appreciate this," Connor said humbly. "I suppose I always knew, deep down, that Mike was a pretty unsavory character, but, well,...we worked for the same company and saw quite a lot of one another. I can't help feeling a little guilty though for having been his friend." He sighed heavily. "I still can't believe he did what I know he did, or that he is what I now know he is. The old brain wants to reject it all, because it's just too much to take."

Dow grasped Connor's shoulder, squeezing it. "I know," he said softly. "I know."

"Matt knew Mike would choose the elastrator, didn't he?" It was more a statement than a question. "It's too bad he isn't really castrated. The other ways would have been permanent and that's what he deserves. But this way…"

"There was never any intent to really castrate him," Dow explained "We just wanted to scare the hell out of him with a big production, humiliate him and make him hurt a little bit too in the process. He's not really going to be in enough pain to require morphine when that elastic is cut off. We just want him to *think* he will be. And no permanent damage will be done in only a couple of hours, but Matt wants him to think he may never be functional again."

"Too bad," Connor said. "I think I would have preferred to see him castrated for real…I almost left my two little girls in his care once, but something nagged at the back of my mind about doing that, and I hired a woman to baby-sit instead. That turned out to be one of the good decisions I made in life, I guess. Believe me, I've made more than my share of bad ones!"

"Maybe you're about to embark on another good decision," Dow commented.

"Maybe I am," Connor said seriously, a faraway look of contemplation in his eyes. "Maybe I am, at that!"

Connor glanced over at Michael in the passenger seat. He was sitting on his spine, legs extended, rubbing his hand back and forth between his legs, moaning. "I can't feel my balls, Connor," Michael whined. "It's like they're dead!"

Connor chose his words carefully. "The sooner the elastic comes off the better. I was told you wouldn't need any painkillers and you don't actually have to go to a hospital either. You aren't even really castrated. They just wanted to scare you and make you hurt a little bit."

"You're not shittin' me, are ya man? Michael asked hopefully. "Matt said..."

"I know what Matt said. I was there. But while we were loading everything back in the Jeep, Dow told me the whole thing was designed to scare the shit out of you. And it worked! They scared the shit out of me too! I...punched you in the gut because I was so pissed off at you...and you know what a temper I have. But what they did after that was a bit much."

"There's the last roadblock just ahead," Michael said. He looked in the side mirror. "They're still behind us."

"How much you bet they stop following us after this last roadblock?" Connor asked.

"I hadn't thought about it, but that's probably a good bet," Michael said. "They wouldn't have any reason to escort us any further, would they."

In the rear view mirror, they saw Matt's car grow smaller and smaller after they passed through the roadblock. "Looks like we're on our own now," Connor said. "As soon as I'm sure we're completely out of their sight I'm going to pull over somewhere and cut that damn thing off of you. According to Dow, the sooner you get it off the better."

"The hospital's not that far."

"It's a good fifteen or twenty minutes if the roads are clear. And they might not be. It could take another hour or more to get there. You really think you should take that risk?"

Michael hesitated. "You're probably right. I wasn't exactly looking forward to explaining this rubber band to anyone, anyway. You got something you could cut it with?"

"I've got a pack of single edge blades in my toiletry bag. And there's the lantern in back there so I can see what I'm doing. Connor hesitated as though he were deep in thought, then looked at Michael, shaking his head. "I don't know Mike. I'm beginning to have second

251

thoughts about this. I know you need to get that thing off as soon as possible, but what if the blade won't do the job, or…"

"Aw come on Cooper! I need to have you do this for me! There's nothing sharper than a razor blade and that lantern will give you plenty of light to see. You gotta do this for me!"

"You're sure you want me to?"

"I'm sure."

"Okay then." Connor hesitated as he smiled to himself in the dark interior of the Jeep. "I'll do it."

Connor pulled off onto a side road, that the wind had swept reasonably clear of snow. He drove a short distance up the road then turned the Jeep around so it was facing the highway, and turned off the engine.

"We're going to have to do this outside, unfortunately," Connor said. "There's no way for you to stretch out in here. "I'll get a blanket and the lantern,…and the razor blades."

Spreading the blanket out in the middle of the road behind the Jeep, he told Michael to drop his pants and lay down on the blanket. "Hold your dick up out of the way," he barked, shining the powerful lantern on the target area. "Ready?" he asked.

"Do it! Just get it off!"

"Connor ran the blade lightly over the thick elastic cord then increased the pressure, slicing deeply into Michael's testicle. Michael didn't even flinch. *'Numb nuts,'* Connor thought, grinning. *'They really are!'* He sliced through the elastic and it split apart with a loud 'pop' that startled both of them.

"Oh shit," Connor said. "I think I nicked you when that thing popped open. Don't move. I've got a first-aid kit with some bandages under the front seat." He got in the Jeep, started the engine and drove off slowly, looking back in the rear-view mirror at what he had left behind.

He saw Michael sitting upright on the blanket with an arm outstretched toward the Jeep. The lantern clearly highlighted the slick shine of blood flowing from the deep gash he had made. He thought he heard a scream, but wasn't sure. He wondered briefly what was running through Michael's mind then dismissed it as irrelevant.

"Nobody's going to miss you, Mike," he said. "Nobody's going to care."

He turned west, back toward Annapolis Royal, thinking he had just been through the longest day in his life.

CHAPTER TWENTY-TWO - JANUARY 11, 2005

The sound of someone banging around in the kitchen woke Connor. *'Cripes,'* he thought, opening his eyes in the nearly dark room. *'What time is it anyway!'*

He saw that the fireplace could use another log. The flimsy camp cot he had slept on creaked in protest as he unzipped the sleeping bag and crawled out to stoke the fire. A fine shower of sparks flew up the chimney and onto the hearth when he dropped a log onto the grate, one landing on top of his bare foot. He brushed it off with a hissing intake of breath then spit on the tips of two fingers, bent over, and massaged the spit onto his foot.

The unmistakable odor of coffee brewing reached his nostrils, instantly wiping out his desire to crawl back into the sleeping bag. *'Coffee,'* he thought, slipping into the jeans and shirt he had taken off the night before and hung over the back of a chair. *'How long has it been since I've had a cup of coffee?'* Eagerly anticipating a mug of the steaming hot brew, he hopped into his heavy winter socks then opened the door to the kitchen.

Matt was finishing the last bite of his slice of bread and butter when Connor walked through the door. He paused before greeting Connor to give the patiently waiting Buddy a piece of crust he had broken off, along with a loving pat.

"Morning!" Matt said. "We don't stand on ceremony around here; everybody helps themselves. Coffee mugs are in the cupboard to the right of the sink, milk in the fridge."

"Thanks," Connor said, once he was seated at the table with the coffee in front of him. He gave Matt a level look. "Thanks for everything."

"Roads pretty clear last night up to Kentville?" Matt asked, noncommittally.

"Uh…yeah, I guess," Connor hedged.

"Hmmm. You didn't have time to go all the way to Kentville and back in the amount of time you were gone. So what did you do with Cooper?" Matt asked, looking Connor in the eye.

Connor quickly decided to be truthful, up to a point. "I left him a little way up a side road. But I cut the elastic off him first, and left him with a blanket and a lantern." Connor nervously plucked at the lacy edge of a doily in the center of the table, taking a sip of coffee to allow himself time to think. *'The whole truth? Do I dare?'*

"Did you leave him with anything else by any chance?"

Connor studied the oily looking dark liquid in the mug in front of him. "Yes." His voice was barely audible as he told Matt how he had cut deeply into Mike's scrotum with the razor blade then left him bleeding profusely. "I left him with what could be a mortal wound, but I didn't wait around to see. You'll probably want me to leave as soon as possible, and I will. I know you didn't plan on Mike dying."

Matt got up from the table, pushed his chair in then leaned his arms over the back of it, studying Connor.

"I wanted him dead. But I knew I couldn't be the one to do it. You were used, Connor. I used you. *We* used you. We all wanted that bastard dead. If you had taken him up to Kentville you would have disappointed all of us." Matt paused, looking around at all the familiar things in the kitchen before continuing. "Disappointed,...that's not a strong enough word for what we would have felt. It's easier to describe how we felt when we *knew* you had done something to him because you got back too soon. Satisfied. That's a soft word too, but it's the right word. You satisfied us. We were satisfied that he would never hurt another child, we were satisfied that it was over, we were satisfied with the justice of it."

Connor stared at Matt as the substance of what he was being told sank in. He was waiting for the expected fury to rise inside him, blinding him to everything but a necessary physical release. He has been *used!* Used as the means to someone else's end! But for some reason he couldn't fathom, there was no feeling of outrage, only a feeling of relief and...sadness, as he recognized his gullibility.

"We don't want you to leave," Matt said sincerely. "If you hadn't taken care of Cooper we wouldn't have been able to trust you, and we wouldn't want you here. That may sound like a strange way to think, but there's a simple logic behind it. You see, basically good people have no tolerance for basically evil people. The bleeding hearts in this world who would condemn you, me, and all the rest of us, for what we did to a basically evil man, like to think of themselves as good people; but they aren't. They aren't at all. They perpetuate evil by championing the cause of evil - doers, at the expense of all the good people in the world. Human rights they call it; as though the victims of evil people are something less than human. Do you understand what I'm trying to say Connor? You're a stronger man, morally, than I am. You had the guts to do the right thing. "It's a better, safer world without a Michael Cooper in it."

Connor didn't know if he wholly agreed with Matt, but had to admit he didn't feel the slightest bit of remorse. Maybe in this case, he decided, the role of avenger suited him, but he hoped he would never have to play that role again.

"I'll stay," he said quietly. "Gladly. I have no where else to go."

When Matt went out to the barn, Connor poured himself another cup of coffee, relishing some quiet time to himself. It didn't last long. He heard someone coming down the stairs, and a small, matronly woman in a faded robe, with her hair piled in an untidy mess on the top of her head came into the kitchen. "Morning," she said, barely glancing at him as she reached bleary-eyed for a mug in the cupboard and poured it full of coffee. Without another word, she exited out the kitchen door into the cold entry room.

Richard was next down the stairs, greeting Connor cheerily, pouring himself coffee and refilling Connor's cup. "Better make a fresh pot," he said as he emptied the pot into two fresh mugs and set them on the table. "Everyone will be in here in a few minutes looking for coffee and breakfast," he chuckled.

Connor watched Richard with interest. He certainly seemed to know his way around a kitchen, Connor thought, simultaneously cooking a huge pot of oatmeal, beating a bowl of eggs with a whisk, slicing bread and tossing together sandwiches. "You feeding an army here?" he asked.

"Just about!" Richard laughed. "I like to get in here early and get all the lunches made for school while breakfast is cooking. There's fourteen of us here today, counting you, and ten of us head out for school every day now. Except for Mickey. He's my 3 year old and he just goes every other day."

"Ten people here go to school?"

"Yup! Everybody but Ruth, that's Matt's wife, Michael, and my wife, Doreen. They stay here and take care of the place, all the animals you know, and bake the bread and fix the supper. There are five kids," he said, pouring out glasses of apple juice, "and five adults who teach classes. You'll be meeting everyone soon. Breakfast time can be a real zoo around here. You'll be glad when we're all gone!"

The woman with the tousled hair came back in from the entry room, deposited her empty cup on the counter and patted Richard on the back on her way past. A sweet- faced little girl with long, dark hair came into the kitchen almost on the woman's heels, looked curiously at Connor then smiled shyly. Richard handed her a coffee mug, which she filled from the pot on the stove, and she too disappeared into the next room.

"Isn't she a little young for coffee?" Connor asked.

"Oh, she's taking that into the living room for old Nate Taylor," Richard replied as he stirred the oatmeal on the stove.

Next into the kitchen were two blond youngsters, a boy and a girl, followed by a very attractive, petite woman around his own age, Connor thought, and a tall slender man a few years older. Richard introduced Connor to everyone, but just as they were about to question him as to who he was and what he was doing there, the kitchen was invaded by a noisily babbling toddler, a little girl and a very pregnant woman. These last three were obviously Richard's family, Connor surmised, and the little girl was the reason for all that had happened the night before.

Connor studied her surreptitiously, and what he saw was a fine-boned, delicate, Dresden-doll of a child. Her complexion was like the golden tan of someone who had just spent the winter on a Florida beach, her eyes a deep mahogany flecked with gold. Seeing this little girl, Connor knew beyond a doubt that getting rid of Michael Cooper was the best thing he had ever done in his life!

The woman in the robe with the tousled hair came back in the kitchen dressed in fleece pants and shirt, with her hair neatly secured in a bun at the back of her head. She poured herself another cup of coffee, smiling at, and greeting, all the children then sat down at the table across from Connor. Richard ladled oatmeal into bowls, passing them around to everyone. When he handed a bowl to the little girl with the long dark hair, she morosely took a seat next to the older woman, saying, "I'm not very hungry this morning."

He watched the woman gently take hold of the little girl's jaw, turning the child's head to face her.

"What's the matter, Lindy?" she asked.

The child's eyes filled with tears. "Grandpa Nate says he's going to be leaving."

"Leaving? What do you mean? Where's he going?"

"He's going to move in with Mrs. Henderson."

"But why? He *hates* Bea Henderson!"

The little girl shrugged. "I don't know."

"He'll be miserable living there with her!"

"No I won't," a tall, elderly man said as he walked into the kitchen.

"Nate, what's this all about? Are you unhappy living here? Have we…"

"Being here has been one of the happiest times of my life! But I realize something now that I've been trying to ignore for years…Have you ever heard the expression 'he protesteth too much?' Well, that's me. I've been denying my feelings for Bea most of my life because I always felt she was beyond my reach. I'm uneducated, never went beyond the eighth grade, and I never felt I was good enough for someone like Bea. So I talked myself into the idea that I couldn't stand her. That's not the truth, though. She was a beautiful, wealthy girl twelve years my junior that I didn't think I could ever make happy. But I'm going to give myself the chance now, while I still can. Because I know for sure she wants me too. Now, I know for sure."

The little girl sprang out of her chair and wrapped her arms around the old man's waist. "I want you to be happy," she said, "but I don't want you to go. I'll miss seeing you."

"We'll have two hours together every afternoon," the man said, "because all you kids are coming over to Bea's after school. She has some kind of project cooked up, and you kids are all part of it."

"I know what it is, too!" the blonde girl chimed in. "But I can't tell."

With the focus now off the elderly man, the woman in the fleece set asked Connor to join her in the dining room while everyone else finished breakfast and got on their way.

Ruth closed the dining room door behind her, motioning Connor to take a seat at the table. She sat down next to him, extending her hand. "I'm Ruth," she said, "Matt's wife. And you are?"

"Connor Putnam," Connor said, shaking Ruth's hand.

"That's not a name I recall hearing before. I was out in the barn delivering a calf when everyone got back last night. You were asleep, and so was everyone else when I finally got in. Ruth looked closely at Connor, taking his measure. "You must have been a part of whatever took place last night, otherwise you wouldn't be here. I'd appreciate hearing about it."

"Uh," Connor hedged, glancing around nervously and wondering how much he should say or even if he should say anything at all. There was a tapping on the door and Ruth went to open it, saving Connor for the moment. Matt came in with a plate of scrambled eggs in one hand and a mug of coffee in the other.

"You can tell her the whole thing," Matt said without preamble. "But wait until everyone is gone so you can tell Doreen and Michael at the same time. That way you'll only have to tell it once. Ted, Rachel, the kids and Nate don't know anything and there's no reason for them to know. Except it might be good for Cassie to know that man has gone away and will never be able to hurt her again."

There was another tap on the door. Nate stuck his head through, apologizing for the intrusion. "You about ready to go, Matt? My things are all packed and Ted put them in the back of the pickup."

"You're leaving right now?" Ruth asked, surprised. "What's the rush?"

"It's no quicker than I moved in!" Nate chuckled. "But I wanted to say good-bye, and thank you for everything. Except, I find I don't know any adequate words of thanks."

"Then don't try to find any," Ruth said, going over to Nate and wrapping her arms around him. "We have as much to thank you for, and I know what you mean about words being inadequate." She stood on her toes to kiss him on the cheek. "You always have a home here if you need it."

"I know," he said almost reverently. "And it feels awfully good to know that."

Connor was introduced to the business end of a manure fork when he went out to the barn with Ruth. She fed the cattle while he cleaned out the calving pens. He was struck with how natural and familiar the work felt to him although he knew for certain he had never done anything even remotely like it before. When he had finished, he went to the back door of the barn and looked out.

Michael was on a small tractor, scooping up manure and depositing it on a concrete pad at the side of a huge enclosure that resembled a fortress. Cattle were lined up, side by side, around a large bunker of hay, grabbing huge mouthfuls and barely chewing before swallowing and reaching for more. Struck by the serenity of the barnyard, Conner felt an ache inside him that he couldn't find a name for. He felt he could have stayed there with those animals all day if he had been asked to. Reluctantly, he went back to the house when the chores were finished.

"You can't be absolutely certain he's dead, can you?" Doreen asked fearfully.

"No," Connor admitted. "Not one hundred percent, anyway."

"Then we're going to find out!" Michael exclaimed, abruptly getting up from the kitchen table. "I hate to waste another precious drop of gas on Cooper, but for everyone's peace of mind we have to know. You're coming with me, Connor," he stated in a way that let Connor know there was no room for argument. "We'll get that radio of yours unloaded and take your Jeep. There has to be an end to this."

260

"Almost a dozen cars trying to get through here so far today," the man at the roadblock said. "There's going to be trouble soon. Big trouble. I can almost smell it."

"We figured there would be, sooner or later," Michael told him. "There's a ham radio at our place now, thanks to Connor here, so you can let us know if anyone who doesn't belong here gets through. Whatever you do, don't try a standoff. Keeping people out of Annapolis County isn't worth anyone getting killed."

"So far, we've been able to get people to go back the way they came. There haven't been any kids in the cars that have tried to get through, fortunately. I'm not sure what I'd do if there were."

"You'd let them through and we'd find some way to feed them and keep them warm," Michael said. "And then we'd pray that there's someone watching who knows how to multiply loaves and fishes."

"Amen to that!" the man said.

"We have a little unfinished business up the road a way, but don't expect to be long," Michael added.

"I'll still be here another two hours. If you take longer than that I'll leave your names and license number with my relief and tell him to let you back through." He wrote down the information in a notebook, and waved Michael and Connor through.

"It looks different in the daylight," Connor complained. "This could be the road, but I'm not sure...No, it curves a little way in; the road I went up was straight." He picked up speed then slowed every time he approached a side road. "I don't know," he said, becoming frustrated. "Maybe I should turn up every side road and go about a mile in to be sure. I don't think I went that far, so a mile should do it."

The next side road went off at an angle and there were no tire tracks. "No use wasting time on this one," Connor said. "The road was at right angles to this one." The very next crossroad was the right one. "This is it!" Connor said excitedly. "The center of the road is windswept and look, there are the tire tracks!" He turned right onto the road, squinting into the distance. "I left him right in the middle of the road on a dark gray blanket," Connor said. "We should be able to see it."

They could see a dark mass in the center of the road a few hundred yards away. It seemed to be moving and they watched it disperse at the approach of the vehicle. "Crows," Michael said. "Let's see what they were after."

Frozen blood blanketed the remnants of snow, surrounded by bloody bird tracks. "This is where I left him alright. What could have happened to him?"

"I don't see any car tracks other than the Jeep's," Michael said. "Look, you can see where you turned the Jeep around, and no car has been past that pool of blood." He looked around him, back down the side road toward the highway then began turning counter-clockwise, scanning the desolate winter landscape that would become a fragrant hayfield in the summer. Farther down the road there was a thick stand of trees on the right, and to the left, the trees thinned. A small white house was set back on a slight rise, nearly invisible in its blanket of snow.

"He would have headed for that house down there," Michael said with certainty. He had to leave some tracks. I'll look for them, and you follow in the Jeep. We'll find him; dead or alive."

Cooper must have walked where the asphalt was clear, Michael decided, because he had gone about 50 yards before he saw a partial boot-print. He was puzzled by the lack of blood anywhere, especially since there had been so much of it in the middle of the road back there. If Cooper had been cut as deeply as Connor said, there should be evidence of blood all along the road.

At the driveway to the little house, boot-prints could be clearly seen. The snow was over a foot deep in places, and the tracks looked as though Cooper was almost dragging his left foot. Michael motioned Connor to leave the Jeep in the middle of the road, and join him there in the driveway.

"No sign of blood anywhere," Michael said. "But there was a lot where you left him in the road. It doesn't add up."

"He should have bled to death in a very short time. I can't explain why we aren't seeing any trace of blood!"

The front door of the house opened before the two men had left the driveway to follow Cooper's trail to the front stoop.

"Go away!" a frightened sounding female voice shrilled. "I don't need any more crazies coming around here!"

An overweight teenaged boy joined his obese mother, a rifle pointing at Michael's chest. "You heard! Get out of here!"

"We're looking for someone," Michael said. "His tracks lead right to your front door. The man is a criminal, and he could be dangerous."

The woman and her son looked at one another, and she nodded her permission for him to talk. "He ain't dangerous no more," the boy said. "He's dead. Bled to death, looks like."

"All over my bathroom, he did," the woman added with disgust. "I ain't even got it all cleaned up yet."

"Bled to death?" Connor asked. "We followed his tracks here; there was no blood."

"Look, we didn't do nothing to him, mister!" the boy said, alarmed. "There was blood all over a blanket he had wrapped around hisself when he come here, but we didn't see where he was bleedin' from."

"You let him in. What did he say to you?"

"Said a feller stole his car. He was tryin' to get down to Annapolis to his wife and kids an' this feller stabbed him an' stole his car. Said could he come in an' see how bad he was hurt."

"I don't think he was hurt a'tall," the woman interjected. "We thought maybe his foot was hurt 'cuz he kinda dragged it and there wasn't no lace in his boot. We figgered he undid it you know, 'cuz his foot was all swole or sumpthin'. But there wasn't nothin' wrong with his foot far as we could see!"

"You say he bled to death," Michael said. "How, if he wasn't bleeding when he got here?"

"He sliced his wrists open!" the woman exclaimed. "He come in here an' used our house to kill hisself with a razor blade! He was in the bathroom bawlin' an' carryin' on! Couldn't make out what he was babblin' on about. He had the door locked, an' after it got all quiet in there we got the door open an' he was layin' there dead, blood all over!"

Carol Kern

Michael studied the ground at his feet then looked back up at the woman and her son. "He didn't have a wife and kids in Annapolis, or anywhere else. He was run out of Annapolis last night for raping a little girl, and we wanted to make sure he had gotten far enough away."

"He was a rapist?" the woman asked, clutching her sweater tightly across her enormous breasts. "Do you think he kilt hisself 'cuz he couldn't live with what he done?"

"I guess we'll never know that for sure. Let us get him out of there for you," Michael offered.

"Already done," the boy said. "When I got the bathroom door open, he was layin' there dead with a bright lantern on. At first light, me an' mum got him out a there an' drug him way out back to the woodlot. Can't bury him with the ground froze, so we jist covered him with snow an' dead branches."

Michael nodded. "Maybe we should take a look at him. Can you show us where?"

"I ain't goin' near him again." The boy said adamantly. "We didn't get no sleep last night with that man layin' dead in the bathroom. You kin jist follow the tracks to the woods."

"Make sure you cover him up agin real good," the woman added. "Don't want no ky-otes or sumpthin' gittin' at him an' draggin' his parts around. It'll be bad enough when the ground thaws an' he starts stinkin.' Not lookin' forward to that!"

"We're keepin' his lantern for our trouble," the boy called out as Connor and Michael headed back to the Jeep for shovels.

While Michael carried the shovels, Connor went back up to the woman and boy who were still watching them from their front stoop. He handed the woman a 6-volt battery.

"A spare battery for the lantern, in case the other one runs out," he said.

Mother and son couldn't have looked more pleased, Connor thought, if he had just told them they had won the lottery! "We said a prayer over him when we buried him," the woman said shyly. "Thought it was the right thing to do."

"That was good of you. He probably needed your prayer."

264

The body was easy to find. It was in a depression where the ground sloped between trees, clearly defined by a mound of snow - covered branches and surrounded by footprints.

"We should have asked which end was his head," Connor said. "I only want to see the face. I know it's him, but I still have to see the face."

"My bet is it's that end," Michael said, pointing to the left. "The ground slopes down the other way and I think they'd bury him with his head higher than his feet."

The snow was less than a foot deep over Cooper's face. "Didn't hardly need to bring the shovels," Connor remarked. "That's the shallowest grave I've ever heard of. Maybe we should cover him a little more."

"Any bets as to where we'd find the missing bootlace if we were to look for it?" Michael asked, still staring at Cooper's face.

"I know right where it is. What I can't figure out is why he would do that to stop the bleeding then slit his wrists so he could bleed to death *that* way!"

"The answer to that is buried along with Cooper. Maybe he couldn't stand to die at the hands of someone else. Or maybe he didn't want *that* part of him to be what killed him. Maybe we'll never know and are just wasting our time speculating. I don't care why. I'll never forget the way I found out what he did to Cassie. Never! I'm glad he's dead, no matter how it happened. And I hope he rots in hell!"

Connor covered Cooper's face again then shoveled more snow on top of the branches, tamping it down. "It's finished," he said. He felt as though he had permanently shut the door on one life and was opening the door to another as yet unknown to him.

'*It wasn't just Michael Cooper who died. The man I was died too,*' he thought.

CHAPTER TWENTY-THREE -
JANUARY 12 – 16, 2005

January 12

Bea had unquestionably agreed to every condition Nate insisted upon before he would move in with her. She felt younger and immeasurably happier than she had ever been in living memory. Her lawyer was drawing up all the paperwork, and the wedding ceremony would take place in two days.

Her work with the children made her feel alive again, so much so that she was looking forward to all the young people who would be invading her home every afternoon. She wasn't as accomplished on the piano as Ted, she knew, but she was good enough to accompany her students through rehearsals. Besides, she couldn't let Ted in on everything. She had a surprise for him that would knock his socks off! She had made her discovery by accident, and kept it a secret. Her students knew; there was no way it could be kept from them. But they were sworn to secrecy. Nate knew too, but his attitude was that he was too old for anything to surprise him anymore. He may not have been surprised, but Bea knew he was amazed and delighted, nonetheless.

'This is the best time of the day,' Carin thought strolling hand in hand with Drew along the sidewalk, making the most of the hour they had together after rehearsals. A light snow was falling, almost invisible in the growing dusk. They leaned against a towering elm growing close to the sidewalk, happy to be alone together.

"I can hardly believe that a few days ago I was dying to get back to Edmonton," Carin said softly. "Now I don't think I ever want to go back."

"I'm glad of that; I don't ever want you to," Drew replied.

"School is really different here. We're learning so many new things, useful things, you know? So much of what we learn in school

266

is called 'getting an education', but most of it isn't useful. There's one thing they're *not* teaching us here though, and I'm glad they're not!"

"What's that?"

"Sex education."

Drew felt himself blush. "Did learning that back in Edmonton make you uncomfortable?"

"No. At least not in the way you're thinking," she said, grinning at him. "Back in Edmonton they told us we had all these raging hormones and we had to know everything there was to know about sex so we wouldn't do something dumb. I always felt like there was something wrong with me because I didn't know what they were talking about!"

"You don't have 'raging hormones'?"

"Not that I know of. Do you?"

Drew blushed again. "Sometimes, I guess. Maybe raging hormones is more a guy thing than a girl thing at our age."

"I asked my grandma about it and she said there was no such thing as sex education when she was growing up. She said she was fifteen before she knew where babies came from and she still didn't know how they got there! Can you believe that?"

"She didn't know at fifteen?"

"That's what she says. And she says she sure didn't know she was supposed to have raging hormones, so she didn't have any! She also doesn't remember any girl in her high school ever getting pregnant."

"Maybe girls didn't mature as fast back then."

"Grandma said they were more mature in lots of ways. At fifteen a girl was responsible enough to stay by herself and care for little kids over a weekend. No one would trust a fifteen year old to do that now! And at fifteen, Grandma worked weekends cleaning paint off windows and cleaning up spills and stuff in newly constructed houses. She even waxed and polished the hardwood floors! No one would trust a fifteen year old to do that kind of work unsupervised today either! And she says she still played with dolls then, too!"

"Boy, everything must have been a whole lot different back then."

"Yeah," Carin sighed. "I wish I had lived back then. I think being a teenager would have been a lot more comfortable."

"Then you must be comfortable with the way things are right now. It's like we've taken this giant leap back in time, with several generations living under the same roof together, no TV, no radio, no movies…no sex education!"

Carin laughed. "Yeah, it's really different all right. But I think I like it this way. Don't you?"

"Not all the time," Drew said honestly. "I miss a lot of the things I was used to. But I'd give them all up for you, if you're happier without them."

"Are you going to kiss me again?" Carin asked matter-of-factly.

"I think I'm about to. I know I *want to!*"

"It's okay if you do," Carin said. "As long as it's because you like me and not because of 'raging hormones!'"

January 13

Connor played with the coffee mug in front of him, aimlessly turning and tilting it, unseeingly. He was remembering the conversation he'd had with Michael Cooper on their way past this very farm on which he was now living. He glanced over at Ruth, humming to herself as she put the finishing touches on the cake Richard had made for the wedding tomorrow. Her unexpected question startled him.

"Something on your mind, Connor?"

He cleared his throat. "Uh, yeah. When I first saw the sign you have down by the road that this place is protected by an electric fence," he said haltingly, "I thought farmers must be a very selfish lot, that they were the only ones with food and weren't about to share it. Then I was dumbfounded when Matt turned up the lane here on the way back from that business with Cooper, and invited me to stay here. I realize now how wrong my conclusions were about farmers."

"We didn't plan on helping anyone or organizing anything, initially. And maybe other farmers didn't either. We were basically interested in our own survival, until we realized our survival depended on everyone else's survival. So, don't attribute any purely altruistic motives to what we're doing; there aren't any."

"Uh huh, tell it to the Pope! Connor said." Maybe he'll believe that, but I don't. Is opening your home to other people and feeding them part of your survival plan for yourselves? Is putting in sixteen hour days, half here, half in town, part of your survival plan? Do you have any idea how amazing everything is here? Everybody's working together and they all seem to be enjoying it too! When I drove into Annapolis County I felt as though I was traveling backwards in a time machine or something, and had landed in the perfect era. You know, I think I'd be perfectly happy if 'now' lasted forever."

"Ah, but it won't," Ruth said sadly. "It's just a matter of time before everything is fixed, and up and running again. I think I wish many things would stay the way they are right now. And you know, I was so afraid of what life would be like when the lights went out, I was close to hysteria. Now, I find myself actually enjoying it."

"Richard told me you must have known something was going to happen because you had stored away a lot of food, just in case."

"Oh, he did, did he?" Ruth laughed.

"Yes. So what's the deal? Do you have ESP or something?"

"I honestly don't know what I have, Connor," Ruth said seriously. "I sometimes get to see something before it happens. Not very often, but when it happens it's always something that affects me in some way. Maybe I live in that time machine you felt you were in," she laughed, "and everything has already happened and it just takes us a while to catch up and realize it. Maybe I'm just a little quicker at catching up than most people. I don't think of it as either a gift or a curse, it's just something that *is*, and I really don't think about its source at all anymore."

Without consciously realizing she was doing so, Ruth told Connor about the curious sounds in the house shortly after they had moved in, the scrawled message *'gost here'* on the plank door out back, and how the visions started, something she had vowed she would never reveal to anyone outside the family. "I didn't believe the vision I saw about all the lights and communication systems going out. Not at first, anyway. But when they persisted, I knew I had better take the vision seriously and I did what was necessary in order to be prepared. What bothered me most about the vision was that it was about something bad happening when always before the visions had been about good, or pleasant things. Now I find myself thinking that the vision that frightened me so much was, maybe, actually about something good happening after all. Maybe everyone just needed to be reminded of what's really important in life, and this was a way to make that happen. Maybe. That does seem to be what it's all about."

Impulsively, Connor grasped Ruth's hand and kissed it. There was no need for him to give a reason for the gesture, he knew. And he knew that Ruth knew.

Ruth, flustered, felt herself blush. "Goodness, look at me!" she exclaimed. "I haven't blushed since I had my last hot flash several years ago!" Recovering quickly, she asked, "More coffee, Connor?"

January 14

Bea stood inside the doorway of her dining room waiting to hear the strains of the wedding march on the piano. She felt a little bit silly carrying a small pot of pink cyclamens as a wedding bouquet, but flowers were flowers and she hadn't wanted them cut from the plant. She would have to remember not to throw her bridal bouquet, she thought, giddily.

The rosy pink flowers complemented her dove gray dress and matched the dewy blush on her cheeks. If she didn't look in the mirror again, she could believe she had lost 50 years and was a starry-eyed twenty-two year old girl again, a blushing bride, about to be united in holy matrimony to the man she had loved for as long as she could remember. She was giving up everything she had for him, and it was a very small price to pay. Being with Nate, finally, was the only thing that mattered.

Ted's first notes on the piano startled her. She drew in a deep breath and held it before taking her first step toward the Florida room, and Nate, and the Minister, and the rest of the wedding party. She hadn't wanted anyone to give her away; she was giving herself to Nate. She hadn't wanted anyone to precede her or escort her; she needed no support.

Smiling, her love-filled eyes never leaving his face, Bea walked up to stand beside Nate, where she would vow to remain until death parted them. *'Our days may be numbered, my love,'* she told Nate inside her heart, *'but each one will be the lifetime we didn't have together.'*

She had thought about springing her surprise discovery on her wedding day then thought better of it. *'No, there have to be a lot more people there, a whole lot more! This is our day, Nates and mine. The surprise can wait.'*

"Oh Richard! What a wonderful cake!" Bea gushed. "Just don't let Ruth serve it," she said teasingly, grinning at Ruth. "I don't think I want to wind up wearing dessert for a hat again!"

Ruth laughed. "You aren't the same person who wore the rhubarb crisp a few days ago. I don't know what happened to her, but I'm glad you decided to take her place."

Bea looked radiant in the flattering lamplight. "That old shrew is gone forever," she said. "Nate gave her the boot!"

Carin and Drew sat together on the couch, holding hands and beaming at the obvious happiness of the elderly couple.

"They look so cute," Carin said.

"They're probably thinking the same thing about us," drew responded.

"You think?"

"Yup. Look at them. That could be us someday."

"You think?"

"Yup. The first love is the best and longest lasting."

"You think?"

"Yes, I think. Don't you?"

"I don't know. I don't have any experience with being in love. We haven't known one another long enough to be in love. Have we?"

"I didn't need any time. For me it was love at first sight."

"Really?"

"Really. But I know it wasn't that way for you. I want to believe you will be in love with me some day. Soon. Do you think that's possible?"

"How will I know if I'm in love?"

"You'll want to be with me all the time, your eyes will light up when you look at me, your heart will flutter, you'll feel weak in the knees just thinking about me, your..."

Carin put her fingers to Drew's lips. "I already feel all those things," she said, gazing at him in wonder. "Does that mean I'm really in love?"

"I hope so," Drew said, sincerely. I really do hope so. "But it could just be those 'raging hormones' kicking in!"

Carin backhanded Drew in the stomach, giggling. "You're bad!" she said.

"Sorry to break up the party," Matt said, "but there's school tomorrow and it's getting late."

"There's *always* school tomorrow," Lindy said morosely. "I don't get to spend hardly any time with the cows anymore. They'll forget who I am!"

"There's still time for you to pay a visit to the barn if we leave now," Matt told her. "Michael wasn't expecting any calves to be born tonight, so there won't be any surprises for you anyway."

Bea bent down to give Cassie a hug. "I'm so glad you could be here to share our special day," she told the little girl. Nate had told her all about Cassie and she had insisted the whole family be there for their wedding. Richard's family, after all, was going to be a big part of their future, though they were as yet unaware of that. Mickey came for his hug too, and Bea was happy to oblige. A mischievous imp most of the time, he had his quiet cuddly moments as well. He was a three year old, and that's how three year olds were.

Doreen thanked Bea for taking the time to show her the whole house. "I've been wondering what these beautiful old houses were like inside," she said. "It's incredible! There's so much room, and such beautiful woodwork and carpets. And the furnishings, especially the antiques are, well, words escape me. I thought places like this existed only in the movies!"

Bra's only response was a wide smile. *'Then get ready to be a movie star!'* she thought happily.

Dow and Marilyn insisted on cleaning up after the wedding party while Nate and Bea retired together for the first time. "It's a shame they can't get away together for a real honeymoon," Marilyn remarked, watching the pair ascend the stairs hand in hand.

"They are probably just as happy staying right here," Dow assured her. "Get-away honeymoons are for the young because they can be exhausting. How well I remember!" He winked at Marilyn.

"She's up to something, but I can't figure out what. She's bubbling over with excitement and it's more than just marrying Nate. Do you have any idea what it is?"

"Haven't a clue," Dow said. "But I know what you mean. Two weeks ago she was a bitter, crabby old woman, a real pain in the ass! Now she's an entirely different person, and it happened before she knew she would be marrying Nate."

"Maybe it's this whole lifestyle change we've all been forced to accept," Marilyn said. "I think we're working more than we ever have before, yet we seem to have a lot more free time to ourselves too. I'm finding myself looking forward to working every day, and it hasn't been that way for a long time. Why do you suppose that is?"

"The change, the slower pace. This should be one of the most trying times of our lives, but it's not, is it," Dow said, slipping his arm around Marilyn's shoulders. "We're seeing love in bloom between Bea and Nate, and budding between Drew and Carin, and people seem to be caring about one another in a way they never have. It's not going to last though. You know that, don't you?"

"I guess, she said, wistfully, "we'll all have to go back to making a living at some point, won't we. But this sure feels like a wonderful vacation for as long as it lasts!"

January 15

"Earl Drummond is doing his level best to rile up the other fishermen," Dow told Matt. "Most aren't listening to him, but a few are. There have been some rumblings when they bring their catches in to the food banks."

"Isn't Drummond's family getting food supplies and fuel like everyone else?" Matt asked, continuing to move trays of seedlings into the path of the sunlight streaming through the plastic roof of the greenhouse. "What's his problem, anyway?"

"He's gotten it into his head that you are responsible for the fishermen having to give their fish away instead of selling it. He's selling his, you know, because there are people willing and able to buy it. So, some of the other men figure they should be paid for theirs too. I feel like cutting off Drummond's food supply and I would too if it weren't for his wife and two boys. You know what a stubborn, bigoted cuss he is, Matt. He's like a pit bull once he's got his teeth sunk into something, and I don't think he's about to let go. He could wind up causing a whole lot of trouble!"

"You telling me this because you think I can do something about it, Dow? Or is this a warning to be on my guard?"

"Maybe both. I don't know. There's no one nastier when he's riled, and the man is really riled! And it doesn't make any sense. He's getting his, both ways. His family is being fed and he's being supplied with fuel; all free! And he's selling his fish for top dollar too. The man should be as happy as a pig in shit! Instead he's doing everything he can to cause trouble."

"Some people never seem to be happy unless they're making trouble for someone else," Matt said wryly. "Human nature has many facets, and I guess we have to deal with the ugly side once in a while. I wish the fishermen didn't have to give away their fish and I wish farmers didn't have to give away everything they produce. Lord knows none of them make a descent living even when they sell it. But for right now it has to be that way. We'll just have to convince Drummond and his cronies of that, somehow!"

"How about a fisherman's and farmers meeting at the Legion?" Dow asked. "Maybe everyone together would make a bigger impact on the rebels, take some of the wind out of their sails."

"Set it up," Matt replied. "Drummond must think I'm awfully powerful to have convinced everyone to give up their livelihoods for the time being. What I'd like to know is, if I'm so all-fired powerful, how the hell come am I not rich and famous!"

January 16

Chris and Ted begged off rehearsals for one afternoon to accompany Matt to the farmers' and fisherman's meeting. Ted felt he might be able to get a few points across to the recalcitrant fishermen, especially if Matt or Dow lost their tempers. Chris just wanted to be with the men for a change. It wasn't that he didn't like the rehearsals. He did. But he thought there might be some excitement at the meeting, and he didn't want to miss out on a bit of excitement if he could help it.

There were only half a dozen fishermen at the Legion, and two farmers, when Matt and his crew arrived. But, by the time they were ready to start the meeting, more had drifted in. There were fourteen fishermen and six farmers present, counting Matt. "Not a very good turnout," he said to Dow, "especially of farmers. Do you know which of the fishermen here are in cahoots with Drummond?"

Dow pointed out two he knew of for sure, and another two he thought were possible. "Looks like Drummond is nervous," Dow observed, "the way he keeps rubbing his lips and scowling."

"Maybe they're chapped from all the lip-flapping he's been doing," Matt said acidly. "May as well get started. It doesn't look like any more are going to show up."

"We're aware that some of you fishermen feel you should be getting paid for the fish you catch rather than giving them away," Matt began. "I understand how you feel. It's damn hard for a fisherman to make a living and maybe even harder for most farmers when they're getting paid for what they catch or what they produce. Giving it away means giving away their livelihood. But right now, no one has a livelihood. No one has a paycheck, a pension check or even a welfare check to buy food with. None of you are paying, with money, for the food or fuel you've been receiving. You are paying for those things with your labor; catching fish. Neil Stoddard here is paying with milk. Ed Ramsey with eggs, Dave Kittridge with chicken, Garnet Daven…"

"And what are *you* paying with, Kingsley?" Earl Drummond shouted. "I hear you're not paying at all!"

"Two steers from my place were shipped for slaughter yesterday morning," Matt shouted back."

"Two steers," Drummond sneered. "Two lousy steers! You've got a barnyard full of cattle and you contribute two lousy steers?"

"Two lousy steers, as you refer to them, will provide about a quarter of a pound of beef for about three thousand people, plus a whole lot of soup bones. What do you propose I do, Drummond? Slaughter all the pregnant cows? That would be like asking you to swamp your boat so you can't use it to catch fish anymore!"

"What have you contributed, Drummond?" Dwight Chambers hollered. "You get your box of food for your family every other day at no cost to you just like everybody else, and you haven't contributed so much as a scale off a mackerel!"

"Butt out, Dwight! Nobody asked you for your opinion! I'll contribute something when I'm ready, and I'll be ready when the amount of food and fuel I'm getting equals the value of a load of fish. As long as there are people willing to pay, I'm willing to sell. I'm also willing to pay for my food and fuel, if they'd let me. I don't want no handout. Not like certain people I could mention. You get a kick out of your free food, Kingsley? You commie!"

Ted put his hand on Matt's arm to restrain him before he could respond. He could see Matt's temper flaring, and that wasn't going to do the situation any good. "There are a few facts that need to be brought to light here," he said calmly. "First of all, Matt and his family are not receiving any food from the food bank. He has stored up food over the past couple of years and has ten extra people in his household that he is feeding with food he bought and paid for. He's also sending enough food in every day to the high school to provide a hot meal for twenty kids. He works nine hours a day at the greenhouses growing fresh vegetables for everyone, and he had his own fuel storage so he isn't dipping into the available fuel either. He is doing a whole lot of giving and what he's getting in return is a great deal of satisfaction in knowing he is doing what he can to help keep people from going hungry during this very difficult time. There has been one thing that has been very clear from the beginning. If there is a cost attached to food, only people with money will be able to eat. Food *has* to be free, right now, for everyone, and portioned out equally so..."

"Bull shit!" Drummond roared. "If fat-cat people can pay, why shouldn't they? Why should poor fishermen have to *give* to the wealthy? Huh? Answer *that* you know-it-all smart ass!"

"People who pay are taking more than their fair share!" Ted answered loudly, wondering what it would take to get that across to this thick- headed man. "They are taking food out of the mouths of people who can't pay!"

"That's a crock of shit!" Drummond bellowed, advancing toward Ted.

Chris watched apprehensively as the big rough looking fisherman inched his way closer and closer to his dad. A sudden rush of adrenalin made his ears ring fiercely, blotting out the angry words passing between the two men, and making everything seem as though it was happening in slow motion. He shoved his hands in his pockets as he backed away, his left hand encircling his slingshot, his right hand finding a rock. Without thinking what he was doing, he aimed the loaded slingshot at Drummond as the man made a menacing move toward his dad, the rock landing squarely on Drummond's mouth then dropping to the floor with a thud.

There was utter silence in the room as everyone watched Drummond stagger backwards and land solidly back in the chair he had vacated. All eyes were on him as he removed the bloody hand he had reflexively clamped to his mouth after the rock found its mark. When he opened his hand, a tooth was clearly visible, lying in a slimy pool of blood and spit in his palm. They all watched as he pushed his tongue into the cavity at the front of his mouth, then spit into the palm that held the tooth. He wore a stunned look, as though he had been pole-axed and was just waiting to realize he should fall over.

"You knocked out my toof," Drummond said dazedly to Chris. "Damn ting has been hurtin' like a bashtard for weeks! I'm gonna have a lip swole up like a bitch, but the pus is drainin' an' my toof don't hurt no more."

Everyone seemed to let out his breath at the same time, including Chris. He went over and wrapped his arms around his dad's middle, hoping he wouldn't start bawling. But gee, he had really gotten to be a crack shot with that slingshot, hadn't he? And it appeared he had done the man a favor!

"My teef give me a lot a trouble," Drummond continued. "An' da pain makes me mad at everyting an' don't let me tink straight."

"Why didn't you get yourself to a dentist and get it looked after?" Ted asked.

Drummond lowered his head, looking sheepish. He shrugged. "I'm scared a dentists. I had a bad exp...exp...time wif one once." His missing tooth and rapidly swelling upper lip were making it difficult for him to talk.

A fisherman that Dow had pointed out as one of those who were on-side with Drummond shouted out, "Earl, are you telling us you got us all riled up about givin' away fish 'cause you had a goddamned toothache?"

Drummond looked even more sheepish if that were possible, and shrugged again.

"Kid," the man said, looking at Chris, "hand me that slingshot! I'm gonna knock out the *rest* of his teeth!"

Everyone laughed at that, including Drummond.

Ted wanted to get back to the issue at hand, because even though Drummond was in a better frame of mind, the issue was still unresolved. He held up his hands indicating he wanted to speak, and everyone gradually quieted down. "Everyone is actually paying for the food and fuel they receive," Ted said. "They are paying by contributing their time and their labor. Farmers and fishermen are unquestionably being asked to contribute the most because they are the only source of food. We *know* a lot is being asked of you. But we also know everyone's survival depends on it. If people are hungry they will also be dangerous, especially when they know that people with money have full bellies. We are probably all going to face that danger from outside Annapolis County; it's only a matter of time. But if food isn't free for people within the county, we will be creating that danger within our midst. We can't let that happen."

"You think we're going to be invaded by people from other parts of the Province?" a fisherman asked.

"Yes," Ted said. "I think it's inevitable. "We have our basic needs taken care of here, so I believe there will be many people from all over Nova Scotia who will be trying to take it from us. We don't want people among us who are doing without, and that will be the case if you continue to sell your fish to the wealthy instead of making sure the poor have a fair share."

There was silence in the hall while everyone assimilated the logic of what Ted had said. Drummond hung his head, deep in thought. "You're right," he mumbled, his voice barely audible. He raised his head. "You're right," he repeated loudly. "I'll be givin' my fish to the food bank and sellin' no more."

The assent in the room was unanimous. "So it's all for one and one for all," the fisherman said who had threatened to knock out the rest of Drummond's teeth.

"What can we do to help keep udder people out a da county? Drummond asked.

"Pray for lots of snow to keep the roads closed," Ted answered. "Right now, snow is our greatest ally."

"But I thought he was gonna kill you, Dad!" Chris exclaimed on the way back home in the car. Carin gave Chris a raised eyebrow look, and Chris had the decency to look ashamed.

"You still shouldn't be taking that slingshot to school! It stays home tomorrow, is that understood?" Ted said in a tone of voice that left no room for argument.

"Understood," Chris said sullenly. "But you've got to admit me and my slingshot saved the day!"

Ted, wedged in the front seat between Matt and Connor, was having a hard time keeping a smirk off his face. Glancing at Matt on his left, he saw he was swallowing a bray of laughter that threatened to erupt. To his right, Connor's lips were trembling, and Ted saw him run his hand over his face in a futile attempt to wipe away a grin.

It was too much for Ted. He began shaking with silent laughter that couldn't be contained, that sputtered helplessly between his compressed lips, infecting the two men on either side of him. All three of them began howling with uncontrollable laughter.

"What?" Chris asked from the back seat, smiling expectantly.

"Nothing," Ted managed to spurt.

"C'mon, what?" Chris repeated, beginning to laugh too.

All five children began laughing along with the men, but they didn't have a clue what was so all-fired funny!

CHAPTER TWENTY-FOUR -
JANUARY 16 – 17, 2005

January 16

"We're going to have a storm," Ruth said. "The barometer is falling."

"It's not falling," Matt said, tapping the instrument that hung on the wall by the kitchen door.

"This barometer says we're going to have a storm," Ruth said, tapping the side of her head.

"Well shit, then we are! I've never known your head to be wrong."

"Neither have I," Ruth said ruefully. "I've wished a thousand times my head wasn't such a good judge of atmospheric pressure. I think we're in for a good one according to how much my head is throbbing. Did everyone have to pray so hard for snow?"

"Why don't you take an aspirin and turn in early? You're not getting enough sleep, you know."

"Can't. There'll be another calf coming tonight and I want to keep a close eye on Doreen too. I think she could go into labor any time now. I don't care what the doctor said today! They should have kept her at the hospital. There's going to be a storm, and what if she needs to get back into town tonight and the roads are impassable?"

"You worry too much!" Matt admonished. "I'm sure the doctor knows what he's doing. Doreen isn't due for another three weeks, is she?"

"Supposedly. But it's easy to be mistaken sometimes about when a baby is due. Doreen says she's been feeling a lot more comfortable the past couple of days, and that usually means the baby has dropped. I still remember what it was like when I was pregnant. When I started feeling more comfortable, I was in labor within 48 hours."

"Well worrying about it isn't going to change anything, now is it?"

"I wish I'd gone into town with Richard when he picked her up."

"There wouldn't have been room for everyone to come back if you had."

"There would have been if Doreen had stayed at the hospital which is where I think she should be!"

"Why are you so obstinate!" Matt shouted. "You get hold of an idea and you worry it to death like an old dog with a bone! Get a good night's sleep for a change and maybe you'll have a different outlook on things!"

Ruth had a biting retort on the tip of her tongue, but decided to keep it to herself. The satisfaction she would gain would be at the expense of Matt's ego, and that made the price too high. Sighing, she let Matt have the last word, and went into the family room where Carin was reading the Buddy Book to Cassie and Mickey for the third time.

"Aren't you guys getting tired of hearing that story?" Ruth asked the avidly listening youngsters.

"No," Cassie said. "No," Mickey echoed. "This is the part where Buddy is lost in the woods with Grandpa Nate," Cassie said importantly. "It's the best part."

'*So go away and stop bothering us!*' Ruth thought to herself, smiling at Cassie. She couldn't resist planting a kiss on top of the little girl's head.

Doreen was in the living room organizing the children's clothes for school the next day. Ruth had moved the Martin's into the much larger room after Nate moved in with Bea. Michael had his own room back, and Connor was now using the office as a bedroom, with his ham radio set up on the desk.

Ruth knocked at the entrance to the living room even though the door was open.

Doreen looked up, smiling. "Come on in. It's your house!"

"But it's your room, and I don't want to intrude on your privacy. How are you feeling?"

"I'm feeling great! I seem to have more energy today than I've had for the whole last month put together!"

"I've never asked before, Doreen," Ruth said hesitantly, "but how are you fixed for baby things? Like sleepers, blankets, diapers,…?"

282

"I put away some things I had for Mickey, and for Cassie before that. There's nothing new, except a package of newborn disposable diapers, but it'll do. Babies don't care what they are wearing as long as they are comfortable."

"I suppose you're right," Ruth chuckled. "Babies don't have to make a fashion statement."

"Neither do pregnant women," Doreen said, looking down at her faded, oversize sweatshirt. "I'll be glad to get back into some real clothes!"

"I'd be only too happy to live forever in fleece pants and shirts! There's nothing more comfortable...By the way, where's Richard? He's not still out in the barn with Michael and Lindy, is he?"

"I think he's out in the office with Connor. The two of them are playing around with that radio again." Doreen paused, unsure of how to say what was on her mind. "They have developed a real bond, those two. Richard has always been kind of a loner when it comes to friendships with other guys. He's always been more of a family man than anything. It's good for him to have a close male friend, another guy to talk to. And Connor is really a good person."

"But?" Ruth asked.

"Did I make it sound like there was a 'but' in there somewhere?" Doreen asked, coyly. She looked down at her lap. "But,...I wish they could have gotten to know one another under different circumstances. That would make it easier to tell if they genuinely like one another or just seek one another out because of what they have in common. Contempt for Michael Cooper," she said, looking up at Ruth.

"Wind is really picking up out there," Michael said, coming into the kitchen rubbing his hands together. He held them over the stove a few seconds to warm them. "If we get some snow along with the wind, there might not be anyone getting into town tomorrow."

"Your mother's head says there's going to be snow, Matt said, "so you can pretty well count on it. I've never known her head to be wrong."

"I'm wondering when we're ever going to get our usual January thaw. This is the longest stretch of cold I can ever remember having."

283

"Mmmm!" Matt responded. "Since before Christmas…Where's Lindy? You didn't leave her out in the barn alone, did you?"

"No, she went straight out back. Said she was going to bed."

"She's not coming in to say goodnight?"

"Guess not."

"That's not like her," Matt said, frowning. "There's not something bothering her, is there?"

"Not that I know of."

"Something bothering who?" Ruth asked, coming into the kitchen.

"Lindy. She went to bed without saying goodnight," Matt said.

"Oh, that's my fault I guess. I told her to get to bed early because she begged me to let her see Ginger have her calf,…and, I told her I'd wake her," Ruth added, seeing Matt's disapproving look.

"She's seen enough calves born!"

"That's your opinion, not Lindy's," Ruth said testily.

"If you ask me, *you're* the one who needs to go to bed!"

"I'm going up to the attic," Ruth said, taking a flashlight out of a drawer.

"The attic? What for?"

"For a while," Ruth answered in a tone of voice that clearly meant 'none of your business.'

Matt looked at Michael, who raised his eyebrows and shrugged. "Must be one hell of a storm coming!" he said.

The attic was comfortably warm from all the chimney heat. As Ruth searched for the items she wanted, she pondered the possibility of fixing up the huge space as an apartment for the Martins. Then she remembered why that wasn't practical. The attic was hellishly hot in the summer; no one could live up there.

She found the big plastic storage box of keepsakes she was looking for and hauled it, along with an abandoned wicker laundry basket, down to her bedroom. Then, glancing at the clock on the nightstand, she knew Matt would be coming up to bed before long and she didn't want to have to deal with him. Two more trips down stairs and she had the box and basket in the dining room. Thankfully, there was no one there. She sat in front of the fireplace massaging her aching temples, nearly mesmerized by the dancing flames until she heard Matt noisily clomping up the staircase on the other side of the dining room wall. *'I'll never understand how a man who weighs 160 pounds, soaking wet, can make so much noise going up and down stairs!'* she thought.

Carin found Ruth sorting through the things in the box of keepsakes when she came in to say goodnight. All thought of going to bed left her as she examined the items her grandmother removed, one by one, from the box.

"This was your mother's christening dress," Ruth told her, holding up a delicate hand-crocheted dress faced with a snowy white satin under-dress. There was a matching bonnet and booties, both lined with satin.

Carin was enthralled. "I've never seen anything so beautiful!" she exclaimed.

"My mother, your great-grandmother, made them," Ruth explained. "This was your christening dress too, and Lindy's." Ruth lifted a tiny white satin suit from the box. "This was your Uncle Michael's and Chris's."

"Why did you get these things out to look at them?" Carin asked.

"There are some things in the box I want to give to Doreen, for her baby. I saved some of Michael's baby clothes that he never wore. They were intended for a grandson if I ever had one," Ruth laughed, "but Chris was such a big baby he never could have worn these tiny newborn clothes. So, Doreen shall have them for her baby."

"But what if it's a girl?"

"Oh, it's going to be a boy for sure," Ruth said without hesitation. "Definitely a boy."

"Mom said you told her what her babies would be before any of us were born. How can you know?"

"Can't answer that. Just do," Ruth said.

"What's the basket for?"

"The baby. It will have to do for a bassinette…Enough questions now, sweetheart. Give me a kiss and get along to bed…Love you!"

285

Ruth made one more trip upstairs, this time to the linen closet. Way in the back she found what she was looking for; a large metallic waterproof sheet that was intended to be used in a wilderness survival pack. She had gotten it for Michael several years ago when he went camping for a week. It was still sealed in its plastic wrap, and would finally serve a purpose. *'Now I have to find a way to install this under the mattress pad on Doreen's bed,'* she thought. "Well, it has to be done, so just do it, dummy!" Ruth muttered out loud to herself.

She needn't have worried. Doreen wasn't the least bit insulted. In fact, she was relieved. "I've been worried about what might happen to this mattress if my water broke unexpectedly while I was sleeping," she said. "Can you even replace a mattress in a sofa bed?"

"I have no idea," Ruth said, helping Doreen spread the sheet over the mattress, "but now no one has to worry about it."

In the entry room, Ruth wiped down the wicker basket then sponged it with disinfectant. After another trip up to the linen closet, she slipped a folded quilt inside a pillowcase and fitted it into the bottom of the basket. She placed it near the fireplace in the dining room, then scooped up the little pile of baby clothes, washed and rinsed them in the kitchen sink then took them out to the laundry room and tossed them in the dryer. *'Got to use the electricity for this'* she told herself. *'Got no other choice!'*

"Now I'm ready even if no one else is," she said aloud, lighting a cigarette. She could hear the wind howling outside over the noise of the dryer and wondered how soon the snow would start.

Connor and Richard had two pages of notes on a yellow legal pad after spending almost four hours on Connor's ham radio. There was a lot going on everywhere, and none of it was good news. They had learned from another ham operator that the military base at Greenwood was threatening to forcefully knock apart the roadblock into Annapolis County if it was not done voluntarily by 7 a. m. the next morning. They had apparently already dismantled the roadblock in the middle of Kings County. The base commander had said it was illegal to prevent anyone from using public roads within the Province, and all roadblocks were unauthorized restriction of citizens' rights, unless the Premier authorized the military to take charge. Then, and only then, would roadblocks be permitted, and only if initiated by military personnel.

"Of all the tight-ass, bureaucratic, imbecilic decisions in the world, this takes the cake!" Connor fumed. "Everyone on the military base is protected. They have armed guards, huge generators to power everything and a stockpile of food! But can anyone else protect themselves?...No! It's not *authorized!* What in hell gives those bastards the right to dictate to anyone the way this county is being run when no one has heard of them being put in charge?"

"They may be overstepping their authority," Richard said, trying to calm Connor.

"I told them as much, but they don't seem inclined to listen! They're just going to dictate, and hey, fall in line folks, or else!"

Richard looked helplessly at Connor. He didn't know what to say because he didn't know if anything could be done about the situation.

"You know what I think is going on?" Connor asked, narrowing his eyes. "I think those chicken shits on the base are doing this to protect themselves! The word is out that both the base at Greenwood and Annapolis County have electricity and food, so if they force open the roads into the county, the pressure on the precious soldiers will be relieved."

"How will that relieve the pressure on the base?" Richard asked, not getting the picture.

"Look, if we can't prevent access into the county, this is where the marauding hordes will come; where it's easy pickin's. They won't bother a heavily guarded military base."

"If that's their objective, then what the hell good are they? Isn't it their job to protect people, not subject them to invasion?"

"Supposedly. But they probably figure that by removing the roadblocks they'd be protecting the most important people; themselves!"

Richard screwed up his face, shaking his head. "This doesn't sound right, Connor. It's not the way the military would act. I'm sure of it!"

"You heard the message the same as I did. Whether we want to believe it or not, if there's an order out to dismantle the roadblock, it had to come from the base. It's mostly the RCMP manning those roadblocks, and surely they would verify the source of those orders."

"Well, it it's for real and not some kind of sick practical joke, then there's only one thing we can do. What we've been doing all along; pray that it starts snowing and doesn't stop!"

"Looks like your head was right on target," Michael told his mother when he came in from the barn. "Fine flakes of snow, coming down thick. That usually means there'll be a lot of it." He helped himself to a cup of hot chocolate before giving Ruth the barn report. "Ginger is starting labor. It's early yet; at least ten minutes between pains. With this storm, you're not still planning on getting Lindy up, are you?"

"I promised her I would," Ruth said resignedly. "I certainly would rather not, but I won't go back on my word to her. She's disappointed the last two calves were born while she was at school."

"There won't be school for anyone here tomorrow if it snows all night and the wind keeps up," Michael was saying as Richard and Connor came into the kitchen from the office.

"There's hot chocolate for you on the back of the stove," Ruth said, smiling at the two men. "Help yourselves."

"Anything on the radio?" Michael asked.

"Plenty," Connor responded, setting the two pages of notes in front of Michael. "And none of it good news, I'm afraid."

Ruth and Michael leaned their heads close together as they scanned the information Connor had recorded. There were reported incidents of violence breaking out all over the Province, still seemingly scattered and random, but an alarming pattern was emerging. Farms were being targeted, as they had expected, but the incidents were getting closer and closer all the time and were beginning to surround most of Annapolis County. Cattle were being hauled from barns and slaughtered in farmyards while farm families were held at bay by rifle-toting groups of men. The same thing was happening with pigs, sheep and goats, but cattle appeared to be the preferred target. Chickens were being stuffed into feed sacks and hauled away, and cellars were being ransacked for any remaining

288

stored food. People had been shot at, some wounded, but no rural people had been killed yet, to the knowledge of their contacts.

When they came to the news that the base at Greenwood had ordered the roadblocks removed, Michael and Ruth simultaneously gasped. "What?" Michael exclaimed. "Are they out of their minds? Getting rid of the roadblocks would be the stupidest thing we could do! That would open the county up for anyone to get through and ruin everything we have managed to do here!"

"There has to be some mistake," Ruth said. "I can't believe the military would do that. We have order and security here, which should be the objective everywhere. Why would the military want to destroy that?"

"All I can tell you is what we heard on the radio," Connor said. "My thinking is, if they destroy our roadblock, they believe the pressure will be off them and directed at us instead."

"And I maintain the military wouldn't do that," Richard said. "I think the directive must have come from another source."

"I'm inclined to agree with you, Richard," Ruth said. "It doesn't make sense for them to do that. Can't we make direct contact with someone at the base to confirm this?"

"I've tried. But I'll get back on the radio again and keep trying. For some reason they haven't been answering and that's part of what makes me suspicious of their motives," Connor said.

"If it turns out to be an actual military directive," Ruth said, "there has to be something or someone behind it. The officers at the base wouldn't have the authority to dictate to private citizens without authorization."

"Whatever the source turns out to be isn't going to matter all that much," Connor said on his way out to the office. "The roadblock up in Kings County has been dismantled. That's been confirmed. And if the roadblocks around Annapolis County are dismantled, the source of that directive isn't important. It won't change the result."

"Like I said before, pray for lots of snow," Richard said. "And it looks like our prayers are being answered!"

"I'll shovel a path on the deck while you get Lindy up," Michael said. "It might be tough going through some of those drifts that are building up all the way to the barn, though."

Ruth stopped in the laundry room for a cigarette before waking Lindy. It was a sure bet she couldn't have one after waking her! She'd think about quitting again when everything was back to normal she promised herself, while inhaling with deep satisfaction. '*I substituted hot chocolate for cigarettes all those months and gained a lot of weight. Then I start smoking again and keep on drinking the hot chocolate because now I'm addicted to that too. I can't win!*' Ruth thought.

January 17

It was almost 2 a. m. when Ruth and Lindy returned to the house from the calving. Whole sections of the path to the barn were swept clear of snow, while others were thigh high drifts. '*The corral will be a real challenge for Michael to clear in the morning,*' Ruth thought as she stomped her feet to free some of the snow clinging to her overalls.

Tear tracks were frozen on Lindy's face, and Ruth wrapped her arms around her. "It happens," she said softly, "and there's really nothing we can do about it."

"Ginger looks so sad," Lindy said tearfully. "She keeps sniffing around the pen, talking to her baby, but there's no baby for her to love."

"I know sweetheart. But by this time tomorrow, Ginger will have forgotten all about it. We couldn't have saved that calf, even if our vet had been here. There was no way to know the cord was wrapped around one of the calf's rear legs or that the calf's movements would sever the cord. He accidentally disconnected his own life support."

"I don't want to go to school tomorrow. I want to stay with Ginger, okay Grandma?"

"I don't think anyone will be going to school tomorrow; it doesn't look like the snow will be stopping anytime soon. Get some sleep now, and don't worry about Ginger. Her baby dying bothers you more than it does her. In a way, I'm glad you got to see this happen.

Raising animals has its share of heartbreaks along with the joys, and that's something you need to know. That's reality."

"Reality sucks," Lindy said unhappily as she went through the laundry room and opened the door to the back room. "It really sucks!"

Michael came in the back door, locking it behind him. Seeing a faint light under the laundry room door, he opened it, knowing his mother would be in there smoking. "Looks like Connor has finally quit for the night," he said. "His light's out...You should get some sleep too."

"I guess he didn't get anyone at the base or he would have told us," Ruth said tiredly. "What's going to happen, Michael? What are we going to do if mobs break in here and start shooting the cattle? What..."

"That's not going to happen, Mom. We won't let it," Michael said, putting his arm around her shoulders. "There's still more we can do to keep people out and we'll do it if we have to. All this snow and wind is going to buy us some time. Even if the roadblocks come down in a few hours, the roads will still be impassable unless they are plowed out."

"They'll *have* to be plowed out! We can't just stop delivering food, the kids can't stop school, we can't abandon the greenhouses!"

"Okay, okay! But there are a couple of towns and a whole lot of countryside before they could get down here to us, from *any* direction!"

"Oh, well, now, that makes me feel a whole lot more comfortable about the situation!" Ruth said sarcastically.

"Mom, what do you want me to do about it?" Michael asked helplessly. "I can't make the situation go away just because you want it to!"

"Keep your voice down," Ruth said softly. "You'll wake everybody."

"I'm going to bed. And I think that's what you should do too. Maybe the picture will look a little different in the morning."

Ruth waved Michael off and lit another cigarette. Her head was throbbing and she felt an almost uncontrollable anger rising inside her. This new threat couldn't be happening! It wasn't fair after all their hard work. She wanted to throw something, smash something, do something to let the anger out! Instead, she finished her cigarette then concentrated on breathing deeply until she felt her pulse slowing and some of the anger receding. Picking up the oil lamp, she was about to leave the room when she remembered the baby clothes in the dryer.

"Well shit," she said out loud then laughed at herself. '*My God, I'm becoming Matt!*'

Ruth placed the folded baby clothes in the wicker basket in the dining room then put another log in the fireplace. She was loading more wood into the kitchen stove when Doreen appeared in the doorway, looking frightened.

Ruth knew what words she would hear before they were spoken.

"My water broke," Doreen said.

"Sit down," Ruth said, pulling out a kitchen chair. "I'll be right back."

She hurried upstairs and gathered sheets and towels from the linen closet, and a box of heavy-duty sanitary napkins from the bathroom closet. She was back downstairs in a flurry, handing Doreen a towel and telling her to sit on it. Then she went to the living room to wake Richard.

"Wha…?" Richard muttered as Ruth hissed his name.

"Shhh," she said, finger to her lips. She motioned Richard to get up and follow her.

Out in the kitchen, Richard knew as soon as he saw Doreen there. "The baby?" he asked.

Doreen nodded, grinning. "My water broke. You weren't by any chance dreaming you were swimming when Ruth woke you, were you?" she asked, laughing softly.

Richard noticed that the leg of his pajamas was wet. "I'll get dressed then warm up the car," he said.

"You're forgetting about the storm," Ruth said, looking at Doreen for her reaction. "It won't be possible to get out of here."

"What are we going to do?" Richard asked dazedly.

"I think we're going to have a baby!" Ruth said brightly. "But first we are going to move the kids into the dining room and put clean sheets on the bed. Doreen, you stay put, and Richard, you put the kids in the lounge chairs then help me carry their mattress into the dining room."

Ruth put the chairs in the lounge position while Richard carried Cassie and then Mickey into the family room and placed them in the chairs. Once their mattress was in the dining room, they each carried a still soundly sleeping child back to their own bed and tucked them in.

Richard was visibly upset as he helped Ruth strip the bed and remake it with fresh sheets. "She can't have the baby here!" he whispered. "What if something goes wrong?"

"Don't you dare show anything but absolute confidence in front of Doreen," Ruth whispered back. "You've been through this before, twice, so just be with her the way you were before. Pretend you're in a hospital, if it helps."

"But..."

"No buts. We can't get her to the hospital, and you're going to have to act like that doesn't matter. "We can't let her be scared, Richard. Do you understand that?"

"Yes ma'am."

"I haven't had any labor pains yet," Doreen said, as Ruth and Richard came back into the kitchen. "That's the way it usually is. My water breaks, then it's 2 or 3 hours before the pains start."

"Then we'll just get you back to bed and let you get some sleep," Ruth said, helping her out of the chair. "Why don't you go change out of those wet pajamas, Richard, then you go back to bed too."

"Uh,...these are the only pajamas I have," Richard said, lamely.

"Then put on a pair of pants!" *'Honestly!'* Ruth thought, *'men can be so helpless!'* "What about you, Doreen? Do you have a fresh nightgown?"

"No, I'm afraid this is it," she said apologetically.

"Never mind. I'll bring a couple of mine down for you. They're brand new, never been worn. I seem to be given nightgowns for my birthday or Christmas all the time. But I never wear them. No one seems to notice that I only wear pajamas."

Ruth settled herself in one of the lounge chairs in front of the stove. Doreen and Richard were both asleep in the living room, or at least appeared to be. Perhaps like her, she thought, their minds were in a turmoil of 'what if's.' What if the baby is really almost a month premature. What if it's a mal-presentation. What if Doreen has complications? What if, what if…"

She couldn't seem to keep her mind from drifting back to the contents of Connor's notes, of the messages received over his radio. She could almost feel fear making the hair on the back of her neck rise. The continual rush of adrenalin kept her from dozing off even though she couldn't remember ever feeling so drained of energy. Deep breathing only seemed to make her head pound harder and made goose bumps erupt all over her body.

'*I'm a real mess,*' she thought, getting up out of the lounge chair and going into the kitchen. She decided if she couldn't sleep she'd make some coffee to keep her awake. Her sinuses were blocked, she figured, so she swallowed two sinus relief tablets along with her coffee then took a refilled cup with her out to the laundry room, planning to chain smoke and think, until Doreen needed her.

Matt found her there two hours later when he came downstairs. She was standing, with her upper body sprawled across the washing machine, her head pillowed by her folded arms, snoring loudly.

"Well shit!" he said. "Now I've seen everything!" He shook her shoulder and her legs collapsed from under her as though his touch had turned them to rubber. He caught her before she hit the floor. Her eyes flew open and stared vacantly at him.

"What in hell are you doing?" Matt asked.

Ruth's answer sounded to Matt like a mumbled, "I'm having Doreen's baby. She's at the roadblock going to school with a gun."

"You're talking nonsense," Matt said shaking her. "Have you been up all night?"

Gradually coming out of her stupor, Ruth became aware of a wrenching pain in her back when she tried to straighten it, and her legs didn't seem to want to hold her up. "Oooh!" she moaned. "What happened?"

"What happened is, you fell asleep leaning over the washing machine! Damn fool woman," he said, helping her walk into the kitchen. "Why don't you go to bed like any sensible person would?"

"Because Doreen is having her baby," Ruth said, regaining her senses. "What time is it?"

"Half past five. And Doreen is in bed, asleep. She's not having her baby!" Matt said sharply.

"Get me some coffee," she said, collapsing into a chair.

"No coffee!" Matt said, adamantly. "Get upstairs to bed."

Ruth sighed, holding her head. "Doreen's water broke nearly three hours ago. She's in labor and I'm not going to bed until the baby is born."

"Three hours ago! Why didn't Richard take her in to the hospital?"

"Take a look outside and you'll have the answer to that!" Ruth said testily. "You never know what's going on! Half of everything that happens around here happens at night, but you'd never know! You sleep through it all!"

"I put in a twelve hour day, every day, and that's enough for anyone!" Matt growled, filling a cup with coffee and slamming it in front of Ruth.

"I agree it's enough for anyone," Ruth shot back. "I'm wondering when it's *my* turn to put in a twelve hour day rather than twenty! Try it once like I do, day after day!"

"You don't have to be out in the barn half the night! Michael can take care of that!"

"Michael puts in twenty hour days too! We could use a little relief once in a while!"

"You know I don't know anything about helping the cows when they're calving."

"No, and you don't want to learn either! Because if you knew what to do, then you might have to take a turn doing it!"

"I've got work to do! I don't care to talk to you until you're in a better frame of mind."

"Don't cuss and mumble and stomp on the deck while you shovel through 3 feet of snow," Ruth said nastily. Connor didn't get to bed until after two."

"What was Connor doing up so late?"

"Don't talk to me right now. I'm not in a very good frame of mind, remember?"

Matt gave her a disgusted look. "Of all the impossible, foul-tempered, cussed,…," Matt muttered as he went out the door.

'Yes, I am," Ruth thought tiredly. *'All of the above, and more. I'm scared too!'*

Ruth peeked into the living room at Doreen. She was awake, smiling wanly when she saw Ruth. Richard was asleep beside her.

Doreen nodded at Ruth's questioning look then laboriously crawled out of bed. "I have to use the bathroom," she whispered. That meant climbing the stairs, so Ruth took her arm and assisted her. Halfway up the staircase, Doreen paused, moaning lightly as a contraction nearly doubled her over.

"I have four or five minutes to use the bathroom and get back downstairs before the next contraction," Doreen panted as the pain receded.

Ruth waited outside the bathroom door, incredulous at how considerate women were of their men, especially when they were needed the most. Doreen whispering, so she wouldn't wake Richard. She, always loathing to wake up Matt even though his help was needed. *'What drives women to be so protective of men?'* she wondered. *'It must be a survival thing; men are actually the weaker sex and women know that instinctively. If men had to put up with all the things a woman goes through, they couldn't cope with it. They would fall apart physically and mentally.'*

Doreen came out of the bathroom looking drawn and fearful. "I didn't have as long as I thought I would," she said. "I think I can already feel the baby's head. It's coming fast! Do you think that's because it's premature?"

"It may not be premature at all," Ruth said, helping Doreen back down the stairs. "But even if it is, it's only about 3 weeks early. Michael was 2 weeks early and he was fine. Rachel was over 6 weeks early and she was fine too. The size of the baby is the most important thing." *'Keep talking!'* Ruth told herself, but her next words were cut off by Doreen's moans as another pain assailed her. She leaned heavily on Ruth, nearly toppling both of them. *'Give me strength, God!'* Ruth prayed. As if in answer to her plea, she braced her legs enough to support the two of them then began the torturous walk back to the living room.

Richard woke as Doreen sank heavily onto the bed. "Has the labor started?" he asked inanely. "What time is it?"

"Time to go boil some water," Ruth instructed.

"Boil water. Right!" Richard exclaimed, leaping out of bed. "That's what they always do in movies when a baby is born at home. What's the water for?"

"For keeping a nervous father busy while his wife delivers her baby," Ruth retorted, watching Doreen's face reveal the agony of another contraction. "Don't go anywhere. I was just kidding about the water," she said calmly. "Help her scoot down to the foot of the bed then brace her so she's halfway sitting up."

With Doreen's legs and most of her pelvis over the end of the bed, Ruth knelt and placed several clean towels on the floor and sprayed them, and then her hands, with antiseptic, before cradling the emerging head in her hands. "It's okay to scream when you push, Doreen," she said. "It helps to manage the pain."

"If she does, it'll be a first," Richard said. "She never screamed with the other two." He leaned forward, and seeing the back of the baby's head his face lit up with an anticipatory smile. "Almost here," he crooned. "It's almost over now."

"One more push and we've got it," Ruth said. The words were barely out of her mouth before the slippery baby was in her hands, taking its first breath and beginning to squall at the indignity it was being subjected to. Ruth laid the infant on the towels and sprayed antiseptic on the cord. Quickly tying it in two places with gauze, about 3 inches apart, she severed the cord in the 3- inch span, then lifted the baby just in time to prevent the afterbirth from landing on top of it.

"This ought to go down in the books as the quickest, easiest birth in history!" Ruth exclaimed, as she placed the baby in Doreen's arms. "I'm going to go get a basin of warm water while you two admire your new son. That's no premature baby. He's going to tip the scales at 8 pounds easily!" She lowered Doreen's nightgown then scooped up the towels with the afterbirth before leaving the three of them alone.

Cassie was in the kitchen looking around in confusion when Ruth came in. *'It must be a bit startling to wake up as usual and find yourself in a different place than when you went to sleep,'* Ruth mused. "Go in the living room and see your new baby brother," she told the puzzled child. "He was just born."

Cassie, mouth agape and disbelieving, stood at the threshold to the living room and stared at the naked, squirming infant in her mother's arms. Doreen held out her other arm to her little daughter in invitation and Cassie reverently approached and allowed herself to be encircled and drawn in close. Richard reached across Doreen and wrapped his arm around Cassie too, and the three of them gazed wordlessly at the baby.

Lindy came bleary-eyed into the kitchen as Ruth was filling the basin. "You're up a little early," Ruth remarked.

"I wanted to go see Ginger," Lindy said. "I had trouble getting to sleep thinking about her baby."

"There's another baby for you to go see," Ruth said teasingly.

"Who's?" Lindy asked, trying to remember which cow was next in line to calve.

"Doreen's. In the living room."

"Doreen had her baby here? In the living room? When?"

"Just a few minutes ago. Why don't you go say hello before I chase everyone out of there."

Lindy stood in the living room doorway a few moments before Richard noticed her. "Lindy!" he called out happily. Cassie turned to look at her friend with a beaming smile.

"What is it?" Lindy asked.

"It's a little brown boy and it's all wet and yucky like I was when I was borned!" Cassie gushed. "Come see him!"

"He's tiny compared to a calf!" Lindy volunteered, gazing at the baby in awe. "What are you going to name him?"

Richard laughed. "His name is going to be bigger than he is. It's Theodore, Matthew, Michael, Connor, Christopher, Martin. But we're going to call him Teddy, for short."

"Like my Dad?" Lindy asked shyly.

"If it weren't for your dad and the plan he developed, we wouldn't be here," Richard said seriously. "And your Grandpa, Uncle Michael and Connor are a big part of us being here too. If the baby had been a girl, she would have been Ruth, Lindy, Carin, Rachel, Martin. If we have another girl someday, that's what her name will be."

"And what will you call her for short?" Lindy asked politely.

"We thought probably Ruthie. But we'll have to wait and see. Sometimes the baby decides the name. Like this little guy," Richard said, running a finger over the baby's damp curls. "The three of us decided he was Teddy just a few minutes ago. He'll probably be called Ted when he's older."

"Will I be called Cass when I'm older?" Cassie asked. "And will Mickey be called Mick? And will Lindy be called Linn? And will…"

"Enough, enough," Ruth said, coming in the room with the basin and an armload of fresh towels. "Okay, everybody out except me, Doreen and the baby. We've got some freshening up to do here, and Richard, go get a newborn disposable diaper then how about getting some breakfast going."

"Aye. Aye, Captain," Richard said, saluting.

"And Lindy? There's a wicker basket in the dining room. Bring it here, please."

"Huh!" Richard said. "Lindy gets a 'please' and I get an order! I guess we know who rates around here!" He tweaked Lindy's nose then playfully messed up her hair. "What is your pleasure for breakfast, princess?" he asked. He scooped Lindy up under one arm and Cassie up under the other, both girls giggling.

"The diaper, Richard! The basket, Lindy!" Ruth reminded. "Save the horseplay for later. It's too early in the morning!"

"Spoilsport," Richard said, setting the girls on their feet. "Come on, we better do the lady's bidding." He assumed a poker face, clicking his heels together then breaking into a Charlie Chaplain walk. His antics were too much for Buddy who had come to the living room door to see what all the commotion was about. He danced from foot to foot as though performing a duet with Richard, tail wagging furiously. When he started his staccato bark, both girls fell on him laughing uproariously. And Teddy, exhausted from the ordeal of being born, slept through it all.

"What would you like for breakfast?" Richard asked Matt magnanimously when he came in from doing the morning milking. "Anything you want, and if we've got it, I'll fix it! Ruth just got through delivering our second boy, and he's a dandy! She's in the living room washing up Doreen and the baby. So, what'll it be?"

Matt sat at the table, his face a blank. Deadpan, he finally said, "I think a large helping of crow would be about right."

Richard sat down across from Matt. "Ruth sort of keeps you on a steady diet of that, huh." He remarked. "What's the reason this time?"

"The baby. She told me yesterday afternoon that Doreen was going to have her baby and she wished the doctor had kept her in town. I as much as told her the doctor knew as much as she did."

"You always listen to her about the weather, don't you?"

"Yes, but that's because she always gets a headache when the pressure either rises or falls rapidly. The headache is the predictor, not Ruth."

"No Matt, I think she knows about things. Or at least has a very strong instinct. She knew something was going to happen on the first of this year way in advance and spent a couple of years preparing for it. That's why you're in the fortunate situation you're in now. She knew I wasn't any threat even though I had a gun on her, just like she knew Connor was an okay guy. And she knew Doreen would be going into labor...You haven't heard the news yet about the base at Greenwood ordering the roadblocks dismantled, have you?"

"What!" Matt barked.

"That was the news that came over the radio last night, but I didn't believe the military would do that, and neither does Ruth. I think we should trust her judgment on this, and find out what the real source is. Because the fact is, the roadblock up in Kings County *has* been dismantled, and the one in Annapolis County was supposed to be dismantled this morning."

"Can't we get in touch with someone at the base and confirm this?"

"Connor has been trying. They don't respond at the base, and with all this snow, there's no way to go check on the roadblock either. If the Annapolis roadblock has come down, all this snow is a blessing. But if it's some kind of hoax, the snow just adds to the worry as well as keeping all of us from doing the things that have to be done."

"Just when we think we're over the worst and everything is clicking into place, this has to happen!" Matt said sourly. "If it's not the military giving the order about the roadblocks, who could it be?"

"Maybe the RCMP?"

"It makes even less sense for it to be them. The RCMP is manning the roadblocks!"

"Maybe they got their orders from headquarters."

"I can't see any of the local men obeying that kind of order. They live here, their families are here, so they are all benefiting from having the roadblocks in place. But, if it's not the military or the RCMP, then who? Who else would have any kind of authority to order the roadblocks to come down?"

Richard shrugged and shook his head. "I don't know who it could be. But one thing is certain. As soon as Connor is up, we're going to be back on that radio trying to find out!"

Ruth was hustled off to bed by 8 a. m., too tired and too wound up to sleep, or so she thought. The images in her mind were a jumble of babies, basins, calves, radio static and men with guns. Flipping onto her side, she tried to erase the images by visualizing herself doing mundane repetitive chores such as hanging clothes on a line and sweeping the floor. The last thing she remembered was sweeping up a huge pile of dog hair, with a nearly nude, mortified looking Buddy hovering in the background.

Connor had made contact with the RCMP in Bridgetown. They confirmed that the order to dismantle the roadblocks had come from the military base in Greenwood. The RCMP however, was refusing to abandon the roadblock at the Annapolis County line. They questioned the authority of the military to either give, or enforce, such a directive, unless the order had come from Government.

The base at Greenwood was still not responding. "There's something really screwy here," Connor said. "The RCMP can't get a response from the base either. The base is sending out messages but will not respond or reply to any questions."

Matt, Michael and Richard were all standing around the radio, while Connor tried once again to contact the base. Again, there was no answer.

"Has the RCMP informed the base they will not abandon the roadblocks?" Matt asked.

"They can't get any response in order to give the base a message," Connor said irritably.

"Why don't you try sending out that message," Matt suggested. "They may be receiving but just not answering, for God knows what reason."

"Just send out the message that the roadblock stays, without even knowing if the message is being received?" Connor asked, incredulously.

"Yes. I think it might be worth a try. And while you're at it, give them a piece of your mind for giving orders that endanger the lives of civilians. Lay it on thick! If they *are* receiving, maybe you can piss them off enough to respond. If not, at least you will have gotten something off your chest!"

"I'll give it a try," Connor said, with a lopsided grin. "But once I get started telling them off, don't be surprised if my language turns the air blue!"

"Turn it as blue as you want! It's stopped snowing so I'm going to tackle that lane and most of the yard with the snow-blower. Good luck. It's hell not knowing what's going on!"

Rachel and Ted kept the youngsters busy 'playing school' in the dining room so that Doreen and Ruth could get some rest. Whenever they heard the baby crying though, everyone trooped into the living room to get another look at him and exclaim over his sudden, unexpected appearance.

"Half an hour of labor pains!" Rachel exclaimed. "That's unbelievable. That's almost obscene. I'm jealous!"

"The longest I was in labor was with Cassie," Doreen said, fondly squeezing her daughter's arm. "That was a little under three hours. With Mickey it was less than two. If there's ever another baby, I might skip labor altogether!"

"There has to be another baby," Cassie pointed out, seriously. "We have to have a girl named Ruthie to make it even. Three boys and three girls."

Amused, everyone chuckled, leaving Cassie wondering what was so funny.

It was a quarter to five when Ruth woke, un-refreshed from her long sleep. Her first impulse was to leap out of bed and try to get something together for supper. Then she remembered there had been too many people in the house with too little to do all day for her to be needed for anything.

She rolled over onto her back, relishing the unfamiliar luxury of stretching out in a bed she had all to herself. She turned back onto her other side for another ten minutes of bliss before facing everyone.

It was half past eight when she woke again, confused and disoriented by the dark. She gasped when she turned to look at the luminous dial of her alarm clock. Out of bed like a shot, she thrust her feet into her slippers and was slipping into her robe when Matt came into the bedroom carrying an oil lamp.

"Oh, you're awake," he said inanely. "I thought I'd better check on you."

"I don't know how I could have slept so long," Ruth said, stifling a yawn. "Twelve hours! That's got to be some kind of a record for me."

"You must have been awfully tired," Matt said solicitously. "Just plain worn out in fact. You're not going out to check on things in the barn tonight. I'll go out with Michael, and if there are any middle of the night checks to do, I'll be the one to do them. Michael is pretty tired too."

Ruth smiled her thanks at Matt as she headed for the bathroom. She knew what he was offering to do was his way of saying he was sorry, and she knew, that he knew, her smile said she was sorry too. *'How ironic,'* she thought, *"I've slept so long I'll never get back to sleep tonight. I'm so rested I could spend all night in the barn if I had to, but now I don't have to!'* She considered saying as much to Matt then changed her mind. She would take the reprieve being handed to her even if she didn't need it right now. She knew Matt too well. If she refused the offer this time, it would never be made again!

Michael and Lindy had already gone out to the barn by the time Ruth and Matt came into the kitchen. Ruth could see that Matt was already regretting his offer as he looked out the kitchen window. The snow had stopped, but the wind had been picking up all evening. Tomorrow, the snow plowing would have to be done all over again.

There was no one in the kitchen. "Where is everyone?" Ruth asked, feining interest. She discovered she didn't particularly care.

"Well, they can't be far," Matt said. "I think the younger kids are in bed and Richard is probably in the living room with Doreen and the baby."

"And Rachel and Ted are probably out back, and Connor is on the radio," Ruth completed for Matt. "And Ruth is going to find something to eat while Matt goes out to the barn!"

Matt took the hint, none too gracefully, while Ruth rummaged in the refrigerator, then the cupboards. "Mmmm, bad stuff," she murmured, reaching for the jar of peanut butter. "A peanut budder samich, as Mickey would say, washed down with berry chocklitty miwk." Ruth knew this was not the best thing for her to be eating and she would probably regret it later. But it was what appealed to her at the moment and right then the moment was all that mattered. She slathered peanut butter thickly on buttered bread then added chocolate syrup to a glass of milk until it was a deep creamy brown. Taking a sip of milk then a hefty bite of the sandwich, she wondered why nothing ever tasted as good as she anticipated it would anymore.

She ate desultorily, Buddy sitting expectantly at her knee, ears at the alert every time she took a bite. "You want some?" Ruth asked. Buddy appeared to smile, vigorously sweeping the floor with his bushy tail. She tore off chunks of the sandwich, which Buddy accepted greedily. "I had sort of a half-awake dream about you, Bud," she told the dog conversationally while she fed him bits of the sandwich. "You were shedding your hair something awful, and I was sweeping up after you until I had a whole dog's worth of hair in the dustpan and you were sitting there hairless except for your face. Did you ever look silly!" Buddy acknowledged the humor of the dream with his tail and a yawning attempt at removing peanut butter from the roof of his mouth. Seeing that the sandwich was gone, he trotted back to his place on the couch in the family room. "Fair weather friend!" Ruth called after him.

Ruth listened at the door to the office. Hearing Connor at the radio, she tapped on the door then opened it. He motioned for her to come in with his left hand, his right hand busy writing on a yellow legal pad.

"Say again!" she heard Connor bark as he placed his left hand against the headset and continued writing feverishly. His face was flushed with anger when he finally leaned back in his chair, clawed the earphones from his head and tossed them on the desk.

Ruth stood mute, her eyes apprehensively searching Connor's face. He stared back at her, taking deep breaths and waiting for some of his anger to dissipate before speaking.

"I'm afraid we're in for it," he said apologetically. "Everything that has been accomplished here might go right down the tubes. Damn!" He slammed the top of the desk with his open palm.

CHAPTER TWENTY – FIVE - JANUARY 17, 2005

Ruth had all the adults assembled in the kitchen to hear the latest news Connor had received on his radio.

"The snow has given us one day's grace," Connor told everyone, "and the wind, maybe another two at the most."

Michael looked thoughtfully at Connor's notes. "The report that power is going to be gradually restored in the Province is good news, but on the other hand, the fact that the power we have here has to be reconnected to the grid *isn't* good news. We have an agreement among the people here that power is for essential use only and it appears that everyone is cooperating fully. I can't see that happening on a province wide basis."

"If we are reconnected to the grid before full power is restored all across the Province, there won't be enough power here to keep electrically charged oil furnaces and water pumps operating and we're dependant on those," Matt said. "So, instead of one part of the Province having the power it needs, the *whole* Province will be in a brown-out situation. It's a stupid thing to do!"

Rachel looked perplexed. "I don't understand how hooking up to the power grid will mean we don't have enough electricity anymore! I admit I don't know how all that works, but..."

"I'm not sure either," Ruth said, "but I think I understand the concept. Now stop me if I'm wrong, but I'd like to offer my interpretation of things with a very simplified analogy. Doreen just had a baby. She has enough milk to meet that baby's needs, and if she had to, she could possibly feed another one as well. But she certainly couldn't provide nourishment for every baby in the county. If she were asked to do so, every baby in the county would wind up starving, including her own. So, it's much better for her to just have to feed her own baby. That way, at least one baby lives. Now, substitute electricity for Doreen. There's enough electricity here to meet the basic needs of only a few people. If you tried to make such a limited amount of power available to *everyone*, there wouldn't be enough for *anyone* to survive."

"Is that really the way it would be with the electricity?" Rachel asked Matt.

"Pretty much! The little bit of power being generated here would go out to feed every power line in the Province, and beyond. It would be so dissipated, no one would have enough power to run anything!"

"Then why would they do that?" Rachel asked. "It doesn't make any sense! There are a few thousand people in one part of the Province who get themselves organized enough to make it through all this, and now they are being told they have to share what they have with everyone else so that *no one* has a chance?"

"There's always a chance the power could be fully restored province-wide in a matter of days," Michael explained. "Once that happens, I don't think anyone would object to being reconnected to the grid. In fact, it would mean that people could move back into their own homes. But until the power is fully restored, it would be foolhardy to allow the power here to be taken from us."

"I think the biggest worry we have to face is those roadblocks coming down," Matt said. "Whether we're talking about power, food, water or fuel, everything that's needed, there's only enough for a limited number of people for a limited time. Those armed roadblocks are the only things making it possible for us to 'feed our own baby'. If they come down, our ability to do that is going to disappear, and most likely in a violent manner!"

"There's a big stockpile of food right here," Rachel said. "Surely, if someone comes here looking for food there's enough to share. We've been eating pretty well here compared to a lot of the people, and that makes me feel a little guilty."

"And what would you feel if someone came and took it all away from us? Hungry maybe?" Ruth said. "For almost two years I planned and put food away, enough to feed maybe 10 people for a full year, provided we put in a big garden in the spring. But we've been feeding 13 people, and every day Richard takes enough food from here to provide a meal for 20 students. The stockpile of food is dwindling fast, and the seeds that were to be used for our own garden are now in seedling trays in the greenhouses. We have 4 months worth of food left, at the most, and we've no idea if it's enough."

"But look," Rachel said irritably, "the power could be back on in what…another week or two? Then food deliveries will be coming in and everything will be back to normal, right? We don't need a four month supply of food."

"Unless you know something that none of the rest of us know, Rachel, there may not be any more food to bring in! At least 80% of all the food normally consumed in Nova Scotia comes from somewhere else! All we know for sure is, there's not enough food in Annapolis County to feed the rest of the province for even a day. So, do we let them take it so more people can eat for a day, or do we fight to keep it so we can…feed our own baby! If that roadblock comes down, we will have to fight for our existence. There's no question about that!" Matt said ominously.

"Maybe not," Connor said slowly, narrowing his eyes. He had been studying his notes from the past couple of days, half listening to the discussion around the table, the seeds of an idea germinating in his mind. "If the message we got from the RCMP means what I am beginning to *think* it means, we just might have a way out of this."

All eyes were on Connor as he gathered his thoughts together, filling in the missing pieces of the puzzle. "The orders from the military were to pull down and abandon those roadblocks. That was done up in Kings County, and I think it was done to clear the way for anyone coming down Highway One so there would be unimpeded access to the base at Greenwood. Now, the RCMP Officers who had manned that roadblock informed us that shortly afterwards, a convoy of army trucks came through, headed toward Greenwood. They had to have come from the base in Halifax, and they came right down Highway One the same as I did. They must have felt the roadblock would be an obstacle for them, so they had to get rid of it. But why would a military convoy come from Halifax to Greenwood? Reinforcements? I know that's what we've all been thinking, but there are no reinforcements needed at Greenwood. The base, the town of Kingston and the surrounding area are as secure as we are here! That's the part that was making no sense. There was no reason to transport more military personnel to Greenwood, so I think I'm convinced those weren't soldiers in that convoy!"

"What else would they have been?" Michael asked.

"Politicians," Connor replied. "Probably the Premier and his family, Cabinet Ministers and their families, maybe a few lesser officials. Because, thinking it over, I agree with Richard and Ruth. There's no way the military would give the orders it gave, then refuse to communicate any further, unless those orders for silence came from a high government official such as the Premier."

"Even it that's so," Michael said, "How would that give us a way out? The Premier being in Greenwood wouldn't change the orders."

"I think the Premier gave that order to gain unimpeded access to Annapolis County,...Where there's electricity, food, water and heat."

"Then why would there be an order to reconnect the power being generated here to the grid?"

"I'm not sure, but it could be that the Premier wants to be *seen* to be doing something for the rest of the Province, or it could be just a simple case of ignorance of the way the power system works."

"Well that would fit!" Ruth exclaimed. "The ignorance part, I mean...You know, I think you're right about this, Connor. I can't see the military initiating any action that endangered the safety and security of civilians, especially when those civilians were on the defensive rather than the offensive. So the order would have to have come from a government authority. And they probably have orders not to respond to any communication, or else they're too damn embarrassed by what they're being forced to do."

"If that convoy actually *was* transporting a bunch of politicians, how could we verify that if we can't get any response from Greenwood?" Matt asked.

"By letting them believe we already know the convoy was carrying the Premier and other politicians," Connor said. "We know they are receiving because the last message tonight was from a pissed off radio operator repeating the original order regarding the roadblock, with the added message about reconnecting the power...So, with everyone's consent, I'd like to radio the base and play 'let's make a deal'. We can offer to meet the Premier and his entourage at the roadblock, escort them through, and offer them our...hospitality. In return, they let us keep the roadblocks because that will ensure *their* safety too."

"I don't know," Ruth said. "Letting in a bunch of politicians with a bureaucratic mentality is an awfully high price to pay! They'd want to reinvent the wheel here just when we have it rolling smoothly along."

"I said we could *offer* our hospitality, but I didn't say exactly where," Connor grinned.

"What do you have in mind?" Ruth asked, grinning back at Connor.

"Putting them all up in one of the big B & B's on St. George Street for starters. Then make sure they have no opportunity to interfere with the way things are being run here. I figure they can be convinced their attention needs to be focused on provincial matters rather than local concerns."

"What about feeding them? Everything has already been allocated down to the last crumb."

"Those fat cats will be on a crash diet. It will probably do most of them a world of good! We can come up with extra fish, meat, milk and eggs, so they won't starve. But we positively cannot allow them to pay for anything, just like everyone else. Receiving food at no cost is our great equalizer, so we have to maintain that. But we're also not going to take any fresh or canned fruits or vegetables out of the mouths of people here in order to feed them."

"And what if it wasn't politicians on those troop carriers?" Matt asked. "What then?"

"If it wasn't, we might have a little civil war on our hands," Connor said somberly. There's only one way to find out; bombard them with the message that we know they have brought in the Premier and offer safe passage and accommodation in Annapolis Royal. Any objections?"

"Go for it!" Michael said. "I'll sit in with you for a while since I'll have to make another trip out to the barn a little later, anyway."

"I could spell you in the barn tonight," Matt offered.

Michael looked at his father uncertainly. "That's okay, I can handle it," he said. "I'm not expecting any calves tonight. You may as well get some sleep."

Matt gave Ruth a 'well, I tried' look then encouraged her to turn in for the night too.

"I just slept for twelve hours!" she protested. "I'll need a nap tomorrow afternoon, but that's about it."

"How do you ever expect to get back on schedule?"

"I've never been on one, so why start now? Just go to bed Matt. I can look after myself."

Matt looked at Ruth with concern. She had changed into her usual fleece pants and shirt, which meant she probably intended on going out to the barn. "In case you haven't noticed, you're not a kid anymore," he said critically.

"Thanks for reminding me," Ruth replied, deadpan. "It's been a long time since I've really looked at myself in a mirror, so I tend to forget that I'm actually an elderly person instead of the twenty-five year old that lives inside my head."

"That twenty-five year old better start taking a closer look. She has you doing things you have no business doing at your age. Tell her to smarten up!" Matt said as he headed toward the stairs, "before she winds up killing you!"

"Smarten up, kiddo," Ruth said flippantly to herself as she went out to the office to hear if Connor was getting any response from the base.

"Nothing," Michael said morosely in answer to his mother's raised eyebrows. Ruth perched on the side of Connor's bed, absently plucking at a loose thread on the quilt coverlet as she listened to Connor repeat the message over and over into the microphone.

"Maybe his 'lordship' is sleeping and no one wants to disturb him with a message," Ruth offered.

"Yeah, maybe." Connor removed his earphones and leaned back in his chair. "Have you ever felt 99% sure about something one minute, then 99% unsure about the same thing the next minute?" he solemnly asked.

"All the time," Ruth and Michael said in unison.

"Well, I guess that makes me feel a little better. "I'm having some second thoughts about who was actually on those transport trucks."

"Don't," Ruth cautioned. "Go with your instincts. Personally, I think your instincts are right. Because nothing else makes any sense."

"How so?"

"It was well publicized back before the year 2000 when they had that Y2K scare that all the military bases had stockpiled food and installed generators to take care of their own, 'just in case'. And the plan was to always maintain that level of readiness in case of a national emergency. So we know they are well taken care of on the base and surrounding area, and they would have no reason to stir up other areas that have protected themselves. With everything being so well organized and managed down at this end of the province, and almost a total lack of incidents that would require any kind of control or intervention by authorities, there would be absolutely no rationale for bringing in troops as reinforcements. There's nothing here to enforce. So it *has* to be politicians! The base in Halifax was probably housing them and they saw a way to get them off their backs by sending them here."

"I tend to agree with that," Michael said. "It's the most logical assumption and I think we should go with it."

"Just keep hammering away with the message we know the Premier is at Greenwood?"

"No, just once more," Ruth said. "Let them know it's the last message until tomorrow morning at 8 a. m. And if they don't respond at that time, there will be no further communication from us. Get tough,…then get some sleep."

Connor gave Ruth a lopsided grin. "Let 'em know we won't put up with any more of their silence shit, huh?"

"Right." Ruth paused, "When this is all over with we won't be very popular with the rest of the province you know. We'll be labeled mavericks or outlaws, and we may have a price to pay for saving ourselves and excluding everyone else."

"The price of *not* doing what we're doing would be even greater," Michael pointed out. "We might not be alive to pay another kind of price later on."

Connor's expression sobered. "And what if we're wrong and it's not politicians that landed in Greenwood? What then?"

"I don't even want to think about that," Michael replied. "Like you said earlier, we have a couple days of grace because of the snow and wind. If we need it, that will give us time for an action plan."

Ruth was in the laundry room having a cigarette, contemplating what she could do to fill her time. She knew she wouldn't be going back to bed that night, and she had to do something. Read? She quickly discarded that idea. All the books were in the living room where Doreen and Richard were sleeping. Besides, she'd read all of them anyway. Two or three times, at least. Work on the dollhouse? That was an appealing idea, but she might screw up plans Doreen had and she didn't want to do that. Doreen was enjoying decorating the dollhouse too much. It had become her passion ever since Nate had finished constructing it.

Her stomach growled complainingly at the meager amount of food it had received. Stubbing out her cigarette, she decided to fill it with something nourishing, like oatmeal. That would give her something to do for a little while, anyway.

Ruth hauled the big plastic bag of oatmeal out of the cupboard and looked for the directions for making one serving. The recipe for oatmeal cookies on the package caught her eye and she began scanning the list of ingredients. Almost before she knew her own intention, Ruth had gotten out her largest mixing bowl and had begun assembling everything she would need.

'*A dozen to send over for Bea, Nate and the Marchants,*' she thought as she worked. '*Maybe Richard could take some for his students, and the men plowing the roads would probably appreciate a few. I'd better make a double,...no, a triple batch. Big, soft, chewy, spicy oatmeal cookies, with raisins. Yum!*'

As Ruth stowed away the last of the cooled cookies, the door between the dining room and the kitchen opened. A little face peeked through, sniffing the air appreciatively.

"Something woke me up," Cassie said sleepily.

"The smell of cookies baking, maybe?" Ruth asked, motioning Cassie over to the table. "How about joining me for a cookie and a glass of milk before you go back to bed?"

"My feets are cold," Cassie said, scrunching up in her chair and pulling her nightgown down to cover her toes. Ruth put two big cookies on a plate and poured two small tumblers half full of milk.

"Let me warm them up for you," Ruth offered, picking Cassie up and sitting her in her lap. She lifted one of her legs, placed Cassie's feet side by side on the seat of her chair, then lowered her leg to cover the little girl's feet. "Wow!" she exclaimed. "Your feet *are* cold! It feels like I just laid my leg down on a couple of ice-cubes!"

Cassie giggled. "It feels like I just put my feets in a oven!"

The two of them nibbled on their cookies and took sips of milk, alternately chatting, or not needing to say anything at all. Cassie leaned against Ruth, resting her head on her shoulder with a contented sigh.

"You have a milk moustache," Ruth said, reaching for a paper napkin and dabbing at Cassie's lips.

"So do you, Grandma," Cassie said, as she snatched the napkin from Ruth's fingers and smiling, wiped away a trace of milk at the corner of Ruth's mouth.

'Grandma'. Ruth hugged Cassie close, basking in the warm feeling of contentment with the little girl nestled on her lap. *'Grandma'*. It felt right.

"Want me to carry you back to bed?" she asked reluctantly.

Cassie nodded. "My tummy is happy now."

"My heart is happy that your tummy is happy," Ruth said, with a catch in her voice.

"My heart is happy too, Grandma," Cassie said sleepily. "This is a happy day."

Ruth went into the family room after tucking Cassie back in bed. She took her knitting basket out of the closet then settled herself in one of the lounge chairs, the basket by her side. She selected a large pair of needles and a skein of royal blue nylon yarn. She knew now how she would be spending the rest of the night; she'd be knitting slippers for Cassie.

Connor was awake. In the darkness of the room, the tiny red light on the radio was like a beacon that kept him from drifting off to sleep. It demanded his vigilance, commanded him to stay alert and watchful! An occasional crackle of muffled static pierced the silence, sending waves of fear down his spine, causing him to open his eyes wide and tense his jaw as he listened.

"I've had enough of this shit," he muttered, throwing off his covers. He slipped into his jeans and sweatshirt then shoved his bare feet into his shoes. Raking his fingers through his hair, he opened the office door, walked across the cold entry room and let himself into the sweet, spicy smelling warmth of the kitchen.

"Hey Mom, can I have a cookie?" Connor whispered from the family room doorway.

Ruth set aside her knitting. *'Mom? Is there something about baking cookies that suddenly transports one into a Mother / Grandmother role?'* "Take two," she whispered back to Connor. "They're big."

"Isn't that supposed to be 'take two, they're small?'"

Ruth brought her knitting out to the kitchen and sat down across from Connor. "Can't sleep?"

Connor shook his head. "What're you making?"

"Slippers for Cassie. So she isn't in her bare feet on this cold tile floor."

Connor shoved nearly half a cookie into his mouth at once, gazing speculatively at Ruth as she cast off the stitches on a finished slipper. He thought about his parents who had died together in an auto accident when he was nineteen, and his two little daughters he might never see again, and knew in that moment he would give up his life if he had to for the woman sitting there knitting slippers for a little girl with cold feet, and for the rest of the family too, because of what they stood for.

"I think I can sleep now," he said huskily. Just needed a cookie." He bent and kissed Ruth on the cheek, in passing. "Thanks, Mom." He didn't look back at her, afraid she would see the tears glistening in his eyes.

Ruth set the finished slipper on the table, staring at the door Connor had just passed through. She was aware that something

316

momentous had just passed between them, and that it was for the simplest of reasons. Smiling, she began to cast on the stitches for the second slipper. *'I've acquired quite a sizable family today!'* she thought pleasantly.

Glancing at the clock, she saw that it was not yet 2 a. m. *'These slippers are so quick and easy to make, I'll have a pair ready for Mickey too by the time the kids get up,'* she thought.

Connor lay on top of his bed, fully clothed, wondering how it had happened. He had fallen in love with a whole family, their extended family of different races and religions, and a whole new way of living. He knew he could never go back to the kind of life he'd had before and fell asleep wondering where and how he would fit into the whole scheme of things. If anyone had told him he would soon fall in love with a pretty, slightly overweight Jewish girl half his age who was, right then, just one of the many new people he had met, or that the girl was at that moment laying awake thinking about him, he would have scoffed. Instead, he contentedly slept, unaware.

CHAPTER TWENTY-SIX - JANUARY 18-19, 2005

Ruth carried a mug of coffee and a hot carrot muffin out to the office. It was a quarter to eight, and Connor was still asleep. Gently touching his shoulder, she called his name softly, twice, before he opened his eyes. He smiled at her, thinking she was part of the pleasant dream he'd been having, then closed his eyes again.

Within seconds, his eyes flew wide open. "What time is it?" he stammered huskily, sitting up.

"It's close to eight. I hated to wake you, but thought I'd better. Here," she said, handing him the coffee. "Everyone's gone off to school. Matt cleared the lane earlier and the crews have plowed the roads. The wind is dying down too. It's just you, me, Michael and Doreen here today. I figured you'd want to radio the base at eight. That's why I woke you."

"Yeah, I do," Connor replied, yawning. "Was there some magic sleep potion in those cookies?" he asked sheepishly.

"Cookies have always been a magic potion," Ruth stated, assuredly. "They have been known to dry up tears, take the sting out of a skinned knee, raise self-esteem after some sort of failure, even help get rid of worries that keep you from getting a good night's sleep."

"How about mollifying politicians?"

"That too, if necessary. Have oven, will bake cookies! Especially if they can be used to bait wolves and keep them from our door."

Ruth listened as Connor repeated his message to the base at exactly 8 a. m. He ended by saying if there was no response, he would repeat the message again at noon, and until a response was given, there would be no action to comply with any orders from the base. They waited expectantly for some sign of a response.

"I know they're receiving the message," Ruth said. "The military would have someone manning that radio 24 hours a day."

"Then why don't they respond!" Connor fumed. "What kind of cat and mouse game are they playing, and why?"

"Probably some politician has watched too many spy thrillers and thinks silence is the way to gain the upper hand and keep us on edge."

"Well, it's working," Connor said, bitterly. "Keeping us on edge, that is. But I'll be damned if they're going to get the upper hand."

Ruth gave Connor what she hoped was a look of encouragement. "I'm going to go help Michael with the barn chores. We'll take turns staring at the radio all day if we have to. I'll be back in to relieve you in about an hour, okay?"

"Gotcha," Connor replied. "Meanwhile, I'm going to try to raise the RCMP at the roadblock. This not knowing what's going on is driving me crazy."

Ruth decided to forego her usual cryptic remarks concerning the intelligence level of the vast majority of politicians and their aiding and abetting bevy of senior bureaucrats. Her stomach was feeling a bit queasy and she didn't want to risk making her gorge rise by dwelling on her pet peeve.

Outside, the thin sun did little to dispel the gray gloom that seemed to permeate the bare trees, the buildings and the river in the distance. Even the snow appeared to be gray. Ruth was reminded of a black and white photo she had seen years ago of a bleak country scene in shades of gray that conveyed a brittle message of hopelessness and poverty. Overcome by a sudden feeling of despair, she stepped off the deck onto the shoveled path to the barn and was immediately assaulted by a blast of wind that threw a stinging spray of ice-crusted snow into her face.

Gasping for breath, Ruth muttered, "Okay God, I get the message. Thanks for setting me straight. But, could we have a little more sun please? It helps." She took a deep breath, puckered up her lips and began whistling the theme song from the old Andy Griffith Show, jauntily pacing her way to the barn to the rhythm of the tune.

"They answered!" Connor enthusiastically greeted Ruth and Michael as they returned to the house. He had his parka on, and was hurriedly lacing up his boots. "It's the Premier all right! His family

319

is with him and 22 others. Twenty- six in all. I'm heading into town to get a crew together to figure out which of those B & B's we can put them up at, get some heat going and stuff. We've got to go meet them at the roadblock at 7 p. m. There can be no more than four of us and we'll be accompanied all the way back by am armored guard."

Connor tittered and waggled his fingers in the air. "Ooooh! Cloak and dagger stuff under the cover of darkness! What a pathetic bunch of wooses. As if anyone here thinks they're important enough to want to do them harm!"

"The military guards won't be staying, will they?" Ruth asked apprehensively.

"My guess is they'll head right back to the base as soon as they have escorted all those politicians out of their hair. I'll bet they're delighted to have the opportunity to dump them."

"Oh well, we're used to being dumped on in this end of the province," Michael said. "Other people's garbage, twenty-six freeloaders, what difference does it make?"

"They aren't going to be freeloading," Connor assured him. "We can let them think they are our honored guests until the armed escorts depart. Hell, I can bow and scrape along with the best of them! I've had to do that for years with some of the prima – donna doctors and hospital CEO's in this province. But they'll be introduced to the concept of Trade Bucks, and will have to sing for their supper along with everyone else."

"What about dismantling the roadblocks and reconnecting the power lines. Was anything mentioned about that?" Michael asked.

"No, but I would think both the politicians and the military will listen to reason on both counts. After all, the roadblock will ensure the politician's safety and keeping what electricity we have will ensure their relative comfort and maybe even their survival. They can't possibly be so dense they won't recognize that reality."

"Let's hope," Michael said bleakly. "If nothing else, they might understand Mom's baby analogy."

"Maybe they'll turn out to be real human beings," Ruth said hopefully.

Michael and Connor both looked at her dumbfounded. That didn't sound like anything she would normally say about politicians.

Michael, Ted, Connor and Matt were silent as they approached the roadblock. There were four troop carriers on the other side of the barrier, protected by a semicircle of armed soldiers. The four men were ordered out of the Jeep while soldiers kept their rifles trained on them. They were meticulously searched for weapons, and the inside of the Jeep was nearly torn apart. No weapons of any kind were found, not so much as a pocket- knife.

The soldiers visibly relaxed and appeared to be somewhat embarrassed by the obviously excessive precautions being taken, as Matt complimented them on their vigilance.

At a signal from a senior officer, a private opened the passenger door in the cab of the truck at the head of the queue and helped a uniformed man to descend. When armed soldiers quickly surrounded the man, Matt found it difficult to keep a straight face. Glancing at the other three men, he could see that they were having a similar difficulty. *'This is as ludicrous as Chris and his slingshot,'* Matt thought as he struggled to affect a serious demeanor. Slowly, he walked up to the barricade and met face to face with the Premier.

Matt extended his hand. "Welcome," he said. "We have one of the big elegant old houses in Annapolis Royal all prepared to receive you and your entourage, Mr. Premier." After a short pause, he continued, "The situation in Halifax must be pretty bad for you to feel all these precautions were warranted," he said, sweeping his hand to indicate all the armed soldiers. "Let me assure you, the situation in Annapolis County is very different. There is no looting, no violence of any kind. Our young people go to school every day, everyone has warm shelter and food. I…"

"Where's the county warden?" the Premier snapped. "Why isn't he in charge here? Who are you and these other men?"

"I'm Matt Kingsley," Matt said, nostrils flaring. "I'm a farmer. And these men are my son, son-in-law and a friend who is living with us. We are here to escort you to the rather lavish digs we spent all day preparing for you, so we'd appreciate a little courtesy and…"

"I repeat, why isn't the warden here?"

"Because he isn't aware that you are here," '*you insufferable ass*', he added to himself. "No one in any level of government is running things here." Matt explained. "There are no leaders, per se; we all agree on what needs to be done, and everyone pitches in and helps."

The Premier's eyes narrowed. How did you know I was here? Who leaked that information?"

"Nobody needed to leak anything. We knew the messages we were receiving from the base couldn't have come from a military source so we just put two and two together. It was that simple!" Matt couldn't resist adding.

"What made you think those orders weren't from the military?"

Matt looked at the Premier, organizing his thoughts so that what he said wouldn't sound too insulting. "Under the known circumstances, those weren't orders the military would have given. They would have had no authority to give those orders, so we knew they had to have come from a higher authority."

The Premier's stern look softened measurably. He nodded his acceptance of the explanation and regarded Matt with interest. "Just where do you fit into all this?" he asked almost casually.

"The plan to make certain everyone was cared for, with no one excluded, originated under my roof. We put that plan into action by seeing to it that everyone was informed and included. It works, and everyone works at making it work. It's probably the biggest cooperative movement ever seen in this province because it encompasses every facet of life."

"Well, I'll be looking forward to learning more about your cooperative plan," the Premier said affably.

"You'll be living it, along with the rest of us," Matt informed him.

The Premier gave Matt a dismissive look. "Two officers will be riding along with two of your men," he told him. "And two of your men will be riding in the back of troop carriers. Let's move out. I'm anxious to get my,…uh, entourage settled in."

Two of the young soldiers hurdled the barricade and followed Matt as he headed back to the Jeep. Looking back over his shoulder, Matt saw the Mounties who had manned the roadblock beginning to remove the barricade so the trucks could file through.

"Michael," Matt said heartily, "you and Ted are going to ride back in the troop carriers and these two young men will ride with Connor and me. Maybe you could give those Mounties a hand with those barricades." The pointed look he gave Michael got his message across.

"Sure Dad!" Michael said enthusiastically. "Hey, I've always wanted to ride in one of those!"

Ted grabbed one end of a large sawhorse while Michael lifted the other end, and they carried it to the side of the road.

"You're pretty good at acting like a hick farm boy," Ted told Michael under his breath. "But if you come out with a 'goll-eee' I swear I won't be able to keep from laughing."

Michael gave Ted a 'watch this' look as he brushed past him, headed for the trucks. "Do I ride up front or do I get to ride in the back," he grinningly asked a soldier.

"Uh, in the back, I guess," the soldier said, taken off guard by Michael's friendliness.

Michael and Ted were each assigned to the back of different trucks. In both of them, there were 3 men and 3 women, all obviously civilians dressed in military garb, as well as five armed soldiers. They were assigned seats between the two soldiers on one side, directly opposite 3 soldiers on the other side. The 6 civilians were tucked in near the back of the cab.

Michael treated everyone in the back of his assigned truck to a big smile and an effusive greeting. He immensely enjoyed the paternalistic smiles the camouflaged civilians returned, half expecting someone to pat him on the head. He almost said, 'Golly, this is neat!' but changed his mind and decided instead to just sit there grinning and rubbing his hands together in anticipation.

No one spoke to him during the entire trip in to Annapolis Royal. No one spoke, period. Michael felt a nervous sweat prickling his skin all over and wondered if anyone else on this frigid ride had to pee as bad as he did. He felt like a refugee being transported to a detention camp.

Ted was having a similar experience. He too was getting the silent treatment. But every once in a while, when the truck followed a bend in the road and lined up just right with the moon, Ted caught a friendly look from the soldier sitting opposite him, and he was certain he even saw a reassuring wink. Unlike Michael, he had no feelings of apprehension.

In the Jeep, with Connor behind the wheel, Matt in the passenger seat, and the two NCO's in the rear seat, the situation was very different. The soldiers were talkative, relating their experience to date and drawing out Connor and Matt concerning the setup in the county. Matt stuck to generalities, unsure of how much to reveal or whether or not the military could be trusted. Trying to measure and weigh every word spoken to the two officers made the tension in the Jeep almost palpable.

"Look, one of the NCO's finally said, "you guys are obviously nervous and I don't blame you. These are nerve-wracking times. But I want you to know you are doing us a big favor getting this bunch of assholes off our backs and out of our face. They were holed up on the base in Halifax under military protection because the great unwashed in the city were screaming for their blood. Then they were transferred to Greenwood because the brass said things were quieter here and they would be better protected. They just wanted to get rid of them. And that's what we want to do too. We're dumping them on you."

"Why all the soldiers and guns?" Matt asked. "You should know as well as we do that there's been no violence here."

"We know, but those pantywaist politicians don't. The Premier insisted on all the security. He even expects us to stay in Annapolis Royal and guard him day and night for the duration. However long the duration is."

"Good God Almighty!" Matt barked. "We don't even know where the food is going to come from to feed those…those…, how in hell are we going to feed a bunch of soldiers too?"

"Don't worry, you won't have to. We aren't staying. We want them to think we are though. As soon as they're all tucked in for the night, we're out of there! Oh, and a couple of cases of military rations have been sent down to help feed all those extra mouths. Not great food, but it will keep body and soul together."

"How did you guys figure out the Premier was in Greenwood?" the other soldier asked. "That really threw him for a loop, you know. Talk about paranoid!"

"Just a calculated hunch," Connor replied. "The dictatorial messages, the extended radio silence, the absurdity of the whole thing didn't come across sounding like the military. That, and a convoy of troop carriers bringing in what appeared to be reinforcements to an area that needed no reinforcing,....it wasn't too hard to figure it out."

"What's going to happen with the roadblock?" Matt asked, suddenly remembering.

"The roadblock stays. And the one up in Kings County has already been reassembled. Hell, we want those roadblocks just as much as you do. We have all the families on the base and the people in the village to protect!"

"I read a few years ago that all the military bases would keep a continual stockpile of fuel, generators and food," Matt said. "That so?"

"That's so. We have power, heat, water and food. And we want to keep it that way. Whatever you people did down here in Annapolis County was the best thing that could have happened. We thought we were going to feel a lot of pressure from all sides, but that didn't happen, thanks to you. We've been organized for years. In the time you had, I don't know how you guys managed to get organized at all."

"It was like a snowball," Matt said. "Once it started rolling, it just got bigger and bigger. Funny thing about it too. A lot of people are pretty happy about the way things are now, and they're not looking forward to having everything get back to normal. Except for the food. Food is everyone's biggest preoccupation."

"You know, I'm beginning to feel like a real shit dumping this bunch on you," the older of the two officers said. "What are you going to do with them?"

"Assimilate them," Matt replied. "What else can we do? But they'll have to perform a community service every day if they want to eat, just like everyone else. There's no room here for prima-donnas. Or for people who regard themselves as more important than the next guy. There won't be any luxuries, that's for sure."

"What, no pre-dinner cocktails? No appetizers or linen napkins?" the NCO scoffed "I'm afraid the Premier will be expecting those civilized niceties."

"They'll be living on soup they make themselves, restricted to showering once a week, sleeping eight or more to a room, mostly on inflatable mattresses on the floor, they'll be using an outhouse and working 10 hour days for the privilege of residing in our community," Matt recited.

The two NCO's laughed uproariously. "I wish I could stick around to see that!" they both brayed.

"They'll adapt," Matt assured the two men. "If they don't, I'll sic my wife on them. She can put pompous people in their place better than anyone can. She'd feed a stray cat sooner than she's feed the Queen!"

"That's what I love most about her," Connor said seriously. "The way she takes in all kinds of stray cats and makes them feel like they belong."

"Dogs too," Matt said, missing Connor's point. "Buddy was a stray, you know."

Connor turned the Jeep abruptly into the driveway of an old mansion set back from the road, fronted by a sweeping oval of snow. It was eerily quiet in the neighborhood as he followed the sweep of the driveway around to the back of the house, and parked.

"Uh, look. Act like you don't know anything about what's going on, okay?" the older NCO asked. "The Captain would have our heads if he knew we'd been filling you in on things. He's one of those 'tight ass' types, you know? A by the book, regulation kind of guy? Pain in the butt perfectionist?"

"We get the picture," Connor said. "We never heard you say a word."

Matt got out of the Jeep, took the steps up to the back porch two at a time and opened the back door. The entry room was cold and dark, but warmth and the gentle glow of oil lamps greeted him as he opened the door to the kitchen.

Dow was seated at the table and looked up expectantly as Matt entered. "Everything's cool," was all Matt had time to say before half a dozen soldiers barged in behind him, rifles in firing position. They spread out and began searching the house, while others searched the grounds or guarded the Premier and his fellow bureaucrats.

"Overkill?" Dow asked, smirking.

"Definitely overkill," Matt replied. "Way over. Paranoia disguised as routine precaution."

"Well, we have cookies and milk for all the scared little kiddies," Dow said. "Coffee too, if there are any grownups with them."

"Where'd the cookies come from?"

"Ruth. She had Richard bring them in for his students and some for us. We decided to pool them and save them for the new arrivals."

"I'm inclined to tell you to hide them. Save them for the people they were intended for," Matt said brusquely. "But, seeing as how they're obviously afraid for their lives, a few cookies might make them feel a little more at ease."

The soldiers drifted back into the kitchen, one by one, having satisfied themselves that everything was secure and there were no hidden traps. "The other side of the house is awfully cold," one of the soldiers remarked.

"The heat is zoned," Matt told him, "and they'll only be able to use this side of the house. There's not enough fuel to heat the whole place. That's the situation for everyone."

The soldiers looked in the kitchen cupboards and then the refrigerator. "Not much food here. Not even an egg apiece and no bread."

"We hadn't planned on having 26 more people to feed," Matt said through clenched teeth. "What little there is for them, had to be taken out of someone else's mouth."

The soldier lowered his eyes, embarrassed.

"I suspect they were foisted off on us because the military didn't want to have to feed and house a bunch of extra mouths even though you are probably in a better position to do so than we are here," Matt continued. "We don't want them any more than you do. Nobody feels too kindly toward politicians right now, even though politicians aren't to blame for the situation we find ourselves in."

The soldier looked uncomfortably at Matt then shifted his eyes to the doorway behind Matt, and back to Matt again.

"I know there's someone behind me," Matt said, "and whoever it is I hope he heard every word. We'll do whatever we can for these people simply because they *are* people. But they won't be getting any special treatment."

"None is expected," the Premier said from behind Matt's back.

Matt turned to face him. "I hope that's understood," he said.

"Perfectly well understood," the Premier told him.

"Could someone please show me to my room?" the Premier's wife asked, coming up to stand beside her husband. "I'm exhausted and chilled to the bone. I'd like a nice hot soak and a good night's sleep. In that order...Why aren't the lights on?" she asked, looking around.

'Heaven help me!' Matt prayed silently, closing his eyes and sighing. "We can't use the lights because the small amount of power we have is reserved for refrigeration of food and for pumping water for drinking and food preparation only. There is no hot water for a bath and you'll have to use the outhouse out back instead of the toilets. You'll be sharing a room and beds with several other people and you'll eat twice a day, mostly soup that you'll have to prepare yourselves. And, you will all be assigned a daily responsibility at the school, the food bank, the senior citizen's home, the child care facility or the greenhouses," Matt recited.

All 26 civilians had filed into the kitchen and were listening, dumbfounded to what Matt was telling them.

"That's completely unacceptable," the Premier said haughtily. "That's not a lack of special treatment, that's no way to treat anyone!"

"We should have stayed in Greenwood," his wife whimpered.

"Everyone needs to rest," the Captain said from the darkness of the entry room. "My men are bringing in the bags now, so everyone try to get a good night's sleep and we'll sort everything out in the morning." He spoke with brisk authority, and everyone listened gravely. "I see there's coffee here for everyone. A hot drink will have to take the place of a hot tub for tonight. My men will stand watch through the night, and tomorrow we can head back to Greenwood if that's what you decide you want to do."

"Uh, everybody have a cookie too," Matt said magnanimously, passing the plate of cookies around. Hope was a feeble flame growing inside him. Would the military really haul these pampered specimens of humanity back to Greenwood in the morning? It was beginning to look like a good possibility and Matt was already beginning to feel relieved. He could see relief on the faces of the politicians and their families as well.

By dawn, the military trucks and armed personnel were gone, without a trace that they had ever been there.

CHAPTER TWENTY-SEVEN - JANUARY 19 TO MARCH 20, 2005

Matt arrived at 7 a. m. the following morning to find the big house swarming with irate, gesticulating, swearing politicians. "Looks like a session of Parliament," he said to Rachel, Richard and Carin who had accompanied him. "Guess we better see what we can do to calm them down."

"You!" the Premier shouted, pointing his finger at Matt. "You're responsible for this! You tricked us into coming here then got rid of the military!"

"I got you here to put an end to your foolhardy plan to remove the roadblocks and reconnect our power lines to the grid," Matt began, calmly. "Your asinine plan would have destroyed everything we've established here. By bringing you here I saved your sorry ass so the people here wouldn't freeze and starve as a result of your ignorance and incompetence!" Matt was shouting by the time he finished his invective and cut off the Premier's retort by adding, "Everyone is looking for answers and for leadership. You let them down, and you also interfered with the military doing the job they need to do. Your only concern has been for your own safety, when what you should have been doing all along is everything possible to make the people of this Province feel secure."

Carin looked with pity at the red-faced Premier, his face infused with an unspeakable anger. "We're here to fix you breakfast and show you how to make really easy bread," she said shyly.

The Premier's expression softened as he looked at Carin and her words sank in. "Breakfast? Bread? He muttered. "What has that to do with the fact the military has deserted us?"

"They didn't want you with them," Carin explained. "They wanted all of you out of their hair so they dumped you on us. They only pretended to go along with whatever you wanted so they'd have a way to get rid of you." She paused, looking around. "Anybody hungry?"

Richard fetched two huge stock- pots out of a lower cupboard, filled both about three quarters of the way full of water and set them on the stove to heat. Rachel found a large mixing- bowl, measuring cups and spoons then motioned for several of the women to join her over at one end of the kitchen. She had brought a 10 kg bag of flour with her from the farm, along with milk, butter, yeast, salt and sugar. "This bread is great and so foolproof even a kitchen klutz like me can make it," Rachel said charmingly.

"It's old-fashioned, stick to your ribs oatmeal for breakfast," Richard sang out. "With some dried apples, cinnamon and raisins for you as a special treat for your first day here. The bigger pot is for soup tonight. There should be plenty of spices and seasonings in the pantry there. If a couple of you folks will tackle some of these vegetables," he said, hefting a bag of turnips, carrots and onions onto the counter, "we can get the soup started. We'll cook it slow, and the longer it cooks the better it gets!" He took a large frozen beef bone with plenty of meat still attached from a plastic bag, and popped it into the pot. "Great soup and great bread for supper! Enjoy it, because you aren't going to have quite as much after today. Mostly military rations, from what I understand, because there's not enough food to feed 26 more mouths in this town. What you have today comes from the Kingsley farm."

The women looked soberly at Richard then, shamefaced, looked away. They had heard they were taking food out of other people's mouths, and were suddenly painfully aware of it.

The Premier sat dazedly at the table, holding the hand of his wife seated next to him. Matt and Carin took seats opposite them. "Looks like someone made coffee this morning," Matt said. "Can I get you a cup?"

The Premier looked up at Matt, wide-eyed, and nodded. "We both take it with milk, no sugar," he said softly.

Carin reached across the table and placed her hand on top of the clasped hands of the Premier and his wife. "I had an awfully hard time with this too the first couple of days," she said sincerely. "But I got used to it pretty fast because we all keep so busy doing interesting things. Now, I don't care if we ever go back to the way it used to be.

Life is more interesting now because there's a challenge to it. You'll see."

"I used the bathroom this morning," the Premier's wife confessed. "I forgot."

Carin chuckled. "You aren't the first one to forget and you probably won't be the last one either. Don't worry about it."

Matt placed the mugs of coffee in front of the Premier and his wife. "Every one of us contributes something of himself or herself every day here," he said. "Mainly it's because being useful, being needed and accomplishing something is the best way for us to spend our days." Matt looked the Premier in the eye. "I'd like you to hold a series of seminars for the older high school students," he said. "This is a great opportunity for them to learn first hand how government works, and maybe they can give you some ideas of what they think is important too. What do you say?"

"I...I think maybe I'd like that," the Premier said, brightening. "I always thought I would have liked teaching, and..."

Matt turned to the Premier's wife. "I read in the newspaper some time back how much you enjoyed live theater. There's a production underway and I'm sure Bea Henderson, uh, Taylor, the director, can use all the good help she can get. Interested?"

"Could it be set decoration do you think?" she asked with interest. "Some of the other women here would probably like to be involved in some way with a theater production, too."

"I'm sure that can be arranged," Matt said. "Some one will need to be responsible for food preparation here, and a couple of your people could help with the food bank. I'll explain all about that and..."

Carin leaned back in her chair as the Premier and his wife leaned toward her grandfather, listening to him explain all the things there were to do and how everything was done. She glanced around the huge kitchen, at her mother and Richard, each chatting with a group of polite adults clustered around them, smiling and pleasant as they prepared food for themselves. Were these the same people who had greeted them with outrage only a few minutes ago? Basic needs and simple pleasures, she mused. Adults can be such unpredictable children.

The Premier was interested in Matt's opinion as to the source of the total power outage, and wanted to know how Annapolis County had managed to get organized so quickly after the power went out. "There is speculation of everything from a new band of international terrorists, to space aliens, to an act of God being the cause," the Premier said. "And even though Emergency Measures has been in effect here for years, it has been woefully inadequate. Nothing of this magnitude was ever envisioned. That's why I have been at such a loss trying to figure out what to do, other than seeing to it that the government would survive by safeguarding myself and my Cabinet Ministers."

Matt quickly decided his responses would have to be noncommittal; there was no way anyone outside the family could know about his wife's premonition or the lengths she went to in order to be prepared. After all, there was no one she could have told about it beforehand who would have given her premonition any credence; he hadn't even believed it himself! "Most likely it was terrorists," he said. "At least that's the thinking around here. There have been so many articles in the paper in recent years about how hackers have been able to get through to the records in all government departments and that there is no such thing as absolute security when it comes to computers. Personally, I know next to nothing about them, but I would imagine if it's possible to get into government files it's also possible to figure out a way to shut off the power in North America. If it was terrorists, I don't think Canada was the main target. Most likely it was the U.S., and the fact that almost all of North America is connected to the same power grid meant we were affected too." Matt paused, collecting his thoughts. "As far as getting organized here is concerned, well, we came up with an idea to see to it that people in our immediate area were taken care of and the plan just snowballed. That probably wouldn't have happened in the city, but I would think that something similar would have taken place in most small towns and rural areas because people are used to taking care of one another in emergency situations. They wouldn't have had the same advantage we have here though, because of the Tidal Power Plant."

"You really think it was terrorists? After all that's been done to eradicate them since…"

"September 11, 2001," Matt said, his voice clipped and angry. "And it was far more than just the destruction of the World Trade buildings in New York! Thousands of lives were lost in those buildings, at the Pentagon, and on those commercial airliners that were used as bombs. Not to mention the countless numbers of innocent lives lost since then fighting the war on terrorism."

"That's why it doesn't seem to me that it could be terrorists who did this! They go for the dramatic, the showy;…the big bang with lots of blood, gore and noise, and the biggest possible body count. There's been none of the typical things you see in a terrorist act."

"Maybe they got smarter. Maybe they figured out that instead of destroying a small portion of the U.S. and it's local citizens they could do something far more spectacular and deadly; they could do something that would affect the entire continent! Absolutely everything here runs on electricity. Shutting it down would be the most spectacular act of terrorism ever devised and would have the most far-reaching consequences in terms of human life, the destruction of property and the economy. It would also make reprisals almost impossible to carry out."

"How do you figure it would cause a greater number of deaths and destruction of property?"

"All I have to do is look at us here as an example. Annapolis Royal has a population of just over 600 people. There have been 3 deaths, so far, and one house burned to the ground. That's one death for each 200 people, and one property loss for every 600 people. If those percentages hold true across North America, there could be over a million and a half deaths and half a million properties destroyed. But, unless I'm mistaken, I think the property loss will even exceed the loss of life. Not everyone will be organized the way we are here."

"There was nationwide cooperation in 2001. Surely that will happen again!"

"Don't count on it. *Everyone* is affected this time, not just people in a relatively small area. And no, everyone *didn't* cooperate! Far too many people took advantage of the situation by looting, vandalizing, calling in phony bomb scares, even trying to steal the food provided for the rescue workers. Hard times can bring out the best in good people, but they can also bring out the worst in not so good people. And unfortunately, whether we like to admit it or not, there are a whole lot of not so good people in both the U.S. and Canada. Our overflowing prisons are evidence of that, and it's likely that most, if not all, of those dregs of society are on the loose now."

The Premier paled, swallowing hard. The picture Matt had just painted for him was more frightening than anything he had imagined. Even if the power was fully restored tomorrow, which wasn't likely, it could take years to overcome the damage that had been done. He straightened his spine and took a deep breath as he began to understand the enormity of the situation. With a new resolve, he followed Matt out the back door of the mansion and walked with him to the high school.

Bea bustled into the kitchen at the high school with Dow and the Premier's wife following at her heels. She carried a sheaf of papers on a clipboard cradled in her left arm, and she stretched her right hand out to Richard. "Give me a dollar," she commanded.

Wrinkling his brow, Richard reached deep into his pants pocket, pulled out a loonie, and handed it to Bea.

"Now sign here as witnesses," Bea instructed Dow and the Premier's wife as she flipped through the papers she was holding. "And you sign here Richard."

"What am I signing?"

"You're signing that you gave me a dollar."

"Why did you want me to give you a dollar?" Richard asked as he signed the paper.

Bea made a dismissive gesture toward Dow and the Premier's wife then watched them depart. "For my house. You just bought it. Here, this is your copy of the deed."

Richard began reading the document Bea handed him, still frowning in perplexity. "This is for real," he murmured, looking up at Bea. "Why?" he asked, barely above a whisper.

"I'm going to be moving into Nate's apartment with him," Bea explained. "Not just yet, of course. You won't be taking possession of the house until the power is back on fully, and I still need it for a while for rehearsals. But it's much too big for Nate and me to live in alone. When Dow and his family move back to their own house, we'll just rattle around in that great big place."

Richard looked at Bea in confusion. "That doesn't answer my question. Why are you giving your house to me?"

"I didn't give it to you," Bea said coyly. "You bought it."

Richard stared at Bea, his eyes demanding an explanation.

Bea plucked at a piece of lint on the sleeve of her jacket then raised her eyes to meet Richard's. "The house would never have been for sale if it weren't for the situation we are all in right now," she began. "I had always intended to leave my house and its furnishings to the town to be turned into a museum as a kind of monument to myself. That would have been a very selfish thing to do, I think now." Bea lowered her eyes. "I want to be remembered, you see. The best way for anyone to be remembered is through their children, and their grandchildren, and so on. But I have no children of my own, so I have to choose who my children and grandchildren will be. I...choose you and Doreen for my children, and Cassie, Mickey and Teddy for my grandchildren. If you will have me," she said softly, looking back up at Richard.

"Is this something Nate made you do?" Richard asked, his voice husky with emotion.

"Divest myself of my property, yes. But how I did that was entirely up to me. I chose to do this, Richard. And I chose you and your family because you are a good man that a lot of hard things have happened to, and...because being with Cassie and Mickey every day I have grown to love them and I can't imagine them ever not being a part of my life from now on."

Richard hung his head and watched as a tear dropped onto the toe of his shoe. "I stole that dollar I gave you,...mom," was all he could think to say.

"From who?" Bea asked, teary-eyed.

"I dunno. I got it out of the ashtray of some car on a street close to where I used to live."

"Oh."

"You sure you want a thief for a son?"

"I stole a pair of shoes in a K-Mart once."

"*You* did? In a K-Mart? How come?"

"My feet hurt and I needed more comfortable shoes. I didn't want to stand in a checkout line, so I left my expensive pair of new shoes on the rack and walked off in the cheap shoes. They felt good, but I could never wear them again. I still have them. I don't know why, but I could never throw them away. Maybe it's because they are the only thing I ever stole."

"Now you have two stolen things."

Bea looked at the loonie in her hand. "I'm going to put this in the toe of one of the shoes. It will be there, always, as a reminder to both of us that we are far from perfect."

"No, we sure aren't. We're a couple of bad cats."

"Like mother, like son," Bea said, smiling up at Richard.

"Whatever you say, mom."

Richard would have sworn his feet never touched the floor the rest of that day. He smiled benevolently at all his students and constantly found himself having to resist the urge to hug everyone. It wasn't the gift of the house that made him feel that way, as great as that gift was. It was the gift of all the people who had become a part of his life; the gift of unconditional acceptance and belonging. There was no finer gift in the world, he knew.

Ruth leaned against the gate to the calf pen, gazing in turn at each calf. Her mind wasn't on the calves though. It was far away, leaping from one image to another, inducing feelings of sadness mingled with joy, anger with contentment, and fear with tranquility. '*The sum of nearly 3 months of change,*' she thought.

Restless, she had come out to the barn to escape the too empty house. The calves were undemanding company; they required nothing of her inner self, no conversation, no social amenities, no personal attention. They were her catharsis, as always.

She was greatly missing Richard, Doreen and their children, and Connor would soon be leaving too. She was happy for the Martin's, moving into a home they could only have dreamed about if the lights hadn't gone out. And for Connor too, moving into the big house with them so he could be nearer the greenhouses and gardens that had become his passion, and near the friend with whom he had developed such a close bond. *'I'll have to get Connor to take the dollhouse with him,'* she reminded herself. *'That's where it belongs, with Doreen and Cassie.'*

"I should be happy to get my life back," Ruth said out loud to the calves. "So why do I feel such an ache inside?" Priscilla nuzzled Ruth's hand then tugged on the sleeve of her jacket. Absently, Ruth stroked the calf's neck while she dreamed up various hypothetical plans for the family she had left to her. She didn't want to think about how long that would be; the thought of anyone else leaving was almost unbearable.

"They're awfully cute, aren't they?"

Ruth jumped, her hand automatically flying to her chest. "Oh Lindy!" she gasped. "You startled me! I guess I was daydreaming and didn't hear you come in the barn. You're home early, aren't you?"

"No, I don't think so."

"What time is it?"

"A quarter past five," Lindy said, checking her watch.

"It's staying light out later now. I guess that's what made me lose track of time. Supper is in the oven. A casserole. It should be just about ready, so maybe…"

"Grandma," Lindy interrupted, "you told me you sometimes play a game in your head about the cows and calves, and you said you'd tell me about it. Is that what you were doing just now? Playing that game?"

"No, I was just thinking about things."

"Sad things? You look sad."

"Kind of sad and happy mixed together. Bittersweet is probably a good word to describe the way I'm feeling right now."

"Want to talk about it?"

"I'm missing Richard and Doreen and the kids and already anticipating missing Connor even though he'll still be here for a couple more days. Things are changing back too fast and I want to make time stand still. Or at least slow down a bit. I don't want everybody to leave," Ruth said, smiling sadly at Lindy.

"Are you afraid we're going to leave too?"

"That's what I'm most afraid of," Ruth admitted, stroking Lindy's hair.

"That worries me a lot too," Lindy confided. "So what are we going to do about it? I don't ever want to leave here and I don't even want mom or dad to think about it. How can we get them not to think about it?"

"Everything's getting back to so called 'normal', which means everyone's going to have to be thinking about making a living again," Ruth lamented. "There's no way to say 'stop the world, I want to get off!' and have it happen. I wish we could, but we can't. Of course, if there were some assurance that your mom and dad could make a living here, then maybe..."

"Well we'll just have to think of a way. Because if they move back to Edmonton, it's going to be without me!"

"The teachers told their union to go take a flying leap today," Ted told everyone around the dinner table. "And the school board too. They won't get away with it, of course, but the teachers all like the new curriculum, and *especially* the attitude of the kids toward school! So, they're pressing for a lot of changes. The union wants all the non-teachers out of there and the school board says the new curriculum is out. Could get very interesting."

"I hope the teachers win," Carin said. "I'm learning more than I ever did in my old school. Everything is interesting now; math, science, English, history, you name it! We get to discuss things, figure them out instead of just having to sit there and listen most of the time."

"Maybe the school board and union should be invited to sit in on some classes," Ruth said. "They might be agreeable to taking a good look at what's happening in the schools here, especially when the results are so positive."

Everyone looked at Ruth with a puzzled expression. Saying anything favorable about school boards or unions didn't sound a bit like anything she would normally say.

"Tell me the game you play in your head about the cows, Grandma," Lindy coaxed. They had finished with the nighttime barn chores and Lindy was hand feeding some sweetened grain to Priscilla. "Please!"

"It's really kind of silly," Ruth said, feeling mildly embarrassed. "I try to think what kind of clothes they would be wearing if they were people."

"Huh?"

"Well, look. Take Priscilla for example. If she were a little girl, would you see her in pigtails and overalls or a party dress and patent leather shoes?"

Lindy stared at her grandmother, her eyes beginning to sparkle with amusement and a grin forming at the corners of her open mouth. "Neither," she said. "Priscilla would be wearing a plaid skirt and a white blouse, like a school uniform. And glasses, she'd be wearing glasses!"

"And bobby socks and she'd be carrying a book," Ruth added, chuckling.

Lindy got right into the game. "Pitty-Pat would be wearing a bonnet with a big bow tied under her chin and a diaper with ruffles on the seat! And she'd be sucking a lollipop. A red one!"

"Pammi would be the one in a fancy party dress," Ruth said.

"It would be pink, with lots of ruffles and lace and petticoats," Lindy added, laughing.

"Enough silliness?" Ruth asked.

"No! We can't quit until we've finished dressing all the calves! How did you ever think this up, Grandma?"

"I guess one day when I had too little to do I got to thinking how each calf's personality was different, and that just led to imagining what they would be wearing based on their personality. Kind of a dumb thing for a grandma to think about, huh?"

"I think it's a neat thing for a grandma to think about...did I ever tell you how much I love you, Grandma?"

"No Lindy, I don't think you ever did," Ruth said, with a catch in her voice.

A truckload of fish and another of turkeys was hauled up into Kings County past the roadblock there, and exchanged for a load of potatoes, carrots, onions and apples. That helped stop the random slaughter of cattle and the poaching that was sweeping into the adjoining county. A food distribution system had been organized, modeled after the system in Annapolis County. There were a lot of stored vegetables but too little protein up in Kings County, and just the opposite in Annapolis County, so the exchange was welcomed with cheers from both counties.

Electricity had been almost fully restored by the end of January and Annapolis County was reconnected to the grid by the middle of February. By that time phones were working again and local radio stations were broadcasting. Television followed a week later with news and weather reports, but it would be another month before regular programming would be gradually resumed.

The roadblocks into Annapolis County were dismantled by the end of February. Although staple foods were again being delivered, the supply was still rationed and the county was picking up the cost. Food was still being distributed at no cost to anyone. It had to be; there were still no paychecks and the postal system was still in shambles. Fuel was still rationed, and most cars sat idle. With everyone working in his or her own neighborhoods and food being delivered every other day, there was no reason for anyone to go anywhere. And most people were beginning to like it that way.

The banks would be "deeming" all accounts current as of May 1st, so there would be no interest accrued for the first 4 months of the year, either payable or receivable. This had been done at the insistence of government, to help insure the economic stability of the country.

By the first of March the airlines were operating again, though not on full schedule. They were honoring round trip tickets held by people who couldn't get back home after the holidays. Those tickets were good until April 1st., and that news filled Ruth with dread. She had tried to face the inevitability of five more members of her household leaving, the five she would miss the most, but she couldn't stand to think about it. It was as unthinkable as the prospect of the lights going out had been, only this time she was at a loss as to how to go about planning for it.

Two nights before Bea's production was scheduled for performance, Rachel asked if she and Ted could have a talk with Ruth and Matt after supper. Ruth responded with an obviously nonsensical attempt at evasion, but Rachel persisted.

"It's important, Mom."

"Okay," Ruth said lightly, busily checking the pots on the stove she had checked just a moment ago. She couldn't say any more and didn't dare look at Rachel.

Supper over, the three youngsters were assigned the task of kitchen cleanup, while the five adults retired to the dining room with coffee. Ruth had insisted on the coffee. It was more than just a stalling tactic; it was a prop, something to do with her hands, something to keep her from falling to pieces.

"We've put this off as long as we can," Rachel began. "As you know, the plane tickets have to be used by the first of April, so we've already made our reservations. We leave in 4 days."

Ruth was having difficulty swallowing, and her eyes, like those of Matt and Michael, were fixed on the tablecloth as Rachel continued. "We don't know exactly what the situation is going to be in Edmonton and we've talked the whole thing over with the kids. But we need to talk it over with the three of you, too." Rachel paused. "Is it okay with you if the kids stay here for the time being?"

Three heads popped up, eyes riveted on Rachel.

342

"Ted and I decided we had to go back to put our house on the market and sell our furniture. Then we'd load up all our personal stuff in the van and drive back. We'd rather not put the kids through all that, plus there's school and everything. We don't exactly know how we're going to make a living here yet, or how long we might be a burden on..."

Ruth raised her right hand in a halting motion, indicating that Rachel need say no more. Her left hand was already covering her trembling mouth, but it couldn't stem the tears that had sprung to her eyes. Three speechless heads nodded in unison.

"Welcome home," Ruth finally managed in a whispered sob.

CHAPTER TWENTY – EIGHT - MARCH 21, 2005

The Premier and his wife sat front row center in the high school gymnasium. The Premier had come back from Halifax for the production, but his wife had stayed in Annapolis Royal. She had designed the set along with the help of a couple of carpenters, and some of the minister's wives had designed and sewn the costumes. This day represented both an ending and a beginning for her, and she squeezed her husband's hand tightly as her stomach fluttered from the excitement of it all.

The high school auditorium was the only place large enough to hold all the people they knew would want to attend. The bleachers along the length of both sides of the room were packed and the center was filled with folding chairs. Small children were seated on parent's laps so that more people could have a seat. At the back of the auditorium, people were standing six deep.

Backstage, Lindy perched on the edge of a sawhorse in the corner, looking at everyone in turn. There was her grandmother, dressed as a nun. Lindy smiled to herself remembering how Ruth had said she couldn't possibly sing on stage. As pleased and flattered as she was to be asked, the answer was 'no'. But there she was, not looking like Grandma at all. She had even stopped smoking again.

Lindy watched her mother retying the apron covering her plain blue dress. "Me? Play Maria?" her mother had exclaimed. "Okay, but let me warn you, I'm no Julie Andrews!" *'To me you're better,'* Lindy thought. *'Especially in the yodeling song.'* She knew Bea thought so too.

There was Marissa talking to Connor. "I guess I'm supposed to tell you to break a leg," Lindy heard him say. Marissa, flustered, promptly turned and tripped over some props. Connor caught her before she fell. "I don't think you're supposed to take that literally," he said, laughing. Connor would be opening the curtains, and Marissa played the oldest of the children. Lindy looked over at the boy she had watched rehearse the song and dance with Marissa so many times, Earl Drummond's oldest son, who would be playing the part of the boy who professed to love her, but in the end would betray her. He was peeking through the side of the curtain, smiling as he saw his father grinning proudly back at him through a new set of teeth.

Carin and Drew were standing off by themselves, side by side against the back wall. Their hands were entwined, and Lindy watched as Drew planted a kiss on the tip of Carin's nose. "Hey, we're supposed to be brother and sister," she heard Carin say. "Right," Drew replied. "And that was definitely a brotherly kind of kiss." Carin elbowed Drew in the ribs, and Lindy winced. *'She does that a lot. Funny, he seems to like it!'*

Chris was standing importantly between Cassie and her friend Pammy, making sure they didn't do anything to smudge their makeup. Pammy, half a head shorter than Cassie, was playing the role of the youngest child. She was excitedly hopping from one foot to the other, blonde curls dancing, in contrast to the serious looking Cassie in pigtails. "Are you nervous or something?" Lindy heard Chris ask the bouncing little girl. "Nope," she replied, balancing on one foot. "My mom says everyone's gonna love me!" Cassie smiled her agreement at that, and her smile deepened when her best friend added, "She says they're specially going to love Cassie too!" Lindy remembered how pleased her grandma had been when she learned that Bea had included Cassie in the stage family.

Lindy jumped when Bea touched her on the shoulder. "Sorry darling, I didn't mean to startle you," Bea said soothingly. "Are you nervous?" Nate, standing next to Bea, looked questioningly at Lindy.

Lindy shook her head. "I've just been kind of watching everyone and thinking."

"You aren't by any chance the *other* secret surprise Bea is so excited about, are you?" Nate asked. "I promise I won't tell anyone if you tell me."

"That's not fair Nate!" Bea exclaimed. "You know Lindy wouldn't keep anything from you!"

"Yes I would. I promised you I wouldn't tell anyone, and I won't. But I can tell you, Grandpa Nate, that I'm really not any kind of surprise."

345

"If you aren't part of the production, then why are you backstage instead of out in the audience with your grandpa, Michael and everyone else?"

"Because I'm the page turner and I'm going to have the last word," Lindy said, as though that explained everything.

The Premier, sitting amid the din of people conversing and finding seats, was lost in his own thoughts. The past two months had been a revelation to him. There had been none of the bowing and scraping from the people of Annapolis Royal that he had been used to and had considered his due. He had discovered what it felt like to be humbled, stripped of pretentiousness and self-importance. The young people he had set out to inform about government had wound up informing him that his only purpose for being was to see that their collective tax dollars were spent wisely and well. They told him political leaders had forgotten that and things had to change. *'Without us, you are nobody,'* one young lady had said.

At first he had been angry. Then gradually he began to see the truth of what he was being told. He had been guilty of ruling rather than governing; it had been his will rather than public need or public good that had ruled his decisions. As tough as the students were though, they couldn't hold a candle to Matt Kingsley's wife, Ruth.

He would never forget the day he spent at the Kingsley farm, where Ruth confronted him and demanded an explanation for the rationale behind every government policy she considered to be unreasonable, illogical, ill-conceived or just plain stupid. She had listened attentively to what he thought were reasonable answers then shot everything full of holes with the rapid-fire accuracy of a sharpshooter.

"Politicians listen to big business because it makes them feel like big shots hob-nobbing with the rich and powerful," she had said. "You are trying to build our economic base from the top down and you wonder why everything keeps falling apart. Support at the bottom is what's needed. Small, independent fishermen instead of huge corporate owned trawlers that rape the ocean. Small diversified farming instead of corporate owned factory farms. Stop thinking big and start thinking small!"

The Premier sighed, shifting in his seat. His wife smiled at him and squeezed his hand. He looked around him, marveling at the contentment he saw on the faces of young and old, rich and poor, at the simple prospect of enjoying an *amateur* production in a school auditorium. '*They have organized a society here that is immune to outside forces. And they have given me a model to work with,*' he thought. The magnitude of the problem all over North America was mind-boggling, and the blame was universal. Everyone had lusted after 'Mistress Technology' and she had proven to be a duplicitous whore. And that made governments the whore - masters.

'*Think small. Think basics. Prop up the structure of society from the bottom.*' He had always considered the rhetoric that people were the greatest resource of a country a lot of crap. In his experience, people were individually self-serving, greedy, demanding and opportunistic. But collectively, their labor was the only real wealth in the world. He now understood the reality of that, now that he had stopped looking in the mirror, admiring himself. And he was convinced that the greatest resource was also the solution to rebuilding the economy of the country. Government and money would be needed, yes. But the people themselves were the real solution.

His reverie was broken by a smattering of applause, as Ted and Lindy took their positions at the piano on the floor of the auditorium just below the right side of the stage. When the auditorium lights were switched off, it was as though the switches controlled the voices of the people in the audience as well. In the hushed silence, all eyes were riveted on the brightly lit stage that came into view as the curtain opened. The Premier wondered absently how many people besides himself were stricken with a lump in the throat and tears in their eyes as the introductory notes sounded on the piano and the words from the song they all knew so well burst forth from the diminutive woman in the center of the stage. "The hills are alive with the sound of music," Rachel sang, to a collective intake of breath from the audience.

The production was based loosely on the film, with scripting from memory since there were no scripts available. Emphasis was on the music itself as a means of carrying the story. Most of the dark, terrifying side of the film was eliminated, except for the betrayal by the young zealot. It was, in its essence, a depiction of the new life the people had created for themselves; the very same people who filled the auditorium with enthusiastic applause after every song. It ended with everyone eager for more, always the sign of a successful production. And there *was* more!

Lindy and Ted joined the cast on stage for a standing ovation. When the applause finally died down, Bea motioned everyone to be seated, then spoke into the microphone that Nate had handed her. "There's more to come," she announced to deafening applause and cheers.

"Everyone has heard that there is a special surprise," she began as soon as her voice could be heard above the uproar. "When I began selecting the cast for this musical production, I discovered an untrained voice so perfect, so pure, it was astonishing. I knew immediately that voice had to be heard, and that it would have its debut here, at the end of our musical. I also knew there was only one song perfect enough for the introduction of this voice. It's a prayer; the most beautiful prayer ever set to music."

Bea turned and looked at all the cast members assembled on the stage then held the microphone invitingly in front of her. After a few breathless seconds, a little blonde boy stepped forward and accepted the microphone from Bea, holding it exactly as she had shown him. He stepped forward to the edge of the stage then smiled shyly at the audience and closed his eyes. There was absolute silence in the auditorium.

"Aaaa ve Mariiii ia," Chris sang reverently, feeling the power and the awe of the Latin words, even though he didn't understand them. He sang, unaware of the gasping sobs that could be heard all over the auditorium, especially from the people on the stage. Even little Pammy stood quietly enthralled as the bell-like voice rang out, sending shivers through the crowd.

When Chris opened his eyes as the final note melted away, it was to a stunned silence. People began slowly getting to their feet before the applause began. Once it started, it seemed to Chris that it went on forever, as he was surrounded and congratulated by everyone onstage, especially his family.

Lindy rushed to the front of the stage from where she had been standing near the wings to hug and congratulate her little brother, and retrieve the microphone. Then she handed the microphone to Bea and waited patiently for it to be her turn to speak. Bea was dabbing at her eyes with a lace-edged handkerchief with one hand and juggling the microphone in the other, trying to regain her composure. Lindy came to the rescue, taking the microphone from Bea and telling her, "Blow! Your nose is running down your face!" The applause from the audience had died down enough for Lindy's amplified words to carry. Her motherly admonishment had been heard by everyone in the auditorium and the spattering of applause that followed changed to howls of laughter.

Bea blew her nose then retrieved the microphone from Lindy. "Settle down everyone, because we're not quite through yet!" she announced. "We're going to end the evening with a few words from a young lady who has something to say other than that my nose needs blowing."

Light laughter and applause accompanied Lindy as she took the microphone from Bea and walked out to stand on the center apron of the stage precisely as Chris had done. Her serious demeanor commanded everyone's attention as she scanned the audience from left to right.

"Since I'm the only one in my family who can't carry a tune, except for my Grandpa Matt who sings about as bad as I do, I've been asked by my Grandma to give everyone a message. Most of you have heard by now that my grandma had a premonition that the lights would go out on New Year's Day. She wants you to know how scary that was for her to know, and at the same time how thankful she is that she did know. She believes there are probably many other people who had the same premonition, and the message is that we should all be prepared for anything. The world isn't the same for us anymore, and hasn't been for several years. We need to remember that, and not let down our guard. But that doesn't mean we should live in fear, or isolate ourselves from the rest of the world the way we had to do here for a while. Because if we did that, we would be helping to create the

349

kind of world that all the terrorists, past, present and future want to see created. Instead, we must go on with our normal lives, because working together and helping one another is the best way to defeat acts of terrorism and to show the world that no act of terrorism will ever defeat the freedom loving spirit of the people of the Americas or anywhere else where people are free!

"That's my Grandma's message to you, but I have something of my own to add if that's okay with you."

Lindy received a hearty round of applause, whistles and cheers, and waited patiently for the noise to abate before continuing.

"Tonight has been a celebration of '*us*'," she began. "All of us, and all that we have been through together. I know something now that I didn't know before. I know that heroes are really just ordinary people who do extraordinary things simply because they need doing, and that they come in all ages and all sizes. And when I look at all of you here, do you know what I see? I see all kinds of heroes!

"You know, I used to think we celebrated New Year's Day at the wrong time of year. Nature shows us the cycle of life in the seasons, and celebrating a new year when life is dormant always seemed to me to be the wrong time.

"Why not celebrate the new year in the spring with its promise of rebirth and a new life beginning, I always wondered. Or, why not in summer when that promise is being fulfilled? Or in fall, the time of giving thanks and renewing hope? Why winter?

"Well, for the first time in my life I think I understand why. When life is dormant, it's not really dead. It only appears to be. Life is just waiting, planning, building up energy so it can spring to life again.

"When the lights went out, it seemed like the worst possible time of the year for that to happen. It was the hardest time for sure, but it was also the best time, because everything was dormant and it gave us room to think, to get together, and to plan how we were all going to get through this. That wouldn't have happened in any other season, because no other season has the same needs winter has.

"Winter drew us together and helped us sort out what's really important and what's really not. Now that spring is here, everything is changing back to the way it used to be. But we have all changed

350

too, and I don't think we will ever completely change back to being the way we were before the lights went out. Because now we all care about one another more, and we are all a little stronger than we were before. So I'm thankful that if the lights had to go out, they went out on New Year's Day.

"And now I'd like to say something to all of you on this first day of spring that we didn't think to say to one another all through the winter because we didn't know if we could say it and really mean it. Now we know we can. Happy New Year, everyone!"

EPILOGUE

Four days after the lights went out the Special Forces Squad surrounded the isolated shack in the foothills. The Squad Commander entered the hovel alone, leaving his men stationed outside.

The familiar stench in the small dingy room assaulted him; a combination of filth, rot and decay he knew he would never become accustomed to. It was the smell of poverty, ever present in this forlorn wasteland.

He gazed down at the swarthy-faced corpse on the narrow cot. The face was not one he knew. The needle and syringe still protruded from the bend in the left arm, its contents having snuffed out a young life before it could be removed.

Turning his attention to the computer, he touched the mouse and watched the screen spring to life. *'Happy New Year America'* in dripping blood-red letters was superimposed over a drooping American flag for several seconds then disappeared as the disc erased itself.

His first impulse was to curse his stupidity then he realized it didn't matter. There would have been many ways built into the program to erase the disc. No one would ever have been allowed to know how it had been done; that would make it too easy to undo.

He picked up the letter in the printer tray and began reading. When he finished the letter, he read it through a second time, glancing thoughtfully at the emaciated body on the cot from time to time. Reaching in his pocket, he removed a cell phone and pressed the key that would put him in contact with the man waiting on the other end.

He reported his findings then read the letter aloud in its entirety. The instructions he was given in return were brief and decisive before the connection was terminated.

He was near the door when, on impulse, he turned and faced the cot, clicked his heels together and saluted the genius mind that had designed the way to bring a continent to its knees with the touch of a keypad. "What a waste," he whispered.

As he closed the door behind him, the order he gave his men was curt. "Torch it," he said, looking straight ahead. There would be a hero the world would never know existed.

THE END

The Buddy Book – *Home At Last!*

I hung around out of sight, watching until I was sure it was safe. Those people looked all right, but I had learned the hard way that it was better to be cautious.

There were several big buildings and I couldn't sense any movement or sound coming from any of them. What I saw was a bearded man doing something to a tractor out in the yard and occasionally muttering to himself, and a boy carrying a bucket of apples into the smallest of the buildings.

The boy was whistling through his teeth. It was a pleasant, friendly sound that seemed to beckon me from my hiding place beneath a big tree with drooping branches. I had gone a long time without food, and I knew I had to find something to eat soon. I could feel myself growing weak from hunger.

Feeling reassured, I stepped out from under the branches. Slowly, I walked over toward the man then sat down a few feet away from him. I tensed when he looked at me, but knew instinctively I had nothing to fear as soon as he spoke.

"Well, what have we here?" he asked. His voice was friendly and he kept talking to me as he fiddled on his tractor with wrenches and other tools. I wondered why he didn't stop what he was doing, get me something to eat then put me in the car and take me home. That's what had always happened before when I was lost.

I've always had a habit of getting lost. I like running and chasing things better than just about anything else. Rabbits are my favorite things to chase. They leap and change direction often, making the chase interesting and a lot of fun. Cats and squirrels are fun too, if there aren't a lot of trees around. But they don't know how to play fair. They always run to a tree and climb it, ending the great chase game much too soon for my liking. Raccoons, porcupines and skunks are fun to chase too, but I've learned the hard way to be careful about getting too close to any of them.

Rabbits are definitely the most fun, but they are also the reason why I get lost so often. Sometimes the chase game can last for hours and I wind up so deep in the woods that I'm completely lost. My people get very angry with me if I'm off on a chase and don't return home before dark. They are especially angry if I am gone for several days. I always feel ashamed and tell myself I will never run so far again, but I always do. Because a chase game isn't over until it's over. And it isn't over until I lose the sight and smell of the rabbit, no matter how far I have to run until that happens. And now I was the most lost I had ever been in my life!

As I sat there waiting to be fed and taken home, I saw three cats come out into the farm- yard through a small hole in the big barn door. I was instantly alert, every muscle in my body tingling in anticipation of the chase that would come when the cats spotted me. But ... they didn't act like any other cats I had ever seen. They just lazily walked right up to me, sniffing the air and staring me right in the eye.

Nothing like that had ever happened before, so I didn't know what to do. My whole body was quivering because all three cats were close enough for me to pounce on. While I was making up my mind which one it would be, one of the cats suddenly lay down right in front of me and began rolling back and forth in the dirt. Then another one sat down and began licking its paws. And, to my horror and amazement, the third cat began rubbing up against me, purring! I was used to cats not playing fair, but these cats clearly didn't understand the rules of the chase game at all!

I decided I had come upon a crazy place, with cats that didn't run and people that didn't give me food then take me home. That wasn't the way things were supposed to be. I was supposed to be taken home where my people would yell at me and tell me I was bad while beating me with a stick. Then I would be locked up in the dark shed and would stay there until my boy let me out. That was the way it was supposed to be, because that was the way it had always been.

Slowly, carefully, I moved away from the man and the strange acting cats. I walked over toward the house then stopped just before rounding the corner. I'd heard a door open, then shut, and footsteps coming toward me. A woman appeared from around the corner of the house and stood frozen in her tracks as soon as she saw me. I could smell her fear.

No one had ever been afraid of me before, and her fear made me uncomfortable. Not knowing what else to do, I sat down, tried my best to look like I was smiling, and lifted a paw in her direction.

"The dog's okay," the man called to the woman. "The cats have been all over him and he didn't seem to mind a bit."

"Do you know who he belongs to?" the woman asked.

"Never saw him before," the man answered. "He's wearing a collar but it looks as though his tag is missing. Why don't you see if he is hungry or thirsty then maybe call around to see if anyone in the area knows where he lives."

"Are you hungry?" the woman asked me.

In reply, I lowered my paw, whined softly and swished my tail back and forth in the grass. *'Now we're getting somewhere,'* I thought. *'Finally things are going to happen just the way they always have.'*

But I was wrong. After feeding me a most wonderful meal of raw meat and cooked rice followed by a drink of cool, fresh water, the woman fixed a bed for me. It was in a small room inside the house with lots of boots and coats and wonderful, interesting smells. I could smell chickens and some other kinds of birds, but mostly I could smell the people who lived there, and I could smell cows.

I was alone in the room, lying on the fragrant feed sacks that were my bed, waiting to be taken home, when I heard footsteps on the porch, and the door was suddenly opened, revealing the whistling boy I had glimpsed earlier. He entered the house noisily, banging the door shut behind him. The boy stopped short when he saw me, staring wide-eyed for what seemed to me to be a very long time. I was delighted when I saw a big grin slowly spreading across his face. I got up off the feed sacks, walked over to the boy, and was rewarded with a gentle pat and then a big bear hug.

"Dad told me there was a dog here," the boy said. "But he didn't tell me it was the dog I have been looking for. I hope we never find your owner; I want to keep you."

He proceeded to tell me how his dog had been very old and had died several years before. And how ever since then he had been looking for the right dog, but could never find one that felt right. Until now.

"I'm going to give you a name," the boy told me. "You're ... Buddy. No, Buddy Bear, because you look like a big, cuddly, friendly bear. Buddy Bear it is. But I'll just call you Buddy for short."

I cocked my head sideways, looking hard at him. He seemed so happy, I hated to hurt his feelings. He was nice enough; so were the man and the woman. But sooner or later they would have to know that I couldn't stay with them. This was not my home, these were not my people, and my name wasn't Buddy Bear.

I rested on the feed sacks, dozing off and on, waiting to be taken home. The man and the boy came in and out of the house several times, both stopping to pat me on the head or scratch behind my ears as they went about their business. Their kind words and gentle touch, along with a full stomach, made me drowsily content to wait.

When the woman came through the door that led to the part of the house where the people lived, keys jingling in her hand, I was instantly alert. I followed her out the back door and ran to wait for her beside the car. *'Finally,'* I thought. *'I am going to be taken home!'*

"You like riding in a car, do you?" the woman asked as she opened the back door of the car for me. I scrambled inside and leaped up on the back seat, trying my best to smile. "I guess it's okay if you come along with me," she said. She called out something to the man, but I couldn't hear what she said with the door closed.

We drove down the lane then out onto the paved road. The woman kept talking to me but I didn't pay attention to what she said. I was too busy looking at all the houses and trees and cows passing swiftly by, and trying to catch a glimpse of my home. All of a sudden the car slowed and the woman pulled in and stopped beside many other cars all standing in a row.

She rolled the back window down a few inches then told me to stay and be good; she would only be a few minutes. Many other people were walking about, getting in and out of cars. I didn't see any people I knew, or hear any cars I knew the sound of either. When the woman returned, she placed some interesting smelling bags in the back seat with me, and we were soon back on the paved road again, flying past more houses, trees and cows. *'Soon,'* I thought. *Soon I will be home again!'*

When the car finally stopped, I found myself not back home again, but back at the farm with the man, the woman, the boy and the strange acting cats. Puzzled, I reluctantly followed the woman into the house and plopped down onto the feed sacks, prepared to wait again. Clearly, these people did not know what was expected of them. I would have to find another way to get back home.

After what happened that night though, I decided I wasn't in any great hurry. I had already been away from home a long time, so a few more days wouldn't matter, I told myself. You see, I was invited inside the house where the people lived, fed another wonderful meal then was permitted to lie on a rug near a warm stove. And later, the boy gave me a delicious, crunchy bone then sat beside me on the rug, talking to me and stroking my head. I had never been allowed inside my people's house. My bed was a mat on the dirt floor of a cold, dark shed. I never minded that because it was what I was used to. But, lying on a rug next to a warm stove was much nicer, and the food was better than any I'd ever had before. I must admit, too, I loved having my head stroked and my ears scratched, so I decided I would stay another day or two before trying to find my way home again.

I spent all the next day with the boy. We ran everywhere together; down the lane and back, through the pastures and even into the woods. I played the chase game with the boy and we ended every run with a tackle and a laughing tumble in the grass. I didn't know how to play ball or fetch a stick. When the boy picked up a stick to throw, I cringed and lowered myself to the ground, expecting a beating. But the boy quickly turned and threw the stick far into the woods. Then he sat down in the grass next to me and wrapped his arms around me.

"Someone used to hit you with a stick, didn't they," he said, sadly. "Well, no more sticks. No one is ever going to hit you again. It doesn't matter that you don't know how to play ball or fetch. It doesn't matter if you don't know how to do anything except run with me, because I love you just as you are. You're my Buddy Bear."

Early the next morning, the boy and I ran together to the end of the lane. Very soon, a big yellow bus stopped, and the boy stepped inside then turned and told me to run back to the house. I knew about yellow busses. My boy got on a yellow bus too, and returned later the same day. But this was not my boy's bus. This one had a different smell and sound. I watched as the bus moved slowly down the road then I turned and trotted back to the house. The woman opened the back door for me and gave me one of those delicious, crunchy bones she got out of a box on the counter. I happily took the treat over to the rug in front of the stove, and stretching out and soaking up the heat, I noisily devoured it.

I was drowsing contentedly when I heard the jingle of keys in the woman's hand. "Come on Buddy, we're going for a ride," she called. I leaped to my feet and followed her excitedly out to the car. After a long ride, we stopped in front of a building and the woman hooked a lead strap onto my collar before letting me out of the car. I was suddenly frightened and nervous, trying to pull away as she led me inside the building, even though she kept talking to me softly, telling me everything was going to be okay.

I had thought I was being taken home, but instead, the woman led me into a small, strange smelling room, where a man lifted me onto a slippery table. He felt all over my body and looked in my eyes and ears while talking to the woman.

"When did you say he showed up at your place?"

"Early Saturday afternoon. I called about a dozen people to see if anyone had heard about a lost dog, and notified the radio station too. Thought I'd better bring him here to get him checked over."

"Did you want to leave him here in the holding pens?"

"Oh, no! I'll take him back home with me. I just wanted to make sure he wasn't sick or anything, and maybe have him get vaccinations and whatever else he needs."

"He's in pretty good condition; a little too thin maybe, a bit malnourished, but that's to be expected if he's been on his own for a while."

"About how old do you think he is?"

"He's young; not quite two years old, I'd say."

"And what breed, or mix of breeds I guess I should say. Obviously, he isn't a purebred."

The man looked me over very carefully. "I can see evidence of about four different breeds," he said. "The size and body structure are like a Husky, the slightly wavy hair and his eyes are like a Border Collie, the ears and muzzle are like a German Shepherd and the short, fluffy tail that curls over his back and the set of his mouth that makes him look like he is smiling, is like a Samoyed. Altogether, he's a very handsome dog!"

"We think so too; especially my son, Michael. You know we've been looking for another dog ever since old Sultan died, and Michael has already decided this is the dog he wants. We will certainly try to find his owner, but at the same time we hope his owner never shows up. Michael thinks the dog was abused and has led a pretty hard life. If he got lost and is trying to find his way back home, we're lucky he stopped off at our place on his way."

"If you ask me, the dog is the lucky one," the man said.

Back at the farm, I followed the man around and sat near him as he did things with fences and gates. I kept watching to see if the cats would come out of the barn and want to play the chase game with me. But I didn't see them at all that day. Bored, I stretched out on the porch in the path of the sun, soaking up the warmth in the chilly air. I was about to doze off when I heard the sound of the yellow bus far down the road. I leaped to my feet and ran down the lane as fast as I could, loudly greeting the boy as he stepped off the bus. He hugged me hard then we ran together back up the lane to the house. After he fixed himself a sandwich, which he shared with me, the two of us played the chase game until it was dark and time to go inside.

I soon discovered that the best time of day was when I heard the yellow bus coming down the road. As soon as I heard it, I would run down the lane as fast as I could to meet the boy. Every day was the same. He would stroke my head and hug me. Then the two of us would run back up the lane to the house and share a sandwich. After that, we went back outside and ran some more until dark.

Finally there was a day when the boy didn't have to leave in the morning on the big yellow bus. That was good. I missed him all those hours he was away. He told me we had the whole weekend to be together, and he was going to introduce me to the cows.

I knew what cows were. I had come across them many times in my travels. Mostly, I tried to avoid them, after having one old cow catch me on her horns and flip me in the air when I tried to take a shortcut through her pasture. It was an experience I didn't care to repeat, so I was pretty nervous walking out into the field with the boy, where a bunch of cows and calves were eating grass or lazing about.

But there seemed to be something different about these cows. There weren't horns on any of them, and they all looked alike. All of the cows had white faces and dark, reddish brown hair, but they each smelled a little different from one another. As we walked among them, some of the calves came over and touched noses with me, while the mama cows watched nervously. But they didn't run at me, snorting and pawing the ground the way other cows had before. I was just beginning to feel very easy walking among the cows when the boy startled me.

"Oh no!" he yelled suddenly.

I looked around, frantically. What was wrong?

"Some of the cows have broken through the fence and are heading for the road," the boy yelled as he started running. "Come on Buddy, help me round them up!"

I ran alongside him and we jumped the broken fence together. Then the boy pointed and hollered. "Go that way." I did as he told me, while he ran around the other side of the cows. I seemed to know exactly what I was supposed to do, but I don't know how or why. I ran back and forth along the edge of the road, driving the cows back through the fence. It was so much fun that I kept on driving the cows until I had driven them all the way into the barnyard. Then I stood guard at the gate so none of the cows could escape and waited for the boy to catch up.

Soon he arrived, panting, and he closed the gate. Then he treated me to one of his smiles and a big hug.

"Wow Buddy, if I ever had any doubt about you being the right dog for me, which I didn't, then you sure took care of that just now! Come on. Let's go tell Mom and Dad what you did."

The boy was so excited telling about rounding up the cows that he made me excited too. We were racing around the yard showing how we had done it, and I was suddenly so happy I was jumping up and down, loudly joining in the telling, until the boy and I collapsed in a heap together. I was petted, praised, hugged and given a bone with lots of meat still on it. I had never felt so good in my life!

A little while later the man and boy went to fix the fence and the woman went back in the house. I stretched out on the porch with the bone between my outstretched paws, content to just lay there for a while. One of the cats approached, eyeing the bone, and I growled at her softly, letting her know it belonged to me and I wasn't interested in sharing. She made a wide berth past the bone then came back and snuggled up against me. For some strange reason I let her.

As the two of us lay there together drowsing in the thin fall sun, a faraway sound made me suddenly alert. A car had turned into the lane. It was a familiar car, remembered from long ago. I never forgot the sound or smell of any car that had ever driven into the yard at my home. Locating a familiar car and waiting beside it was almost always the way I managed to get back home when I was lost. With growing excitement, I leaped off the porch and ran to greet the car.

When the car door opened, I leaped in past the man behind the wheel and settled into the seat beside him. The man quickly got out of the car then peered back in at me, shaking slightly and obviously puzzled. I could smell his fear. I hadn't meant to frighten him, but clearly I had.

The woman came out of the house and the two people stood chatting for a while, looking at some papers in a big book. I sat on the front seat of the car, waiting to be taken home.

"I'm sorry, I'm really not interested," I heard the woman say, and the man turned back to the car.

"Your dog thinks he wants to go home with me," the man said. "He jumped in the car as soon as I opened the door. He must like to ride in cars."

"Yes, he must," the woman said. "Come on out of there, Buddy. You can't go for a ride in the man's car."

I didn't understand why she was making me get out of the car, but I did it because she asked me to. The man got back in his car and began to drive back down the lane. I went with the woman back to the house, but didn't go in. I looked where I had left my bone, but it was gone. And the cat was nowhere in sight.

Sighing, I lay back down on the porch. But as I saw the car that was supposed to take me home turn out of the lane and onto the road, I leaped to my feet and ran down the lane after it. By the time I got to the road, the car was out of sight. Its scent was still strong though, and I began following it.

I trotted a long way down the side of the road, following a scent that was growing weaker and weaker. It was getting dark and I was getting tired, so I climbed down into the ditch, looking for a place to rest for a while. No sooner had I closed my eyes when I heard the sound of another car I knew. Leaping up to the side of the road, I waited for the car to see me and stop.

But it didn't stop. I chased the car for quite a way, but it was moving too fast for me to keep up. Tired, and now hungry and thirsty too, I slowed to a walk. I could still smell that last car I knew, and the smell seemed to be growing stronger.

Then I saw it. It was standing still in front of a house on the other side of the road. I waited impatiently for another car to go by, then dashed across the road and ran up to the car, sniffing all around it. It was a car I knew, all right, but I couldn't remember just where or when I had smelled it before. Its sound would help me remember, but it wasn't making any sound then. It was just sitting there, quietly.

I crawled under a nearby bush and lay down to wait for someone to come out to the car. Many times before when I waited for a familiar car to take me home, the wait had been long. I was hungry, but I had been hungrier many times before. Thirst was more of a problem, after all the running I had done. But I didn't dare leave my watch to go in search of water; the car might leave without me.

Luck was with me; I didn't have to wait long after all! An old man came out of the house and headed toward the car. I ran to greet him just as he opened the car door, shoving past him and leaping up into the front seat. He was startled and I felt bad about that. I really didn't like scaring people.

"Well, I know you!" the old man finally said, half laughing. "You're a long way from home youngster. Looks like you want a lift, huh? Well, I'm going right by your place so I'd be glad to give you a lift home."

I remembered the man, but wasn't sure where I had seen him before. He had given me part of a sandwich from his lunch-pail once. That much I knew, and that was enough. Settling into the seat beside the man, I closed my weary eyes for the ride that would take me home.

The car stopped and the old man opened the door for me. I followed him out of the car and slunk low to the ground, awaiting the harsh words and shame from my people that would soon follow.

But, ... looking around, I saw that I wasn't back home after all! I was back at the farm where the man and woman and boy lived! They were coming out of the house, all three of them, happily calling 'Buddy'! Then I was being hugged and stroked and exclaimed over and taken in the house for a drink and my dinner.

Later, as I lay stretched out on the couch with my head in the boy's lap, he told me how they had been searching for me for hours and had been afraid they would never see me again. I listened to his sad sounding voice, and was sorry for making him worry. I was content to be there with him, but ... I still wasn't home.

The next day the boy put a new collar on me and attached a tag that jingled when I moved. There had been a tag on my old collar that had jingled the same way, but I lost it when my collar caught in some bushes while chasing a rabbit through the woods. I lost the rabbit too.

For quite some time after that I was content to stay on the farm with the boy, almost forgetting that I had to get back home. I no longer wanted to ride in the car with the woman because it was just a ride, not a ride home. Winter had set in, and aside from running to the end of the lane with the boy in the morning, and meeting him again later, I spent most of my time stretched out on the rug next to the warm stove, soaking up its wonderful heat. Once in a while I ventured a short distance into the woods, following the scent of a rabbit, but never went far enough to get lost.

Then one day in the middle of winter it grew warmer outside. It was a 'thaw' I heard the man say. As I made my morning rounds among the buildings and to check out some of the outlying fence posts, an overwhelming urge to get back home overcame me. I trotted around to the barnyard where the cows were sunning themselves with their new calves by their sides. Touching noses with one of the new baby calves, I said goodbye to the gentle cows and crawled under the gate.

'*Home,*' I kept thinking, '*home,*' as I crossed the field that led down to the road. I climbed between the strands of wire, snagging my coat and leaving a clump of hair hanging on a barb. The side of the road was wet and piled high with dirty snow, so I stayed to the fields, easily walking on top of the still crusted snow. I felt good; I was going home. I had been away a long time and my people would be very angry. I felt a great need to hurry, so wherever I could I broke into a run, wishing at times that the boy were running with me. I would miss our runs together; my boy never wanted to run.

I traveled all day, stopping only long enough for an occasional drink from a stream wherever water had broken through the ice. I crossed many roads, climbing over the banks of snow on either side, and didn't allow myself to be distracted by anything; not houses or people, or other dogs or small animals I would have liked to chase. I was going home, and nothing would stop me.

As the day wore on it began to grow colder. The sun disappeared behind a cloud and a chill wind began to blow. I knew it would soon be dark, so I looked for a place to shelter for the night. What I found was a big tree right in front of a house. Its thick branches of needles kept out most of the wind, and underneath there was a soft bed of dried needles where the snow had never reached. Curling myself into a ball with my nose tucked under my tail, I was prepared to wait out the night.

Only ... I didn't have to! Before long my sleep was interrupted by the sound of a car pulling up beside the house. It was a sound I knew well, having heard it many times before. Dashing out from under the tree, I ran up and greeted the man who was opening the door of a small truck with a big box on the back. When I jumped up onto the seat the man frowned at me and, leaving the door open, went around to the back of the truck and took something out. He went up to the house and handed the people there the thing he was carrying, then put something in his pocket and came back to the truck.

The man climbed inside the truck and looked at me hard, still frowning. I raised one front paw in his direction and tried the best I knew how to smile.

"Ah, now I remember you!" the man exclaimed. "It's your smile that would charm a man out of his dinner that did it! You're a long way from home pal. I suppose that's why you jumped in my truck; you want me to take you home. But I'm not headed that way, not until tomorrow. So how about if you come home with me for the night?"

That's what I did. He was the 'fish man' and he shared his fish supper with me. He also shared his bed with me, after checking my coat for mud, litter and bugs. The next morning I rode with him to the fish market, and after loading the back of his truck, we set off on his rounds.

He made a lot of stops. Though I was anxious to get home, I was careful not to show my impatience. That would have made me seem ungrateful. The nice fish man was, after all, taking me home!

When at last he turned up the lane to … not my home but the farm where the boy lived … I began barking loudly, trying to tell the man *'No, this is not my home!'* He just looked at me and laughed, not understanding at all!

I was still trying to tell him this was not my home long after the truck stopped and the man had opened the door and was motioning for me to get out. But when I saw the woman come running over to the truck, I realized how happy I was to see her and tried to jump out into her arms. We both fell to the ground.

"Buddy, Buddy," she crooned, while massaging my ears. "Oh thank God you're back and okay! No one got any sleep last night; we were all so worried about you." She hugged me close and kissed the top of my head even though she was on the ground getting covered with mud.

She bought a lot of fish and we both thanked the fish man. Then we went inside and the woman gently brushed the tangles and mud from my coat until it was dry and clean. All the while she told me how they had all looked for me all day; she and the man up until the time the boy returned from school, then the boy and man up until dark. The boy had refused to go on the bus this morning, and he and the man were out looking for me right then.

I was stretched out by the woodstove when the boy and man returned for lunch. We had a joyful reunion and then the boy curled up on the rug next to the stove with one arm draped across me. We slept that way until the woman woke us for supper.

As time passed, I was mostly content living on the farm. The man, the woman and especially the boy all treated me with kindness. I was never hungry or thirsty, never cold, and I had a comfortable rug near the stove and even a couch to lie on. I ran with the boy every day then was petted and hugged, and no one ever yelled at me or hit me or told me I was bad. Yet, there was a feeling deep inside me that something was wrong; something was missing. When that feeling came over me, I couldn't explain it or resist it. The insistent urge to get back home seemed to overpower me, and even though I had grown to love these people as much as they loved me, I knew I could not stay with them. They were not my people and I was not their Buddy Bear. Although I eagerly answered to that name when called, and enjoyed hearing it spoken so lovingly, I knew I had another name and another home; my *real* name and my *real* home!

One morning, after accompanying the boy to the bus, I trotted as usual back up to the house, prepared to spend most of the day relaxing by the stove, waiting for his return. But the air was warmer than usual, and a soft breeze tickled my nose with the enticing smell of damp earth mingled with the odor of animals emerging from their winter nests. Without giving the rug by the stove another thought, I ran up into the woods, anticipating the wonderful game of chase I knew awaited me there.

A squirrel scolded me from its perch on a branch high over my head. I didn't give it a second glance because it was obvious that squirrel wasn't going to play fair. Besides, I had spied a movement deep in the woods at the base of a large tree, and I was off and running before I even knew what kind of animal it was. I gave a shout of joy when I saw it was a rabbit, my favorite thing in the world to chase. The rabbit leaped into the air when it heard me then was on the run even before it hit the ground. With little yelps of happiness escaping from me every now and then, I jigged and jagged in hot pursuit after the rabbit. The chase game was on!

At first the ground was level, but then it seemed as though I was running steadily uphill. The rabbit stayed just far enough ahead of me to make the chase game exciting, but I soon began to tire from the steep climb. So did the rabbit. He began pausing every now and then to catch his breath, alert and wary. I paused when he did, laying in wait for the chase to continue. The rabbit didn't seem to know that I wasn't interested in catching him. I could have pounced on him and ended his life any time I wanted to, but that would have ended the fun. I was only interested in the chase.

The day was growing darker and colder but I didn't mind at all. We were running downhill by then, and the going was much easier. I was surprised when the rabbit suddenly stopped and flopped over on its side. Carefully creeping forward for a closer look, I saw that the rabbit's eyes were closed and his body was slightly twitching. Then the twitching stopped and the rabbit was completely still. I didn't understand why the rabbit had stopped running so suddenly, so I nudged him with my nose, but still he didn't move. Resigned to the fact that the chase game was over, I picked the rabbit up in my mouth and turned to carry my prize back up the hill.

The rabbit was heavy to carry and was making my mouth dry. I realized I was very thirsty from running so long. Dropping the rabbit in an area that was clear of brush and trees, I stood very still, listening for the sound of water. I thought I could hear water, but it was different from any I had heard before. Then, looking back the way I had come, I saw more water than I had ever seen before. It stretched as far as I could see off in the distance, and was pounding and spraying into the air when it ran up against some big rocks. It was frightening to see. As thirsty as I was, I did not want a drink of that strange acting water.

It was growing colder and strong gusts of wind had begun blowing icy flakes of snow into my eyes and nose. I snapped at the flakes, but they didn't do much for my thirst. Picking the rabbit up again, I trotted as quickly as I could up the hill and into the shelter of the woods. There were still many patches of snow in the woods, and I chewed several mouthfuls even though their icy coldness made me shiver. I was beginning to feel worried and a bit scared too when all of a sudden I smelled a familiar smell that filled me with happiness. It was the smell of wood burning, just like the smell from the stove at the farm where I had been staying until I could get back home again.

I shouted out my happiness before picking up the rabbit again, and my call was answered by a man's faint shout from deep in the woods. "Hello! Over here!" I followed the smell of the wood smoke, and found a man sitting with his back up against a tree, close beside a small fire. He smiled when he saw me, but his smile quickly disappeared.

"Are you all alone?" the man asked. "I thought maybe you were bringing me some help." Then he noticed the rabbit I still held in my mouth. "Maybe you are bringing me help of a sort," he said, taking the rabbit from me. I watched as he took a knife from his pocket, skinned the rabbit then put it on a stick and held it over the fire.

"You picked a sorry old man to hook up with little buddy," the man said. I cocked my head and looked at him, wondering how he knew to call me by the name the people at the farm had given me. I was certain I had never seen the man before. "A sorry, foolish old man," he continued, "who had absolutely no business going off into the woods alone. Now look at the fix I'm in. Broke my leg, can't walk back out of here, can't find any more wood dry enough to burn and don't have any more matches anyway. But you brought me something to eat, some fine company so I won't feel so alone, and maybe a bit of hope too. Someone should have seen my truck on the side of the road by now and will come looking for me. And maybe they'll even find me before I freeze to death."

The man shared the rabbit with me then we watched silently together as the fire dwindled away. "I have an idea that might help both of us," the man said. He pulled me close, opened his coat then wrapped it around me and closed it again. At first I was alarmed at being so tightly enclosed, but the warmth from the man felt good and the wind couldn't reach inside the coat. I decided I was more comfortable from the warmth than I was uncomfortable from the closeness, and as the man curled up by the dying fire, I rested my head on his shoulder and drifted off to sleep.

Both the man and I woke, cold and stiff, as it began to get light. We could hear the voices of men shouting in the distance. "Hello! Hello! Nate!", the voices shouted. The man tried to shout back, but his voice was little more than a weak croak. I started shouting myself, struggling to free myself from the coat before the man could open it. As soon as I was free, I ran in the direction of the shouting voices then led the shouting men back to the man who had shared the rabbit and his warmth with me all during the cold night. Before long, both the man and I were in a big car that made a loud, frightening noise. He was lying stretched out in the back, and I was on the seat in the front next to the man driving. We were flying down the road so fast everything was a blur. I cringed against the back of the seat, wanting the frightening noise to stop

When we finally came to a stop and the car stopped making the noise, I relaxed slightly. The man I had spent the night with told the driver to check my tags. "We have to get this little guy back home safely," he said. "I don't know how he happened to find me in the woods, but he saved my life. He was like a guardian angel, appearing out of nowhere and bringing me food, warmth and comfort, telling me to hang on and not give up hope of rescue. I would have frozen to death if he hadn't been there to keep me warm, and if he hadn't gone running to you, you may never have found me in time. Promise me you'll make sure he gets home safely."

I was left alone in the car, with the window rolled partly down, as all the people went into a big building. As soon as they were out of sight, I squeezed through the open window and began to run. I had to get away from that frightening car before it began to make its terrible noise again. I ran past many houses and across many roads, always listening for the sound of a familiar car or a familiar voice, all the while looking for a familiar face. There was nothing, and no one, I recognized. I kept on the move most of the day, stopping now and then to drink from a puddle or rest for a few minutes. The sun felt warm on my back and there was no wind, but my feet were sore and I was very hungry. I had decided to head into the woods to find a rabbit to eat when I saw something that looked familiar. It was a big yellow bus traveling down the road. I knew it wasn't the one that stopped for the boy at the farm, and it wasn't the one that stopped for *my* boy, but I decided to follow it just the same. I thought it might lead me to a bus I knew the sound and smell of.

The bus was already gone by the time I got to the place where it had stopped. At first I was disappointed, but then I picked up a smell that filled me with excitement. I could smell my boy's bus! It had been there! And I was sure I had picked up the faint trace of my boy's smell too! Although I was very hungry, I didn't want to leave in search of food in case my boy or the bus returned while I was gone. So I crawled under a bush by the side of a building to wait.

It seemed as though I waited for a very long time. It grew dark and very cold. The wind began to blow too, and I thought about being snug inside the coat with the old man in the woods, and about lying on the rug in front of the stove at the farm, with the boy's arms wrapped around me. I also thought about my own home, and my bed on a mat in the cold, dark shed. I thought and dozed, thought and dozed, --- and waited.

It was a long time after it was light again before I heard the approach of a bus. It stopped in front of the building, and as its door hissed open, many talking and laughing little boys and girls spilled out of it. I was immediately alert for the sight or smell of my boy, but he wasn't among the people who got out of the bus. Before long another bus arrived, then another and yet another. But my boy didn't get out of any of them. I was beginning to think my boy's bus wouldn't be coming, when suddenly, unbelievably, I heard it! And right behind it was the bus that picked up the boy at the farm where I had been staying until I could get back home again.

Almost beside myself with happiness, I waited eagerly at the door to my boy's bus, waiting for him to come out. When I didn't see him or catch his scent, I ran to the other bus to find the boy from the farm. But I didn't see him or catch his scent either. In desperation, I ran back and forth between the busses, sniffing, searching then finally making the only decision I knew was the right one to make. I scrambled onto one of the busses just before it closed its door, and leaped into the seat behind the driver.

"Hey!" the man yelled. "What the ---!" When he turned to look at me I tried my best to smile. "Well, I know you!" the man said. "What are you doing so far from home? Ran off and got yourself lost again, did you? You're at the wrong school and you're a little late though if you're looking for your owner. I pick him up earlier than I pick up these little kids, and he goes over to the high school in town." The man looked at me thoughtfully as I sat there trying to smile at him. "How about if I just take you home," he finally said. "It's probably against the rules, but you look like you could use a good meal and a warm bed."

I was bristling with excitement and happy anticipation as the bus raced past houses and barns and trees, finally turning into the lane that led to the farmhouse and the people I knew deep inside were my *real* family, waiting for me in my *real* home. And I knew my *real* name was Buddy Bear, --- and I was home at last!

ABOUT THE AUTHOR

Carol Kern is an American who moved to Nova Scotia 25 years ago to experience a different lifestyle. She lives on a farm in the beautiful Annapolis Valley with her husband and son, where they raise purebred Hereford cattle.

A prolific writer, she has published well over 200 articles, essays and editorials in regional and national agriculture and tourism magazines over the past 20 years, as well as writing scripts and developing characters for a local Theme Park, and writing, producing and directing several "young players" productions for the local theater.

All Kinds of Heroes is her first novel, for which she "deeded" her farm, animals and some of her experiences to the characters in the book.

Printed in the United States
1174800001B/326-423